Praise for *His Fair Assassin 1: Grave Mercy*

'Like in *The Hunger Games* Ismae is a female assassin . . . A fantasy based on the rough contours of history . . . *Game of Thrones*-style' *New York Times*

'Historical fiction and adventure readers alike will tear through this series opener about killer nuns, tr̶e̶a̶s̶o̶n̶ a̶n̶d̶, o̶f̶ cour̶s̶e̶, romance' *P̶u̶b̶l̶i̶s̶h̶e̶r̶s̶*

'T̶h̶e̶ f̶i̶r̶s̶t̶ i̶n̶ a̶ gripping new trilogy that will appeal to fans of *The Hunger Games* in particular. We love it' *LoveReading*

'LaFevers' ambitious tapestry includes poison and treason and murder, valour and honour and slow love, suspense and sexuality and mercy. A page-turner – with grace' *Kirkus,* starred review

'With characters that will inspire the imagination, a plot that nods to history while defying accuracy, and a love story that promises more in the second book, this is sure to attract feminist readers and romantics alike' *Booklist,* starred review

'Well-written and filled with fascinating, complex characters who function realistically in this medieval world' *School Library Journal,* starred review

'A blooming romance . . . makes for a heady, ferocious page-turner' *The School Librarian*

'Sweeps the reader up in a page-turning tale of clashing factions, dangerous ambitions and simmering romance' *Books for Keeps*

Praise for *His Fair Assassin 2: Dark Triumph*

'The prose's beauty inspires immediate re-reads of many a sentence, but its forward momentum is irresistible. An intricate, masterful page-turner' *Kirkus,* starred review

'Brimming with powerful emotions, thrilling sword fights, and accurate period detail, this tightly plotted tale will enthrall readers of romantic historical fantasy' *Publishers Weekly*

'Beautifully written with a strong female protagonist. It is sure to bewitch fans of Philippa Gregory and Lauren Kate' *LoveReading*

'If you thought that Ismae was a dark and troubled character in *Grave Mercy*, then wait until you get to know Sybella . . . Highly recommended reading for anyone looking for exceptional storytelling' *YA Book Reads*

Praise for *His Fair Assassin 3: Mortal Heart*

'Both a powerful tale of political intrigue and a heady supernatural romance, this memorable adventure will entirely satisfy devotees of this series' *Publishers Weekly*

'LaFevers again mesmerises her readers through the political struggles of 15th-century Brittany and the intrigues of the followers of Mortain' *School Library Journal*

'[LaFevers] offers readers worthy heroines: fair assassins whose emotions and choices are as rich and complex as their fearsome abilities' *Booklist*

GRAVE
MERCY

ROBIN LAFEVERS

ANDERSEN PRESS

This edition first published in 2019 by
Andersen Press Limited
20 Vauxhall Bridge Road
London SW1V 2SA
www.andersenpress.co.uk

2 4 6 8 10 9 7 5 3 1

First published in 2012 in the UK by Andersen Press Ltd
First published in 2012 in the United States of America
by Houghton Mifflin Books for Children

British Library Cataloguing in Publication Data available.

ISBN 978 1 78344 823 4

Printed and bound in Great Britain by Clays Ltd, Elcograf S.p.A.

For Mark,
who first showed me what
true love looked like.

✦ Dramatis Personae ✦

ISMAE RIENNE
HER FATHER
GUILLO THE PIG FARMER
THE HERBWITCH

At the Convent
THE ABBESS
SISTER THOMINE, martial arts instructor
ANNITH, a fellow novitiate
SISTER SERAFINA, poisons mistress and convent healer
SYBELLA, a fellow novitiate
SISTER WIDONA, stable mistress
SISTER BEATRIZ, instructor in womanly arts
SISTER EONETTE, convent historian and archivist
SISTER ARNETTE, arms mistress
SISTER CLAUDE, sister in charge of the rookery
SISTER VEREDA, the ancient seeress
RUNNION, traitor to Brittany and Ismae's first kill
MARTEL, French spy and Ismae's second kill

The Privy Council
VISCOUNT MAURICE CRUNARD, chancellor of Brittany
MADAME FRANÇOISE DINAN, the duchess's governess

MARSHAL JEAN RIEUX, marshal of Brittany and the duchess's tutor

CAPTAIN DUNOIS, captain of the Breton army

The Breton Court and Nobility

ANNE, Duchess of Brittany, Countess of Nantes, Montfort, and Richmont

DUKE FRANCIS II (deceased)

BARON LOMBART, a Breton noble

GAVRIEL DUVAL, a Breton noble

BENEBIC DE WAROCH, the Beast of Waroch and knight of the realm

RAOUL DE LORNAY, a knight of the realm

BARON GEFFOY, a Breton noble

LADY KATERINE GEFFOY, his ladywife

MADAME ANTOINETTE HIVERN, mistress of the late Duke Francis II

FRANÇOIS AVAUGOUR, a knight of the realm

ALAIN D'ALBRET, a Breton noble with extensive holdings in France, and one of Anne's suitors

CHARLES VIII, king of France

ANNE DE BEAUJEU, regent of France

NORBERT GISORS, ambassador for the French regent

FEDRIC, DUKE OF NEMOURS, one of Anne's suitors

MAXIMILIAN OF AUSTRIA, the Holy Roman emperor, one of Anne's suitors

Chapter 1

BRITTANY 1485

I bear a deep red stain that runs from my left shoulder down to my right hip, a trail left by the herbwitch's poison that my mother used to try to expel me from her womb. That I survived, according to the herbwitch, is no miracle but a sign I have been sired by the god of death himself.

I am told my father flew into a rage and raised his hand to my mother even as she lay weak and bleeding on the birthing bed. Until the herbwitch pointed out to him that if my mother had lain with the god of death, surely He would not stand idly by while my father beat her.

I risk a glance up at my husband-to-be, Guillo, and wonder if my father has told him of my lineage. I am guessing not, for who would pay three silver coins for what I am? Besides, Guillo looks far too placid to know of my true nature. If my father has tricked him, it will not bode well for our union. That we are being married in Guillo's cottage rather than a church further adds to my unease.

I feel my father's heavy gaze upon me and look up. The triumph in his eyes frightens me, for if he has triumphed, then I have surely lost in some way I do not yet understand. Even so, I smile, wanting to convince him I am happy – for there is nothing that upsets him more than my happiness.

But while I can easily lie to my father, it is harder to lie to myself. I am afraid, sorely afraid of this man to whom I will now belong. I look down at his big, wide hands. Just like my father, he has dirt caked under his fingernails and stains in the creases of his skin. Will the semblance end there? Or will he, too, wield those hands like a cudgel?

It is a new beginning, I remind myself, and in spite of all my trepidations, I cannot extinguish a tiny spark of hope. Guillo wants me enough to pay three silver coins. Surely where there is want, there is room for kindness? It is the one thing that keeps my knees from knocking and my hands from trembling. That and the priest who has come to officiate, for while he is naught but a hedge priest, the furtive glance he sends me over his prayer book causes me to believe he knows who and what I am.

As he mutters the ceremony's final words, I stare at the rough hempen prayer cord with the nine wooden beads that proclaim him a follower of the old ways. Even when he ties the cord around our hands and lays the blessings of God and the nine old saints upon our union, I keep my gaze downcast, afraid to see the smugness in my father's eyes or what my husband's face might reveal.

When the priest is done, he pads away on dirty feet, his rough leather sandals flapping noisily. He does not even pause long enough to raise a tankard to our union. Nor does my father. Before the dust from my father's departing cart has settled, my new husband swats my rump and grunts toward the upstairs loft.

I clench my fists to hide their trembling and cross to the rickety stairs. While Guillo fortifies himself with one last tankard of ale, I climb up to the loft and the bed I will now share with him. I sorely miss my mother, for even though she was afraid of me, surely she would have given me a woman's counsel on my wedding night. But both she and my sister fled long ago, one back into the arms of death, and the other into the arms of a passing tinker.

I know, of course, what goes on between a man and a woman. Our cottage is small and my father loud. There was many a night when urgent movement accompanied by groans filled our dark cottage. The next day my father always looked slightly less bad-tempered, and my mother more so. I try to convince myself that no matter how distasteful the marriage bed is, surely it cannot be any worse than my father's raw temper and meaty fists.

The loft is a close, musty place that smells as if the rough shutters on the far wall have never been opened. A timber and rope bed frame holds a mattress of straw. Other than that, there are only a few pegs to hang clothes on and a plain chest at the foot of the bed.

I sit on the edge of the chest and wait. It does not take long. A heavy creak from the stairs warns me that Guillo is on his way. My mouth turns dry and my stomach sour. Not wanting to give him the advantage of height, I stand.

When he reaches the room, I finally force myself to look at his face. His piggish eyes gorge themselves on my body, going from the top of my head down to my ankles, then back up to my breasts. My father's insistence on lacing my gown so tight has worked, as Guillo can look at little else. He gestures with his tankard toward my bodice, slopping ale over the sides so that it dribbles to the floor. "Remove it." Desire thickens his voice.

I stare at the wall behind him, my fingers trembling as I raise them to my laces. But not fast enough. Never fast enough. He takes three giant strides toward me and strikes me hard across the cheek. "Now!" he roars as my head snaps back.

Bile rises in my throat and I fear I will be sick. So this is how it will be between us. This is why he was willing to pay three silver coins.

My laces are finally undone, and I remove my bodice so that I stand before him in my skirt and shift. The stale air, which only moments before was too warm, is now cold as it presses against my skin.

"Your skirt," he barks, breathing heavily.

I untie the strings and step out of my skirt. As I turn to lay it on the nearby bench, Guillo reaches for me. He is surprisingly quick for one so large and stupid, but I am quicker. I have had long years of practice escaping my father's rages.

I jerk away, spinning out of his reach, infuriating him. In truth, I give no thought to where I will run, wishing only to hold off the inevitable a little longer.

There is a loud crash as his half-empty tankard hits the wall behind me, sending a shower of ale into the room. He snarls and lunges, but something inside me will not – cannot – make this easy for him. I leap out of his reach.

But not far enough. I feel a tug, then hear a rip of cloth as he tears my thin, worn chemise.

Silence fills the loft – a silence so thick with shock that even his coarse breathing has stopped. I feel his eyes rake down my back, take in the ugly red welts and scars the poison left behind. I look over my shoulder to see his face has gone white as new cheese, his eyes wide. When our glances meet, he knows – *knows* – that he has been duped. He bellows then, a long, deep note of rage that holds equal parts fury and fear.

Then his rough hand cracks against my skull and sends me to my knees. The pain of hope dying is worse than his fists and boots.

When Guillo's rage is spent, he reaches down and grabs me by the hair. "I will go for a *real* priest this time. He will burn you or drown you. Maybe both." He drags me down the steps, my knees bumping painfully against each one. He continues dragging me through the kitchen, then shoves me into a small root cellar, slams the door, and locks it.

Bruised and possibly broken, I lie on the floor with my battered cheek pressed into the cool dirt. Unable to stop myself, I smile.

I have avoided the fate my father had planned for me. Surely it is I who has won, not he.

The sound of the bolt lifting jerks me awake. I shove

myself to a sitting position and clutch the tattered remains of my chemise around me. When the door opens, I am stunned to see the hedge priest, the same small rabbit of a man who'd blessed our marriage only hours before. Guillo is not with him, and any moment that does not contain my father or Guillo is a happy one by my reckoning.

The priest looks over his shoulder, then motions for me to follow.

I rise to my feet, and the root cellar spins dizzily. I put a hand to the wall and wait for the feeling to pass. The priest motions again, more urgently. "We've not much time before he returns."

His words clear my head as nothing else can. If he is acting without Guillo's knowledge, then he is most assuredly helping me. "I'm coming." I push away from the wall, step carefully over a sack of onions, and follow the hedge priest into the kitchen. It is dark; the only light comes from the banked embers in the hearth. I should wonder how the priest found me, why he is helping me, but I do not care. All I can think is that he is not Guillo and not my father. The rest does not matter.

He leads me to the back door, and in a day full of surprises, I find one more as I recognize the old herbwitch from our village hovering nearby. If I did not need to concentrate so hard on putting one foot in front of the other, I would ask her what she is doing here, but it is all I can do to stay upright and keep from falling on my face in the dirt.

As I step into the night, a sigh of relief escapes me.

It is dark out, and darkness has always been my friend. A cart waits nearby. Touching me as little as possible, the hedge priest helps me into the back of it before hurrying around to the driver's bench and climbing in. The priest glances over his shoulder at me, then averts his eyes as if he's been burned. "There's a blanket back there," he mutters as he steers the nag out onto the cobbled lane. "Cover yourself."

The unyielding wood of the cart presses painfully into my bruised bones, and the thin blanket scratches and reeks of donkey. Even so, I wish they'd brought a second one for padding. "Where are you taking me?"

"To the boat."

A boat means water, and crossing water means I will be far from the reach of my father and Guillo and the Church. "Where is this boat taking me?" I ask, but the priest says nothing. Exhaustion overwhelms me. I do not have the strength to pluck answers from him like meager berries from a thorny bush. I lie down in the cart and give myself over to the horse's jolting gait.

And so my journey across Brittany begins. I am smuggled like some forbidden cargo, hidden among turnips or in hay in the back of carts, awakened by furtive voices and fumbling hands as I am passed from hedge priest to herbwife, a hidden chain of those who live in accordance with the old saints and are determined to keep me from the Church. The hedge priests, with their awkward movements and musty, stale robes, are kind enough, but their fingers are unschooled in tenderness or compassion. It is the herbwitches I like most. Their chapped, raw hands are gentle as lamb's wool, and the sharp, pungent smell of a hundred different herbs clings to them like a fragrant shadow. Often as not, they give me a tincture of poppy for my injuries, while the priests merely give me their sympathy, and some begrudgingly at that.

When I awake on what I reckon to be the fifth night of my journey, I smell the salty tang of the sea and remember the promise of a boat. I struggle to sit up, pleased to find my bruises pain me less and my ribs do not burn. We are passing through a small fishing village. I pull the blanket close against the chill and wonder what will happen next.

At the very edge of the village sits a stone church. It is to this that the latest hedge priest steers our cart and I am relieved to see the door bears the sacred anchor of St. Mer, one of the old saints. The priest reins his horse to a stop. "Get out."

I cannot tell if it is fatigue or disdain I hear in his voice, but, either way, my journey is almost done, so I ignore it and clamber out of the cart, sure to keep the blanket clutched tight around me lest I offend his modesty.

Once he secures the horse, he leads me toward the beach, where a lone boat waits. The inky black ocean spreads out as far and wide as my eye can see, making the vessel seem very small.

An old sailor sits hunched in the prow. A shell bleached white as bone hangs from a cord at his neck, marking him as a worshiper of St. Mer. I wonder what he thinks of being woken in the middle of the night and made to row strangers out into the dark sea.

The sailor's faded blue eyes skim over me. He nods. "Climb in. We en't got all night." He thrusts an oar at me, and I grasp it to steady myself as I get into the boat.

The small vessel dips and rocks, and for a moment I am afraid it will tip me into the icy water. But it rights itself and then the priest steps in, causing the hull to sink even lower.

The old sailor grunts, then returns the oar to its pin and begins rowing.

We reach the small island just as dawn pinkens the eastern horizon. It looks barren in the early, spare light. As we draw closer, I see a standing stone next to a church and realize we've come to one of the old places of worship.

Gravel crunches under the hull of the boat as the old sailor rows right up onto the beach. He jerks his head toward the stone fortress. "Get out then. The abbess of St. Mortain be expectin' ye."

Saint Mortain? The patron saint of death. A tremor of unease washes through me. I look at the priest, who averts his eyes, as if looking at me is too great a mortal temptation.

Still clutching the blanket close around me, I climb awkwardly from the boat and step into the shallows. Torn between gratitude and annoyance, I curtsy slightly, careful to let the blanket slip from my shoulder for the merest of seconds.

It is enough. Satisfied at the priest's gasp and the old

sailor's cluck of his tongue, I turn and slog through the cold water to the beach. In truth, I have never flashed so much as an ankle before, but I am sorely vexed at being treated like a temptress when all I feel is bruised and broken.

When I reach the patchy grass that grows between the rocks, I look back toward the boat, but it has already put out to sea. I turn and begin making my way to the convent, eager to see what those who worship Death want of me.

Chapter 2

Two ancient standing stones mark the entrance to the convent. The chickens in the courtyard are just now beginning to stir, scratching in the dirt for their breakfast. At my approach, they cluck and flutter away.

I pause at the door, wishing I could find a corner and sleep until my head clears, but the sailor said the abbess is expecting me, and while I do not know much about abbesses, I suspect they are not fond of waiting.

My heart beats wildly as I raise my hand and knock. The heavy door opens at once, revealing a short, plain woman covered in black from head to toe. Without saying a word, she motions me inside.

I follow her through a sparsely furnished room, then down an equally austere corridor that leads into the heart of the convent. My guide knocks once on a closed door.

"Enter," a voice commands.

My guide opens the door and motions me inside. The furnishings are simple but sturdy, and early morning light pours in through the east-facing window. My eyes are immediately drawn to the woman who sits at the large desk in the middle of the room. She wears a black gown and wimple, and her pale face is striking in its beauty.

Without looking up, she motions me toward one of the chairs. My footsteps echo lightly among all that space as I approach her desk. I clutch the blanket tight around me, then sit.

The abbess lifts her gaze from her work, and I find myself staring into a pair of eyes as cool and blue as the sea. "Ismae Rienne."

I flinch, startled she knows my name.

"Do you know why you're here, child?"

I do not know what answer she is looking for, I only know that I am overcome with a sudden desire to earn her approval. "Because I displeased my new husband?"

"Displeased him?" The abbess gives a delicate snort that makes me like her even more. "From what I hear he practically wet his braies in fear of you."

I feel the familiar shame rise up in my cheeks and I look down at my lap.

"The fault lies not with you, daughter." She says this so gently it makes me want to cry. I have never shed a tear, not throughout all my father's beatings or Guillo's mauling, but a few kind words from this woman and it is all I can do not to bawl like a babe.

"So tell me," she says, drawing a quill and ink pot close. "Do you know the circumstances of your birth?"

I risk a glance at her face, but she is focused on what she is writing on her parchment. "Only that my mother did not wish to bear me. She went to a herbwitch for poison, hoping to purge me from her womb."

"And yet you lived." She looks up. The words are quiet but hold the power of a shout in the stillness of this room.

I meet the abbess's steady gaze. "And yet I lived."

"Do you have any idea what that means?"

"You mean other than having to spend my life in the shadows, dodging blows and staying out of sight so as not to cause others undue fear?"

"Yes, other than that." Her voice is dry as bone. She leans forward, her eyes alight with some purpose. "Did they not claim, Ismae, that you were sired by Death Himself?"

I nod cautiously.

"Well, and so. After many trials, you are now here."

"Trials?" I ask. "Is that what my life has been? A series of trials to be passed?"

"You come to us well tempered, my child, and it is not in my nature to be sorry for it. It is the well-tempered blade that is the strongest."

"And who exactly is *us*?" My whole body stills, waiting for her answer.

"You have found refuge at the convent of St. Mortain. Although in truth, Mortain is older than any saint, older even than Christ."

"One of the old gods we now call saints," I murmur.

"Yes, one of the old gods. One not easily cast aside by the Church. And so we call Him saint, but as long as we serve Him, He cares not what He is called."

"How does one serve Death?" Am I to spend my life collecting bodies in the bone cart?

The reverend mother does not flinch. "We carry out Mortain's will when He wishes to alter the warp and weft of life's weave for some purpose of His own."

I look at her blankly, not understanding what weaving has to do with Mortain. She sighs and pushes away from her desk. "Perhaps some refreshment is in order."

I want to beg her to tell me more of what being Death's daughter might hold, but I suspect this woman does not suffer fools gladly, so I hold my tongue.

She takes a flagon of wine and two crystal goblets from the cupboard behind her desk. She pours the wine into the goblets and hands one to me. The cut crystal is finer than anything I have ever seen, and I hold it gingerly, afraid it will shatter in my hands.

"Here at the convent, it is our job to train those who are sired by the god of death. We teach them to perform their duties quickly and efficiently. Usually, we find that He has given His daughters some special skill or art. Abilities that will aid you as you carry out His work."

His work. The words are ripe with possibility. I take a sip of wine to steady myself. It is sweet and crisp on my tongue.

"If I may guess a little about you?" the reverend mother asks. I nod, and she continues. "You never get sick with the ague or the chills or the flux. Even the plague leaves you untouched, is that correct?"

I feel my eyes widen at her uncanny knowledge. "How do you know such things?"

She smiles. "And I know you can survive harsh beatings

and heal within days. Do you also have dreams that foretell death?"

"No." I shake my head, sorry to disappoint her. "But sometimes I can tell when people are going to die."

She tilts her head to the side. "Go on."

I look down and study the wine in the goblet. "I can see them fading sometimes. It's like watching a flame grow dim in a lantern. And once, I saw a mark. On the blacksmith. He had a faint black smudge on his forehead in the shape of a horseshoe. Three days later he was dead."

She leans forward in her chair, eager now. "How did he die?"

"He was kicked in the head by one of the horses as he worked."

"Ah." A pleased smile hovers at the corners of her mouth. "Mortain has given you powerful gifts." She takes up the quill and makes a notation on the parchment in front of her. Small beads of perspiration begin to form on my forehead and I take another sip of wine to steady myself. It is hard to air old secrets.

"So," she says, looking back up at me. "You are well equipped for our service."

"Which is?"

"We kill people." The reverend mother's words fall like stones into the quiet of the room, so shocking that my body goes numb. I hear the splintering of crystal as my goblet hits the floor.

The abbess ignores the shattered goblet. "Of course, many

die without our help. However, there are those who deserve to die but who have not yet encountered the means to do so. At Mortain's bidding, we help them on their way."

"Surely He does not need our help?"

Anger flares in the abbess and for the first time I feel the iron will I have only vaguely sensed before. "Who are you to say what the god of death needs or doesn't need? Mortain is an old god and has no desire to be forgotten and fade from this world, which is why He chooses to bestir Himself in the affairs of man." She stares at me for a moment longer, then the tension leaves her, like a wave going out to sea. "What do you know of the old gods?" she asks.

"Only that they were once the nine old gods of Brittany but now we call them saints. And we must leave them an occasional offering or prayer if we do not wish to offend them or incur their wrath."

"You are close," the abbess says, leaning back in her chair, "but that is not the whole of it. The old gods are neither man nor God, but something in between. They were the first inhabitants of our land, sent to do God's bidding in this new world He had created.

"At first, the relationship between gods and man was a difficult one, the gods treating us much as we treat cattle or sheep. But soon we learned to honor them with prayer and offerings, which led to harmony between us. Even the early Church, when it arrived, was content to let us honor the old gods, although we learned to call them saints then. But lately, that has been changing. Just as France has gobbled up most of the smaller kingdoms and duchies so it may claim all their power for its own, so too does this latest pope work to extinguish any trace of the old ways, wanting all the prayers and offerings for his own church.

"So now more and more put aside the old ways and traditions that honor the gods of Brittany. But not all. Some still raise their voices in prayer and make their offerings. If not for that worship and supplication the old gods would fade from this world. Surely you can understand why Mortain would not wish that. He feeds off our belief and worship much as we feed off bread and meat and would starve without it.

"So, it is our job to believe and to serve. If you choose to stay here and take the vows, you will be sworn to serve Mortain in any way He asks of you. In all things. In all ways. We carry out His will. Do you understand?"

"Is that not murder?"

"No. You would not expect a queen to wash her own clothes or lace her own gown; she has her handmaidens for that. And so it is with us; we serve as handmaidens to Death. When we are guided by His will, killing is a sacrament."

She leans forward then, as if eager to tempt me with what Mortain offers. "If you choose to stay, you will be trained in His arts. You will learn more ways to kill a man than you imagined possible. We will train you in stealth and cunning and all manner of skills that will ensure no man is ever again a threat to you."

I think of my father and of Guillo. I think of all those in

the village who worked so hard to make my life a misery. The young boys who threw stones at me, the old men who spat and stared at me with terror in their eyes, as if they expected me to snatch the souls from their old, wrinkled bodies. The younger men who fumbled clumsily at my skirts in dark corners, guessing correctly that my father cared not for my safety or reputation. It would be no hardship at all to kill the likes of them. I feel like a cat who has been dropped from a great height only to land on her feet.

As if plucking my thoughts from my head, the abbess speaks again. "They won't all be like them, you know."

I look up in surprise and she continues. "Those Mortain sends you to kill. They won't all be like the pig farmer."

My ears are deaf to her warning. I am certain all men are like that, and I would kill them all gladly.

But she presses further, to be sure I fully understand. "He will ask for sacrifices, but it is not your role to question. Only to serve with love and obedience." A whisper of emotion crosses her face, a memory of some pain I can only guess at. "That is the nature of our service," she says. "Unquestioning faith. Can you do that?"

"What if I say no?"

"Then you will be taken far from here and given to a kind, gentle man in need of a wife."

I weigh the choice that is no choice at all. To be removed from the world of men and trained to kill them, or to be handed to one like a sheep. "If you think I am fit to serve, Reverend Mother, I will do so gladly."

She smiles and leans back in her chair. "Oh, you are fit to serve. You have already passed the first test."

Something about her smile makes me uneasy. "I have?"

The abbess nods to the shattered goblet on the floor. "Your wine was laced with poison. Enough that a sip would kill a man twice your size. You experienced slight discomfort, nothing more."

I am shocked into silence as she so easily confesses to poisoning me, and I remember the warm, dizzy feeling I had earlier.

"Now come." The abbess stands, walks over to the door, and opens it. "Annith will get you settled. Welcome to the convent."

Chapter 3

When I step out of the reverend mother's office, a girl just slightly younger than I am is waiting. Just like the abbess, she is strikingly fair, with eyes the color of the shifting sea and wisps of pale hair escaping from her veil. Next to her I feel shabby and tattered, as if my very presence is a sacrilege in a convent full of beauty. But the girl smiles at me and tucks my arm through hers as if we have been friends since birth. "I am Annith," she says. "Let's get you to the infirmary."

As much as I want to go with her, as much as I want to embrace this new life set before me, I hesitate. There is something I need to understand first. "Wait."

Annith tilts her head to the side. "What?"

"If I hadn't passed the test, would she have let me die of poison?" A chill scuttles across my shoulders at how close I came to meeting Death face to face.

Annith's face clears in understanding. "But, no! The abbess would have fetched a bezoar stone to neutralize the poison or called for a tincture of amaranth to revive you. Now come." She tugs gently at my arm, and she is so certain and reassuring that it chases away my last remaining doubt.

Our footsteps echo faintly off the stone walls as Annith leads me down a corridor. Doors line the walls on either side of us, and I wonder what secrets these rooms hold and how soon I will be allowed to learn them.

Annith stops when we reach a long chamber with clean, white walls and a row of beds. Fresh air pours in from the window and I hear the sound of waves casting themselves upon the rocky shore beyond. A nun in a midnight-blue habit works at a table with a mortar and pestle. At our arrival, she carefully puts her task aside before turning to greet us.

She is of middle years, and her black wimple does not flatter her olive skin. It does, however, match the faint mustache on her upper lip. I am filled with relief that she is not beautiful like the others. At least I will not be the ugliest one here.

"The reverend mother sends a new patient?" The note of eagerness in the nun's voice strikes me as unseemly.

"Yes, Sister Serafina," Annith says. "She has had a bad beating, with many bruises. Possible broken ribs and injuries to her internal organs."

I stare at Annith with new respect. How has she learned all this? Did she listen at the door? Looking at her fresh, delicate face, I find it hard to imagine her doing anything so deceitful.

The nun wipes her hands on a linen cloth and goes to a plain wooden cupboard to retrieve a glass flask. It is not as elegant or ornate as the crystal goblet, but it is every bit as fragile. Even so, she thrusts it into my hands and motions me to a wooden screen in the corner of the room. "Evacuate into that, if you please."

I stare stupidly at the flask. The nun looks at Annith. "Was her hearing affected, do you think?"

"No, Sister." Annith's face is solemn, the picture of dutiful respect, and yet I am sure I can sense a faint spark of humor.

Sister Serafina turns back to me. "Piss," she says, a little loudly in case Annith is wrong about my hearing. "I need you to piss into the flask so I can tell if you have any internal injuries."

Mortification fills me at this request, but Annith gives me an encouraging nudge. I hurry over to the privacy of the screen and find a chamber pot. I lift my skirts, position myself, and pray I will hit the flask.

The nun speaks again. Her voice is low, but my hearing is sharp from so many years spent listening for my father's moods.

"Did the reverend mother test her?"

"Yes," Annith tells her. "With the wine."

"Praise Mortain!" She sounds well and truly grateful, and I cannot for a moment imagine why. When I emerge from behind the screen, there is a look of exultation on her plain face. As she takes the flask from me, admiration shines in her eyes, as if she's just discovered I am not simply a plow horse, but a finely blooded mare. "Annith will settle you in one of the beds while I mix a tisane to hasten your healing." She is still smiling as she turns back to her work table.

"Over here." Annith's hand is gentle on my elbow as she guides me to one of the beds. It is covered in clean white linen, and I am terrified of sullying it. "Take off your clothes,"

Annith orders. "I'll get you a clean shift."

I remember the reverend mother's command for obedience, but I find I cannot bring myself to do what she asks. Just as the dust from my ragged gown will mar the clean linens, I am sure the sight of my hideous scar will mar Annith's view of me. I have known her for mere minutes, but already I am afraid to lose her affection.

She returns to my side holding a shift that bears the clean, crisp scent of lavender. Seeing me still clothed, her face softens. "Do you need help?"

"No." I wrap my arms around myself. "It is just . . . I . . . my flesh is scarred and ugly and I don't wish to offend."

"Nonsense," she says, and pats my arm. "Here at the convent of St. Mortain, we all have scars." As she turns away to give me a moment of privacy, I cannot help but wonder what her scars might be.

I slip out of my old, torn chemise, certain I can still smell the reek of pigs where Guillo touched it.

"Matrona's curse, was it?"

I flinch at Sister Serafina's voice. Desperate to cover myself, I yank the new shift over my head so quickly that I become dizzy. I wait for the sensation to pass before turning to the nun. "Pardon me?"

She gestures to my back. "What your mother used, child? When you were in her womb?"

"I do not know the name of the herbwitch's poison."

"I do." Her eyes are full of compassion. "Only Matrona's curse would leave such a scar. Now, into bed with you."

Annith hovers as I climb into bed, then leans over and tucks the covers around me. When she is done, Sister Serafina hands me a small cup of foul liquid she swears will make me feel better. I drink the tisane – which tastes of rotten berries and old hay – then hand the cup back. This feeling of being fussed over is new and I cannot tell if I like it or not.

Annith settles herself on the stool next to my bed, then glances over her shoulder to assure herself the nun has returned to her work table. "You may not be able to tell," she says in a low voice. "But Sister Serafina is delighted by your arrival. Other than herself, no one here is immune to the effects of poison, and she can scarce keep up with supplying the convent. It will most likely be one of your primary duties when you are healed, helping her in the workroom."

"With poisons?" I ask, not sure I understand her correctly.

Annith nods, and I glance back at the nun, who is busy once again at the work table. My head is full of more questions, but as I turn back to ask one, I realize that the bed against the farthest window is occupied.

At first, I am glad, glad I'm not the only one for them to fret over. And then I see that the other girl's wrists are tied to the bed.

Panic rises in my chest, sharp and hot. It must show on my face because Annith turns and follows my gaze. "It is only so she won't hurt herself," she hurries to explain. "She was brought here three nights ago, thrashing and screaming. It took four nuns to restrain her."

My eyes are drawn back to the girl. "Is she mad?"

"Mayhap. Certainly those that brought her here thought so."

"Was she given the same test as I was?"

"She isn't well enough to be tested yet, but she will be once she is better."

When I look back at the girl, I see her eyes are open and she is staring at us. Slowly, she smiles. It is even more disturbing than her bound wrists.

Chapter 4

I awake sometime later to a hand stroking my hair. The touch is gentle and comforting and I marvel at the sensation, a touch that doesn't hurt. Clearly the tisane has worked.

"Poor poppet," a low, throaty voice croons. Because I am half asleep, it takes me a moment to realize the voice is not Annith's nor even Sister Serafina's. I come fully awake then. The far bed is empty, the wrist ties dangling loose to the floor.

"Poor poppet," the girl kneeling by my bed murmurs again, and fear stirs in my breast.

"Who are you?" I whisper.

She leans in closer. "Your sister," she whispers back. Her words sear away the last dregs of sleep. Her hair is a wild tangle of midnight-black falling down her back and shoulders. The faint moonlight reveals a bruise high on her cheek and a cut on her lip. I wonder if she got those from the nuns or if she had them when she arrived.

"Do you mean you were sired by Saint Mortain as well?"

She laughs softly, a terrifying sound that sends goose bumps scuttling across my skin. "No, I mean we have been sired by the very devil himself. So says my lord father."

It is exactly what the villagers have claimed about me all my life, but I find the words no longer ring true. The reverend mother's revelation has altered something deep inside me, awakened some hope that slumbered hidden all these years. Suddenly, I am eager to convince the girl that she is wrong, just as the reverend mother has convinced me. I push myself up so that I am sitting rather than lying. Her hand falls from my hair.

"Your lord father is wrong." My whisper is so fierce it scratches my throat. "We have been sired by Mortain. Chosen by Him to do His bidding. Your father, the Church, they all lied." As I stare into her haunted, broken face, I grow desperate to convince her, to take this small flame of promise from my chest and light it in hers.

A spark of interest flares in her eyes, then is quickly quenched. She cocks her head toward the door. "They are making the rounds. Farewell." She jumps to her feet, then onto the bed next to me, and begins leaping her way down the row.

"Stop!" Sister Serafina cries from the doorway. The note of command freezes the blood in my veins, but the girl does not even pause. She leaps gracefully as a young deer, making her way to the open window, an almost playful glint in her eye.

Two more nuns appear behind Sister Serafina, all of their attention focused on the escaping girl. "Stop, Sybella," the tallest one calls out. Her voice is low and musical and as soothing as I imagine a mother's caress would be. The fey girl falters, as if that voice has some power over her. With an effort, she leaps to the next bed, but her movements are slower, clumsier.

"If you stay," the lovely voice continues, "we will find a way to give you back your life."

The girl turns and anger flares in her eyes. "You lie!" She takes the last three beds in as many leaps and arrives at the window. Without knowing why, I am afraid for her. I am certain that if she goes out that window, her madness will burn her up and leave nothing but bitter ashes behind.

"Wait!" I add my voice to the others. She stops, and the nuns grow still. Everyone holds her breath. "Don't you wish to learn the arts of Mortain?" I ask. "How to kill those who have done this to you?" I do not know why I am so certain someone has caused this insanity in her, but I am.

She is quiet so long I am afraid she will not answer, and then she does. "What are you talking about?"

"She has not yet spoken to the abbess," the musical-voiced nun says. "She was too wild when she first arrived."

"May I tell her then? If it will keep her here?"

The nuns glance among themselves, an unspoken conversation in which options are weighed. Finally, one nods. I turn to the girl. "Are you so eager to go back to where you came from? To your lord father?"

In the darkness of the bedchamber, the shadows on her face seem to deepen. "No," she whispers. "But I will not be held prisoner by a clucking passel of busybodies who pry and poke."

I glance uneasily at the nuns, but they are unperturbed by her assessment of them. "They mean well," I assure her.

Her quiet laughter is so full of scorn it nearly curdles the air between us. "Good intentions are only lies the weak tell themselves. I will not be caged."

But where else will she go? "They have promised to teach me of poison," I say, hoping I am not getting Annith in trouble by revealing this. "And other ways to kill a man." I share what the abbess told me, her words still bright in my mind. "They will train us in stealth and cunning, and give us such skills that no man will ever be a threat to us again."

Sybella turns toward me, a glint of interest in her eyes, but that is all I know of this new life I've been promised. I look helplessly at the nuns.

Annith steps easily into the opening I have made. "They will teach you of all manner of weapons," she says, coming more fully into the room. "They will show you how to wield a dagger and a stiletto. How to shoot an arrow and draw a sword."

"That is a lie," Sybella says. "No one would teach a woman such deadly skills." But I can see how much she wants to believe.

"It is not a lie," Annith swears.

It is working. With her eyes on Annith, Sybella steps down from the bed. "Tell me more," she demands.

"They will teach you how to caress a man's throat with a garrote so that when he expects your soft lips, he will feel the deadly bite of wire instead."

Sister Serafina speaks next. "We will teach you to make poisons." Her voice is as gentle as the lulling waves. "Poisons that grip the gut and force a man's life to dribble from him into a slop pail. Poisons to stop the heart or squeeze the humors from the body. Bloodwort to congeal the blood so it can no longer move through the veins. We will show you subtle poisons that take days to fell a man, and those that kill within seconds. And that is just to start."

There is a long pause and we all hold our breath, wondering what Sybella will choose. When she speaks, her voice is so faint I have to lean forward to hear it. "Is there a poison that will make a man's member shrivel and fall off?" she asks.

When Sister Serafina answers, her voice is full of a grim determination that makes me love her. "We will create one, you and I. Now, come. Get back into bed and we will tell you of all this and more."

Sybella studies us for a long moment, then shrugs, as if staying here is of no consequence to her one way or the other. But we are not fooled.

She comes to stand next to my cot. "Scoot over," she orders.

Surprised, I look at Sister Serafina, who indicates it is up to me. I glance back at Sybella. Our hold on her is so fragile, I cannot say no. Besides, the convent bed is finer than any pallet I have ever slept on, and it is almost wide enough for two. I make room for her, and she crawls under my covers to lie down next to me. As we lie together in the narrow bed, the nuns lull us to sleep with gentle voices, singing their song of darkness and death.

When I wake, there is pale golden sunlight streaming into the room. I sit up, surprised to find I am alone. Not only is

Sybella gone, but there is no nun clucking at the worktable or fussing with the beds.

Just as I am wondering what I am supposed to do next, Annith appears, as bright and lovely as the morning itself. She smiles when she sees I am awake and sets the tray she is carrying on the work table. "How do you feel?" she asks.

I flex my arms, my toes, raise my shoulders against the soft linen of my shift. "Fine," I reply, surprised that this is true. The healing tisane of Sister Serafina's is indeed a small miracle.

"Would you like to break your fast?"

I find that I am starving. "Yes," I say, and she brings the tray over to me. She hands me a tankard of small ale and a loaf of bread fresh from the convent ovens. There is even a pot of goat cheese. I spread the cheese on the bread and take my first bite. It is the most delicious food I have ever eaten. My hunger, which has been asleep for my entire trip across the kingdom, rises up now, and I devour the breakfast in a matter of seconds. Annith looks at me in concern. "Do you want more?"

I start to say yes, for I have learned never to say no to food, then realize I am already full. "No," I say, pleased when I remember to add, "thank you."

Annith smiles and lowers herself onto a stool by my bed. As she smoothes her skirts around her knees, I long to ask her about Sybella, but I am afraid. Afraid of what might have become of her during the night. I feel a pang of guilt at my own peaceful slumber.

"Once you are feeling up to it," Annith says, "you are to join Sister Serafina in her poisons workshop."

Poisons. The word makes me throw back my covers and swing my feet to the floor. "I am ready now."

Annith's brow wrinkles in concern. "Are you certain? You've been here only a short while."

"Yes, but I had five days to recover from my injuries during my journey, and in truth the tisane and the breakfast have done much to restore me." I am as hungry for this work I have been promised as I was for the bread. "I would love to begin now, if it is allowed."

"Of course! To rest or to work, the choice is left to you." Annith fetches me a gown from the wooden cupboard. It is a dove-gray habit, like hers, and as I slip it over my head, I can feel myself slipping into this new life that I have been given.

Annith helps me comb my hair, her fingers gentle even among all the tangles. When I am presentable, she leads me from the room and down the confusing maze of corridors. She opens a thick door and we step outside. I blink against the bright sun, then hurry to follow her. She leads me to a small stone cottage downwind from the convent. "I am not to go in," she explains, "as I do not have your gift. But you may enter; the good sister is expecting you."

"She is?"

Annith's eyes sparkle. "She suspected you would want to start right away." Then she bids me goodbye and heads back toward the convent. Alone on the doorstep, I knock.

"Who is it?" a voice calls out.

"It is Ismae," I say, wondering if I need to explain further who I am since I am not sure if she knows my name.

"Come in!" the voice says cheerfully.

I open the door and step inside.

The maids in my village talked of falling in love with a man at first sight. That has always seemed naught but foolishness to me. Until I enter Sister Serafina's workshop. It is unlike anything I have ever seen, full of strange sights and smells, and I tumble headlong into love.

The ceiling is high, and the room has many windows. Two small clay ovens sit on the floor. In front of the fireplace is a range of kettles, from one big enough to cook a goat whole all the way down to one so small it could belong to the fey folk of hearth tales. A large wooden press takes up an entire corner of the room. Fragile glass containers and globes sit beside squat earthenware jars and silver flasks. The most striking thing in the room – a writhing mass of glass vessels and copper tubes – sits alone on one of the worktables. Two flames burn beneath it, and the whole thing hisses and bubbles and steams like a large, deadly viper getting ready to strike.

"My still," Sister Serafina says with great pride. "I use it to boil and reduce substances to their essence, removing all the extra matter until nothing but the poison remains." She motions me over to the table, and I come eagerly, ducking under a low-hanging clutch of roots drying in the rafters. A strange and pungent combination of smells reaches my nose; rich, earthy notes combined with a cloying, sickly sweetness, and a strong acrid smell lurking underneath.

On the table is a bowl of withered black seeds and a pile of shiny red ones. Large round pods the size of rosary beads are scattered next to drying tubers that look like a man's organ. Seeing those brings Sybella's question of last night back to me.

Sister Serafina studies me closely. "How are you feeling?"

I start to tell her that I can hardly feel my injuries any longer, then I realize she means how am I feeling among all the poisons. "Fine," I say. To my surprise, I am smiling.

"Then let's get to work." She shoves a bowl of round green pods in front of me. They are misshapen lumps covered in soft, flexible prickles. She takes up a small pointed knife. "Cut them open and extract the seeds, thus." With a deft flick of the blade, she guts one of the pods, and three fuzzy seeds spill out. She pinches one between her fingers and holds it up to me. "One of these will make a man so sick, he will wish to die. Three of these will kill him." Then she hands me the knife, places the seed back on the table, and returns to her distillery.

The knife handle is smooth and well balanced, a thing of beauty, but the seed pod is tough and fibrous, and my hand is not as skilled as the nun's. It takes a long time before the point of my knife pierces the hard shell and breaks it open. I glance up to find Sister Serafina watching me. Unable to help myself, I flash a smile of victory at her.

She gives me a toothy grin, and then she turns back to her work and I turn back to mine.

That night, I attend dinner in the refectory with the

others. It is a large stone chamber with arched doorways and long wooden tables. I see there are less than a dozen girls in all. At thirteen and fourteen, Annith and I appear to be the oldest. The youngest looks to be no more than five, although Annith assures me they do not learn anything of the killing arts until they are older. All of them bear a fair measure of beauty. Perhaps Mortain sires only comely daughters.

"There are even more of us," Annith tells me. "We have half a dozen full initiates of Mortain, but they are all away, carrying out His wishes."

Eight nuns file in and head for a large table set apart on a dais. As we eat our dinner, Annith tells me of the nuns I have not yet met. There is the horse mistress and the weapons mistress and the mistress of martial arts, as well as an ancient nun whose only duty is to tend the crows in the rookery. Another nun is charged with teaching history and politics. The last one, a woman who may have been pretty once but now reminds me of a peahen, instructs us in courtly manners and dancing. "And," Annith adds, her eyes growing bright and her cheeks pink, "womanly arts."

I turn to stare at her in surprise. "Womanly arts? Why do we need instruction in *that*?" I hope the small flicker of panic I feel does not come through in my voice.

She shrugs. "So we may get close to our victims. How else are we to see if they have a marque? Besides, all our talents and skills must be well honed so we may serve Mortain fully." It sounds like a lesson she has been made to memorize.

"Is that all of them, then?" I ask.

"Sister Vereda is not only old but blind as well. She never eats with us and keeps to her rooms. She is our seeress and speaks with us only when she has had a vision."

I feel someone watching, and look up to find the reverend mother's cool blue gaze on me. When our eyes meet, she lifts her goblet in private welcome. The immensity of it all surges through me, leaving me dizzy with my unexpected good fortune. This is my new life. My new home. The one I have prayed for ever since I was old enough to form words. A deep sense of gratitude fills me. *I will make the most of this chance I have been given,* I vow, and I raise my goblet in return.

Chapter 5

It is a full week before I see Sybella again. What they did to calm her, not even Annith has been able to find out.

She first appears among us at the dinner hour. The entire refectory falls silent when Sister Widona, the nun with the melodious voice and a talent for taming the convent's horses, appears in the doorway with Sybella at her side.

When the nun leaves to join the other sisters at the main table, Sybella stands for a long moment looking down at our table, proud and scornful. The younger girls are too awed by her to do anything but stare, but Annith scoots over on the bench to make room for her. Sybella ignores her and instead sits next to me. I am exquisitely uncomfortable at this. Annith has been so kind to me, I cannot bear for her to be shunned like that. And yet...there is something about this new girl, and I am filled with a dark joy that she has chosen to sit next to me. I glance down at my plate so Annith will not see my secret pleasure.

Sybella is thinner than when I last saw her, but her eyes are less wild, and the shadows are nearly gone. Her haughtiness, however, is untouched. She sits on the bench, her back rigid, and looks neither to the right nor to the left.

Proving she is a saint, Annith offers the branch of friendship once more by asking, "May I get you some stew?"

Sybella glances disdainfully at the food in front of the rest of us. "I do not eat pig slop."

Her words are as shocking as a slap to Annith's face. Annith's cheeks pinken. "I assure you, neither do we. Sit there and starve for all I care." It is the first time I have seen Annith provoked into a temper.

Sybella does exactly that; she sits and stares at the wall while the rest of us eat our dinners. It has a severe dampening effect on everyone's appetite, except mine. Having eaten only turnips for years – and old, rotten ones at that – I am always hungry.

After a few minutes of this, Sister Widona rises from the main table, goes to the stew pot that hangs in the hearth, and ladles up a portion. She carries it over to our table and sets it in front of Sybella. "Eat," she orders. Sybella looks up, and the power of their gazes clashing is nearly audible.

When Sybella makes no move toward her bowl, Sister Widona leans over and speaks softly into the girl's ear. "Eat, or I will force it down your throat."

Her words shock me, for I cannot see these gentle nuns doing anything as heavy-handed as that, but the threat works. Staring mulishly at the nun, Sybella begins shoveling the stew into her mouth. Satisfied, the nun returns to the dais.

And so our training at the convent begins, and everything the nuns promised Sybella and me on that first night comes to pass. We study the human body as thoroughly as the physicians at the great universities, poring over drawings of human anatomy that make us blush. But despite our modesty, we learn where the weakest parts of the body hide. How skin is attached to muscle, and muscle bound by sinew to bone, and how these connections can best be severed.

We become well versed in all manner of fighting, with our hands and feet, our elbows, even our teeth. We are trained in every weapon imaginable: knives and daggers, garrotes. We practice with throwing rondelles – small, razor-edged disks – until we can strike our targets accurately. We shoot short bows and longbows – if we can draw them. If we cannot, we are forced to strengthen our arms until we can. Crossbows too are part of our training, for they are highly accurate when one needs to strike from a distance.

Where I truly excel is in the poison workshop with Sister Serafina, the soaking and stewing, pressing and distilling, learning the nature of all the deadly substances and how best to coax their poisons from them and combine them for the desired effect.

But, of course, not all our lessons are so compelling. There are long, boring stretches spent studying history and politics and memorizing the noble families of Brittany. We also study the royal houses of France, for according to the nuns, France is the biggest threat to our country's independence, especially since our duke banded together with other great lords in an attempt to depose the French regent. The deed has not gone unpunished, and hostilities have broken out once again between our countries.

We novices must also learn how to dress in finery and maneuver without tripping. We practice smiling mysteriously and become masters of the seductive glance, peering out from beneath our lashes, our eyes full of promise. These particular lessons make me feel so ridiculous that I often dissolve into fits of laughter and am sent from the room in disgrace.

I alone of the older girls must have extra lessons. Since I am new to the convent and not noble born, I do not know how to read or write, skills the nuns assure me are required to serve Mortain, for how else will I read Sister Serafina's recipes or the instructions that tell me who to kill? I spend long, frustrating hours alone in the scriptorium practicing my letters over and over again.

While the nuns are strict taskmistresses, they are kind too, rarely raising their voices or shaming us. Mayhap they know that treating us well makes us want to please them all the more, or mayhap they suspect we have had too much shame in our lives already.

I take to this new life like a fish to water, Sister Serafina says. Within the passing of a season, my nightmares grow infrequent and I find myself thinking less and less of the realm of man beyond the convent's walls. Indeed, it is as if that whole world has ceased to exist.

Chapter 6

THREE YEARS LATER

November is known as the blood month, the time of year when animals are slaughtered for winter. How apt, I think, that my first assignment comes now.

Not wanting to announce my presence to the stablekeep, I steer my horse to a copse of trees just beyond the tavern, then dismount. I pull my cloak tight against the chill wind coming off the sea and slip Nocturne a carrot pilfered from the convent kitchens. "I will be back soon," I whisper in her ear.

I turn from my horse and make my way through the trees and shadows to the tavern. Anticipation bubbles through me, so strong it is all I can do to keep from running to the door and throwing it open. Sybella was first sent out nearly a year ago, and I had despaired of ever getting an assignment of my own. At least I am better off than Annith, who is still waiting. I had thought she would surely be given an assignment before me.

I shove that puzzle aside and focus on the task at hand. This is a true test of all I have learned at the convent. I must be ready for anything and know that I will be judged accordingly.

When I reach the door, I pause, listening to the murmur of voices mingling with the clatter of crockery on the other side. The tavern is doing a brisk business this evening, with the men in from the fields early and the fishermen back with their day's catch. Good. It is easier to go unnoticed in a crowd. I slip inside. At this late hour, the men are well into their tankards and are far more interested in the dicing going on in front of the fire or in catching the attention of some serving wench than they are in me.

The room is poorly lit, which suits my purposes well. Keeping close to the shadows near the wall as I have been taught, I make my way to the stairs that lead to the second floor, where rooms can be had for the night.

First door on the right, Sister Vereda said.

I am so focused on reaching the stairs and on the instructions going through my head that I do not see the big oaf who has risen from his bench until I run into him.

"Oho!" he cries as he grabs my arms to keep me from falling. "I've found a tasty morsel for my dinner."

His hood is drawn close around his head, shadowing his face, and his straw hat hangs down his back, marking him as one who toils in the fields. Annoyance flickers in my chest. I have no time for delays; I am eager to try my wings. I start to tell him to get out of my way then realize that he could be part of the test the abbess has set for me. I cast my eyes downward. "Someone waits for me upstairs."

It works too well, for I can feel his gaze on me growing warm. Interested. Instead of stepping aside, he draws closer, backing me up against the wall. My heart beats frantically at being trapped like this, but I force my mind to calm, reminding myself that he is likely just a peasant who is nothing to me. I shove against the oaf's chest, which is as hard as iron from days spent pushing a plow in the fields. "I will get in much trouble if I am late." I am sure to make my voice waver slightly so he will think I am afraid.

After a long moment, he steps aside. "Hurry back down to Hervé when you are done, eh?" he whispers in my ear. His big, greedy hand slides down and slaps my rump, and test or no, it is all I can do to keep from gutting him then and there. Keeping my eyes down so he cannot see my fury, I nod, then hurry on my way as he returns to his bench.

At the top of the stairwell, a serving maid struggles with a heavy tray. By the time I reach the landing, she has paused in front of a door. First door on the right.

Jean Runnion's door.

Use the tools and opportunities Mortain places in front of you. It is one of the first lessons we learn at the convent. "Is that for Monsieur Runnion?" I call out.

Startled, the maid turns her head. "Yes. He asked for his dinner to be served in his room."

As well he might. He has good reason to stay hidden. Bretons have long memories where traitors are concerned, and we do not forgive easily. I hurry forward. "I will take the tray to him," I offer. "He is in a foul mood tonight."

The maid is suspicious and frowns at me. "How do you know this?"

I give her a cold smile. "Because his man warned me of such when he came to fetch me for the evening."

A look of contempt appears on her face. I am torn between pride that she finds my pretense believable and annoyance that she thinks me a harlot. It is exactly as Sister Beatriz said it would be: People hear and see what they expect to hear and see. But just because we have been trained to use that to our advantage does not mean I like it.

The maid shoves the tray into my hands and I have to grab quickly to keep it from tumbling to the ground.

With one last swish of her skirts, she clatters down the stairs, leaving me alone with only a thick oaken door between me and my first assignment.

Three years of lessons crowd my head at once, bumping into each other like an unsettled flock of pigeons. I remind myself that there is nothing to fear. I mixed the poison with my own hand. It contains a slow-acting toxin, one especially chosen so that I will be far away before the traitor dies, giving me enough time to escape should something go wrong. To everyone else, it will merely appear as if he is in a deep, wine-sodden sleep.

But nothing will go wrong, I tell myself. Shifting the weight of the tray, I rap on the door. "Your dinner, monsieur."

"Entré," comes the muffled voice.

I open the door, then juggle the tray again so I can close it firmly behind me. Runnion doesn't even look up. He is sprawled in a chair in front of the fire, drinking from a cup of wine. A jug sits on the floor next to him. "Just put it on the table," he instructs.

The years have not been kind to him. His face is deeply

lined and his hair lank and gray. Indeed, he looks almost ill, as if his guilty conscience has eaten away at his soul.

If so, I am surely about to do him a favor. I set the tray down. "Would monsieur like me to refill his cup before I go?" I ask.

"Yes. Then leave," he commands. His dismissive manner makes me even happier that he will not be able to order anyone else around after tonight.

As I move toward his chair, I lift a hand to the finely woven net around my hair and slip one of the pearls from it. I bend over to pick up the wine jug, pausing to look at his face. There is a great dark smudge around his lips, as if Mortain has pressed His thumb into the blackness of the man's soul and smeared it along his mouth to say, *Here, this is how he will die.*

Thus reassured, I slip the pearl into the wine, swirl the jug twice, then pick up Runnion's cup and fill it.

I hand it to him, and he takes a sip, then another. As I watch, Runnion looks up from his cup and scowls at me. "Where is the other girl?"

I have overstayed my welcome. "She was busy downstairs and asked me to come."

Even as his bleary eyes move to my traveling cloak, I begin heading toward the door. I want to be away from here before his wine-soaked mind begins to draw any conclusions.

"Wait!" he calls out, and I freeze, my heart beating wildly in my chest.

"Leave the jug," he orders.

I look down and see that I still carry the wine jug in my hand. *Careless!* "But, of course, monsieur," I say, then set the jug on the floor next to him. I risk another glance from under my lashes, but he's turned back to the fire.

At the door, I pause one last time, waiting until he takes another sip of wine, then another. I cross myself and bow my head, commending the traitor's soul into Mortain's keeping. As I reach for the door, it bursts open. A large form stands there, outlined by the torchlight from the hallway. His hood is still pulled up close around his face, but I recognize the hulking figure of Hervé.

Merde! Could he not have waited till I went back downstairs?

I step away from the door and throw a look over my shoulder to gauge the distance to the window. Hervé follows my gaze and swears when he sees Runnion, who looks as if he has passed out in a wine-sodden stupor. While Hervé rushes to Runnion's side, I take the opportunity Mortain has provided me and bolt for the window.

It is a long ride back to the convent, but my sense of triumph keeps me warm. I want to crow to the heavens that I have served my god and my convent well, but Sister Serafina has told me many times that pride is a sin, and so I do not.

Plus, it would frighten my horse. I reach down and pat Nocturne's neck, just in case my exhilaration is making her uneasy.

The one sour note in my triumph is the oafish peasant who came upstairs. Part of me wishes I'd stayed to fight with him, tested my skills against his, for surely he would be no match for one trained such as I. We are allowed to kill in self-defense, whether the opponent has a marque or not, and I could have avenged myself for his overly familiar groping.

However, since the whole point of this first assignment is to demonstrate my obedience, I think I have made the right choice in walking away.

The thrill of success is still humming through my veins when I reach the ferryman – the same one who rowed me out to the convent when I first arrived. Tonight, he takes Nocturne and has his son – who is nearly as ancient as he is – return the horse to the stables. As I climb into the waiting boat, his eyes slide away from me, afraid that if he stares too long, he might come to know what I've been up to.

I cannot wait to lay my success at the reverend mother's feet. I want to prove to her that she was right to take me in, that she chose wisely in offering me a home. I want her to see that I have passed her test.

That I was picked over Annith brings me joy, even as my heart breaks for her. But perhaps the abbess has seen some special skill or spark in me, one that makes me shine brighter than Annith and the others.

The boat crunches up onto the stony beach and I step out, doing my best to keep my fine gown clear of the surf. "Thank you," I say; I wave goodbye to the ferryman, but he is already rowing back out to sea.

Eager to make my report to the abbess, I hurry toward the convent. As I pass the standing stone, I kiss the tips of my fingers and press them to the cold rough surface in a quick prayer of thanks to Mortain for guiding my hand.

The sun is just beginning to rise, but the chickens are already at their morning scratching. The reverend mother too is an early riser and already sits at her desk. I knock on her open door.

She looks up from her paperwork. "You're back."

"Yes, Reverend Mother."

She puts down the unopened letter she was holding and gives me her full attention. "It went well?"

I try not to preen. "Very well. It was exactly as you and Sister Vereda said. The marque was clear upon the traitor, and the poison was just beginning to work as I left."

"Good." She nods her head, satisfied. "You are safely returned to us before any will know he is dead. An easy, clean first kill, as it should be. No one saw you?"

"No one. Except for the maid, who thought exactly what Sister Beatriz told us she would think." I hesitate, filled with regret that Hervé has tainted my first assignment but knowing I cannot risk omitting him from my report, in case he is part of the test. "And a farmer from the fields who tried to delay me. For a dalliance, I think."

The corner of her mouth quirks up in amusement. "I trust you were able to take care of that?"

"But of course, Reverend Mother."

Her eyes narrow. "Did you kill him?"

"No! He was not assigned to me, nor did he bear a marque."

"Good." She seems pleased with my account. "Do you wish to rest for a few hours before joining the others?"

"No, thank you." I am far too excited to even think of sleep.

She smiles, as if she knows full well why I cannot sleep. "Very well. Once you have changed, report to Sister Thomine in the courtyard. Leave your clothes on the bed, and Sister Beatriz will fetch them shortly." She gives a nod of dismissal, then cracks open the seal on the letter in front of her. Just before I step into the hall, she calls out, "Ismae?"

"Yes, Reverend Mother?"

"Your second test will come soon," she says, not looking up from her correspondence. "It will not be this easy."

I cannot tell if her words are meant as a promise or a warning, so I take them as both. In the dormitory, I change quickly and leave my finery on the bed. As I lace up my plain gray habit, I glance out the window. Sister Thomine is leading the others in evasive techniques. Well and good, as I need to discharge some of this pent-up excitement. I hurry out to join them.

Four of the younger girls are grappling together, and Sister Thomine has paired herself with Annith. When she sees me, she waves me over, glad to pass off this duty to someone else. Annith is highly skilled in this art.

As she steps away, I bow formally to Annith. She returns the bow, then takes her stance. As I take mine, I suppress a snort of laughter. If only that oaf from the tavern could see me now.

And then Annith comes at me in a quick flash of supple muscles and sleek limbs as she steps inside my guard and wraps her arms around my neck. "How did it go?" she whispers.

"Perfectly." I bring both my arms up and jerk them outward, breaking her grip. "As smooth as Sister Beatriz's finest silk."

Annith feints to the side, then grabs my arm and twists it behind my back. "There were no difficulties?"

I grit my teeth against the pain. "None. Except for bit of lip from a serving maid and a grope from a drunken oaf, but that was all. I even saw the marque of Mortain," I whisper.

"But you have not yet received the Tears of Mortain!" she says, relaxing her hold.

"I know." I try to keep the smugness from my voice, but it is there all the same. To distract her, I step sharply back to knock her off balance, then spin out of her loosened grip and continue moving until I am behind her with my right arm tight against her throat. "Don't worry, though. I'm sure it will be your turn soon."

"Girls!" Sister Thomine calls out. "Enough chatter, unless your plan is to talk your victims to death."

Annith reaches up and pinches a spot at the base of my wrist. My hand goes numb and she slides out of my grasp. I try to hold on to her with one hand, but she is slippery as an eel and evades my hold. "No news of Sybella yet?" I ask as I shake off the numbness.

Annith springs behind me. Like a whipcord, her arm comes around my neck. "No, none of the sisters will breathe a word. And if Reverend Mother talks of her, she does so only when I am asleep and cannot listen at the door. It is as if Sybella has ceased to exist," she says just before she tries to choke me.

I tuck my chin under to block her attempt. "I'm sure she'll be fine." My words are thick and garbled under her grip at my throat. "This is her third assignment, after all."

Annith grunts, and I know her thoughts turn to their familiar concern – why others have been chosen and she has not. She grabs my arm, spins around in front of me, then levers my body over her shoulder. For one brief moment I fly through the air. The painful landing on my back forces all the breath from my lungs, and I gasp like a caught fish.

"Fourth," Annith says, looking down at me. "It is her *fourth* assignment."

Chapter 7

"Careful!" Sister Serafina scolds. "Don't let it boil or it will turn to resin and be of no use."

"Yes, sister." I keep my eyes fixed on the small flask I hold over the flame. Tiny bubbles have begun to form along the sides of the glass, but it is not boiling. Not yet.

"Excellent," she says from just behind my shoulder. "Now put it over here to cool."

Using iron tongs, I lift the flask and set it on a cooling stone. We are brewing up a fresh batch of night whispers. In its current volatile state, it will kill anyone who breathes its fumes, causing the lungs to harden and become rigid and brittle as glass.

Anyone except for Sister Serafina and me. We are immune.

"Once it cools," she says, "we'll add it to this candle wax, and then—" A knock on the door interrupts her. "Don't come in!" she calls out in alarm.

"I won't." It is Annith, who surely knows better than to enter.

"Reverend Mother has asked that Ismae come to her office right away."

The thrill of this summons makes my heart flutter. The only time I have been called to her office since I arrived is to receive news of an assignment. Without waiting for the nun to dismiss me, I hurry to the stone basin, where I begin scrubbing the last traces of poison from my hands.

Sister Serafina heaves a sigh of annoyance. "How the holy mother expects me to supply all our poisons without help is surely one of Mortain's great mysteries."

I glance sideways at her. "You'd think she would send Annith instead."

Sister Serafina pins me with a severe look. "The reverend mother has her reasons. Now go. Do not make her wait."

I go, being sure to curtsy so as not to antagonize her further. She thinks she has told me nothing, but it is just the opposite. I now know that there is an actual reason that Annith has not been sent out. And if Sister Serafina knows what it is, surely Annith and I can find out as well.

On my way to the reverend mother's office I straighten my veil and brush a bit of dust from my skirts. I pause at the door, take a deep breath and compose my features, then knock.

"Enter."

When I step into the office, the sight of a man sitting there is as shocking as a clap of thunder in the quiet room. His hair is white, as is his neatly trimmed beard. A heavy gold chain with a bejeweled pendant winks at me from the fur collar of his thick brocade robe.

"Come in, Ismae," the abbess says. "I'd like you to meet Chancellor Crunard. He is a patron of our convent and acts as the liaison between us and the outside world."

He is also head of one of the oldest and noblest families in Brittany and a hero of the last four wars. He has fought long and hard for our independence. Indeed, every one of his sons has died fighting against the French. I sink into a respectful curtsy. "Good day, my lord."

He nods a brief greeting, his eyes giving away nothing of his thoughts.

"We have another assignment for you," the reverend mother says, and a fierce triumph rises up in me at this newest opportunity to prove my worthiness.

The abbess leans back in her chair and folds her arms. "What has Sister Eonette told you of our political situation?" She asks the question lightly enough, but, with the reverend mother, everything is a test. She will not care how many of Sister Eonette's lectures I have missed because Sister Serafina needed my help or because I was stuck in the scriptorium, struggling with my letters.

I fold my hands primly in front of me. "Our beloved Duke Francis died nearly two months ago, harried unto death by the aggression of the French regent. He and the other nobles fought hard to halt France overreaching her authority, but they were defeated. Because of this defeat, our duke was forced to accept the Treaty of Verger, the terms of which are favorable to the French and make it difficult for our country to maintain its independence."

The abbess looks pleased and casts a glance at the chancellor as if to say *See?*. He nods, then raises his eyebrows in a question. At her assent, he speaks, the deep rumble of his voice jarring in this place where I have only ever heard women. "What of our young duchess? What do you know of her?"

I shift slightly, uncomfortable with this strange man quizzing me. "I know that her hand in marriage has been promised to half the princes in Europe and that she has vowed to keep our country's independence." I cannot help but feel sympathy for our poor duchess. "She has been sold to the highest bidder, for all that she is noble born."

The chancellor's eyes widen in surprise and he gives the abbess a quizzical look. "Is that what you teach them?"

"Not in so many words, Lord Chancellor, but you must understand that those who are drawn to Mortain's work, by their very natures, have no love for the married state or for forced or arranged marriages. Indeed, many have joined our convent to escape those very things." The abbess's cold blue gaze clashes against the chancellor's tired brown one, and some unspoken thing passes between them. Chancellor Crunard looks away first, and the abbess turns back to me.

"We have reason to believe that the French are sending a spy to meet with Baron Lombart in an attempt to purchase his loyalty. The port Lombart controls will be critical should war break out again between our countries. We wish you to intercept this contact before he meets with Lombart. We cannot afford to lose another of our nobles to the French."

My heart quickens at this new task. It is much more complex than the tavern, a true test of all I have learned, and I am eager to pass it.

"You will accompany Chancellor Crunard as his paramour at Lombart's hunting lodge in Pont-Croix this evening," the abbess says. I sneak another glance at the chancellor. He is so old, I am sure everyone will see through this deception. If anything, they will think I am his daughter. "Now," the abbess continues, "there is much to prepare – ah! Here they are," she says at the knock on her door.

Without waiting for an invitation, Sister Arnette and Sister Beatriz enter the room.

"Go with the sisters and they will see that you are given what you need for tonight. When they are done, they will take you to Sister Vereda. She has Seen this, Ismae, and will tell you all you need to know. Then you will meet Sir Crunard in the courtyard."

"Yes, Reverend Mother." I dip into another curtsy. As I follow the two nuns from the room, I struggle to keep from skipping in my excitement.

"We will go to the armory first," Sister Arnette announces as we step into the hallway.

Sister Beatriz protests. "I think we should dress her first. How will you know what she can carry if you do not first see her gown?"

"True enough," Sister Arnette says, but the sigh that escapes her makes me think she holds no greater love for Sister Beatriz's womanly arts than I do.

Even so, when we enter Sister Beatriz's inner chamber, I gape. It is the first time I have been here, and gowns of every sort hang from pegs or are folded in stacks, silk upon velvet,

velvet upon brocade, in every color imaginable. Sister Beatriz's eyes are already searching among the finery. "Ah. This one might work." She plucks a russet velvet gown from a stack. It has a gold and green embroidered stomacher, and I have never seen anything so fine. She holds it up to me and squints, then shakes her head. "Makes you look sallow." I am not sure what sallow is, but it is a lovely gown and my eyes follow it longingly as she tosses it aside.

Next, she holds up a gown of vermilion brocade. Not caring for the brightness of the color, I mutter, "Why not just paint a sign on my forehead?"

"You think appearing in stark black like a crow among peacocks will aid your stealth?" she asks.

"No, sister."

She gives a snort of satisfaction that I have taken her point, then begins pulling down dozens of gowns from the pegs. But they are too loose or too short or the color does not suit her. Or me. At last she takes down a claret velvet gown and holds it up. She and Sister Arnette exchange a glance. "It is perfect for her, no?"

"Except it is missing a bodice," I point out.

Sister Beatriz waves my concerns aside. "The bodice is just cut low, in the Venetian style, the better to display your womanly charms."

Sister Arnette studies the gown, her fingers tapping against her chin while she thinks. "I can work with that," she finally says, and my heart sinks. I am not sure *I* can work with it. Or *in* it, as the case may be.

But that is the end of the discussion, and Sister Beatriz shoves the gown at me. "Try it on so we may see if it fits." She motions me to a dressing screen in the far corner. I hold the gown as gently as a newborn babe, afraid my fingers will crush the soft fabric.

Behind the screen, I quickly slip out of my habit.

"Here." Sister Beatriz drapes a delicate piece of linen over the screen. "You will need a finer shift under that."

Painfully aware of the two older women on the other side of the screen, I slip out of my old chemise, shivering in my nakedness. I am relieved when I finally have the new shift on, then I quickly step into the rich velvet skirt and tie the ribbons at my waist. I slide my arms into the tight sleeves and marvel at how perfectly they fit, as if they'd been made for me.

As I ease the bodice up over my shoulders, I see that Sister Beatriz is right. It does cover my bosom, but only barely. I have always known that I must on occasion pass as a noblewoman, but I am loath to dress as a harlot. "I don't think this will work!" I call out, too embarrassed to emerge from behind the screen.

Then Sister Beatriz is there, swatting my clumsy fingers aside and doing up the lacings herself. "It is perfect. It will capture every man's attention so that no one will bother to watch what your hands are doing. Now come with me, Sister Arnette is waiting in the armory. Here are your slippers and cloak. I'll dress your hair when she is done with you."

Even though the armory pales by comparison to Sister Beatriz's dressing room, I much prefer it. Indeed, it is one of my favorite rooms at the convent. In addition to every size and shape of knife and dagger, it holds razor-edged rondelles, used to kill from a distance. Crossbows of all dimensions hang from the rafters, and rows of bolts are lined up on trays. Garrote wires are looped from hooks, as are all manner of leather harnesses and sheaths for concealing the weapons on our bodies. A sharp metallic tang hangs in the air and mixes with the scent of goose fat used for polishing the blades.

Sister Arnette grabs my hand and pulls me to an entire wall lined with knives. She gives my tight sleeves a quick glance. "We'll never get blades under those. Here." She tosses an ankle sheath at me. As I bend over to strap it on, my womanly charms nearly tumble out of my bodice. *Merde.*

Once the ankle sheath is secure, I am handed a thin stiletto encrusted with jewels. I nearly drop it in surprise. "'Tis so fine."

"It is all the rage in Venice. But this will be your main weapon tonight." She produces a finely wrought bracelet that looks like heavy cord dipped in gold and wrapped round and round. She grasps the ends, then pulls, uncoiling it to reveal a length of thin, deadly wire.

"You have only to put your hands to his neck for an embrace. If you move quickly enough, he will not know what's happening until it is too late. If need be, you could even do it in the darkened corner of a crowded room."

She re-coils the bracelet and hands it to me. I slip it on my wrist.

Sister Beatriz studies me thoughtfully. "Perhaps I should rouge her nipples with red ocher."

"Sister!" I am well and truly shocked. Annith has warned me that Sister Beatriz has the makings of a fine lightskirt, but I have missed too many of her classes to see this side of her.

"Don't be tiresome." She dismisses my distress with a wave of her hand and turns to Sister Arnette. "If she raises her arms like so" – the old nun raises hers as if putting them around someone's neck—"her bodice will gape. Since Venetian women rouge their nipples, we should do the same to hers, don't you think? To keep the disguise complete?"

Sister Arnette gives me a sympathetic grin. "I think if he catches sight of her nipples, it won't matter whether they're rouged or not. He'll be dead within seconds."

It is Sister Arnette who leads me to the convent's inner sanctum, where Sister Vereda resides, and I am glad, for I am heartily sick of Sister Beatriz. At the seeress's door, the nun pats my arm.

"Good luck," she says, and I do not know if she means for my assignment tonight or my visit with the ancient nun. Sister Arnette leaves and I turn back to the door. Before I even knock, a voice calls out, "Come in."

I step into the seeress's quarters, which are as dark and warm as a womb. There is a faint reddish glow from a charcoal brazier. Sister Vereda has no need of light, but her old joints are fond of heat. I peer into the darkness to try to see her better. She cocks her wimpled head to the side and studies me with her blind eyes. It is unsettling. "Come closer," she says.

I fumble my way across the darkened room, the heavy, unfamiliar skirts hampering me as much as the lack of light. "Reverend Mother says you have Seen my assignment this evening and can give me directions so I may strike true."

"Strike true? Is that your heart's desire then?"

"But of course! Mortain and His convent have raised me up from a root cellar and given me a more glorious life than I could ever have imagined. I will repay that debt in every way I can."

She stares at me in silence, her milky white eyes unnerving. "Remember, true faith never comes without anguish."

Before I can respond, she reaches into a small pouch at her waist, pulls out a handful of something – it looks to be small bones and a tangle of feathers – and tosses it on the brazier.

Flames spring to life and an acrid tang fills the room. Sister Vereda stares into the small fire as if reading the red-gold flames reflected in her unseeing eyes.

"Twenty paces, then up a staircase. Small for a man, and wiry, like the fox he resembles. The dust of Amboise clings to his boots, and a red ruby given to him by the French regent winks in his ear. Martel is his name. That is who Mortain has marqued." The flames sputter out, and Sister Vereda's eyes return to their milky white.

Not knowing what else to do, I curtsy. "Yes, sister. Mortain's will be done."

Next, she lifts a small box from the shelf under the brazier. Her eyes may be blind, but her fingers are nimble and quick, and she opens the small leather case and pulls from it a heavy bottle. It is of deepest black, its polished surface catching small sparks of light from the embers so that it looks as if she holds a piece of night sky filled with stars.

"Even though you are not a full initiate, the reverend mother says that you are to receive the Tears of Mortain. Kneel," she orders as she pulls the stopper from the bottle.

Keeping my eyes on the sharp, tapered point of the stopper, I kneel at her feet.

"By the grace of Mortain, I grant you Sight so you may see His will and act on it. Do you promise to obey the saint and act only when He bids it?"

"I do."

She dips the point of the stopper into the contents of the vial, then gropes gently for my face. "Open your eyes wide, child."

Even though I am sore afraid of that sharp wand, I do as she commands. She moves it unerringly toward my eyes, one single heavy drop hanging from the tapered end, and I pray her hand is steady.

There is a touch of warmth, then my vision blurs and all the colors and light in the small room run together. My eyes grow warmer and warmer until I fear they will burst into flames. For a moment, I am afraid she has blinded me, but then the sensation passes and the heat and the blurring cease, and I can see again. It seems to me that everything is somewhat brighter now, all the edges sharper, as if the same milkiness that clouds Sister Vereda's gaze has been ripped away from my own.

But it is not only my sight that is different. My skin, too, has changed, and I feel the air as an almost solid thing against my arms and face. I am aware of Sister Vereda in a way I was not before; I can *feel* her, feel the spark of life that shines so brightly within her.

"These Tears of Mortain are a gift to those of us who serve Him," she explains as she returns the vial to its box. "They allow us to experience life and death as He does. Now go," Sister Vereda says. "And may Mortain keep you in His dark embrace and guide your hand with His own."

Chapter 8

Chancellor Crunard has claimed this chateau is nothing but a hunting lodge, but to my eyes, accustomed as they are to a poorly thatched cottage and the austere world of the convent, it looks like a palace. The only thing the nobles appear to be hunting is one another, whether for spirited gossip or furtive liaisons behind the tapestries.

The chancellor pats my arm. "Relax, my dear," he says. "Or else they will wonder why my new paramour is scowling so." His wry smile causes me to blush. Prettily, I hope.

"Your pardon, milord." It had seemed a most far-fetched notion when the abbess first explained it. Surely no one would believe that I was with Chancellor Crunard in *that* way. But the truth is, there are many such pairings throughout the hall, older lords and nobles sporting young maids on their arms just as they sport jaunty feathers in their caps or jeweled daggers at their hips.

Our host, Baron Lombart, approaches, and Crunard introduces us. Lombart is fat and old and reminds me of the boar who used to hide in the woods near my home. I murmur some polite nicety and wonder if my new garrote would be able to slice through the thickness of his neck.

I suspect Crunard has guessed the drift of my thoughts,

for he nods in the direction of the crowd. "Entertain yourself for a bit, my dear. The baron and I have business to discuss."

It is my cue, and joy at being released surges through me. I am only too happy to let the tides and currents of the mingling nobles carry me to the edge of the room so I can slip away to my assignment.

As I move toward the door, curious glances brush against my skin. I feel one particular gaze linger too long, so I stop and pretend to make conversation with two gentlemen nearby. One of them stops talking and turns his protruding eyes to me. I give him a withering glance and continue on my way.

When I reach the doorway, no one is watching, so I slip from the room. The hallway is dark compared to the brightness of the great hall, and cool. I am glad to be away from the smell of too many bodies and warring perfumes. I count off twenty paces and am not surprised to find a wide, sweeping stairway, just as Sister Vereda predicted.

When I reach the first door at the top of the stairs, I draw into myself, as I have been taught, letting everything around me grow still, and then I cast my senses into the room beyond. The Tears of Mortain have done their job well, for I am certain there is no spark of life burning behind that door.

The next chamber is as cold and empty as the first, but when I stand in front of the third, I feel the faint trickle of life, warm and pulsing.

Anticipation bubbles through me, and it is all I can do to keep from charging in, daggers drawn. Instead, I put a hand to my heart to calm it and quickly run through Sister Beatriz's instructions. This will be the hard part, acting the coquette.

With one last deep breath, I force a smile of breathless anticipation onto my face and open the heavy wooden door. "Jean-Paul?" I whisper into the room, then stumble slightly, as if I've had too much wine. "Is that you?"

Standing at the window, Martel whirls round to face me. He is just as Sister Vereda said he would be, not much taller than I, his hair the reddish brown of a fox. I stumble toward him, and barely have time to register his scowl of alarm before he steps away from the window and grabs my shoulders. "What are you doing here?" He gives me a rough shake and I let my body go slack, as if I can barely manage to stand on my own.

"I am looking for Jean-Paul. And you, sir" – I tap him lightly on the chest—"are not him." I squish my lips into a pout and pray I do not look like a hooked fish. I am close enough to see the ruby he wears in left ear.

Looking down at my bodice, the fool relaxes. Are men truly such idiots that they cannot resist two orbs of flesh? Martel glances at the door behind us and licks his lips. "Perhaps, after I conduct my business, I can come to demoiselle's aid," he suggests. His eyes stray again to my bodice, and the dagger at my ankle calls to my clenched hands. *Not yet*, I tell myself. *Not yet.*

"That is a very kind offer." I let my eyes wander up and down his body, as if assessing his charms. In truth, I am searching for the marque. His forehead is clear, as are his lips. Uncertainty raises its head. I sigh as if smitten. "But Jean-Paul," I say, then sigh again. I tilt my head, considering. "Well, as you say, he is not here. Mayhap monsieur will do." *As if I am a mare in heat,* I think in disgust, *and any stallion will suffice.*

Martel steps closer. I swallow the distaste that rises up in my throat and wind my arms around his neck. *There!* Just where his shirt meets his jaw line, a dark shadow marks his skin. He sees the spark of interest flare in my eyes, and his own heat with desire. I allow my body to press even closer against his. He licks his lips again. "As soon as I am done... Perhaps you can wait in the next chamber?"

"My pleasure, milord," I say. He nuzzles my ear to seal our agreement. While pretending to play with the hair at the nape of his neck, I slip the bracelet from my wrist. Just as his nuzzling starts to move dangerously low, I yank the hidden wire from the bracelet. Before he can guess what is happening, I loop it around his neck, spin out of his embrace, step to his back, and pull tight, a move I have practiced with Annith a hundred times.

His hands scrabble at his neck, tearing at the silver wire. The sounds he makes are ugly and desperate and fill me with uncertainty. Then I remember that this man is betraying my country, my duchess, and I pull tighter, praying to Mortain for strength.

He grants it. After a short but spirited struggle, Martel sags against me. Before he is completely gone, I lean in and put my lips to his ear. "We punish those who betray our country." My words are as soft and tender as a lover's caress, and Martel shudders as death claims him.

Just as I relax my grip, a thick warmth rises up from his body and rubs against me, like a cat rubbing its owner's leg. Images fill my mind: a fleet of ships, a sealed letter, a heavy gold signet ring, my own breasts. The warmth swirls briefly within me, then dissipates with a sudden *whoosh*, leaving me chilled and shaken.

What in Mortain's name was that?

His soul.

The words come unbidden. Almost as if someone else – the god, perhaps? – has spoken them.

Why has no one at the convent warned me of this? Is this one of the glories of Mortain that Sister Vereda spoke of? Or something else? For I cannot decide if I have just been violated in some way or granted a sacred trust.

But I have no time for reflections. I shove my questions aside and brace myself against the man's body, trying to balance his weight as I unwrap the garrote from his neck. I wipe it clean on his doublet, then retract the wire into the bracelet. With both hands free, I prop the body up against the window and peer down to the courtyard, praying that the cart Chancellor Crunard promised is there.

It is.

I grasp the traitor by his collar and begin the difficult task of shoving his body through the window.

For a small man, he is surprisingly heavy. I struggle with

his dead weight, trying to maneuver it onto the casement. After a final heave that leaves me breathing hard, the lifeless body tumbles from the window. There is a moment of silence, then a thud as the body hits the waiting cart. I peer out in time to see the driver lift the reins and urge the horses forward.

I do not know where he will take the body or what he will do to keep it concealed, but that is not my task.

Flushed and shaky after my brush with Martel's soul, I long to sit down in one of the chairs and compose myself. Or fall to my knees and pray for understanding. But I must get back to Crunard so we may take our leave.

I push away from the wall and move toward the door, then hear a footstep in the corridor outside. Too late! Someone is coming. Baron Lombart, perhaps? Hoping to meet with Martel?

I try to think. Should I seduce him or kill him? Of course I would prefer to kill him, but I cannot – not unless he tries to kill me or I see the marque.

The latch on the door lifts and I step back a few paces, gripping my arms and hunching my shoulders, already slipping into the role I must play. Once again, anticipation burbles through me. Or perhaps it is panic.

When the door opens I cry out, "Jean-Paul? What took you so long? I'd almost given up on— Oh. You are not Jean-Paul," I say accusingly.

"No," he says, then closes the door softly behind him. "I am not, but perhaps I can help you," he offers.

And indeed, he is not Jean-Paul, nor Baron Lombart. This man is much taller than the baron, and where Lombart had gone to fat, this man is all lithe muscle. His rich brown cloak is clasped in place with the silver oak leaf of Saint Camulos, the patron saint of battle and soldiers. Under that he wears an unadorned black doublet that is elegant in its simplicity. He steps farther into the room, and I begin to feel trapped. Afraid of what his sharp gray eyes will see in my face, I fold my arms so that my breasts rise up enticingly. "As you are not Jean-Paul, I do not think you can help me." Even as I speak, my eyes search his face, his neck, praying for the marque that will allow me to dispatch him. But there is none. Or none that I can see.

"But I am here and he is not." The man's eyes, as dark and shifting as storm clouds, roam over my body, but there is no heat there. His keen gaze dismisses me and moves to the window.

I take a step closer to distract him. "Ah, but I do not wish to play Jean-Paul false, my lord, even though your charms are many." In truth, he is not charming so much as dangerous, and I would have said anything to turn his attention from that window.

Almost as if reading my thoughts, he crosses to it and peers outside. I hold my breath. *Sweet Mortain, please let the cart be gone from the courtyard!*

The man's regard flicks back to me, cutting straight to the bone. "You wound me, demoiselle. I am sure I could make you forget all about Jean-Paul."

Still playing the coquette, I tilt my head to the side, but something is wrong. He is saying the right words, but his eyes do not match his flirtatious tone. A deep note of warning sounds inside me. "B-but I do not want to forget about him," I say as if insulted.

He takes three giant strides toward me, his entire demeanor changing as he grabs my shoulders. "Enough with the games. Who are you? What are you doing here?"

I let my body go slack, as if I'm weak and frightened. "I might ask the same of you. Who are you and what are you doing here?"

"Gavriel Duval. And if you are looking for a tryst, I can accommodate you." He pulls me closer, so that I feel the heat rising off his body, warm and smelling faintly of some spice. "But I do not think that is what you are looking for."

He knows! I can see it in the depths of his eyes. Somehow he knows what I am and why I am here.

I panic and begin to babble. "I am sorry, milord, but I am waiting for Jean-Paul. I will leave you to your moment of quiet and be on my way." With a nimble twist of my body, I slip from his iron grip. It is artlessly done, but I am free and fleeing for the door.

Once in the hall, I run all the way to the stairs. I take them two at a time, then pause a moment to compose myself. I look over my shoulder, but there is no sign of Gavriel Duval. I straighten my skirts and square my shoulders, then enter the great hall. Upon seeing me, Crunard extricates himself from his conversation and makes his way through the crowd to my side. He arches an eyebrow. "Is everything as it should be?"

"It will be once we are away from here," I say.

As he escorts me to the door, I feel a pair of eyes boring into the back of my head. I know if I turn and look, they will be the color of storm clouds.

Chapter 9

At the convent, the reverend mother looks at me sharply as she leans forward. "You are certain he said Duval?"

"Yes, Reverend Mother. That was the name he gave. Although perhaps it was false? He also wore the silver oak leaf of Saint Camulos," I add, in case that will help in any way.

The abbess glances at Crunard and he nods reluctantly. "Duval does serve Saint Camulos, as do most knights and soldiers."

"Even so," she says. "It would be easy enough to get hold of such a pin to round out the deception."

Crunard shifts in his chair. "But if it *was* Duval..." he says.

"There could be other reasons for his being there," the abbess points out.

"There could," Crunard agrees grudgingly. "But it is also possible we have caught a very big fish indeed."

The abbess turns her piercing blue gaze back to me. "How did he react to finding you in the room?"

"He assumed I was there for a liaison of some sort and was flirtatious at first. Then he grew angry." I want to look away, afraid she will be able to tell just how poorly I played my role with him, but trying to avoid her will only make her pay closer attention.

"Tell me everything he said. Everything."

And so I repeat the conversation for her, word by word. When I am done, she looks at Crunard, who shrugs. "It could mean nothing; it could mean everything. I no longer claim to know all the duchess's enemies. They hide too well among her allies."

"But Duval..." the abbess says, shaking her head. She leans back in her chair and closes her eyes. I cannot tell if she is thinking or praying. Mayhap both. While her eyes are closed, I take a deep breath and long for my own bed. Tonight's duties have been exhilarating, but draining too. That Duval saw through my deception has left me shaken. I had thought there was little more for me to learn, but tonight has proven me wrong. I vow to pay more attention to Sister Beatriz's lessons in the womanly arts. Perhaps Annith and I can even practice on each other.

"So," the reverend mother says, coming out of her reverie. "This is what we shall do. Baron Lombart's guests will be staying the week. Chancellor Crunard was on his way back to court, but he has had a change of heart, haven't you, Chancellor?"

He nods, then spreads his hands. "I fear my horse has gone lame."

The abbess smiles. "So, of course, he will return to Lombart's with his young guest. And you" – her eyes pin me to my chair—"will return with him and find a way to engage Duval again. Preferably alone. With luck, you can convince him to play a game of seduction with you, a liaison or some such—"

"But, Holy Mother—"

Her face grows cold and distant. "Did you or did you not vow to use every skill you possess in the service of Mortain?"

"Of course, but—"

"There is no but. Your feminine artistry is as much a part of your arsenal as your dagger or beloved poison. Duval must be watched. You yourself have found evidence of that. The closer you get to him, the more you will learn. Perhaps you will even be able to coax truths from him under the guise of pillow talk."

I am certain I could no more coax secrets out of the dark, angry Duval than I could coax the abbess to dance a gavotte in the streets of Nantes, but I keep that to myself. I have already performed poorly tonight and I am afraid if I argue she will think I am no longer fit to serve the convent. Then a thought occurs to me. "Why not just eliminate him now and avoid the risk altogether?"

"Did you see the marque of Mortain on him?"

I hesitate, then answer truthfully. "No. But Martel's was nearly hidden under his collar. Perhaps Duval's hides as well."

She smiles, and too late I see I have played right into her hands. "All the more reason to get close to him, no?"

I cannot begin to fathom why Mortain insists on concealing these marques of His so that I must play hide-and-seek.

"Ismae," she says, serious once more. "Duval is one of the duchess's most trusted advisors. It is critical we know where he stands."

"He has her ear and trust in a way few others do," explains Crunard.

"And if he is betraying us, he will feel Mortain's punishment soon enough." The abbess's face is grim. "Perhaps even at your hand—"

She is interrupted by scuffling at the door. The abbess only has time to frown before the door bursts open. My breath hitches sharply in my throat as Gavriel Duval himself strides in.

Annith is right on his heels. "I am sorry, Reverend Mother! I told him you'd left instructions not to be disturbed, but he wouldn't listen." She sends the intruder a scathing look.

"Yes, I can see that," the abbess says. She sends a quick questioning glance my way. When I nod, indicating he is who I saw at Lombart's, she turns back to the man glowering in her doorway. "Well, Duval, come in. Don't hover at the door."

Duval comes farther into the room and I nearly flinch at his heated gaze. In truth, the man is angry enough to breathe fire. "Abbess. Chancellor Crunard." He gives a perfunctory nod to both. His anger eats up all the empty space in the room. "We have a few things we must discuss."

The abbess raises an eyebrow. "Is that so?"

"Yes. The incompetence of your novices, for one." He places undue emphasis on the word *novice,* I think.

"Twice now, she" – he jabs his finger in my direction—"has interfered with my work. The convent cannot keep sending out agents who destroy valuable sources of information."

"Twice?" I challenge him, for I have seen him only once before.

"The tavern." At my blank look, he hunches his shoulders and leers. "*Hurry back down to Hervé when you are done, eh?*"

The oaf! *He* was the oaf at the tavern. My fists clench at the memory.

The reverend mother speaks, her cold voice drawing his attention back to her. "The convent has always acted alone in carrying out Mortain's will. Are you suggesting we need your permission?" Her tone implies he should not be suggesting any such thing.

He folds his arms across his chest. "I propose only that some thought be applied to your actions. Twice now you have gotten to men before I did. And while you and your saint are interested in meting out retribution, I am interested in information that can guide our country out of this wretched hole we are in."

"You wanted them for questioning." The reverend mother's flat tone does not reveal whether she feels remorse for having disrupted his plans.

Duval nods. "I am sure, given the right incentive, they could have led us to the puppet master pulling their strings."

Crunard sits forward in his chair, suddenly alert. "Surely they come from the French regent?"

"Perhaps," Duval says cautiously. "But she is working with someone at court and I would like to know who."

Crunard spreads his hands in invitation. "Will you share your suspicions with us?"

"Not at this time." Duval speaks quietly, but his refusal is shocking just the same.

Crunard recovers first. "Surely you're not suggesting we are not trustworthy?"

"I suggest no such thing, but it would be unwise for me to voice any suspicions I have without sufficient evidence. Unfortunately" – he sends me another scathing glance— "someone keeps destroying my evidence."

Mouth pursed in thought, the abbess folds her arms in her sleeves. "How do you propose we rectify this? Are we to consult with you every time the saint bids us act?"

Duval runs his hand through his hair and turns to the window. "Not necessarily. But we must find a better way to coordinate our efforts. Because of your novice's actions, the duchess has lost valuable information."

I feel as if I've been slapped. "*Might* have lost," I correct under my breath.

He looks at me in surprise. "Excuse me?"

I willingly bow to my god and my abbess, but I'll be damned if I will bow to this man. I raise my head and meet his gaze. "I said *might* have lost. It is not certain that these men had any vital information."

He strides toward me then, coming so close that I must tilt my head back to meet his glower. He places his hands on the arms of my chair, imprisoning me. "But we will never know, will we?" His voice is soft and mocking and he is so near I feel his words move across my skin.

"Duval!" The reverend mother's sharp voice breaks through our tense silence. "Stop intimidating my novice."

He flushes and pushes away from my chair.

"I was not intimidated," I mutter under my breath.

He glances angrily at me but says nothing. A small tic begins at the base of his jaw. He appeals to Chancellor Crunard. "Tell them. Tell them how delicate the balance is. How each bit of information has the power to sway that balance."

"He has no need to tell me," the abbess says sharply.

Crunard spreads his hands. "Then you know it is true. The circling vultures grow bold. The regent of France has forbidden that Anne be crowned duchess. It is our enemies' wish to make her France's ward so that they may claim Brittany for their own. They also claim the right to determine who she will marry."

Duval begins pacing. "Spies are everywhere. We can scarce keep track of them all. The French have set up a permanent entourage within our court, which has made some of the border nations uneasy."

Crunard adds, "Not to mention that their presence makes it impossible to see our duchess crowned without their knowledge. But until we place that crown upon her head before her people and the Church, we are vulnerable."

I cannot help but feel sympathy for our poor duchess. "Surely there is some way out of this mess?"

I have addressed my question to the abbess, but it is Duval who answers. "I will forge one with my bare hands, if need be," he says. "I vow that I will see her crowned duchess, and I will see her safely wed. But I need information against our enemies if I am to accomplish this."

The room falls so silent that I fear they will hear the pounding of my heart. Duval's vow has moved me, and that he has made it on sacred ground proves he is either very brave or very foolish.

At last the abbess speaks. "I will concede your greater experience in the matter of gathering information," she says.

At her words, Duval relaxes somewhat. The fool. The look she has given him is one that all of us at the convent have learned to fear, and I, for one, do not care for the gleam in her eye one bit.

"Your concern for our country is admirable, and it is true that few are as committed as you." Her compliments lull him further into an illusion of safety. "And," she continues, "I know you are as anxious to help us as we are to help you."

Duval's face creases into a frown as he tries to recall expressing such a thing. My heart swells with pride at how neatly the reverend mother is boxing him in. She glances at Chancellor Crunard, who gives a slight nod.

"We will be happy to work with you. And in order that we may do so more smoothly, we will place Ismae in your household for the next few weeks."

The shock of her words forces all the air from my lungs, which is the only thing that keeps me from shouting, *No!*

Duval sends me a horrified look – as if this has somehow been my doing! He opens his mouth to protest, but the abbess talks over him.

"We need someone at court. I don't like being so far away when there is such turmoil surrounding our duchess. Posing as your mistress, Ismae will have access to all the people and information the convent requires. More important, she will be in a position to act when needed. And" – she gives him a beatific smile—"coordinating our respective duties will then be possible."

I cannot help but admire the neatly set trap she has built around him. I would admire it even more if I had not been the bait. "But, Reverend Mother—" I start, but she silences me with a look.

Duval, however, does not owe her the same blind obedience. "You are mad," he says simply, and the reverend mother's face hardens. "I shall do no such thing. I do not have time to play nursemaid to one of your novitiates."

"Then any chance we have of coordinating our efforts is lost," she says, her entire demeanor cold and distant.

"You are blackmailing me," Duval says, aggrieved.

"No, only agreeing to the cooperation you yourself have requested." And there it is. He is well and truly trapped, and he knows it.

When he huffs out a sigh of resignation, I know she has won.

"I will not claim her as mistress. We shall say she is my cousin."

That barb finds its home. *Am I so very repugnant?*

The abbess looks incredulous. "And who will believe you? Your family and its ties are too well known for that to work."

"Besides," Sir Crunard adds, "no one would place an unwed maid in your care without female family members to chaperone. It is much more believable that you have simply taken a mistress."

I clear my throat, and the abbess raises an eyebrow, giving me permission to speak. "Would it not work for me to be installed in his kitchens? Or as a maid?"

She waves her hand, brushing away my suggestions. "You would not have access to court then, which is the whole point of this exercise."

"Except," Duval points out, "I am not known to favor mistresses. Not to mention that if I did, it would certainly not be one who was greener than a winter apple."

I set my teeth at his words. I am not *that* unpolished.

Reverend Mother leans back in her chair and *tsk*s. "You exaggerate, milord. Ismae has been well trained in all things, including how to act as a man's mistress."

Clearly now will not be a good time to confess to playing truant during most of Sister Beatriz's lessons.

"But more important," Duval continues, "with the way things are at court, I cannot assure her protection."

"I do not need protection," I say, offended at such a suggestion.

"No, she does not," the abbess agrees. "She merely needs an opportunity to act."

"You would leave such life-and-death decisions to a novice?"

"Of course not," Reverend Mother snaps. "We leave such life-and-death decisions in the hands of Mortain, where they belong." She turns to me. "You'll leave with Duval within the hour. Go pack a small bag to take with you. We'll have the rest of your things sent to his residence in Guérande. You may go."

Dizzy at the speed with which my world has been turned upside down, I stall, trying to think of one last argument I can make. I have joined the convent to withdraw from the world of men, not to be thrust upon the mercy of one.

The abbess leans across her desk. "Have you forgotten your vow for complete and unyielding obedience in all things?" she asks in a low voice. "You are but a novice. You still have much proving to do before you can take your final vows."

I swallow my remaining protests and go to my room to pack.

Chapter 10

Before I finish packing, there is a knock at my door. When the reverend mother walks in, I am stunned into silence. She has never visited my quarters before.

She closes the door behind her, eyes alight with a cold, blue fire. "You see how conveniently this aligns with our plans, don't you?"

It is true. Duval has given her an opening to carry out the very subterfuge she'd been planning minutes before he burst into her office. "It is what you wanted, Reverend Mother."

"It is what Mortain wants, child," she says sharply. "Or else it would not be so easily arranged. Settle your mind to this, Ismae. Even if Duval is guilty of nothing more than a temper and poor manners, this arrangement will serve us well, for there are many at court who bear watching. I would know with whom Duval spends time, who his allies are, what correspondence he sends. And receives. Keep an eye out for anything from the French regent. Be truthful with him whenever possible. It will be the quickest way to lull him into trust. I am not overly fond of coincidences and would like to better understand why he was in that room. He has complete access to the duchess, and her complete confidence as well. I want to be certain he is serving her interests."

"Is that whose interests we serve, Reverend Mother? Does serving the duchess serve Mortain? I am not being impudent," I rush to add. "I truly do not understand."

Her face softens. "But of course it is the same, child. Every day thousands of Breton voices beg our gods to keep them safe from the French and to keep our duchess strong. You can be certain France does not pray to our gods. Nor will the French honor the old saints as we do should they succeed in conquering our land. France is too closely aligned with the current pope, who would see all forms of worship but his own purged from the world. Of course Mortain does not wish that."

She lifts her hand from the folds of her gown and I now see that she carries something wrapped in soft, worn leather. "You have made only two kills, not three, but you are close to completing your training. This assignment is your final test. Once you pass it, you will only have to say your vows to be fully committed to this convent."

Dismayed that she would think otherwise, I meet her gaze, willing her to see the truth of my words. "I am fully committed already, Most Holy Mother."

"I know. Which is why I am giving you one of Mortain's own daggers."

I blink in surprise. I have never heard of such a dagger before.

"Full initiates carry them, and since you will be acting as such, I would see you properly armed with a misericorde." She unwraps the leather and reveals an ancient dagger with a handle made of antler and chased with silver. The blade is a handbreadth long and worn with age. "This knife possesses an old, ancient magic, one of Mortain's greatest gifts," she says, holding it out to me. When I take it in my hand, it is warm.

"On a living man," she continues, "the misericorde needs only to pierce the skin in order to release the soul from the body. Because the dagger was fashioned by Mortain Himself, only a cut or scratch will send a person's soul to Him, quick and sure. It is meant as a weapon of grace – a way to invoke death and release the soul from painful days spent lingering and pondering one's sins and wrongdoings."

Awed by the power of this gift, I slip it through the slit in my gown and attach it to my waist; the weight of it is reassuring against my leg. This talk of souls has also reminded me of Martel. "Reverend Mother, as Martel's soul left his body, I felt it rush through me. Is that . . . normal?"

The abbess stares at me a long moment, then frowns slightly.

"But of course. It was your first encounter with a soul, yes?" When I nod, she continues, "The encounter was no doubt powerful and unexpected, as it is no small thing to experience a soul in all its richness." She reaches out and puts her hand to my cheek as a mother would her babe's. "You came to us a lump of clay, and we molded you into an instrument of Death. Duval is the bow through which we will launch you at our common enemies. Go now, and make us proud. Do not shame us with doubt or hesitation."

And indeed, I am filled with remorse at her words. I am naught but a tool of the convent, to be wielded at need. Who am I to question those who have raised me up from the cellar floor?

I am a handmaiden of Death. I walk in His dark shadow and do His bidding. Serving Him is my only purpose in this life, and I have let my annoyance drive that duty from my mind. It will not happen again.

Instead of heading directly to the courtyard, I take a quick detour to tell Annith goodbye. Sybella did not have time to say farewell, and I would not have Annith suffer that twice.

She is in the rookery, helping the elderly Sister Claude. She startles at my approach, her eyes widening as she takes in my traveling cloak and satchel. She presses her lips firmly together and she turns away.

I pick my way across the bird droppings to where she is resealing a small parchment with beeswax. Guilt at having been chosen before her – yet again – fills me. I try to lighten the mood. "Sister Claude will catch you," I tease.

Annith keeps her attention firmly on hiding the signs of her snooping. "And I will argue that this is what they have trained me for."

"True enough."

Silence stretches out between us as she finishes her task. When she speaks, it is as if she is pushing bitter pips off her tongue. "You are going out again."

There is no answer I can give her but the truth. "I am to become a member of Viscount Duval's household."

Her head snaps up, her interest caught in spite of her disappointment. "The one who burst in on the reverend mother this morning?"

I nod. There are still no voices in the courtyard, so I quickly tell Annith of the night's events and what transpired in the abbess's office. When I finish, she tosses the resealed message down on the table with disgust. "It should be me," she says with quiet fierceness.

"I know. I can only think that the abbess must have something truly special she is saving you for."

"It is because I failed at the lesson with the corpse."

It is the only one of the convent's lessons at which Annith failed to excel – the time we were made to practice our skills on corpses. Sybella and I had our pasts to give us strength for the task, but Annith did not. "Faltered, not failed," I say. "And you did it in the end. Sister Arnette said you passed. That cannot be it. Mayhap it is simply because you are younger?"

"I am only a year younger than you and Sybella. And Sybella was my age when they first sent her out." She glares at me, not wanting my words of comfort. "Do they know how many classes you've skipped?"

"Sister Serafina needed my help in the workshop!"

"Even so," she sniffs. "I am better at dancing and coquetry, not to mention I can beat you seven out of ten times in our practices."

Her words pluck at my own worries. This assignment will not be a case of quickly slipping in and then out again undetected. It will be a prolonged deception before those who can easily sniff out an impostor. "I am sure she knows that," I say, and hope that it is true.

Her haughty expression crumples. "If it is not the corpse, then it makes no sense," she whispers, and I feel her despair as if it were my own.

"Have you asked the abbess?" I would never take such a risk, but Annith is far more at ease with the reverend mother than I am.

"And have her question my faith and dedication to Mortain?" she scoffs. "I think not."

I hear a male voice in the courtyard, reminding me where my current duties lie. "I must go. Please don't let us part in anger."

She steps closer and throws her arms around me. "I am not mad at *you*."

I hug her back and wonder how long it will be until I see her again. "Perhaps you will join me at court soon?" I suggest.

"I will pray for it nightly."

I glance at the resealed parchment on the table before her. "No word from Sybella?"

"None." Then her face brightens. "Perhaps you will learn of her at court."

"If so, I will send word." We hug one last time before I hurry from the rookery.

I clutch my small bundle of possessions and make my way toward the beach where Duval waits for me, his brown cloak whipping about his boots in the stiff breeze. He does not look any happier about this arrangement than I am, but from where I stand it is all his fault.

When he puts his hand on my elbow to help me into the boat, all the holy resolve I have wrapped myself in disappears and I jerk away, nearly tipping us both into the water.

"Don't be an idiot," he growls.

But I am in the boat and he is no longer touching me, so I consider myself the victor in our exchange.

I settle myself on one of the planks and stare out at the sun sparkling on the blue water. I amuse myself by wondering if Duval can swim and if I dare put it to the test.

"This is not my doing, demoiselle," he says. "So you can save your prickly temper for the abbess."

"It is most certainly your doing. If you had not seen fit to criticize the work of the convent, I would not be here now." That is not the entire truth, for even before he burst into her office, the abbess was plotting to put me in Duval's path again, but he does not need to know that.

He is silent for a while, the only sounds the lap of the water against the boat and the creak of the oars. As he rows, I cannot help but study him, this man in whose hands my fate now rests. His brooding eyes are the light gray of a winter sky. His chin is covered with whiskery stubble, which makes his firm, well-shaped mouth stand out all the more. Unbidden, the word *mistress* echoes through my mind, and I shiver. A sense of foreboding washes over me. He is not Guillo, I remind myself. Indeed, he is as different from the pig farmer as can be.

Duval is the first to break the silence, and I count it another small victory. "Did Martel say anything before he died? Make a confession, perhaps?"

"A confession?" I allow a touch of scorn to seep into my voice. "We are handmaidens to Death, milord, not confessors."

He shrugs in equal parts irritation and embarrassment. "I do not claim to know what your mysteries involve. Either way, did Martel have any last words as he looked into your face and saw his fate?"

Since Martel's last words were of seduction, a red-hot poker will not drag them from me. "He said nothing of importance."

"Are you certain? Perhaps it sounded like nothing to you but will have meaning for me. Tell me his exact words."

Merde, but the man is persistent. Or is he concerned that the traitor named him? If so, I will not give him the satisfaction of saying yea or nay. "He talked only of meeting someone, that is all. How is it again that you came to be in that room at that exact time?" I ask sweetly.

His jaw twitches. "Are you suggesting what I think you're suggesting?"

I shrug my shoulders.

He stops rowing and leans forward, bringing his face close to mine. "I have served my country in more ways than you can imagine, and I serve it still. Do not ever doubt that." His words are sharp and pointed and intended to slice my doubts to ribbons. And while they have the ring of truth to them, a traitor of his caliber would be very good at lying.

Still glaring at me, Duval begins to remove his cloak. For a moment, panic flutters in my breast and I wonder what he is doing. But he is only hot from his rowing, and he thrusts the garment at me. "Try not to let it get wet," he says.

Without thinking, I take the thick, rich wool in my hand. A flash of silver catches my eye, and I run my finger along the oak leaf pinned to the cloak. The old noble families of Brittany have always dedicated at least one of their sons to the patron saint of soldiers and battle. I cast my mind back to the enormous tapestries that line Sister Eonette's chamber walls, tapestries upon which the sisters of Mortain have recorded the family trees of all the Breton nobles throughout the centuries in bright silk thread. I do not recall seeing the name Duval embroidered there. Is it a family name? Or the name of his holding? For the first time, I wonder who exactly he is other than a favorite of the duchess who has earned the abbess's and chancellor's suspicions.

As he rows, his chest strains against the fine velvet of his doublet. The muscles in his arms bunch, then stretch, with every pull on the oar, and I cannot help but think that even with all the training the convent has given me, he could easily best me in a hand-to-hand fight.

Not liking the direction of those thoughts, I cast my gaze out to sea, certain I have been consigned to a special version of hell.

Chapter 11

The old sailor is at the beach waiting to help pull us ashore.

Duval jumps off, then holds his hand out to me. I eye it warily.

He raises one sardonic eyebrow. "My cloak?"

Flustered, I shove it at him, then leap from the boat, ignoring the hem of my gown as it drags in the water. He slips the cloak around his shoulders, then begins walking to the stables. "I have only one horse, as I was not counting on company. Do you prefer to ride in front or back?"

Both of those choices are unacceptable to me. "The convent keeps a stable of horses here on the mainland for assignments," I inform him. "I will use one of those."

"Excellent. We will make better time that way."

I turn to the sailor. "Would you please saddle up Nocturne?" The abbess and I did not discuss this specifically, but surely she does not expect me to ride behind Duval the entire way to Guérande. And, even if she does, she is not here to gainsay me.

The sailor nods and goes off to collect the horses. I can feel Duval studying me; it makes my skin itch. After a moment, he shakes his head, as if unable to believe the trap that has been sprung upon him. "They will think me a besotted fool."

I shrug and keep my attention fixed on the stables, willing the old sailor to return with our horses as quickly as possible. "If the boot fits, milord..."

He snorts. "I am many things, but besotted with you is not one of them."

Before I can make a further thorn of myself, the old sailor appears leading both our horses, and we busy ourselves making ready for our journey.

Under Duval's critically observant eye, I become all thumbs, and it takes me longer than it should to secure my satchel behind the saddle. When at last I am done, I lead Nocturne to the mounting block and, with the help of the old sailor, hoist myself into the saddle. Duval is already seated on his horse and waiting. "Ready?" He does not bother to mask his impatience.

"Yes." Before the word is halfway out of my mouth, Duval slaps his reins and his mount leaps forward.

Glowering at his back, I reach into the small pouch at my waist, take a pinch of salt, and toss it onto the ground, an offering to Saint Cissonius, the patron saint of crossroads and travelers. Only then do I urge Nocturne to follow.

Duval slows his horse long enough for me to draw alongside him. "Have you ever been to court before?" he asks. "Is there any chance you will be recognized by anyone?"

"No."

"No? You do not even ask who is in residence at court.

How can you be so certain no one there will know you? If you are recognized, it will throw our plans into disarray."

Stung that he thinks me so witless, I toss my low birth across his path like a challenge. "No one will recognize me, milord, because I am naught but a turnip-farmer's daughter. You may rest assured that none of those in residence in Nantes will have ever seen me before."

"Guérande," he corrects. "Anne's court moved to Guérande in order to escape the plague in Nantes."

"Even so, I will not be recognized."

He shoots me a glance out of the corner of his eye. "I thought you were supposed to be the daughter of Death?"

"I am," I say through clenched teeth. "But I was raised the daughter of a farmer. There was dirt under my fingernails for the first fourteen years of my life. It has most likely seeped into my blood."

He gives another snort – of derision or disbelief, I cannot tell. "It seems to me," he says, "that being sired by one of the old saints puts your lineage into a class all its own, a class as untouchable by the nobility as the nobility is by turnip farmers.

"Now come, we must reach Quimper by nightfall." Ensuring he has the last word, he puts his heels to his horse and breaks into a gallop.

It takes me a while to catch up.

We ride all day. In the newly cleared fields, sheaves of wheat hang from a cross, begging for Dea Matrona's blessing on the harvest. Cattle graze nearby, feasting on the remaining stubble in the ground, one last fattening before slaughter. Indeed, the slaughter of animals for the winter has already begun and I can smell the copper tang of blood in the air.

A few stone cottages are scattered throughout the countryside, squat and stubborn against the encroaching wilderness. Most doors have a polished silver coin nailed to them, an attempt to discourage Mortain from casting His gaze on their households, since it is believed He will go to great lengths to avoid His own reflection. Those that are too poor to afford that small protection hang hazel twigs, in the hope that He will mistake them for the real bones He has come to collect.

The road is empty except for a handful of travelers heading to market in some nearby village. They carry bundles on their backs or push small carts. All of them step aside when they hear our horses coming.

There is little enough to distract my thoughts from circling back to Duval.

I am painfully aware of him riding in front of me, solid, commanding, angry. No matter where I steer my mind or my gaze, they always come back to him.

Mistress. The word whispers through me, taunting, beckoning, laughing. That I will have to pose as such is almost more than I can bear. And that I shall do so in front of half the Breton nobility is laughable. I pray that a messenger from the convent will come galloping up behind us to tell me it is a cruel jest and that Annith will go in my stead. But all I hear is the drip of the heavy mist as it falls upon the leaf mold on the forest floor, the creak of our saddles, and the faint jingle of harness.

Near mid-afternoon we reach a small wood. The thickness of the trees forces us to slow our horses to a walk so they may carefully pick their way through the branches and brambles. Under the canopy of leaves, it grows cool. I pull my cloak closer, but it does nothing to warm me.

It is not that kind of chill.

Death is nearby. I feel it in my bones, the way an old sailor's aching joints warn him of a brewing storm.

"What?" Duval's voice breaks through the shroud of quiet. He has noticed my distraction. His hand moves to his sword hilt. "Do you hear something?"

"No, but there is something dead nearby."

His eyebrows shoot up and he reins in his horse. "Dead? A man? A woman?"

I shrug. This has never happened to me before and my own ignorance frustrates me. "It could be a deer, for all I know."

"Where?"

"That way." I point off to the side of the road, through a faint opening in the trees.

Duval nods, then steers his horse over and motions for me to take the lead. Surprised that he gives a hunch of mine so much weight, I move ahead and let my sense of death lead me.

The trees are closer here, their soft, delicate branches waving overhead like rich green feathers. Just past an ancient standing stone, its surface mottled with lichen and moss and corroded by time, the sense of Death grows stronger. The freshly dug grave is well hidden by dead branches and a scattering of leaves, but I could find my way to it blindfolded. "Martel," I announce, certain of who is buried there.

I begin to dismount and immediately Duval is at my side, helping me. He reaches up and puts his hands on my waist. I bite back a gasp of surprise as the warmth from his hands seeps through his gloves and my gown to my skin, driving away some small portion of the chill Death has brought. He lifts me from the saddle and as soon as my feet touch the ground, I pull away from him. I am all business, as if he has not just touched me more intimately than I have ever been touched in my life, and I head toward the grave. "This must be where Crunard's men buried Martel."

Duval follows me and stares down at the freshly turned earth as if he would will Martel's secrets to ooze up from the ground. "On the battlefield," he tells me, "they say a man's soul lingers for three days. Is that true?"

"Yes." A plan is already taking shape in my mind, an idea that might remedy one of the mistakes of which I am accused.

"Would that you could speak with men's souls," he murmurs.

I glance up at him sharply. Has he pulled the very thought from my head?

He looks at me in surprise. "You *can* speak with souls?" he asks, as if the words are writ plain on my face.

While I do not like that he can read me in such a manner, I am eager to try this new skill and show him I am not as green or useless as he seems to think. "I can."

"Can you communicate with Martel's?"

And although I have been planning to do that very thing, his asking it of me makes me balk. "Are men subject to your probing even after death?"

He has the grace to look sheepish. "I mean no disrespect to the dead, nor would I ask you to break any of your vows. But if I am to find our duchess a way out of this mess, I must use every tool at my disposal."

Even souls. Even me.

"I will try, but he has been dead for more than a day, and I am accustomed to dealing with souls when they are fresh."

"Thank you." The look of gratitude changes his face, softening the harsh planes and making him appear younger than I had thought. He moves a respectful distance away, and I kneel and bow my head.

In truth, I have never done this, have no idea how to do it. I know only that I am compelled to try. I am eager to understand what it was I felt with Martel's soul yesterday. Was it merely the richness of the experience, as the abbess claimed? Or did his soul truly share his last thoughts and feelings with me? I want to fully comprehend all the gifts Mortain has bestowed upon me. Besides, if Duval is a traitor, as the abbess and Chancellor Crunard suspect, perhaps Martel's soul will reveal that to me.

I close my eyes and take a deep breath. I think of the thin

veil that separates the living and the dead, of how tenuous it is, how very fragile. Once I have it pictured firmly in my mind, I search for an opening, a seam, any gap that might allow me to push aside that veil. There. A small corner turns up. I reach for it with my mind and gently peel back the barrier that exists between life and death.

Martel's unhappy soul is just on the other side. A towering wave of cold crashes over me. Hungry for life, the soul rushes to me. It rolls against my warmth, much as a pig trying to coat itself in mud. It is happy to see me, pleased even. And then suddenly, it is not.

It has recognized me. Knows that it was my hand that sundered it from its earthly body. It grows agitated, writhing against me, trying to escape my will. But I do not give way. This is not some innocent dead who deserves grace and mercy, but a traitor who surely earned whatever punishment Mortain saw fit to administer.

The thoughts and images the soul contains have begun to disintegrate. There is nothing but fragments and snatches, nothing I can grasp as a true memory. I bear down with my mind, willing the soul to gather itself, its memories. *For whom did you work?*

There is an angry swirl, an eddy of ice. I see the purple and yellow of the French crown, a fleur-de-lis plain on a servant's breast. Pleased with my success, I try again. *Who were you to contact?*

There is a brief flash of ships, and then the image is gone, broken into a thousand pieces as Martel's soul shifts. Now it tries to force its will on me, but the power it holds over life is nothing compared to the power I hold over death. I shove the icy coldness of Martel's lingering soul from me and bring down the barrier, so that it is once again solid between us.

When I open my eyes, I am shivering. I am so cold I cannot even feel the rays of sun, and then Duval is next to me, his hands on my elbows, pulling me to my feet. "Are you all right?" Concern is etched on his face, but I cannot stop my teeth from chattering long enough to assure him I am fine.

He lifts the woolen cloak from his own shoulders and places it around me. The heat from his body still clings to the rich fabric, and I close my eyes and let my body drink it in.

"Your face is so pale that, truly, you look as if you are dead too." He pulls the cloak tighter about me, grabs me by the hand – how warm his fingers are! – and drags me to a larger patch of sunlight. And still I shiver. Duval places his hands on my arms and rubs them up and down, trying to work some warmth back into them.

I am too stunned to even breathe, and my arms tingle as if they have long been asleep and are only now awakening. Appalled, I pull away. "I am warm now," I say, my voice stiff. I avoid his eyes, afraid he will see the confusion in mine. That he is good at playing the gallant is only to be expected. His kindness to me means nothing. He is kind to his horse as well. In truth, his chivalry could be a plan to lure me into a false sense of trust and security.

"I would never have asked that of you if I had known—"

I cut him off. "I am fine."

His eyes search my face to see if I am telling the truth. I try to shift his attention away from me. "He could tell me nothing," I say.

"What?" Duval is clearly perplexed.

I nearly laugh at how thoroughly my discomfort has swept his purpose from his mind. "Martel told me very little."

"A little is better than none," Duval says, remembering. "Go on."

I am still slow-witted from my encounter with the soul and try to decide just how much to tell him. I busy myself with removing his cloak from my shoulders. "Images. Fragments. Nothing that made much sense." I pause; I want to clutch each bit of information to myself, gain any advantage I can over this man, but the reverend mother's instructions still echo in my ears. "There was a fleet of ships—"

"Ships?! Describe them to me."

When I do, he swears and begins to pace in the small clearing. "The French fleet."

It is exactly as the abbess and Crunard have feared. Martel was trying to find port for the French so they could launch their attacks.

"Are you well enough to ride yet?" he asks. "This news adds some urgency to our journey."

In answer, I turn and head for my horse.

Chapter 12

We make Quimper just after nightfall, the bonfires in the fields lighting the last of the way as the local plowmen celebrate Martinmas. Once we are inside the city, Duval leads us to a small inn where the innkeeper clucks and fusses over us as if Duval is an honored guest. At last, dishes of braised rabbit and mugs of spiced wine are placed in front of us, and then the innkeeper retires to the kitchens. We fall on our meal in silence. Indeed, Duval has not said much since my encounter with Martel's soul, but I can almost hear the wheels of his mind turning, much like a millstone, grinding down bits of information, until they can fit in some pattern only he can discern.

All this silence is fine with me, as I am as tired as I have ever been, and my backside is bruised from the day's grueling ride.

When we finish our meal, the innkeeper returns and leads us up the narrow stairs to our rooms. My chamber is next to Duval's, but after a quick search I find no connecting door, so I relax somewhat. Even so, it takes longer than it should for me to fall asleep. I can feel Duval on the other side of the thick wall, the flame of his soul bright and steady and so very different from the sisters with whom I've shared my nights with for the last three years.

We are on the road the next morning before daybreak. Once we clear the town, we ride hard and do not stop until noon. In truth, I think Duval would gladly ride straight through, but the horses need the rest.

As do I. However, I will let him think it is the horses he is coddling, not me.

While he tends to them, I stretch my legs and try to work out the stiff muscles in my back. Once our mounts are watered and settled, Duval rifles through his saddlebag and pulls out a small bundle. He tucks it under his arm and comes to stand next to me in the small patch of sunlight I have found.

It galls me that I am painfully aware of every movement he makes, from shrugging his cloak over his shoulder to pulling off his worn leather gloves. His hands fascinate me, and I remember the feel of them against my waist, along my arms. I force my gaze away.

Unaware of the turmoil inside me, Duval unwraps the bundle, which turns out to be a wedge of hard cheese. He breaks it in half, then holds a piece out to me. "Eat."

With a murmur of thanks, I take the cheese, hating that I must now rely upon him for food, just as I once relied upon my father and had thought to rely on Guillo. I am overcome by a childish desire to throw the cheese back at him and refuse to eat it. But I am no longer a child, and I have a responsibility to my convent, my saint, and my duchess. I take a bite of cheese and vow to arrange for my own provisions at the next inn.

The clearing is quiet except for the faint burbling of the brook the horses have drunk from. The silence feels thick and awkward to me, but any attempt to make small talk seems equally so. Wondering if he feels it too, I sneak a glance in his direction and am appalled to find him watching me. We both wrench our eyes away, and even though I am no longer looking at him, every part of me is aware of his proximity, of the faint heat coming off his body in the damp autumn air, of the scent of leather and whatever soap he washed with that morning. I hate that I am conscious of him in this way and I dredge through my heart, trying to find where I've hidden all the resentment and suspicion I hold him in. "What did you want with Runnion back at the tavern?" The question springs from my lips, artless and unsubtle.

His forehead wrinkles in thought, as if he is weighing some thorny dilemma. When at last he speaks, it is only to ask a question of his own. "What do you know of the man you killed there?"

I blink in surprise. "It is not my place to know anything of those I kill. I merely carry out Mortain's orders."

"And that sits well with you? Not knowing who or why?"

It does, but his question makes me feel lack-witted for not knowing more, for not *wanting* to know more. "I do not expect you to understand the duty and obedience required of those who serve Mortain," I say, my voice prim and pinched.

"How does the convent decide whom to kill?" he presses.

I study his face closely, but I cannot tell if he is questioning the convent or just me. "Surely that is the convent's business, milord, not yours."

"If I will be sponsoring you at court, I will not be kept in the dark, only to find myself cleaning up bodies and making explanations."

I raise my chin in annoyance, for in my mind that is exactly the role I have assigned to him. "The abbess will communicate with me through letters, and sometimes – sometimes the saint makes His wishes clear to me directly."

"How?" His question is sharp, urgent. He is hungry to understand this puzzle.

I shrug and try to regain control of this conversation. "What does this have to do with Runnion?"

He is silent for a long minute, so long I think he will not answer. When he does, I wish that he had not. "Doesn't it worry you, that you understand nothing of how they make their decisions? What if they make a mistake?"

"A mistake?" My cheeks grow hot at the suggestion. "I do not see how they can, milord, since their hand is guided by the saint Himself. Indeed, to suggest such a thing reeks of blasphemy to me."

"It is not the saint I doubt, demoiselle, only the humans who interpret His wishes. In my experience, humans are all too fallible." He is silent again briefly, but his next words cause the cheese I have eaten to curdle in my stomach. "Runnion was working for the duchess."

"No! He was a traitor! I saw the marque on him myself."

Duval jerks his head round to stare at me, eyes sharp with interest. "The mark of a traitor, demoiselle? What does that look like?"

Even as I reel from this revelation, I realize how neatly he has tricked me into divulging more than I intended. "That is not something I can share with you."

"I seem to recall your abbess speaking to us both of cooperation."

"In worldly matters, yes, but she said nothing of betraying the sanctity of our rituals." I look pointedly at the silver leaf on his cloak. "Would you share with me the rites of Saint Camulos?"

He ignores that question, for he knows I am right. "Your abbess's definition of *cooperation* differs greatly from mine," he mutters. "Consider this. Runnion had betrayed the duke three years ago, during the Mad war, but he had come to regret that action. In truth, he wished to make amends for his betrayal. That was how he came to work for us; as a means of earning his way back into his country's good graces."

I feel as if I have been turned to stone by one of Saint Arduinna's arrows. "You lie."

"No, I do not." He looks me square in the eye and what I see there looks disturbingly like truth. "Perhaps, demoiselle, your saint is more complex than your convent would have you believe. Now, come, I think the horses have rested enough."

Chapter 13

Duval's revelation about Runnion plagues me for the rest of the afternoon. If Runnion was truly innocent, why did the convent send me to kill him? Had they not known of his work for the duchess? Or do they know something Duval does not?

And if Runnion was working for the duchess, why had he borne the marque? Why had Mortain not removed that stain from the man's soul?

I fear the answer lies in my actions. By striking him down, did I rob him of his chance to earn forgiveness?

I shove that disturbing thought from my mind. Mortain is all-knowing. Surely He would have seen the man's intention and spared him if He thought Runnion worthy.

I am still wrestling with the Runnion matter when Duval steers us across a thick stone bridge. The town is small and crowded, but Duval seems to know where he is going and leads us through the cobbled streets until we reach an inn.

We dismount, and the ostler arrives to take our horses. Duval gives him instructions for their care, then offers me his arm. As I take it, I wonder what folly decreed that women cannot walk unassisted. Inside, the innkeeper rushes forward to greet us, and Duval tells him of our needs for the night.

The innkeeper directs someone to take our things to our rooms, then leads us to the inn's main hall, where dinner is being served.

The hall is a large room, larger even than the refectory back at the convent. In spite of the room's size, a low ceiling and dark timber beams make it feel small and close. A fire burns in the hearth, and the place smells of smoke, new wine, and roasting meat.

We choose a corner table, as far away from the other diners as we can get. I hurry forward so I can take the seat that affords me the clearest view of the door. Duval's lips quirk in amusement.

A serving maid sets a flagon of wine and two cups on the table, then withdraws. I do not even let him quench his thirst before I launch my questions at him. "If Runnion was working for the duchess, what was he doing at the tavern?" I know the convent cannot make such a mistake. There is some other element in play here, and I am determined to ferret it out.

Duval lifts his goblet and takes a long drink before answering. "He was bringing me word on whether England would commit troops to aid our fight against the French."

I feel as if Annith has just landed a kick to my gut. I want to accuse him of lying again, but his eyes are steady, and there are none of the signs of deception that I have been taught to look for. Besides, his answer makes sense. The duchess had been betrothed to England's crown prince before he disappeared from the tower. "If that is the case, then I cannot believe the abbess knew that he was helping you."

Duval shrugs. "I would like to believe she had no knowledge of his true purpose. The alternative is most disturbing."

"Your suspicions are ill founded," I snap. I take my goblet and drain half of it, as if the wine can wash the foul taste of his mistrust from my mouth.

As I set the goblet down, Duval leans across the table. "Now, I have shown good faith and answered your questions, and I would have you answer one of mine. I want to know more of these marques and how they work."

"I am sorry, but I cannot share such things with you."

He leans back and his eyes grow as cold and stark as the winter sky. "That is unfortunate, demoiselle. For until I learn more of how the convent makes its decisions, I will have to regard it – and you – with suspicion."

I give him a false, brittle smile. "It seems we are both bound by duty."

The serving maid arrives at that moment, breaking our impasse. She sets down loaves of fresh crusty bread, a roast capon, two bowls of stew, braised turnips and onions, and a wedge of cheese. Famished by the day's long ride, we dig into our supper.

Once the worst of my hunger pangs have been appeased, I risk another question. "And what of Martel? Do you claim he worked for you too?"

"Could it be you are asking me for more information, demoiselle? When you have refused to give me so much as a morsel in return."

It sounds unfair when he puts it like that. I soften my voice so he will think I regret this, but, of course, I do not. "I will share what I know with you, but I cannot reveal the secrets of our order."

He looks away, a small muscle in his jaw tightening. He is silent for a long moment, then turns back to me. "Very well. I will tell you of Martel, but only in the interest of showing you why you must stay your hand until you have gathered all the facts.

"Martel did not work for us, no. But I believe he could have been persuaded to tell me who at court was working for the French regent."

I take a sip of wine to cover my distress. "Feeling a twinge of conscience yet?" Duval asks.

"No," I lie.

A shadow looms near the door and pulls my attention from Duval. The largest man I have ever seen steps into the room. Half a head taller than Duval, he is travel stained and road weary and looks like an ogre who has strayed out of a hearth tale. His face bears the roughened texture of pox scars; his nose – broken at least twice – is a lumpen knob. His hair is shaved close to his head, and his eyes are creased in a permanent squint.

The man's iron gaze sweeps across the room and lands on Duval. His eyes narrow, and he strides in our direction. Every muscle in my body tenses, and my hand creeps to the dagger at my waist. Duval catches the movement. His eyes widen in surprise, then he glances over his shoulder.

He is up on his feet in an instant, heading towards the stranger at full tilt. They crash into each other with the force of two tree trunks colliding. It takes a moment for me to realize their blows are those of joyful greeting and not attempts to pummel each other into the ground. I let out a slow breath and remove my hand from my knife.

As they finish pounding each other, I notice a small cluster of stable boys and apprentices hovering in the doorway, pointing at the stranger. Duval nods his head in their direction, and the giant man rolls his eyes good-naturedly before turning and greeting them. They smile and talk excitedly among themselves until the innkeeper shoos them back to their duties.

Duval then drags the stranger to our table. The man does not improve upon closer inspection. His light blue eyes are startling in his scarred face and put me in mind of a wolf. In truth, he may be the ugliest man I have ever seen.

"Ismae," Duval says. "This is Sir Benebic of Waroch, otherwise known as the Beast. Beast, this is Demoiselle Rienne."

My eyes widen in surprise, for even we at the convent have heard the tales of the Beast of Waroch, of his ferocity and valor in battle, his extreme disregard for his own life that causes some to think he is mad. "Greetings, my lord."

The Beast of Waroch reaches for my hand and lifts it in a gentle grip, then makes a courtly bow. His pretty manners surprise me, as they do not match his face. When he speaks, his voice is low and rumbles like far-off thunder. "I am honored to make your acquaintance, my lady."

"I am not noble born," I murmur, embarrassed.

"Every maid Beast meets is a lady as far as he is concerned," Duval explains.

Beast straightens and lets go of my hand. "Only those who do not run away from me in terror," he says with a grin. He intends it to be rakish, but it looks more like he is baring his teeth before an attack. I like that he does not apologize for his looks, that he throws them down like a gauntlet. It is an approach I admire, and I immediately warm to him.

Of course, the number of French he killed in the last war does not hurt his cause any, either. During the Mad war, it was his bravery that inflamed the imaginations and hearts of the peasantry and moved them to take up whatever arms they could find – pitchforks, poleaxes, shovels, scythes – and drive the French out of our country. If it were not for Beast's inspiration and the peasants' aid, the French might be here still.

"Sit, sit." Duval shoves Beast onto the bench and takes a seat beside him. "I did not expect you back so soon. Nor to find you here."

The men's eyes meet and an unspoken message passes between them. "We made good time," Beast says, then signals the innkeeper for another cup. The innkeeper is only too glad to oblige this legend come to life in his inn.

"We? De Lornay is with you?" Duval asks.

"Aye. He lost the coin toss and is seeing to the horses."

"Would this be de Lornay?" I ask, staring at the man who has just entered the room. He is tall also, although he is closer to Duval's height than to Beast's towering stature, and he too is clad in road-stained riding leathers, but that is where any similarity ends. He is perhaps the most beautiful man ever – fair of feature and graceful, he looks like an archangel who has fallen from heaven. By the time he reaches our table, he has a small army of serving wenches following in his wake, eager to do his bidding. Disgusted, I avert my gaze and take a swallow of wine.

Duval rises to greet him, and I feel Beast watching my face. "You do not care for de Lornay's beauty, demoiselle?" Beast asks.

I wrinkle my nose. "I am not impressed with pretty men in general, my lord."

He grins maniacally and raises his cup to mine. "I knew we would get along," he says, then drains his cup. Warmed by his words, I do the same.

When Duval presents me to de Lornay, the other man makes no attempt to kiss my hand, nor does he call me lady. In fact, he all but ignores me. Beast leans in close again. "Pay no heed to this knight of Amourna's manners."

I glance sharply at de Lornay to see how he takes this slight, for to call a true knight naught but a lover of women seems a grave insult. But de Lornay merely shoots Beast an annoyed look and takes a seat. The innkeeper arrives and sets another jug of wine and more cups on the table, then shoos the cow-eyed serving maids away and leaves us to our dinner.

De Lornay reaches for the jug. "Did Runnion find you?"

Duval tosses a disgusted glance my way. "No. He met with an unfortunate accident before we could speak."

De Lornay pauses in the middle of filling his cup. "Truly?"

Duval nods, and I stare at my dinner, doing my best to look incapable of causing an unfortunate accident. I remind myself that I have done nothing wrong, only allowed Mortain to guide my hand.

"What happened to him?" de Lornay asks.

Duval waves the question aside. "I am more interested in why you are here. I thought you had business in Brest once you returned."

De Lornay and Beast exchange glances. "The baron was not there. He is on his way to Guérande for the convening of the estates," Beast explains. "As are we."

"What?" Duval says. It is the first time I have seen him nonplussed.

Beast frowned. "You did not want us to attend? We thought you would need our support."

"I am not aware that a meeting of the estate has been called! The duchess hadn't planned on calling all the barons together until she had a firm solution to this crisis to put before them. Are you certain?"

"Yes. The message arrived in Brest just as our boat landed. It bore the Privy Council seal."

Duval takes a huge gulp of wine, as if fortifying himself.

"Which means someone on the council has ignored the duchess's wishes and called the meeting himself." The table grows silent at this dire implication.

"Could she not have changed her mind?" I cannot help but ask.

Duval glances at me as if he had forgotten I was there. "No," he says gently.

De Lornay turns to study me. "You picked a fine time to launch a romance," he tells Duval.

"Demoiselle Rienne is my cousin, not a romantic liaison," he says. "As such, I expect you to extend her every courtesy." There is no mistaking the warning in his voice and I cannot help feeling a small glow of gratitude.

De Lornay's striking dark eyebrows shoot up in disbelief. "Cousin?"

"Cousin," Duval growls. "I am launching her at court."

De Lornay whistles. "To what purpose? Other than to cause gossip and speculation among the entire court?"

Duval grins, a quick flash of white teeth. "Is that not enough of a reason? However," Duval continues, "your news changes everything. We should retire so we can get on the road at first light." He stands and looks down at me.

It takes me a moment to realize that supper is over and I am being dismissed. He holds out his arm, in case I have not caught his meaning.

I narrow my eyes at him. Does he truly think I do not know his plan? That I will sit quietly in my room while he talks of kingdoms and traitors with these friends of his? Well and so, if he is that stupid, let him think I will do exactly as he wishes.

I smile sweetly at him. "Of course, milord." I rise to my

feet and bid the others goodnight. As Duval escorts me from the room, I school my features into a mild, placid expression. At my door, he bids me a polite goodnight and leaves. I close the door and lean against it, listening. When I am certain he is gone, I open the door and peer out into the hallway. It is empty.

Quiet as a shadow, I slip out of my room and hurry to find the servants' stairway.

Chapter 14

I descend the narrow stairway and pass through a small, cramped antechamber, then come to a thick door. The kitchens, no doubt. It is late, and if the saint is with me, most of the workers will be done for the night. I push the door open, a ready excuse at the tip of my tongue. But there are only two boys inside, over in the scullery corner scrubbing pots nearly as tall as they are.

I wink at them, then hold my finger to my lips and offer them two copper coins. Their eyes brighten at this unexpected largesse. They snatch the coins from me with red, raw fingers and nod their acceptance of our bargain. Their loyalty thus purchased, I make my way to the door that will lead me to Duval's secrets.

It opens onto another short hallway between the kitchens and the dining hall. Perfect. I slip into the hallway, hide myself among the shadows, and inch along the wall toward the dining room.

Duval is just returning to his seat. Beast looks up and grimaces. "Catch that wench's eye and order more wine, will you? She is too awed by my pretty face to heed my call, and Lord Dandy here will not do it."

"Most likely because she'll try to follow him back to his

bedchamber," Duval mutters.

Ignoring Duval's jab, de Lornay leans across the table. "Are you really going to flaunt this girl before the entire court? Your bloodlines are far too well known for such a deception."

Duval snorts. "I am hoping they will hear *cousin* and think *mistress.*"

"They would if it were anyone but you," de Lornay scoffs. "You may as well be a monk with as few women as you take to your bed."

Beast tilts his head to the side. "What is truly going on? Politics is your mistress, not some rustic from the country, no matter how charming she may be."

I blush in the darkness, glad there is no one to see.

"And therein lies the rub," Duval says. "No one will believe us, as I tried hard to explain to the abbess of St. Mortain."

My limbs go rigid with shock as he exposes my true identity to the others. He must hold them in even greater regard than I thought. Or my safety in less.

Beast gapes at him. "That girl is from the convent of St. Mortain?"

Duval grimaces into his goblet. "One of Death's hand-maidens, my friend."

Beast whistles. "Has she been set on you?"

"She says no, as does her abbess. But the girl is about as trusting as the French regent, so I have my doubts."

Mayhap he is not as foolish as I think.

Duval refills his goblet and recounts the story of how he was ensnared in the reverend mother's trap. When he is done,

Beast throws back his great, ugly head and laughs, frightening the serving maid even more.

Duval stares morosely into the dregs of his cup. "It is not funny."

"Oh, but it is," de Lornay says. "The master of more plots than a whore has lovers has been neatly caught in someone else's."

Duval waits patiently for his friends' mirth to pass. In truth, he is handling it much better than I would. I would have clouted them both by now.

"If you've quite finished . . ." he says.

"Sorry," Beast murmurs, wiping his eyes with his massive fist. "What will you do?"

"Lie as convincingly as I can and pray she doesn't kill someone important."

This glum reply sets off Beast's laughter anew until Duval has to reach out and kick him to get him to shut up. "You're scaring the other patrons," he mutters. "Now, tell me what news you bring from England, since I was not able to hear it from Runnion."

"Runnion truly did not reach you? What happened to him?" de Lornay asks.

Duval jerks his head up toward the ceiling and my room.

Beast's eyes widen. "*She* happened to Runnion? But I thought the convent served Brittany?"

"It does, or so I believe. But there has been a breakdown in our communications, which is why they've saddled me with this green stripling of a novitiate."

De Lornay leans forward, his face aflush with curiosity. "Have you bedded her yet?"

Beast's face takes on a rapt look. "They say to lie with a handmaiden of Death is the sweetest end imaginable."

"They do?" Duval looks momentarily surprised. Which is nothing to how I feel at this announcement. No one at the convent has thought to mention this to me.

De Lornay shakes his head. "That is but a rumor," he says with great authority.

The other two turn to look at him.

He shrugs. "I didn't realize she was from the convent until the next morning, when the corrupt commander was found dead."

Although it is small of me, I cannot help but wonder who he *has* lain with. Sybella? Or one of the older initiates?

"Enough." Duval holds up his hand. "I would have your news from the English king."

Beast's face grows somber. "He would not speak to us himself," hc says.

"Or so his chancellor claimed," de Lornay adds. "We could never be sure which it was."

"Either way, official channels were closed to us."

"What about unofficial channels?"

"Ah, that is where we learned much, and most of it contradictory." There is a long moment of silence, then Beast speaks. "The English king is considering an offer from the French regent. She will pay him an annual pension if he will not stand in the way of France invading Brittany."

Duval strikes the table with his fist, making us all jump. "Even after all the aid we gave him in his struggle for the crown?"

Beast nods. "Even after."

"There is some good news," de Lornay offers.

"It would have to be very good to counter that," Duval says.

"Well, for one, the French regent is reluctant to pay the fifty thousand crowns the king is asking for. But more important, the English king let it be known that he would put aside the negotiations and lend us aid if we would give him the four Breton cities the French still hold."

Duval lifts his goblet and studies it. "Everyone has a price, it seems." He falls silent a moment, then shakes his head. "I fear the age of kingdoms and duchies is coming to an end. France is eating its way through Europe like a beggar at a banquet." He leans back and fixes his companions with a considering gaze. "The French regent is doing her best to outfox our every attempt to join with our allies. The question is, is she simply being cautious and anticipating our moves? Or does she have specific knowledge of our plans?"

Beast and de Lornay exchange a look. "I thought we were the only ones who knew our plans, outside of the Privy Council."

"Exactly," Duval says. "Which is what makes it such a burning question. If someone is feeding our secrets to the French, it is one of Anne's closest advisors. And now we must wonder if that traitor is the same one who called this estate meeting or if there is a second traitor we must deal with."

They all digest this somber question in silence, then Duval lifts his goblet and drains it, grimacing at the dregs he'd forgotten in the bottom. "To bed, I think. We've an early start."

They stand up and clatter out of the room, and I turn and begin making my way back to my own chamber. I had hoped to learn something that incriminated Duval. Instead, I have learned just the opposite. Even when I am not present, his story is the same.

Why, then, would he not discuss this in front of me? Unless he truly does not trust the convent? I bite back a sigh of frustration. Things would be much easier if I could just prove him traitor and be done with it. But no matter how I turn each word and gesture upside down, looking for hidden meaning and betrayal, I can find none.

We are up early and on the road before dawn. Duval has sent Beast and de Lornay on ahead. I know that he chafes at our slower pace, but there is naught I can do about it.

Recent rains have made the countryside wet and muddy, which further hampers our progress. As dusk falls, it becomes clear that in spite of Duval's best efforts, we will not make Guérande by nightfall. Resigned, he turns off the main road and heads toward La Roche Bernard.

La Roche Bernard sits on a rocky outcropping overlooking the Vilaine River. Its greatest feature is the new chateau the Geffoy family built after their last castle had been razed to the ground in the first war of succession.

At the chateau, we are escorted to a great hall filled with

rich, colorful tapestries and a roaring fire. A rotund man with sandy hair and beard leans in close to an elegant woman as if he's hanging on every word she says. When the steward announces us, the woman pulls back and looks demurely into the fireplace, while the gentleman – the baron, I presume – rises to his feet and hurries to greet us.

"Duval! What a pleasant surprise this is," Baron Geffoy says, but his face gives lie to his words. In truth, there is a harried look about him that has me wondering if Duval isn't precisely the last person he wishes to see right now. "We are graced with all sorts of visitors from court. Madame Hivern is staying with us for a few days."

Duval's head snaps up, and his cold gray eyes zero in on the lovely woman by the fireplace.

The baron lowers his voice. "Being at court right now is too painful for her, as you well know."

"So she keeps claiming," Duval murmurs. There is an angry, bitter note in his voice that I have not heard before. I glance again to the fireplace. Madame Hivern sits with her head bowed, the very picture of pious contemplation – indeed, it is the same pose I adopt at the convent when I fear I have been caught whispering to Annith or Sybella.

"Baron, I would like you to meet my cousin Demoiselle Rienne."

Geffoy smiles knowingly at the word *cousin*. "I am pleased to make your acquaintance," he says. An unsavory gleam appears in his eye. "Please make yourself comfortable in my home, my dear," he says. "Will you be joining us for dinner,

Duval? Or are you too exhausted from your journey?"

Duval's eyes are still pinned on Madame Hivern when he answers. "We would join you and hear the news at court." Surely the woman can feel him looking at her. Why does she not glance up?

Almost as if hearing my thoughts, she lifts her head just then. Although her charming expression never changes, her hostility toward Duval is palpable.

"Excellent! I will have someone show you to your rooms so you may refresh yourselves." The baron leans in close to Duval. "I will be sure you and your *cousin* have adjoining rooms, *mais oui?*"

His vile wink has my hand itching for my dagger. Perhaps sensing this, Duval grabs my elbow and escorts me to the stairs.

My chamber is large and well appointed. I cast a longing glance at the immense canopied bed that I cannot enjoy for hours yet. I sigh with regret, then turn to make myself ready for the evening. As I disrobe, my mind returns to the baron's unease at seeing Duval, Hivern's hostility, and Duval's tightly controlled reaction. Mayhap I will learn something of importance tonight.

At least the mystery of what lies between Duval and Hivern will provide some small measure of entertainment during dinner. I cannot help but wonder how much of Duval's wish to dine in the great room has to do with her. Even from far away, I could tell she is very beautiful; her skin pale, her hair the color of spun gold and dressed in an artful style. The elegant Hivern has made me exquisitely aware of every lesson on court manners and womanly charms I have missed.

I catch my reflection in the small oval of polished silver hanging on the wall. We could not be more different. She has the feel of a delicately wrought treasure. I, on the other hand, am dark and serious; a faint frown draws my brows together. In my mind, I can almost hear the mocking laughter when the baron and his wife learn of my fakery and deception. I will not let that happen. I relax my scowl, which improves my looks somewhat but not nearly enough.

I dip the linen cloth into the warm water – scented faintly with rose petals, a true luxury – and take the opportunity to wash my face and arms and anywhere else I can reach.

I travel with only one gown grand enough for this evening, so, with reluctance, I put it on. I have not grown any more fond of it since I wore it last. And while I have no fancy headdress such as Madame Hivern wears, I do have my hairnet with the pearls. I smile at this reminder of the dark skills I possess that Hivern does not.

As I poke the last stubborn tendril of hair into place, there is a knock at my door. I open it to find Duval, ready to escort me to dinner. He takes in my greatly altered appearance, much as I take in his. He has changed from his riding leathers to an elegant black doublet with fresh white linen at his neck. I wonder briefly if black is a signature color for him. He eyes me thoroughly, and I grow a bit flustered under the warmth of his gaze. "I am not certain I would let my cousin appear in public in such a gown," he says at last.

"Your cousin has no other choice available to her, milord."

A look of resignation settles over his face. "And so our lots are cast." He holds out his arm. "Come, let us join the others."

After a moment's hesitation, I gingerly place my hand on his sleeve. Annoyed by these courtesies I must endure, I look for a way to torment him. "Madame Hivern did not seem especially pleased to see you," I point out. "Nor the baron, come to that."

He snorts, and the earthy noise catches me off-guard. "Madame Hivern and I do not see eye to eye on many things. The baron's discomfort is somewhat newer." Then he looks down at me, a faint air of amusement touching his eyes. "You do know who she is, do you not?"

I curse my own ignorance. It is even worse than being assigned to Duval's care. "No," I say shortly. "I do not."

Duval gives a short bark of a laugh. "That, dear assassin, is the late duke's mistress."

I gasp in surprise. "The French whore?"

He glances at me sharply. "Why do you call her that?"

I shrug as I try to peer ahead into the room, full of lewd curiosity now that I know who she is. "That is what the sisters at the convent called her," I tell him.

There is a long, heavy moment of silence. When I look back at him, his whole demeanor has shifted and the amusement is gone from his face. "Yes," he says. "And just so you are clear, I am the French whore's son."

I feel as if a giant cavern has just opened up at my feet as Duval's words clang through my head like a great bell. He is one of the duke's bastards. Half brother to the duchess.

Chapter 15

Duval tugs my arm and pulls me into the great hall. It is ablaze with a roaring fire and candles burning brightly in heavy silver holders, but I hardly register any of this as my mind scrambles back to Sister Eonette's tapestries. The French whore is listed there, along with her five children by the late duke, but they are listed by first name only, and the name Gavriel is common enough.

Did the abbess know that I was going into this blind? Was this part of her test? Or was there merely a mistaken assumption that I would know the duke's bastard by the name Duval?

As if from a great distance, I hear Baron Geffoy say, "Here they are now." With effort, I try to concentrate on the introductions. "Viscount Duval, Demoiselle Rienne, this is my ladywife, Katerine." She is a drab peahen of a woman with sharp, intelligent eyes, and I warm to her immediately.

"Her brother, Anthoine de Loris, and my steward, Guy de Picart. And, of course, Duval, you already know the charming Madame Hivern."

The clash of Duval's and Hivern's gazes as they meet is as loud as the opening parry of any duel, but what makes my breath catch is the brief glimpse of pain I see in Duval's face before he shutters it. It is so fleeting, I cannot help but wonder if I have imagined it.

When Hivern puts her hand out for Duval to kiss, he dons his formal court manners like a suit of armor and bows over it. "As always, your presence leaves me speechless, madame."

"Would that were so," she mutters. Baron Geffoy shifts in discomfort while his wife's brows rise slightly in surprise.

Duval's eyes narrow. "I am glad to see you have taken my advice and removed yourself from court."

Hivern's smile is as sharp as a knife. "Oh, but I have not. I am only taking a little break to visit with my dear friends and draw comfort from their company." She lifts a delicate linen handkerchief and dabs at her eye.

"My pardon." Duval's voice is drier than bone. "I did not mean to remind you of your loss."

She waves her hand in the air and I cannot tell if she misses the irony in his tone or simply chooses to ignore it. "It is always with me. I am just so grateful to Baron and Lady Geffoy for offering their hospitality, far from the painful reminders of my dear Francis." Her voice catches slightly, as if she is about to cry, and I am struck by the sense that they are acting out parts in a masque.

As if to distract from Madame Hivern's sorrow, Lady Geffoy directs us to take our seats at the table, and I use the moment to try to collect my wits. With Duval's revelation, so many small details fall into place. The abbess's and Crunard's incredulity that Duval would try to pass me off as his cousin; Beast and de Lornay's reactions, as well. In truth, remembering causes me to blush and squirm at how stupid they must have thought us. No wonder Beast thought me noble born, for although Duval is a bastard, he is a royal one.

Humiliation courses through my veins. I reach for my wine goblet and take a healthy swig, wishing I could drown my ignorance. As my thoughts begin to settle, I become aware of the tinkle of crystal, the smell of braised meat and strong wine. The table is laden with all manner of food and delicacies, but they are as tasteless to me as the dust kicked up by our horses.

Lady Katerine artfully steers the conversation to hunting and recent jousts, people and events I am not familiar with. I let it recede into the background until it is naught but the buzz of gnats hovering over a stagnant pond.

I try to remember everything the convent told us about the French whore, for that is how they referred to her always and why I did not recognize her by the name Hivern. She was the mistress of the old French king when she was but fourteen. When he died, she became mistress to our duke. Over their many years together, she bore him five children: three sons and two daughters.

Duval's arm rests next to mine on the table, his long elegant fingers playing with the stem of his glass. When his fingers tighten suddenly, I force my thoughts to the conversation going on around me.

"That is the fourth tournament this year that my dear François has won," Madame Hivern is saying to the baron. "He has few equals in the jousting lists."

Baron Geffoy casts an admiring glance at Duval. "Except perhaps for his older brother. If I remember correctly, he was never beaten—"

"Those days are long gone," Duval says, abruptly dismissing the baron's attempt at flattery. As Duval lifts his goblet and drains it, there is a brief moment of awkward silence. Lady Katerine tries to brush over it.

"We have had uncommonly good hunting this year," she says, but once again Madame Hivern turns the conversation and begins prattling of François and his prowess at hunting and how he speared a wild boar single-handedly in last week's hunt.

Is that what lies between them? Does she favor François so much that it has driven Duval to hate her? It happens thus in families sometimes, especially the noble ones, where favor translates into titles and holdings. I glance over at Duval, but he looks pointedly at his plate, cutting his venison with angry, precise movements.

I turn my attention across the table to Madame Hivern. Her gown is the color of emeralds and is cut even lower than mine, leaving her entire shoulders exposed as well as revealing the profuse swell of her womanly charms.

"Gavriel, dear," she drawls. "Who is this maid of yours again and why is she staring at me as if I am a five-legged calf?"

I blush furiously, for I had thought them all so involved in their conversations and plots that they wouldn't notice my scrutiny.

Duval tosses me a glance, as if to show he is bearing my presence with little grace. "Forgive her, madame. She was raised in the country and is no doubt struck dumb by your beauty and elegance."

"As are we all," Baron Geffoy adds, completely missing the deep irony in Duval's voice. Lady Katerine, however, does not.

"Is she what caused you to stray so far from your young duchess's side?" Hivern smirks.

Duval lifts his goblet and takes a sip of wine. "I did not *stray* anywhere. I had business to attend to on behalf of the duchess."

Madame Hivern looks sharply at me. "Where did you say you were from?"

"She didn't," says Duval, and while I do not like that he is speaking for me, I cannot even pretend to understand what is going on between them.

"Have you news of the French?" Baron Geffoy asks. He is no longer jovial but tense and bristly, and for the first time since meeting him, I think I would not want to face him in pitched battle. "There have been rumors of their troops amassing in the north."

Duval gives a firm shake of his head. "No. There have been no troop sightings or even signs of scouting parties. Your information is mistaken. The duchess has the matter well in hand."

Madame Hivern leans forward, eyes glittering. "Does she, Gavriel? Does she truly? For it does not appear that way from where I sit."

Across the table their eyes meet. "That is because you choose not to see it, madame." His words are tight and hard, like stones from a catapult. "As always, you see precisely what you want to see and no more." He casts his unflinching regard toward the head of the table, where Baron Geffoy pays careful attention to the slices of pheasant on his plate. Duval stares at him for a long moment before returning his attention to Hivern. "Beware, madame," he says softly. "Politics can be far more dangerous than you know." It takes me a full beat to recognize that this is no general advice but a very specific warning. But of what?

She, too, appears puzzled by his words, but before she can speak, Duval turns to me. I barely keep from recoiling at the simmering fury in his gaze. "Since we leave at first light, it would be wise to retire early." He rises and holds his arm out to me and I quickly get to my feet, thank Lady Katerine for her hospitality, and let Duval lead me away.

Duval escorts me from the room, his lightly banked fury propelling us at a rapid pace, and I am nearly breathless when we arrive at my chamber. I start to ask a question, but he cuts me off with a curt goodnight, opens my door, and fair shoves me inside, then shuts it with unmistakable finality.

I am alone, and grateful for it, but angry too. It is not *my* fault he and Hivern have nearly come to blows.

I cannot guess what lies between them, what sort of falling-out they have had. It seems far too heated a feud to be based on Duval's resenting his mother's affection for his brother. And how does Geffoy play into all this? For he sat there looking as guilty as Annith did when she was caught snooping through Sister Beatriz's love poems.

Or was that it? Is the baron contemplating a liaison with Madame Hivern, and is Duval trying to discourage it? De Lornay claimed Duval had the morals of a monk, so perhaps that is at the heart of his and his mother's animosity: he believes she is taking another lover far too soon after his father's death.

My tired fingers are graceless and clumsy as I fight with the laces on my bodice. At last they come lose and I remove it, shivering as the cold air brushes my skin. I step out of my skirt and, clad only in my shift, hurry over to the enormous bed and climb under the thick covers, welcoming their warmth.

I can hear Duval pacing in the next room, restless and agitated, his anger rolling in under the door like some foul miasma off a fetid marsh. I push it from my mind. Who his mother takes as a lover cannot be of interest to Mortain.

Sometime later, I am awakened by angry voices. At first, I think they are in the room with me, then realize they come from Duval's chamber. The door is thick, so I catch only snatches.

"...you will ruin everything for us..."

"Have you so little respect for my father that you would..."

"...has nothing to do with..."

It is Madame Hivern. She and Duval are arguing.

That brings me fully awake and just as I throw off the

covers so I may go and listen at the door, I hear another door slam with a thud. After a brief moment, there is a sharp, brittle crash from Duval's room, a shatter of crystal that brings me to my feet. I have only ever heard that sound once before, in the abbess's office, and before my head knows what my feet are doing, I am flying to the door, my hands fumbling at the bolt.

Duval sprawls in a chair by the fire, his head thrown back and his eyes closed. An open decanter sits at his elbow, and the rich fruity scent of wine mixes with the lingering traces of Madame Hivern's rose perfume. Firelight glints off the shards of broken crystal on the floor, and I stop, afraid I'll slice my feet to ribbons. "My lord?" I whisper, dread beating in my breast.

Duval's head snaps up, his eyes filled with bleak despair. He quickly looks away, but too late. I have seen his expression, and sympathy for something I do not even understand pierces my heart. "I heard a crash..."

He raises one sardonic eyebrow at me, his face now a brittle mask. "And thought to save me from attacking crystal while clad only in your shift?"

I flinch at his mocking tone. Truly, why had I rushed in? Even if he had been poisoned, what could I do? *His soul,* I think, relieved that a reason has come to me. *If he were to die, I must learn all I can from his soul before it departs.*

He glances at the empty decanter at his elbow. "Unless you are checking to see if your poison worked? Am I one of your targets, then?" The weariness in his voice suggests he would not mind so very much.

And while I did not like Hivern before, now, for some inexplicable reason, I hate her. "Are you drunk?" I try to put as much scorn into my words as he did.

"No. Yes. Perhaps a little. Definitely not enough." The bleakness is back and he turns to stare into the flames.

I am torn between wanting to leave him to wallow in his despair and wanting to rush to his side and chase that look from his eyes. That I long to do this appalls me, sets panic fluttering against my ribs.

"I suggest you return to your room," Duval says, his gaze still fixed woodenly on the fire. "Unless you have come to practice your lessons of seduction on me?" His mouth twists in bitter amusement. "That could well entertain me till sunrise."

I jerk my head back as if I have been slapped. "No, milord. I had thought only to pray for your soul if Madame Hivern had seen fit to poison you. Nothing more." And with that, I turn and flee the room, then bolt the door against the disturbing glimpse of both his soul and mine. Whatever games are being played here, he is a master at them, and I will do well to remember that.

Things are strained between us the next morning. I won't meet Duval's eyes nor he mine as we take our leave and gallop from the yard. The sun rises, and the early morning mist swirls up off the ground in gentle eddies, like steam from a simmering pot. Our awkward silence follows us on the road to Guérande. Nocturne doesn't like that I hold myself so rigidly, and she whinnies. I force myself to relax my shoulders.

For his part, Duval acts as if I don't exist. At least as far as La Baule. Then he turns in his saddle, his face stiff with discomfort. "I am sorry I insulted you last night. I was angry with Madame Hivern, and you presented an easy target. Please accept my apologies." Then he turns forward again, leaving me to gape at his back.

No one has ever apologized to me before. Certainly not my family, or the nuns. It is disturbing, this apology, as if my feelings matter when I know that they do not. It is what Mortain and the convent want that is important. Even so, I cannot help but whisper, "I accept," mostly to myself. Or so I think – until I see Duval nod once, then put his heels to his horse.

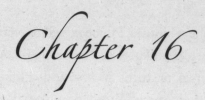

Chapter 16

Even though I grew up only three leagues away, I have never been to Guérande. My father went, many times, and he used each of those to taunt me with what he had seen. I had thought he exaggerated in order to rub my nose in what I had missed. Now I see that he did not.

The town is entirely enclosed within thick stone walls that stretch as far as my eye can see. Eight watchtowers loom at regular intervals. I understand now why the duchess has chosen this city for her headquarters. Surely those walls are impenetrable.

Provided the enemy comes from without.

As we draw closer to the city, I see a crowd near the gate tower. Legions of servants and carts piled high with household goods block the road. Knights and noble lords mill about on horseback, their horses prancing impatiently at the delay. Duval mutters an oath. "I will not reach the palace till midnight at this rate."

"Are they refugees?" I ask, remembering the desperate families and townspeople who had been displaced by the Mad war.

Duval looks at me askance. "No. They are here for the Estates Assembly. Come, we will try the north gate."

Before he can wheel his mount around, a trumpet sounds from behind. A standard-bearer approaches, his gold and blue banner snapping briskly in the crisp autumn air. A long entourage snakes behind him on the road, the outriders and trumpeters heralding its arrival. People and horses do their best to make way, but it is a narrow road and there is nowhere to go.

The knights do not slow down. They gallop full tilt into the crowd, forcing people to leap from the bridge or risk being trampled. I recognize the banner at once; it is that of Count d'Albret, one of the wealthiest Breton nobles and one of the duchess's suitors. A most insistent one, according to Sister Eonette.

The count is surrounded by men-at-arms, so my only impression of him is one of great girth and a lathered horse with far too many spur marks upon its flanks. It is enough for me to take an immediate dislike to the man. Even so, I am surprised by the intensity of Duval's reaction – his eyes grow dark and flinty, while his lip curls in disgust. I cannot help but note that there are now two people we both heartily dislike – Madame Hivern and Count d'Albret – and I am reminded of Sister Eonette's maxim that our enemy's enemy often makes a good ally.

Duval tears his gaze away from the count and looks to the road. "I think we can get through now," he says, then puts his heels to his horse. It leaps forward. Caught off-guard, I do my best to follow, but I am not as quick. Nocturne balks, then bolts out in front of an approaching horse. My hands are so full trying to manage Nocturne that I barely spare a glance for the other rider. As she struggles to regain control, she utters a foul oath at her mount.

The familiar voice is like a pail of icy water down my back. I whip my head round, but she has already passed. All I can see are her slender shoulders and the defiant tilt of her head. Until she turns round to send me a scathing glance, annoyance writ plain on her face.

Sybella.

My heart begins to race even as the rest of the riders converge on the road between us and she is lost to my eyes. Jubilation surges through me. She is alive! And in Guérande! That is more than I knew before. It is enough to lighten my heart as I hurry to catch up to Duval.

Once we are inside the city, our horses clop down the cobbled streets. Stone and timber houses jut jauntily into the street, like gossiping housewives. Shops line the narrow lanes, their shutters drawn up to display bolts of wool and silk, perfumed oils, and all manner of goods. We pass candlemakers' stalls and food stalls. I look longingly at the latter. Our breakfast was hours ago.

"Try not to gawk," Duval says, amused.

"I am not gawking," I say, piqued that he has caught me.

"You most certainly are. Have you never been to a town before?"

"Not one this size," I admit reluctantly.

Duval shakes his head. "At least you will have no trouble playing the country rustic."

It is clear that Duval wants to gallop through the town, straight to court. He holds himself in check, however, as we are boxed in by townspeople and pedestrians clogging the streets and hurrying about. Trying to avoid these, we turn down a side street. Duval mutters an oath as we come upon an overturned cart blocking the road. Bags of grain and flour spill out onto the cobbled street, and the driver studies the broken axle in dismay.

"This way," Duval orders, turning into a narrow alley.

We have gone but a few paces when Duval gives a garbled shout. He reaches for his sword as three men drop seemingly from the sky into his path. Another one lands directly behind him, on the horse itself. The beast stumbles, but he is battle trained and quickly recovers. The stallion prances and snorts, nearly trampling one of the assailants. Duval shoves his elbow deep into the belly of the attacker behind him, dislodging him from the horse. "Turn back!" Duval shouts.

But I am not some simpering maid to flee at the threat of a fight. There is a ringing of steel as Duval draws his sword, then he is swinging at a second man who is trying to pull him from his saddle. Even as the wet, soft *thunk* tells me the blade has connected with flesh and bone, I am reaching for the long knife at my ankle.

But too late.

Two – no, three – more men emerge from the shadows. Nocturne prances and rears. One of them grabs my bridle, then has to dance backwards to avoid Nocturne's flailing hooves. I free my knife and regain my balance. I kick my right foot out of the stirrup, swing my leg over the saddle, and send both feet into the face of my attacker. He reels back, giving me just enough room to get my long knife between us.

But my movements have unbalanced me again and I am pitched from the saddle. I use the momentum and throw myself forward, landing neatly on my feet. I lunge to meet the bandit.

He does not see my knife in time.

His eyes widen as it sinks into his belly. I brace myself, but there is no whisper of soul. Not a killing blow, then. There is a sucking sound as I pull the blade out, but before I can strike again, another man is upon us.

I duck low to avoid his short sword and spin out from under his swing. There is a whinny from Nocturne as the blade misses me and cuts along her flank.

A hot wave of fury crashes through me and I straighten for my next strike but my hand explodes in pain as one of the men's kicks finds its target. My knife clatters to the cobbles.

The two men draw together, silent but deadly, as their companion writhes on the ground, his hand clamped to his middle to keep his guts from spilling onto the street.

I reach through the slit in my skirt, hand closing around the smooth, worn handle. When I pull the misericorde free, the bandit on my left laughs at the puniness of my weapon.

I smile.

One nick, the abbess said. Just one scratch. And while I am loath to use a weapon of grace on two men such as these,

I am certain Mortain will forgive me, as we are allowed to kill in self-defense.

I settle into my fighting stance.

The man spits out a mouthful of blood, then rushes forward with his short sword thrust out. *Merde*, but he is stupid. Does he truly think I will just stand here and wait to be skewered?

I duck under the out-thrust blade and roll onto the ground, swiping at the man's ankle as I pass. When I come up on my knees, there is a puzzled look upon his face. He stops moving and slowly sinks to the ground, like a puppet whose strings have been cut. There is a flutter of his passing soul, but it disappears quickly.

His companion's eyes widen at this uncanny trick. If he is smart, he will run, but he is not. He panics and lunges forward. I leap back and get the misericorde between us. It connects with his bony knuckles, just a scratch, but he stiffens, and then looks from his cut to my face.

"You cannot win against Mortain's own," I whisper. Then he, too, settles to the ground, as if giving a deep curtsy. Another fluttering of soul, then nothing. I frown at my lack of connection with their souls and wonder if that is another gift of grace with the misericorde, that the victims' dying thoughts remain private.

The sound of steel scraping on stone pulls my attention back to Duval. Three of his assailants are down; the fourth is backed against the wall. As I approach, the remaining bandit glances my way. It is the merest slip, but Duval uses the distraction to force his way inside the man's guard and strike him on the head with the butt of his sword. The man's eyes roll up in his sockets and he slides to the ground.

"I will save *you* for questioning," Duval says, then turns his attention to me. "Are you hurt?"

I glance down and see that one of the blades has sliced through the fabric of my gown. A faint line of red wells up on the meaty part of my arm. "Just a scratch. And you?" I ask, because it seems polite.

"Fine," he says curtly. His gaze moves beyond me to the three men I've dispatched. "Sweet Jesu!" He hurries over to where they lie and kneels to feel for their pulses. "All of them dead," he announces.

"I know." I try to keep the pride from my voice. A sense of triumph races through me and I am nearly giddy with it. I have bested three men, and though the test was harder than any at the convent, I passed with flying colors. Even better, I fought as well as Duval. I wonder how to compose my message informing the abbess of this without sounding as if I am bragging.

"What happened to your horse?"

My spirits crash back to earth at Duval's question. I whirl round, shocked to see that Nocturne is lying on the ground, her sleek black side drenched in sweat and heaving like a bellows. "She was only scratched," I tell him as I rush over to kneel beside her. The acrid tang of bitterroot fills my nose and there are flecks of bloody foam upon her lips.

"Poison." Even as I say the word, I can feel the fevered heat coming off of her. "No mere bandits, then. They wanted us dead." I run my hand down Nocturne's silky flank, trying to comfort her. "Do you have so very many enemies?" I ask Duval.

"It would appear that I do," he says. "The better question is, should I be flattered that they set seven upon me? Or does that mean someone knew I would be traveling with a skilled fighter?"

The full implication of what he has said hits me. "Are you suggesting the abbess sent them? Or Chancellor Crunard?" I am barely able to keep the disbelief out of my voice.

He shrugs. "It seems whoever sent them knew that both of us could fight."

I am tempted to ask if he also suspects Beast or de Lornay, but then I would have to reveal that I overheard their conversation, and I am not willing to do that. Not yet.

Is it possible that Duval had sent them on ahead to arrange such a thing? Would he have staged an attack in order to rid himself of me?

"We must put her out of her misery," Duval says gently.

His words remind me of what I must do, and while I long to ease Nocturne's suffering, I am saddened beyond reason that I must bid her farewell.

"Would you like me to do it?" Duval's voice is nothing but kind. There is no hint of condescension in it, but I act as if there is. Getting angry is the only way I can bear this. "I am trained in death," I remind him. "I need no help."

"None of us are trained to kill those who have served us well and faithfully," he says. "It is a special agony all its own, and I would spare you if I could." There is a note of sorrow in his voice and I know – *know* – that he has had to do this very thing. His sympathy makes the pain of losing Nocturne worse, as if my feelings for her are not some childish affection I should have put aside long ago. "I am not weak." To prove my words, I reach down and grasp my knife handle.

"I never said that you were." His voice is still gentle, as if he sees how much this is hurting.

Which only makes me resolved to prove that it is not. "If you will cease your endless prattle, I will do it." I feel rather than see him step back, and I am suddenly able to breathe now that he is no longer near. I turn my full attention to Nocturne, wanting to find some way to let her know how much I will miss her.

I place my cheek along her neck, breathe in her familiar horsy scent. "Thank you," I murmur in her ear. "For carrying me so faithfully, and for being my friend." I whisper this last part so softly that I am afraid she will not hear. But her ear twitches, and I know that my words have reached her. She gives a faint whinny, as if to let me know she understands. "I hear there are many carrots where you are going," I tell her. Then, before I can falter, I grasp the misericorde and put it to her throat.

Nocturne's spirit leaves her body in a red-hot gush. A faint breeze rustles by, bearing the scent of sweet green grass and the sense of galloping into the wind. I lay my head down on her neck and pray I will not weep.

Then Duval grabs my arm and pulls me to my feet. If I didn't know he had nerves of iron, I would have said there was a faint glimmer of panic in his face.

"What are you doing?" I wrench my arm out of his grip.

He stares intently at the cut on my arm. "If one blade was poisoned, why not all of them?" As I look at him blankly, he gives me a little shake. "*You* might have been poisoned too."

Now that he has mentioned it, there is a faint burning sensation in my arm. I glance down at the cut. "I am fine," I assure him.

"You cannot know that. Perhaps even now it is working its way to your vital organs." He takes my arm again and keeps a firm hold on it as he leads me to his horse.

He does not know I am immune to poison, and I am reluctant to share this. If he himself was behind our attack, better not to hand such secrets to him. When we reach his horse, he stops long enough to feel my brow. "No fever yet," he mutters.

"I am fine, I told you."

He ignores my protestations and puts his hands around my waist. I barely have time to gasp before I am perched on the horse's back, the imprint of his hands still burning against my skin. He springs up into the saddle, then takes the reins in hand. "Grab hold of me or else you'll tumble off," he instructs over his shoulder.

Gingerly, I place my hands along his sides.

"Hold on," he repeats, then puts his heels to his horse.

We fly forward, and I barely have time to grab the thick folds of his cloak to keep myself from spilling off.

He gallops back the way we've come. The overturned cart is gone now and there is no sign of anyone nearby. He takes a side street, then another, and soon we come to a wider street with finer houses.

Duval pulls up in front of one of them. His horse has barely come to a full stop before a groomsman rushes out to take the reins. Duval dismounts only long enough to introduce me to his steward, then remands me into the keeping of his housekeeper, Louyse, a round, pleasant-faced woman who welcomes me cheerfully, if curiously.

When he starts to give her orders to send for a doctor, I stop him. "Milord. If I had been poisoned, I would be dead by now."

He scowls at me and begins to argue, but I cut him off. "Look how quickly it felled my horse. Surely someone my size would be dead already."

His face clears somewhat at my words. "Perhaps. But why would only one of their blades be poisoned?"

"I do not know. I only know that I am well, and that is enough."

He nods curtly. "Very well. Louyse will see that you have anything you may need." He surprises me by taking my hand. *It is for the servants*, I tell myself. *To convince them of our masquerade.* "Promise me you will send for a doctor if you start to feel ill."

I want to laugh at his concern. No, I want to wrap it

around me like a blanket and use it to soothe my most recent loss. Instead I say, "I promise," knowing it will cost me nothing.

Then he leaps onto his horse, calls four of his men to ride with him, and leaves. As they clatter out of the courtyard, I realize I do not know if they head for the palace or back to the scene of our attack. My desire to know is so strong, I take one step forward as if to run after them, but then I notice Louyse's puzzled look.

I give her a wan smile, and she smiles back broadly. "Come, demoiselle. You are no doubt weary from your journey."

I marvel at how well trained she is, for I am certain she heard Duval say *poisoned*, and yet she neither sends me curious glances nor asks me any intrusive questions.

Instead, she leads me inside. A great hall looms to my left, and the sun sparkling through the oriel window casts a glow on the tapestries covering the wall. It occurs to me that I should at least try to search Duval's home now that he is gone, but, in truth, I cannot muster the desire. I am tired down to my bones, and my movements feel as if I am wading through water.

Perhaps there was poison on the blade, after all. If so, this feeling will pass quickly, much quicker than some malaise of the heart, which is what I fear it is. Nocturne's death shouldn't gnaw at me so, but it does, and I hate how weak I am.

Louyse continues up a wide center staircase to a bed-chamber. It, too, has glass windows, and thick velvet drapes keep out the chill. There is a fire burning in the hearth, and a large tub sits nearby. A serving maid is just emptying a bucket of steaming water into it.

My spirits lift somewhat at the thought of a bath. I have not had a bath since the convent and am in sore need of one.

There is a light knock on the door and a footman appears bearing my satchel. Louyse motions for him to put it on the bed, then shoos both him and the maid from the room. She takes a step in my direction. "May I help you with your gown?"

"No!" The small spurt of panic I feel at exposing the scars on my back gives more force to the word than I intend. "Thank you," I add, more graciously. "But I am convent raised and more comfortable disrobing in private." My heart is beating quickly. I have not given a single thought to the assistance of a maid.

Her eyebrows raise only slightly, yet another sign of her excellent training. "Very well. I shall leave you to your bath then." And with that, she leaves.

When she has quit the room, I ease myself onto the bed. All sense of triumph has fled and I feel nothing but the keen loss of Nocturne and the awareness of how very far from home I am.

Chapter 17

I come awake with the fine hairs at the nape of my neck lifting in warning, every muscle in my body tensing with anticipation. As my mind fumbles with the unfamiliar surroundings, my hand reaches for the stiletto under my pillow.

A voice heavy with weariness rumbles through the silence. "You can leave that pretty little prince sticker of yours where it is."

Duval. I am tucked up in his house in Guérande. My hand relaxes its grip on the handle. "You don't *stick* with it," I correct automatically, much as Sister Arnette does. "You shove and twist."

A low, warm chuckle fills the chamber, and my skin ripples slightly. Annoyed, I want to rub my forearm to ease the sensation, but I am not ready to let go of my knife just yet.

Duval sits in a chair with his back to the lone window. Has he come to take advantage of me? Here, where the only ones who will hear my protests are those loyal to him?

For I *will* protest, I assure myself.

"I said put your dagger down." This time there is a hint of steel in his voice rather than laughter.

"You must be mad to think I'll just sit here in the dark, defenseless—"

"What exactly do you feel you must defend against? I have not made any move toward you."

And there he has me, for I cannot say what I must guard against, only that I feel threatened in some way.

"You have exactly five seconds to put your dagger away before you find it at your lovely throat." He thinks to browbeat me into obeying him, but his words have the opposite effect. I am filled with a desire to test my skills against his. We have both dispatched three men today. How would we fare against each other? The thought has something dark and unsettling unfurling inside me. I shove my stiletto back under the pillow, afraid I will use it without cause.

Lying down feels too vulnerable, so I sit up. Duval's broad shoulders are silhouetted by the faint moonlight coming in through the window and I want desperately to see his face so I can discern what he is about, but it is cast in shadow. Besides, he isn't even looking at me. His head is leaning back against the chair, and the faint slump to his shoulders hints of his fatigue.

"Why are you here?" I ask.

He turns his gaze to me, and although his eyes are still hidden in the shadows, I feel them as surely as any touch. My skin ripples again, and this time I do rub my arms.

"What is my fair assassin so afraid of? I wonder."

"I'm not afraid."

Duval tilts his head to the side. "No?" He studies me a long moment, then rises out of his chair. I hold my breath as he crosses to my bed. "Are you afraid I will draw closer, perhaps?" His voice is pitched low, little more than a purr. My breath catches in my throat, trapped by something I long to call fear but that doesn't feel like fear at all. Every inch of my skin is thrillingly, painfully aware of the soft linens and bedcovers between us. They are thicker than any gown I have ever worn, and yet I feel unbearably exposed.

"Perhaps you worry I might touch you," he muses. I watch, mesmerized, as his hand reaches toward me, hovers over the foot of the bed. Under the covers, my skin twitches in anticipation.

When his hand comes down and grasps my ankle, it takes every bit of willpower I possess to keep from jerking away. His grip is firm, and it is as if the heat from his hand burns through all the layers between us. My ankle throbs, and the sensation creeps up my leg and spreads throughout my entire body, until every inch of my skin is alight with – what? Fear? Anticipation?

We stare at each other, the moment stretching out, swallowing up all the moments that came before it. "However will you play the game of seduction if you flinch so?" His voice is soft velvet along my skin. "You will be hard-pressed to gain my secrets if you cannot bear my touch." Then he swears and pulls his hand away from me. "What is your convent thinking, sending such an innocent out in the world to play the strumpet?"

My heart thuds painfully in my chest as Duval returns to his chair. He knows. He knows the abbess has sent me to spy on him. Has probably always known. It was only I who thought we were fooling anybody.

Duval settles back and studies me, as if I am some complicated knot he must untangle. I try not to fidget.

"So why *are* you here?" I cling stubbornly to that question.

"Your abbess was correct. It does not matter what we call you – people are drawing their own conclusions. When I arrived at court this evening, two nobles congratulated me on my new mistress. It is stupid to fight this."

"Perhaps my wits are addled from sleep, but I still do not understand why you're here."

Duval sighs. "So my attendants will note I visited your bedchamber tonight and draw their base conclusions."

"Surely we don't need to continue the charade under your own roof?" I say, glad to have something concrete to argue over.

"Surely you are not willing to risk your life or our duchess's future on everyone in my household being completely loyal?"

"I cannot believe you do not trust your own household," I say, but it is a lie. I am not surprised.

Duval leans forward and places his elbows on his knees. "The French have bought any number of Breton nobles, Ismae. It is only a matter of who and how much. If I were the French spy-master, I would certainly make an effort to place a spy or two in the house of every one of Anne's trusted advisors."

"Then surely they would all bear the marques of Mortain for their treachery."

"And yet, they do not. As I have said, I suspect your saint is more complex than your convent would have you believe."

Anger, prickly and welcome, flares inside me. "How can you know they do not bear the marques? They are not visible to you."

He smiles then, a genuine smile. "That is why I am presenting you at court tomorrow. It will prove most amusing, I'm sure. However, I recommend that you consult with the duchess before you begin assassinating her courtiers with abandon. Now, go back to sleep," he says. "I will sit here for another hour, then return to my own chamber."

It is clear he will not budge until he is good and ready. I settle back down under the covers, too aware of his presence, of the lack of space between us. Of only the thin linen of my nightshift covering me. I clear my throat. "Did you learn anything of our attackers?" I ask.

"Sleep now, Ismae. We will talk more in the morning." His voice is low, naught but a faint rumble in the night air.

I am certain I will never fall back to sleep, and yet I do. And when I awake in the morning, he is gone. It is as if he was never there at all.

When Louyse comes to help me dress, I am unable to meet her eye. Does she know that Duval spent a good portion of the night in my room? If so, she gives no indication. She is either remarkably discreet or truly unaware.

With a pleasant "Goodmorning, demoiselle" she sets a ewer of water on the stand and lays a fresh chemise on my bed. As she moves to the garderobe to collect my gown, I slip quickly out of bed, eager to get into my chemise while she is not looking. When she returns with my gown, she blinks in surprise but says nothing. The woman is well trained.

I step into my skirt and she moves behind me to fasten it. "The viscount is in his study," she says, lacing up the back of my gown. "He asked that you join him when you are ready."

"Very well." I hope she does not hear the reluctance in my voice.

The door opens again and I flinch slightly at this intrusion, but it is only the serving girl Agnez bringing me a tray so that I may break my fast. Once I am fully dressed and brushed, and after I assure them – twice – that I can manage my breakfast unattended, they finally take their leave. I close my eyes and allow myself to savor the solitude, even just for a moment. But the knowledge that Duval is waiting robs me of whatever peace it might bring. I tear a corner from the loaf of bread on the breakfast tray and nibble at it, hoping it will calm the roiling nerves in my gut.

Feeling restless and awkward, I pace as I nibble, unable to stand still. It is as if sometime during the night I have outgrown my own skin. Duval's presence still lingers, like the faintest trace of perfume, and my ankle still bears the memory of that touch. I find myself wishing for a great throbbing bruise instead. That I would know how to deal with better than this.

Agitated, I go to the window and throw open the shutters, welcoming the chill morning into the room. Closing my eyes, I breathe in, pulling the sharp cold air deep into my lungs. I will it to clear my addled wits and am pleased when it does. But even with my wits restored, I cannot discern Duval's strategy.

He could easily have made me his mistress in truth last night.

With the spell he cast over me, I am not even sure I would have fought very hard. And yet he did not. Is he that honorable? Or is it but one more way to keep me unbalanced, to keep me wondering what his next move will be?

With a grimace of disgust, I toss the remaining bread out into the courtyard below and turn from the casement. *It is a strategy,* I tell myself. *And an excellent one at that. But I will not let myself be lulled into a false sense of accord between us.* I cross the room to the bed, then withdraw my blades and sheaths from where I have hidden them under the mattress. Only when I have strapped them firmly in place do I go to find Duval.

He is in his study behind a large desk. Gone is the travel-stained man I journeyed across the country with. In his place is a finely dressed courtier in a doublet of dark blue. He has shaved the whiskery stubble that lent such a dark and dangerous air to his face. A pot of ink and half a dozen quills are on one side of him, stacks of parchment on the other, and his fingers wield a quill with quick, bold strokes.

When he looks up, I am sorely vexed to be caught staring, so I step inside the room, holding my head high and fighting the shyness that plucks at me. "Good morning." My voice is cool and remote.

"I will be with you in a moment," he says, returning his attention to the letter in front of him.

Torn between annoyance and relief, I saunter to the two trestle tables that have been set up to hold the overflow of papers and maps from his desk. A map of Brittany is spread out, and small, colored pebbles are scattered across it. I squint my eyes and see a shape and pattern to the pebbles. The dark ones mark the towns and villages that France took easily during the Mad war. Is he trying to determine where the French will attack if they do not get their way? A shadow passes over my heart. *Sweet Mortain, not another war.*

Duval finishes his letter and sets it aside before looking up at me. "How did you sleep last night?" There is a gleam of amusement in his eyes – eyes that are very nearly blue from the reflected color of his doublet – that I do not care for.

"Poorly, I am afraid, milord. My sleep was much disturbed."

"I am sorry to hear that," he says, even though he knows full well he is the cause. Before I can point that out to him, he holds up his hand. "Peace," he says. "We have much to discuss this morning before I leave and very little time."

It costs me to let him have the last word, but I nod in agreement nevertheless.

Duval tosses his quill on the desk and leans back in his

chair. "I was correct. Someone has called the meeting of the estates without the duchess's knowledge or consent, and she is most aggrieved. All the barons of the realm are now gathered here in Guérande like eager vultures. Even worse, the French envoy will no doubt witness the entire spectacle and report back to the French regent."

"Perhaps he will bear a marque," I say with hope. "Then I can kill him before he carries tales back to the French."

Duval grimaces. "By all means, if you see a marque on the French ambassador, kill him with my blessing along with Mortain's. However, if you think that will stop the leak of information from our court to France, you are more naive than you appear."

I bristle at his words, wanting to argue that I am not naive, but it has become clear that the convent has woefully underprepared me for this assignment.

Or perhaps it is the convent that is underprepared. It is a most unsettling thought, and I push it away. "Did you learn anything further from the footpad who attacked us?"

A grimace of embarrassment crosses his face. "No." He rises to his feet and stalks to the window. "I'm afraid I clouted him a bit too soundly. He has yet to wake up."

"Did you search through his belongings? Was there nothing that hinted at who they were or why they were there?"

"No. They had no standard or signed note of instruction stuffed neatly in their purses." His mocking tone prods me to my feet as well.

"Of course not. But had they been paid? What coin did they carry? Were their cloaks of Flemish wool, or their boots of Italian leather? We can learn much from these details."

Duval's brows lift in respectful surprise. "They carried French coin, but that tells us little, as half the coinage in the realm is French. Their cloaks were of cheap make, but their boots were of the finest leather, so they made some attempt at concealing their origins."

I try not to look smug, but before I can enjoy my small victory, he changes the subject.

"I have a number of meetings today. As you can imagine, the duchess has much to sort out with these newest developments, and I would be there to offer her guidance."

"Will they not question my presence, my lord?"

He looks at me in amusement. "They would indeed, demoiselle, which is why you will not be there."

"But what am I to do? Shall I question the footpad when he awakes? Or perhaps I should attempt to learn who it was that called for the meeting of the estates in the first pla—"

He raises his hand to stop my flow of words. "None of those. In fact, you will have a meeting too, of sorts." I do not like the smile playing about his mouth. "A seamstress, one of the duchess's, will be here shortly to fashion a gown for you to wear tonight when I present you at court."

"A . . . gown!" I splutter. He cannot be serious. He cannot think I will sit and be poked and prodded with pins and silk while he is off attending to matters of state. "That is not in our agreement, my lord."

"A good subterfuge requires preparation and attention to detail. Surely the convent taught you that much? If you are appear tonight as my mistress—"

"I thought we had settled on cousin," I say stiffly.

He leans against the wall near the window and folds his arms across his chest. "You must realize the futility of that now. My bloodlines on both sides are too well known for me to pull a cousin out of my lineage like a conjurer's trick."

My cheeks flame red at this reminder of my earlier blunder. He purses his lips and taps his finger against them, studying me. "In fact, that is what you can do once your gown has been properly fitted. You can study the noble families of Brittany so that when you meet them face to face tonight, you will not make similar mistakes."

I raise my chin. "I have already studied them, my lord, but unless they carry their shields or colors or display their coats of arms, I have no way of recognizing them."

"True enough, but you will forgive me if I am somewhat leery of what you learned at the convent. I would like to be certain you possess the basic facts of the situation."

A hot bubble of anger rises up inside me, but I force it back down. At first I think it is his arrogance that has made me angry, but then I realize I am angry because he has planted tiny, wicked seeds of doubt within me.

He strolls to a chessboard near the window. There is a game in progress, I see – but, no, there are far too many pieces for that. There are, in fact, twice as many pieces as in a regular game.

"Do you play?" he asks.

"No." This is a lie. I do play, just not very well.

"I am surprised," he says. "I would think the convent would find chess a useful tool for their novices."

"They do." Honesty compels me to admit it. "But it is not one of my strengths."

A corner of Duval's mouth lifts in amusement. "Too impatient, perhaps?"

I force myself to unclench my jaw. "So I was told," I mutter.

Ignoring my discomfiture, he reaches down and lays a finger on top of the white queen. She is flanked by a small cluster of white pieces. Surrounding her are dozens of dark pieces. "The French," Duval says, "press hard against us. They look for any excuse to step in and swallow us whole. They not only wait but actively plot and plan. If they can create discord within our ranks, they will cheerfully do so and use that as a justification to help themselves to our country. I know they are paying off some of our barons, but I do not yet know which ones. I am working on gathering that information."

"That is precisely what the convent explained to us, my lord." With the exception of the barons being bribed by the French regent, but I will bite off my tongue before admitting that to him.

"There are two things we must do," he continues, as if I have not spoken. "Secure a strong marriage alliance for the duchess, and see her crowned. Both are made more difficult by the French envoy's presence here at court. What do you know of Anne's suitors?" he asks.

"That she was dangled like bait in front of all the princes in Christendom and promised to nearly half of those," I say.

Duval's lips twist in a sour smile. "Precisely so. However, the one who is most determined to ensure that promise is kept is Count d'Albret. His suit has some support among the Privy Council, as well as among the barons. He has a number of large holdings and thousands of men-at-arms that he can call upon to fight against the French. It does not hurt his cause any that his half sister, the duchess's governess of many years, sits on the Privy Council. She is much in favor of his suit. The duchess herself, however, is greatly opposed to the match, as am I."

"Why?" I ask, genuinely curious.

He looks at me, incredulous. "You have seen the man."

"Not truly. He was surrounded by his outriders yesterday. I only caught a glimpse of his bulk and his poor lathered horse."

"Yes, well, he treats his wives much as he does his horses, but he goes through wives much faster."

His words strike a chord of memory. "Six," I say, remembering Sister Eonette's teachings. "He has had six wives so far. Indeed, he has gained much of his wealth and many of his holdings through those marriages."

Duval plucks a black knight from the board and scowls at it viciously. "You will forgive me if I mislike those odds."

I gape at him. "What are you suggesting?"

His jaw twitches. "Only that marriage and childbirth are hard on women, especially d'Albret women. Besides, I harbor suspicions of his role in our final and losing battle with the French."

"But I thought d'Albret rode to our rescue with four thousand troops?"

"Yes, but he was supposed to charge the center with those troops during the battle, and instead they hung back. I cannot decide if it was due to the normal chaos of battle or some ulterior purpose."

I am quiet a long moment as I ponder the many reasons d'Albret would be a most unsuitable match. "But surely he is not the only one of Anne's suitors who wants to claim her hand? She has been promised to so very many."

Duval drops the chess piece back on the board, then holds up his hand. "The Spanish prince is too ill right now to think of pursuing his betrothal agreement, although his royal parents have offered fifteen hundred troops to aid us. The English prince went missing from his tower over five years ago and is unable to follow through with those betrothal plans. Two of the other contenders are already married, although they are seeking annulments from the pope even as we speak. That leaves the Holy Roman emperor. He is by all accounts a good leader and a decent man, as well as a powerful ruler over both Germany and the Holy Roman empire. But he is mired in wars of his own and cannot send us any aid. Further, if we betroth Anne to the Holy Roman emperor, France will call it an act of war, and we will need troops to defend the alliance."

"Thus the plea to England for support."

"Exactly so. And we still do not know which side the English king will favor."

I stare at the board, painfully aware just how desperate the duchess's situation is. "She is well and truly under siege then," I murmur.

"That is a most excellent assessment of the situation, I'm afraid." Duval's gaze lingers on me for a long moment before he reaches toward the board once more. He lifts up a discarded white pawn and sets it in front of the white queen.

"Who is that, my lord?"

When he looks up, his eyes are so dark they seem almost black. "You," he says, our eyes holding for a long moment. "I can count you among those loyal to the duchess, can't I?"

"Of course, my lord," I murmur, struggling against the unexpected warmth his words bring me. *But,* I remind myself, *I am not the issue. Better for me to ask if* I *can count* him *among those loyal to the duchess.* Instead, I look back down at the board and wonder what piece Duval has assigned to himself.

Chapter 18

I stand among a gaggle of women who are clucking and honking like a flock of geese. They are tugging and pulling and patting and smoothing until I fear I will scream. Instead, I stare out the window at the lengthening shadows and wonder how they would react if they knew what I planned to hide under this fine skirt and these elaborate sleeves.

Louyse gives a final tug, then steps back. "You look a wonder, demoiselle." There is a warm glow in her old cheeks.

Young Agnez clasps her hands together as if in prayer. "It is the finest thing I've ever seen."

I want to dismiss their foolish prattle, but as I finger the heavy silken brocade, I cannot help but agree. I do not know where these seamstresses have found this gown or whose it was supposed to be, but it is mine now, and I must remind myself that assassins should take no pleasure in their finery and frippery.

But surely even a knight can admire his armor?

"Go get the mirror from the master's chambers," Louyse tells the others.

"That is not necessary," I tell her. "I trust what you have done."

"*Pish.*" Louyse flaps her hand. "You should see how lovely

you look."

I realize then how much she misses having a lady of the manor. I also realize that she does indeed know that Duval has spent the night in my room and is much pleased by it. The housekeeper appears to have a taste for romance, and I do not have the heart to take that from her, so I keep silent.

Agnez and the other two women return to the room, lugging the heavy mirror between them. When they lean it against the wall, Louyse takes my hand and gently pulls me toward it. "There." The triumph in her voice is unmistakable.

"Well? What do you think?" Young Agnez is practically bouncing on her toes in her excitement.

Slowly I lift my eyes to the image in the mirror and for one heart-stopping moment I do not recognize that person. It is most certainly not me, for my complexion has never been that fine nor my cheeks tinged with such a becoming shade of pink. The dusk-colored gown has done something to my eyes, and they shine back deep and luminous. I am filled with a ridiculous desire to lift my skirts and twirl to see how the fabric moves. Instead, I scowl at my image and turn away abruptly. "It will do," I say, and I harden my heart against the women's falling faces. "Now leave me, please. I would like a few moments alone before I go."

"But your hair," Louyse says, her old face uncertain now.

I soften my voice. "Thank you, but I can dress it myself. You forget that I am convent raised and all this vanity sits poorly on me."

"Ah." Her old face clears with understanding, and she

reaches out and pats my hand. Then she shoos the others from my room as she leaves, and I am blessedly alone. At least for a moment. I allow myself another quick look in the mirror, and – with no one to see – I do give a twirl, savoring the thick drape of the heavy skirt and the way the fabric ripples like water.

Feeling foolish, I turn my back on my mirror and hurry to the bed and snatch up the net of gold and pearls. I hastily twist my hair into a knot, then secure the net around it.

Next, I go to the mattress and reach for my weapons. The moment my fingers touch my ankle sheath, certainty flows in my veins once more. I strap it in place, then take up the wrist sheath. There is barely enough room for it under the tight sleeve, but after a long struggle, I am able to make everything work. I slip the lethal golden bracelet onto my wrist, then put my hand to my waist. At the comforting touch of the misericorde, I smile, and a sense of purpose settles over me. Surely Mortain will make His wishes known to me tonight, and I will be able to deal with our country's traitors in a manner suited to their crimes.

I am still smiling at that thought as I go to meet Duval. He is waiting for me at the foot of the staircase, and when I appear at the top of the steps, he forgets what he is saying to his steward and stares as if he has never seen me before. Even though this may well be an act, it pleases me more than it should. It cannot *all* be an act, for Duval is master at having the last word and would never knowingly grant me such an advantage. "That will do for now," he finally tells the steward.

"Good evening, milord," I say as I descend the stairs, trying to tamp down the bubble of pleasure.

When he takes my arm, he looks at me with suspicion. "What is wrong?" he asks.

"May I not smile without arousing your misgivings?"

"No," he says with a wry twist to his mouth.

"You need not look so distrustful; I am but practicing my role for tonight's masquerade. If we – if *I* – cannot convince the court of my role, then I will have no access to the duchess's enemies and will fail in the task the convent set for me. I have no intention of failing." The unwelcome truth is, until Chancellor Crunard returns, Duval is my only ally at court. Furthermore, the Breton nobility does not take kindly to the lowborn prancing among them. The last commoner to reach so high had been hung from the gibbet when his aspirations proved greater than his birth.

"What shadow just crossed your face?" Duval asks, and I curse his eyes that always see too much.

"I was thinking of your father's late chamberlain."

Duval grows somber. He tucks my arm closer against his. "That will not happen to you." His words sound almost like a vow, which discomfits me greatly.

To distract us both, I cozy up to him and flash my most brilliant smile, one I have copied from Sybella. "That is settled then. Shall we go?"

He blinks. "If you are not careful, I will begin to think you are enamored of me."

At his words, something flutters happily in my breast,

pleasure, perhaps, but I am at last finding my footing in this game we play. "It is what we want the court to think, my lord."

The grandeur of the Breton court can scarce be described. The rustle of fine silk and brocades, the whisper of plush velvet and softest leather. The air is heavy with perfume, from the shy scent of violets and bold bouquet of roses to the subtler scents of vetiver and sandalwood. The very air drips with richness and opulence that puts every place I've ever been to to shame.

I cannot imagine a gathering where I would be less at home; a turnip mislaid in a rose garden. I feel Duval's eyes upon me and risk a quick glance at him. "What?" I ask, reaching up to discreetly adjust an escaping tendril of hair.

He bats my hand away. "Leave it. It looks charming thus."

My cheeks grow warm at this unexpected compliment. Then he leans down. "Just how many of those pearls are poisoned?"

The warmth of his breath tickles my ear in an unsettling manner, but his words embolden me, reminding me of my purpose. I turn back to the gathered nobles with a lighter heart. Surely now that I am here, Mortain will reveal His wishes to me.

It is like watching a large group of birds of prey, all hooded eyes and hungry gazes, all waiting to pounce. What tasty morsel they hunger after, I know not. Gossip? Intrigue?

The nobles cluster in small groups, much like the chickens at the convent when they find a nest of slugs. All of the ladies are as poised and graceful as Madame Hivern, and while there are varying degrees of beauty, the style is the same: bold and well practiced, artfully achieved, demanding to be noticed.

"First things first, I think," Duval murmurs. "I must introduce you to the privy councilors so you do not kill one of them in error."

"If Mortain wills it, my lord, it will not be in error."

"Even so, I suggest you consult with the duchess before dispatching any of them." He leads me to two older men standing a bit removed from the others.

It is easy enough to guess who they are. The man on the right is built like a bear and stands as if he has been riding a horse for a fortnight. Surely he must be Captain Dunois. There is something about his quiet, unassuming strength that makes me inclined to trust him at once, a sentiment that I remind myself has no place in this game we play.

The other man is taller, with iron-gray hair and a surfeit of square yellowed teeth that put me in mind of a braying ass. He must be Marshal Rieux, and it is clear from the way he stands and surveys the room that he is much in love with his own opinion.

Captain Dunois greets Duval warmly, but Marshal Rieux is vexed and takes no pains to hide it. "You picked a fine time to disappear," he snaps.

Duval meets the older man's eyes steadily. "Indeed, I would never have left if I'd known someone would call an estate meeting over my sister's wishes."

Marshal Rieux doesn't flinch. "The barons have every right to be addressed and apprised of the situation, and sooner rather than later."

I glance at Duval. Does that mean that the marshal called the meeting? If so, he would surely bear a marque, but he does not. Or at least, not one that I can see.

Duval takes a step toward Marshal Rieux. "So it was you who called the meeting?"

Marshal Rieux's manner grows cold and distant. "You forget yourself, Duval," he snaps. "You are naught but a bastard, tolerated only for your sister's sake. You do not have a formal place on the council, or a voice. You are in no position to demand answers from me." Without giving Duval a chance to respond, he turns on his heel and stalks away.

Captain Dunois watches him a long moment before turning back to Duval. "Were you intending to have that effect on him?"

Duval gives an irritated shake of his head. "No, he is just more prickly than a damned hedgehog. Was it Rieux that called the meeting, do you think? Is that why he grew so angry?"

"No, I think he grew angry because he did *not* call the meeting and does not like being reminded that someone disregarded not only Anne's authority but also his own."

"Since Chancellor Crunard has been away from court nearly as long as I have, that leaves Madame Dinan. But to what purpose? Does she mean to put her half brother's marriage proposal before the barons? Surely she knows Anne will refuse him. What does she gain by forcing the issue in such a manner?"

Captain Dunois shrugs. "Perhaps it is intended as a show of support and strength to deter our French guests?"

"French plague is more like it," Duval mutters. "Perhaps now is as good a time as any for us to greet the French parasite."

Dunois bows. "You will forgive me if I do not linger to watch the resulting tempest," he says, then takes his leave.

With a sigh, Duval begins leading me across the room. "If the French ambassador bears a marque, do feel free to kill him at once. It would save us all a great deal of trouble."

Only too pleased at the chance to open myself to Mortain's will, I let Duval steer me to the far corner of the hall where the French envoy sits like a fat brown spider, patient and cunning, tending his carefully woven web. He is a hatchet-faced man surrounded by smirking, fawning courtiers. He makes no move to acknowledge us as Duval and I approach, but I feel him study us all the same.

When we reach the envoy, Duval looks contemptuously at those gathered round him. "Still here, Gisors?" That Duval does not even feign politeness surprises me. I thought honeyed words a requirement here at court.

The French noble spreads his hands. "But of course. I am here to oversee the wardship of young Anne."

"Anne is no one's ward," Duval counters. "You are here to guard France's interests and care nothing for our duchess." While Duval's words are sharp, he delivers them almost cheerfully, as if he enjoys tearing down the carefully constructed web Gisors has built.

"Tsk-tsk. So little trust, Duval."

Duval narrows his eyes. "Says the wolf as he sniffs at the door."

As Duval keeps Gisors distracted with conversation, I study the French envoy intently, looking for any hint of a marque, but I see nothing, not the faintest smudge or shadow anywhere.

When Gisors finally turns his hooded gaze on me, I am struck by how very green his eyes are. Those eyes travel languidly down my body and back up again, but he says nothing to acknowledge my presence. Under my hand, the muscles in Duval's arm stiffen, and he glances at me. When I give a little shake of my head, his mouth flattens in disappointment.

Completely unaware of our silent exchange, Gisors says, "I hear Anne has received correspondence from the Holy Roman emperor. What did he have to say?"

"I believe that is between the Holy Roman emperor and the duchess." Duval's mild voice is at odds with the tension in his arm.

"Since he is petitioning for a betrothal that the French Crown forbids, it is most certainly our business as well."

"Brittany is a sovereign nation, and our duchess free to choose whom she pleases."

I peer up at Duval from under my lashes. This is not quite true and I wonder if Gisors will call the bluff. He does.

"And I would remind you of the Treaty of Verger," the envoy says. "Furthermore, young Anne has not yet been crowned duchess."

"A mere formality," Duval replies, "since that treaty you're so fond of quoting agrees that she keeps the duchy and will rule over it as duchess."

"Only if she marries whom the French Crown says she should marry."

"We have yet to see a serious offer put forth by you or your regent," Duval points out.

"We have given you two."

"A foppish minor baron and a doddering sycophant older than her father." Duval flaps his hand at the far wall, where for the first time I notice an old, gray-bearded courtier dozing in a chair. "Neither is remotely suitable."

Gisors gives an indifferent shrug. "Then we are at an impasse."

"Again," Duval says, then gives a curt bow and escorts me away. As we pass beyond Gisors's hearing, I glance once more at the dozing figure against the wall. It takes me a moment to realize that his spirit is growing dim, like a candle flame shrinking and sputtering before going out. "It is just as well the duchess is not inclined to accept France's candidate for a husband. That one over there will be dead within a fortnight," I tell Duval.

He stops to stare at the aging courtier. "He is marqued by Mortain?"

"No, he is merely dying of old age or some slow disease."

"You can tell this from looking at him?"

I nod, pleased that he is impressed with my gifts. Before Duval can say anything further, a large hand clamps down on his shoulder.

"That is quite a subtle touch you have there, Duval, to have angered two men in so short a time. First Marshal Rieux and now the French envoy."

We turn to find a brute of a man just behind us. He is tall and fat, and a bristly black beard covers his face. Amid all that blackness, his lips stand out like wet pink slugs. His hooded eyes study me with the hungry intensity of a hawk. Something cold and chilling slithers in their depths, and then it is gone, so swift and fleeting I do not know if it was truly there or was simply my own dark fears awakening.

Duval's greeting is less than warm. "Count d'Albret," he says. "What brings you to Guérande?"

This is the man the late duke promised his twelve-year-old daughter to? I can scarce wrap my mind around it.

D'Albret casts Duval a sly look. "Always the wit, aren't you, Duval."

"One hopes so," Duval mutters, his voice dry as bone. "Allow me to present my cousin, Ismae Rienne."

I look demurely down at the floor and sink into a curtsy.

"Ah, yes. I, too, have a cousin," he says. "I am quite fond of her." D'Albret reaches out, takes my hand, and brings it to his slack, fleshy mouth. Revulsion, sharp and hot, spikes through me and it is all I can do not to reach for my knife. As his wet lips press against my hand, I shudder. Duval places a bracing hand at my back, and I am grateful for something to focus on besides d'Albret's touch. "*Enchanté*, demoiselle," the count murmurs.

"The honor is all mine, my lord," I reply. As soon as his grip on my hand has loosened, I snatch it back and bury it in the folds of my gown where, unable to help myself, I wipe it on my skirt.

Count d'Albret smiles at me as if we are the closest of friends, as if we share some secret that Duval is not privy to. "Do not let Duval bore you with all his talk of politics and intrigue, demoiselle," he says. "There are much finer pleasures to be had at court." The leer on his face leaves little doubt as to which pleasures he is thinking of.

"My cousin is young and from the country, d'Albret. Surely you can do your hunting in more verdant pastures."

"Nonsense, Duval. I just wanted to make her feel welcome at court. After all, it can be overwhelming, and she will quickly learn how serious and dull you are." D'Albret turns to me. "When he leaves you in a corner somewhere so that he may discuss politics like an old man, I will find you, my dear." And even though this promise will surely give me nightmares, he smiles as if he has just offered me the moon.

Duval stares steadily at the older man, his dislike rolling off him like fog from the sea. It is a wonder the count does not see it.

D'Albret winks at me. "Come find me when you grow bored." And with that, he saunters off.

Once he is well out of hearing, I give voice to my outrage. "I cannot *believe* your father promised that man your sister's hand in marriage. He is so old," I say. *"And vile!"*

The look Duval sends me fair trumpets the words *I told you so.*

"Does he care anything for the duchess herself or is it merely the duchy he is after?"

Duval's mouth quirks in disgust. "The duchy is his first and foremost goal, but I am sure being married to a young maid of Anne's beauty and charm will be no hardship for him." Something dark and dangerous shadows Duval's face, but before I can question him further, he speaks again. "Now, come with me. I have one more person I would have you meet."

Chapter 19

The heat of Duval's hand passes through the silk of my sleeve all the way down to my marrow. I am sorely tempted to throw it off, but I need his solid warmth to chase away the clammy chill d'Albret has left behind.

Duval leads me up a wide stone staircase, then down one corridor, then another. For the first time I get a feel for just how big the duchess's residence in Guérande is. After leading me through many twists and turns, he stops in front of a thick oaken door and knocks. When there is no answer, he lets himself in.

The room is a sumptuous receiving chamber with several ornately carved chairs, thick velvet tapestries covering the stone walls, and a fire burning in the fireplace. "Why have you brought me here?" Duval lets go of my arm and prowls around the room. He looks behind the tapestries at the window, then strides to the small door in the far corner and confirms that it is locked. "Because I would have you meet our duchess face to face and see who precisely it is that you are serving."

The main door opens just then and the duchess herself comes into the room. She is very young, but she holds herself with pride and not a little arrogance. Her forehead is high and noble; her cheeks still bear the slight fullness of her youth. Her brown eyes are keen with intelligence. It would be a mistake to underestimate her, yet because of her youth, I am certain many do.

She is followed by an older noblewoman whom I can only assume is her governess, Madame Dinan. She was strikingly beautiful once, and her bones still hold the truth of that beauty even with her hair gone white. It is hard to believe she shares any blood with Count d'Albret.

Duval bows low and I sink into a deep curtsy. "Your Grace; Madame Dinan," he says.

"You may rise." The young duchess's voice is as clear and true as a bell. She turns to the other woman. "And you may leave us."

Madame Dinan glances at Duval. "Your Grace, I think I should stay. It is not fitting that you are alone, with no chaperone."

"You would keep me from speaking with my own brother?" the duchess asks sharply.

"I would keep you from nothing, Your Grace, only suggest you should have a chaperone, as is fitting."

The duchess glances at Duval, who gives the tiniest shake of his head. "We have a chaperone," she says, indicating me. "You may leave."

The command in her tone is unmistakable, and Madame Dinan rears her head back slightly, nostrils flaring. "Very well, Your Grace. I will wait outside." Her unhappiness with this arrangement is palpable, but whether it is because she resents being left out or because she is truly worried to leave the duchess with her own brother, I cannot tell.

The room is quiet until she leaves, then the duchess crosses over to the fireplace and holds her hands out to the flames. "Was that necessary, Gavriel?" she says. "It is hard for her to take orders from me."

"I understand, Your Grace." Even though he is her brother, Duval remains formal with her, and I wonder if it is for my benefit. "But I wanted you to meet Demoiselle Rienne and learn from her own mouth who and what she is. It is knowledge best kept to ourselves for a while."

The duchess tilts her head, curiosity shining in her eyes. "You do not trust Madame Dinan?"

"Someone called this estate meeting, Your Grace, and d'Albret *is* her half brother."

The duchess wrinkles her nose. "Do not remind me! She presses his suit at every turn until I fear I shall scream."

"We will find you a better marriage, I promise," Duval says.

She dimples prettily at this, making her look impossibly young, and her affection for Duval is plain on her face. In that moment, I am fiercely glad she has a brother to protect her from this marriage they have planned for her. It is unthinkable that she has been promised to d'Albret. Surely it cannot be Mortain's desire to see the duchess wed to such a foul man.

Duval grabs my hand and pulls me forward. "Ismae Rienne is sent from the abbess at the convent of St. Mortain."

The duchess's eyebrows shoot up. "Mortain? The patron saint of death?"

"The very one, Your Grace. It is but another thing your advisors would keep from you." Duval quickly explains the convent and its purpose.

When he is done with his explanation, she turns to me. "You are truly trained in death?"

It feels too bold to meet her gaze, so I look down at the floor. "Yes, Your Grace."

"Sit, sit." She waves her hand and chooses a chair for herself. After an uncertain glance at Duval, who nods, I sit also.

"How do you kill a man, demoiselle?"

I am certain her advisors would be shocked if they could see the hungry curiosity in her eyes. "With a knife. Or poison. Or by strangling. There are many ways. Hundreds of them. It depends on the circumstances and Mortain's wishes."

She leans forward slightly in her chair, her brow furrowed. "How do you decide who to kill?"

"Yes," Duval drawls from where he stands by the fireplace. "How *do* you decide who to kill?"

And there he has me, for while the rites of Mortain are closely held, if Chancellor Crunard can know of them, so can the duchess. Just as I must know what weapons I have in my arsenal in order to do Mortain's work, so must the duchess know what tools are available to her in her struggle to maintain her country's independence. "Your Grace, I would tell you of our mysteries, but our knowledge is sacred and revealed only to a chosen few." I glance at Duval, indicating that he is not one of the chosen few.

When she sees where I am looking, her expression grows unyielding. "I trust my lord brother with my life," she says. "I have no secrets from him and want him to know of these rites as well. Now tell us."

I fair grind my teeth in frustration. Is that why he arranged this meeting, knowing she would demand answers and that I would have to give them? "We are mere instruments of Mortain, Your Grace. His handmaidens, if you will. We do not decide who to kill or why or when. It is all determined by the god."

"You mean saint, do you not?" she asks.

I have forgotten the conventions of the Church that must be followed outside the convent. "But of course, Your Grace. Forgive me. The saint."

She nods graciously. "How, then, does the saint inform you of His wishes?"

"One of our nuns, Sister Vereda, has a vision. The saint communicates through her, then she and the abbess direct our hands."

"How does Chancellor Crunard fit in?" Duval asks.

"He acts as liaison to the outside world and keeps the abbess up to date on the politics at court."

"And you have only the sisters' word that there has been a vision?"

I turn on Duval. "Their word is above reproach. They serve Mortain."

"He raises an interesting question," the duchess points out. "How can you be so certain their visions are correct? How do you know they serve Saint Mortain and not their own interests? And what if they make a mistake?"

"They don't." I direct my answer to the duchess and do my best to pretend Duval is not in the room. "If they did not speak truly, then we would not see the marque of death on our victims and we would stay our hands."

The duchess is intrigued by this idea. "Marque? What does that look like?"

"It looks as if the saint has dipped His finger into the darkness of a man's soul and anointed him with it. Sometimes the marque will show how a man is to die."

"And that is how you will know how to strike here in Guérande, away from your seeress?"

I shake my head. "It is our plan for the abbess to communicate the visions to me by crow. But should I happen to see such a marque without an order from her, I am allowed to strike."

"Mon Dieu!" The duchess sits back in her chair and looks at Duval. "Do all the Privy Council know of this convent?"

Duval shakes his head. "I believe only Crunard works with the abbess. Marshal Rieux has some vague knowledge of it, and Dunois has probably heard rumors among his men, but as he is French, he was not made privy to Breton secrets by our late father. Madame Dinan has no knowledge – or should not – which is why I requested she be kept from this meeting."

The duchess tilts her head and studies me. "Who else knows Ismae's true identity?"

"Only Chancellor Crunard."

"Then I agree we should keep it that way." I stand as she rises to her feet. She holds her hand out to me. "I am glad you are here, Ismae. It is a comfort to know that you and the patron saint of death are helping Duval guard my flanks."

I kiss her ducal ring, awed that the daughter of a turnip farmer is being raised to her feet by her sovereign. "It is my greatest honor to serve Your Grace."

She smiles again, transforming her young face. "I welcome you to my court. Your skills will come in most handily with my fractious barons," she says in jest.

At least, I believe it is in jest.

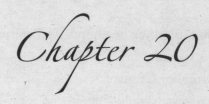

Chapter 20

I lie in bed, my head still buzzing from the babbling voices that filled the court this evening. In truth, I have learned much and nothing at all. Duval is still an enigma, and if he is a traitor, as the chancellor and abbess suspect, I have no idea whom he might work for.

His hatred of both d'Albret and the French envoy is palpable, but of course he could easily fake that. But what of the fierce protectiveness he feels for his sister? I remember the grim set to his mouth, the fury in his eyes, and the anger that fair sparked off him, and I must admit that even he could not feign that. Which turns all my other arguments to dust.

Perhaps Duval is exactly who he says he is, a devoted brother intent on seeing his sister crowned duchess and safely wed to a man who can stand with her against the French. Of a certainty that is what the duchess believes.

Hoping a night's rest will bring clarity, I close my eyes and urge my thoughts toward sleep. Instead, Count d'Albret's thick, fleshy lips rise up in my mind, and my eyes snap open. Guillo. That is who d'Albret reminds me of, why he disturbs me so.

I fear the dreams will come tonight. Whether they will be

the old ones of Guillo or some new nightmare built around d'Albret, I cannot guess.

There is a whisper of sound near the door, and my heart stutters in my chest even as my mind whispers, *Duval*. But my hand creeps toward my stiletto, just in case.

"I thought we had gotten past that." Duval's deep voice stirs the darkness of the room.

I lift my head from the pillow to see where he is. "Perhaps you have, but I have not."

"Do not be tiresome."

I follow the sound of his voice. There. In the faint glow cast by the dying embers, I can see him make his way to the chair in front of the window. I relax somewhat. As unwelcome as he is – and he *is* unwelcome, I assure myself – he will chase away the even more unwelcome dreams. "What are you doing here?"

"Performing my nightly duties to my young mistress."

His words cause something to flutter inside me. I have no idea what it is, but it frightens me almost as much as my dreams. "I am too tired to spar tonight, my lord."

"As am I. Go to sleep. I will sit here but an hour or two, then leave."

I yawn. "So very long as that?"

When he answers, there is a wry note in his voice. "I do have my reputation to protect."

I have no idea what he is talking about. I yawn again, then pinch myself, not wanting to fall asleep. "Why did your father promise your sister to Count d'Albret? With her kingdom as dowry, surely she could have made a better match than that? To someone who wasn't so repulsive."

There is a long moment of silence before Duval answers. "It was a desperate bid to save that very kingdom. Our lord father was short on troops with which to fight the French. D'Albret agreed to supply those troops, but at a price."

"The duchess's hand in marriage."

"Yes. My sister's hand in marriage."

The utter betrayal of this leaves me speechless, for while the price paid was considerably higher, the arrangement was not so very different from my father's bargain with Guillo.

"Perhaps my father thought he would live long enough to assure the marriage never came to pass," Duval says. "I would like to believe that." There is a faint note of anguish in his voice, and I know that he feels the betrayal as sharply as I do.

"I'm sure you are right, my lord," I say, surprised that I feel the need to comfort him.

"I have sworn that no matter how much d'Albret bellows or what he threatens, he will have to step over my dead body to marry her."

I cannot help but admire Duval greatly in that moment and find myself wishing that his father had cared half so much about Anne. Even so, I am not altogether comfortable with this small bit of harmony. Luckily, it does not last long.

"Now, enough questions, Ismae, or else I will have to think of some way to silence you."

At his threat, my mind immediately goes to his disconcerting game of the previous night. From the faint note of humor in his voice, I suspect he is thinking of it also. Not wishing to test that theory, I settle down under my covers and close my eyes. I am certain I will not sleep with him in the room, but the sooner I fool him into believing I am asleep, the sooner he will leave.

I am locked in Guillo's root cellar; my face presses against the floor, and the sharp smell of dirt is in my nose. Something heavy pushes down on me, forcing me farther into the dirt. Straining my neck, I look up. Guillo is before me, fumbling at the front of his braies, leering. The weight on top of me grows heavier, and my arms are wrenched up behind my back, nearly to the point of breaking. I twist round, trying to peer through my hair, and find the flat black eyes of Count d'Albret. His long, careless fingers fumble at my skirts while Guillo beckons to me from the shadows. I struggle and buck against him, trying to throw him from my back, but he grips my arms tighter and forces me back down. "No!" I shout. My hand scrabbles in the dirt until it closes around the handle of a dagger hidden there. I grip it tightly, then roll out of d'Albret's grasp and thrust the knife in his throat.

He swears a black oath and I feel the warmth of his blood trickle down my arm. Now free of his grip, I blink and shove the hair out of my eyes.

Only to find Duval sitting on my bed, staring at me. He holds his hand to his collar, blood seeping between his fingers, the dagger still in my hand.

"God's Teeth!" he says. "I was only trying to wake you. You were crying out in your sleep."

"I was not," I say, then look from his neck to my knife.

"When I tried to wake you, you stabbed me." He sounds sore put out, and I cannot blame him.

"Merde." I am fully awake now and filled with remorse. I toss my knife onto the bed and scramble out from under the covers. While Duval tries to keep the blood from dripping on the bed, I hurry to the washbasin and dip one of the linen towels into the cold water. "Let me see how bad it is," I say, returning to the bed.

"Not serious, I think." He lifts his chin to give me better access. "But you have ruined one of my favorite shirts."

I gently mop the blood on his neck and collarbone. "Then perhaps you shouldn't sneak up on people when they are sleeping."

"You were whimpering and crying. You'd rather I left you to the tender mercies of your dream?"

Heat creeps into my face at the memory of my nightmare. "No," I admit. "Perhaps not." I've wiped away most of the blood and can see a two-inch scratch along his collarbone. "I must resume practicing," I mutter. "I missed."

Duval barks out a laugh. "Only because I have very good reflexes and you were asleep." He grows quiet for a moment, and I become aware of the intimacy of our positions. We sit on the bed, our knees touching. My hand rests at the base of his throat and I can feel the steady beat of his heart under my wrist. His dark eyes study me.

Trying to ease my sudden discomfort, I take the towel from his neck and begin folding it. My wrist still throbs where it has lain over his heart.

"Do you care to share your dream?" His voice is low and warm and like as not could coax secrets from a stone.

"It was nothing. I have already forgotten it."

"Liar." His voice is so soft I am not sure I heard it. Even so, I keep my gaze on the linen towel as I search it for a clean, unbloodied spot.

There is a long moment of awkward silence, then Duval speaks. "I can tend to it from here, I think." His fingers brush against mine as he takes the towel from my hands. He stands up, leaving me alone on the bed, the warmth of his solid body no longer between me and my nightmares.

Feeling miserable, although not sure why, I wrap my arms around myself. "I am sorry, my lord. I did not wish to harm you." The truth of my words surprises me, for it seems as if I have done naught but long to be rid of him.

His smile flashes, quick and surprising in the darkness. "When one consorts with assassins, one must expect to dance along the edge of a knife once or twice. I bid you goodnight."

He leaves the room, and I lie back down on the bed, unable to tell if I am overly warm or chilled to the bone.

The next morning, Louyse bustles in with a cheerful smile and a pitcher of hot water. I have not slept since Duval left and am awake when she arrives. "Good morning, demoiselle."

"Good morning, Louyse." I stretch, then climb out of bed. Since there is no towel this morning, I cup my hands into the basin and splash the warm water on my face. "No word of my trunks yet?" I ask as I hurriedly dry my face and hands on my night shift.

"No, demoiselle," she says as she straightens the covers on the bed.

"In that case, I will wear the dark gray gown today."

When Louyse doesn't answer, I turn and find her staring at a smear of blood on the sheets. Sweet Mortain! What must she think?

Not wanting to acknowledge the blood, I hurry over to the garderobe. She bustles to my side and casts me a look, her face full of concern. "Is demoiselle sure she feels well enough to be up and about today? Would you like me to bring you more hot water? Or I could arrange for a bath, if demoiselle likes?"

"No," I say shortly. "I am fine."

The older woman reaches out and pats my arm. "Do not worry." She lowers her voice. "It will not always hurt so."

With dawning horror, I realize what conclusions she has drawn from the blood on the sheets. My cheeks flame bright red.

My reputation as Duval's mistress has just been firmly established.

Chapter 21

Duval is breaking his fast in the winter parlor. At my entrance, a servant pulls out a chair. I sit stiffly, filled with shame that Duval has seen me having a nightmare as if I were nothing but a child. Nor can I forget the feel of his skin beneath my fingers as I tended his wound. Even worse, I am afraid all of this will show on my face.

"How did you sleep?" he asks politely.

I risk glancing at him, expecting to see a glint of amusement or a smirk. Instead, there is a hint of concern. It is this kindness of his that unsettles me most. I can dodge a blow or block a knife. I am impervious to poison and know a dozen ways to escape a chokehold or garrote wire. But kindness? I do not know how to defend against that.

"Like a babe," I answer. The lie falls easily from my lips as I glance pointedly at his throat.

He fingers the small ruff on the high collar he is wearing this morning. "Mayhap I will set a new fashion at court."

His words prick my conscience. I raise my chin slightly and refuse to utter the apology that hovers on my tongue. It is his own fault for skulking about my room at night. "I have not yet received any message from the reverend mother. Have you word from Chancellor Crunard?"

His face sobers immediately. "No, why?"

I shrug and take a pear from the platter on the table. "I have been in Guérande three days. As urgently as the abbess wanted me here, I would think there should be someone who needed killing by now."

Duval throws back his head and laughs. "You are a bloodthirsty thing, I'll give you that."

I stab a knife into my pear. The golden skin splits, and fragrant juice drips onto the plate. "Not bloodthirsty, merely eager to do Mortain's work. It is why I am here, after all."

"True enough."

"What are our tasks for the day?"

He raises one of his eyebrows at me. "*I* have received word that a messenger has arrived at the palace and requests a meeting with me."

My hand stills. "Who is it?"

"I do not know, as the messenger has cloaked himself in secrecy. He claims he will speak only to me, which is why you will stay here and entertain yourself this morning."

I clench my knife. "I can easily hide, my lord. That will not be a problem."

"Yes, but I have promised the man a private meeting and I would keep my word."

"But what of your promise to the abbess?" I begin cutting the pear with quick, clean strokes.

"I have not said that I will not inform you of what transpires, merely that I have promised him a private audience. Besides, there is still much you are keeping from— Sweet Jesu!"

I look up, alarmed. "What?"

He nods at my plate. "You are supposed to eat it, not disembowel it."

I look down and see that I have sliced my pear to ribbons. I carefully set the knife aside and reach for the bread.

"If it is activity you crave, one of my groomsmen can accompany you if you care to ride. Or you can occupy yourself with" – he waves his hand, searching for some activity he deems appropriate – "needlework."

I stare at him coldly. "I do not care for needlework." I pause. "Unless it involves the base of the skull."

His mouth lifts in amusement and I hold my breath, wondering if he will laugh again. I ignore the small nick of disappointment when he does not. "Then occupy yourself reading some of the histories in my study. I assume the convent taught you how to entertain yourself for a morning. Put some of that excellent training to use." And with that, he removes himself from the table, leaving me to seethe over my breakfast.

Stay, he bids me. As if I am some hound to follow or not, at his command. As if it is he, not I, who is in charge of my actions. I know in my bones that the abbess will want to be informed of any urgent secret meeting. Besides, does not his very desire to keep this meeting secret prove he is up to some deception? When it is over, I will have only his word as to what took place.

Renewed purpose flowing through me, I rise and hurry to find my cloak.

I travel on foot. Saddling a mount would waste precious time and risk drawing questions. I do not know how loyal Duval's servants are or to what lengths they will go to enforce his wishes.

The morning air is crisp and clean; Guérande's merchants are only just beginning to open their shutters. Industrious maids and housewives are already shopping for their day's provisions. No one pays any attention to my passing. When I reach the palace, it is easy enough to gain admittance, as courtiers, nobles, and petitioners come and go as they please. I also suspect the guard recognizes me from last night, although I cannot be certain. My biggest obstacle is finding where Duval's mysterious meeting is taking place.

I stand in the main hallway for a moment, trying to create a map of the palace in my head. As I orient myself, I remember that Duval has private rooms assigned to him. That is surely where he will hold his meeting.

I ask a posted sentry for directions, then hurry up the staircase he points to. The palace is larger than the village where I grew up and far more confusing. Countless chamber doors line the endless hallways and corridors. In the end, I give up and bribe one of the many pages underfoot to show me the way to Duval's chambers. I give him a coin – two when he promises silence – then study the door before me.

There is no antechamber. The door is in plain sight of anyone who walks by, which means I cannot simply stand with my ear to it. There is another door to the right of

Duval's, so I approach it, casting my senses out, trying to see if anyone is in there.

It feels empty, so I slip inside and hurry to the joint wall between the two rooms. I press my ear against it, but the stone is thick, and the men are speaking in low, cautious voices. I turn back to explore the chamber. It is filled with fine furnishings and elegant tapestries, none of which will help me in the least. There is a window, however, that overlooks a small enclosed courtyard. I stick my head out, pleased to see Duval's room also has a window. It is easier to hear through glass than stone.

Once assured there is no one in the courtyard below, I remove my cloak so it will not trip me and step out onto the ledge. Carefully, I inch along the narrow casement until my hand grasps the wood that frames Duval's window. I pause, then flatten myself against the wall so I cannot be seen from inside. I am quickly rewarded for my efforts by Duval's voice, slightly muffled but audible through the thick glass. "If you cannot tell me who you are working for, then we have nothing more to discuss." His voice is as cold and hard as the stone at my back.

"You know well that there are few to trust in the duchess's court. If word of my liege lord's identity were to fall into the wrong hands, it would put many people in jeopardy."

"You cannot expect me to gallop off to a rendezvous with your mystery lord when it could so easily be a trap."

"You may choose the time and place of the meeting, one to your own advantage. But my liege has a plan, a proposal" – his voice sounds like he is smiling—"that he thinks you'll find most intriguing."

There is a long pause as Duval considers, weighing the risks. My ears are firmly fixed on the room beyond, but my eyes search the courtyard below. My fingers and toes have grown numb in the bitter chill of the morning, but I will not leave my post before I hear Duval's answer.

"Why me?" he finally asks. "Why has your liege sent you to me rather than to the chancellor or one of the duchess's guardians?"

"Because blood is thicker than any chain of office. My liege believes that you more than anyone care for the young duchess's well-being."

Interesting that the mysterious lord would think such a thing. Is it empty flattery? Or does the man have personal knowledge of Duval?

The room is quiet as both men weigh and measure each other, and I nearly dance with impatience – I'm desperate to hear Duval's answer and nearly as desperate to be gone from this place before I am discovered.

"Very well," Duval says at last. "I will speak to this liege of yours and hear what he has to offer. Tell me where you are staying and I will have word sent as to when and where we shall meet."

Satisfied that the main thrust of the meeting is over, I peel my fingers away from the window, flexing them to get the blood flowing again. Slowly, for fear of missing a step with my nearly numb feet, I begin inching back to the adjoining room. Stiff with cold, I half fall, half climb back into the chamber, then silently close the shutter. I grab my cloak and rub my arms, trying to get warm again, but only for a moment. I need to be well away from here before Duval concludes his meeting.

I hurry to the door, open it a crack, and peer out into the hallway, then nearly gasp in surprise when I spot Madame Hivern lurking outside Duval's door. Hopefully, the door presented as thick an obstacle to her as it did to me.

I know Duval wanted this meeting to remain secret, but it is my own suspicion of the woman that propels me into the hall. I arrange my face in a flustered look, then step out of the office. "Madame Hivern?" I say, making my voice young and just a bit tremulous.

Startled, she whirls round. "Demoiselle Rienne? What are you doing here?" Her lovely face is wary.

I glance about, confused. "I was looking for milord Duval's chambers. One of the footmen told me they were in this corridor, but I must have miscounted the doors."

Her face relaxes and a smile that is pure condescension appears on her face. "Come, my dear." She reaches out, tucks my arm in hers, and begins leading me down the hall, away from both doors. "Surely you know that the best way to lose a man is to chase him down?" She pats my hand. "Let me share with you the secrets of our trade."

It is all I can do to keep from correcting her disturbing assumption. Nor do I trust this sudden charity of hers. "Madame is too kind." I am pleased that I keep any whiff of irony from my words. In truth, the last thing I want is advice from Duval's mother on how to be a good mistress. However, perhaps I can turn it to my advantage and use the opportunity to learn more about Duval.

The memory of his stricken face the night they argued flits through my mind, and I feel sick at my own deception, as if I am probing a gaping wound. Nevertheless, it *is* why I am here, and I know just what the reverend mother would think of such misplaced scruples.

Ignoring the nobles and courtiers gathered in clusters in the grand salon, Madame Hivern settles us in a corner away from the others. When we are alone, she turns considering eyes on me. "So." She sets her graceful hands in her lap. "Where are you from, my dear, and how did you meet Gavriel?"

I lower my eyes – a young country miss would be nervous, would she not? – and begin twisting my hands in my lap. "My family is of modest means, madame, and would not be known to you."

She tilts her head daintily, but the smile on her face is brittle as glass. "Then how did you come to meet?"

Stick close to the truth to give weight to the lie is what the convent drilled into our heads. "In a tavern, near Brest." I do not fully trust Duval, but I trust his mother even less and will not serve up his secrets on a platter before her.

Her face blanches and she rears back a little, as if she has just been struck. "Please tell me you were not the serving wench."

"No," I say, careful not to smile. "I was passing through on my family's business."

I watch as she mentally combs through the coastal area of Brest, trying to determine what business Duval was up to. After another moment, her lovely mask falls back into place. "You must forgive me," she says. "But my son has kept so completely to himself until now, I scarcely know how to credit your presence."

I make my eyes wide and innocent. "But, madame, clearly the two of you are estranged, so perhaps he has simply not mentioned such relationships to you."

Her mouth grows ugly and flat at this blatant reminder, but she bites back her retort as a servant places a tray of spiced wine in front of us. By the time the servant leaves, she has composed herself. I pick up a wine goblet, and she leans forward, changing the subject. "Not all men are the same, you know. With someone such as Gavriel, I would suggest appearing aloof, not chasing too much. He might see that as suffocating rather than charming."

Her words are sharp, but her voice is sweet, like honey on the edge of a blade, and meant to be cutting. I comfort myself with the knowledge that if Duval ever feels smothered by me, it will be because I am holding a pillow over his face and commending his soul to Mortain.

She frowns and continues her prattling. "Why ever did you think it would be a good idea to chase him down? Is that what girls do in the village you come from?"

"I was not chasing him, madame, merely trying to deliver

a message. It came after he left this morning and I thought to deliver it myself."

Hivern holds up her hands in mock horror. "You are his paramour, not his servant. Do not follow him like a dog follows his master."

My hand tightens on my wine goblet, and I am glad it is silver, not glass, for surely it would shatter under the force of my annoyance with this woman. "Madame, I assure you—"

"Oh, call me Antoinette, won't you? I think we shall be fast friends, you and I."

"Do you think that is a good idea, given the breach between you and your son?"

A hint of cold fury flickers across her face, then is gone. "Perhaps you can help us to heal this rift."

I set my goblet down on the table and give Madame Hivern my most innocent look. "Is that why *you* were looking for him? To call a truce?"

Annoyance crosses her face, and she casts about the room as if searching for a distraction. Apparently she finds one, for her expression softens and her eyes shine with the first true emotion she has shown. "My darling!" Hivern's face is alight with pleasure. "Do come here, I have someone I would like you to meet."

The man who approaches is tall and slender with dark eyes and fine features and is far too young to be her lover, and yet she has called him darling. He gives me a cautious, considering look, then bends to kiss Hivern's cheek.

"Ismae, I would like you to meet my son François

Avaugour. François, this is Ismae, Gavriel's new friend."

If he has heard tell of his brother's "friend," he gives no indication. He bends gallantly over my hand. "*Enchanté,* demoiselle. Any friend of my brother's is a friend of mine."

I murmur some nonsense back, and Madame Hivern pats the seat next to her. "Come join us, my love."

"But of course." François takes the chair close to Hivern so that he faces me. "How can I resist the two loveliest ladies at court?"

I long to roll my eyes at his words, but I peer up at him through my lashes instead.

"Gavriel's friend is not used to such polished manners, François. She has been too long in the country. You should offer to guide her through her first visit to court when your brother is tending to his other duties."

His liquid brown eyes meet mine. "I can think of nothing that would give me more pleasure, demoiselle."

"You are too kind," I murmur, pleased at how easily I have been pulled into the bosom of Duval's family. They must hunger after his secrets as much as I hunger after theirs.

"My son was born and raised at court and can steer you safely through its treacherous waters."

"But surely milord Duval will do that," I protest.

"Duval can do what?" a deep, familiar voice asks.

"Gavriel!" Hivern's voice is full of gaiety that is as false as her heart. "What a lovely surprise. We were just getting to know your friend a little better. She is such a charming thing."

The warm, heavy weight of Duval's hand settles on my shoulder and I am rendered speechless as he bends down and places a kiss atop my head.

"Dearest Ismae," Duval says. "Whatever are you doing here? Not that it isn't a delightful surprise."

Merde. I have been so busy matching wits with Madame Hivern that I have not given any thought to an explanation for my presence here at court.

"She was kind enough to accept my invitation, Gavriel," Madame Hivern says with a sly glance in my direction. "I thought it would be fun to become acquainted."

Duval's hand on my shoulder tightens painfully, then he removes it and gives a perfunctory bow. I do not know how he makes it look ironic, but he does. "My lady mother's generosity knows no bounds." Then he turns his gaze upon me. "Come, demoiselle. I am finished here." He reaches down, grabs my elbow, and pulls me to my feet. Without another look in his family's direction, we depart.

Behind the crackle and snap of anger that burns in his eyes, I catch a glimpse of something else. Something that looks remarkably like fear.

"Was that part of your convent's instructions?" Duval's voice is tight with anger. "To catch the eye of my brother and offer yourself to him as well as me?"

"No, my lord, it was not," I say primly.

But likely only because it hadn't occurred to the abbess.

Chapter 22

Duval escorts me back to his residence himself. He says it is so I do not get lost along the way, but he does not fool me. He wants to be certain I do not circle back to the palace. When he leaves to return to court, I consider following him a second time but then realize it would be foolish, as he will likely be expecting it. Besides, I do not wish to risk running into Madame Hivern again. The thinly veiled venom of her false concern still bubbles through me, as vicious as any poison. I wonder how Duval would feel if I killed his mother, for in truth, that is what I wish to do. He might well thank me.

When I reach my chamber, I find Louyse unpacking my trunks. She turns to me, her old cheeks pink. "Oh, miss! So many lovely things you have."

Indeed, rows and rows of the most beautiful gowns are spread about the room. I am stunned at the riches the convent has provided. Velvets and brocades and the finest silks, all in dazzling colors: deep blue, emerald green, and rich claret.

There is a sound in the doorway and I look up to find Agnez coming into the room holding a large twig cage at arm's length. In it sits a large, rather fiendish-looking crow.

"They sent this along with the trunks, demoiselle," Louyse explains. "We tried to put it in the stables, but it unsettled all the horses, so the ostler insisted we bring it inside. Is it a . . . pet, my lady?"

"Of a sort. Put the cage over by the window," I tell Agnez. As she sets it on the floor, the crow squawks and lunges for her finger. She squeaks and springs back, nearly tripping in her haste to be away from the bird.

"That'll be all," Louyse says to her sharply, although it isn't really the girl's fault.

With one last suspicious glance at the crow, Agnez quickly takes her leave. Louyse shakes her head. "Will you want help dressing?" At my blank look, she adds, "Before you go to court tonight?"

"Perhaps in an hour or so, thank you."

She pauses at the door. "Oh, I nearly forgot. Two letters came with the trunks. They're on the table over there. And the smallest of the trunks is still locked. They do not appear to have sent a key. Would you like me to send up one of the footmen to break it?"

"Let me see what the letters say before I decide."

"Very well, milady." She dips a curtsy, then departs, leaving me alone with a very ill-tempered crow who is trying to shred his cage with his wicked-looking beak.

I hurry to the table and pick up the first letter. Even though I recognize the reverend mother's handwriting, I turn the note over and examine the seal. Annith has a wealth of tricks for opening correspondence, and she has taught me the signs to search for if I suspect tampering, but I see none of them on this seal. It is the same black wax the convent always uses, smelling faintly of licorice and cinnamon, and it is all in one piece, with no smaller, thinner layers to indicate it has been resealed. Satisfied, I tear open the seal, hoping for a new assignment. There are so very many here at court whose throats I would happily slit.

Dearest Daughter,

I hope this finds you well and adjusting to life at court, and I trust your training at the convent is serving you well.

Sister Vereda casts her bones into the flames daily, searching for guidance, but has Seen nothing yet. When she does, I shall send a message. However, if your heart and eyes are open to Him, He will no doubt guide your hand.

Remember that you are also our eyes and ears at court.

Report to me all that you learn, no matter how small a thing it may seem.

In addition to gowns and finery, we have sent a small trunk of the tools and supplies your service to Mortain will require. Vanth bears the key.

Yours in Mortain,
Abbess Etienne de Froissard

My hand crushes the note and in my frustration I cast it into the fire. These are not the instructions I was hoping for. Waiting, waiting. Always more waiting. Had they taught us to wait as well as they taught us to kill, I might be better at it. Sighing, I pick up the second letter. It is from Annith.

Dearest Sister,

I would be lying if I didn't allow how jealous I was at all your new finery. The entire abbey stitched and sewed, altering the gowns to Sister Beatriz's exacting measurements so they would fit you and do the convent proud. Although how they will reflect on the convent when your association with us is secret, I know not, and Sister Beatriz only told me to stitch faster when I pointed that out.

I am near to bursting with curiosity to hear how court is, how many you've killed since you left, and all the other details. I think Reverend Mother suspects I am sore put out that you have been given this task and not me. She has assigned me to work closely with Sister Arnette so that I will not feel left out, but of course, it does no good.

Write me when you can so I can see with my own eyes how you fare, else I shall surely die of boredom. Still no word from Sybella.

Your sister in Mortain,
Annith

When I finish the letter I ache with homesickness, not for the convent but for Annith and her sharp, clever mind.

I would dearly love to put all that I have learned before her and see what she makes of it. I briefly consider writing it all down, then realize Vanth could not possibly carry all the pages it would require.

Instead, I hurry to the cage and see that the crow has a small packet affixed to his left leg. Eyeing him warily, I reach into the cage, crooning in a soothing voice – only to wrench my hand back as he snaps at it with his sharp beak.

"Stop that," I scold. "'Tis my key, not yours." I try again, this time moving more quickly, and pluck the packet from his ankle. His vicious beak just misses my fingers and jabs futilely against the cage. "Traitor," I chide.

I unwrap the packet, and a small gold key on a chain falls into the palm of my hand. Grasping it, I hurry over to the trunklet and fit the key into the lock. I lift the lid and bite back a laugh of pure pleasure. The trunk contains daggers of all sizes: a large anlace to wear against my back, a small easily hidden dirk, a long thin stiletto to slip into the top of my stocking, a needle-like stylet for the base of the skull, and a tangle of leather sheaths so that I may keep them all close at hand. There is a plain garrote as well as one hidden in a fancy bracelet. Sister Arnette has also included a small crossbow, no bigger than the palm of my hand. The quarrels are honed to a fine point.

The sharp metallic tang of my weapons is more welcome than the finest perfume.

But the trunk is deep and holds a second compartment. When I remove the top tray, there is the faint tinkle of glass vials. I pick up a small bottle, its contents the color of the cold winter sky. Mortain's caress, a most pleasant, merciful poison that fills its victims with a sense of euphoria and well-being. I set that bottle on the floor and reach back into the trunklet. There is the deep amber of heretic's lament, a quick-acting poison for those wishing to avoid the excruciating pain of being burned at the stake. A short, squat bottle of thick glass holds the rust-colored scourge, a poison designed with Mortain's harshest judgment in mind: it eats away at the victim's insides and is rumored to be as painful as martyr's embrace. I recognize the blood red of dark tears, which causes the lungs of the victim to fill with fluid until he drowns, and the muddy green of St. Brigantia's bane, so named because Brigantia is the goddess of wisdom and this poison does not kill its victims but instead eats all the knowledge from their brains, leaving them babbling simpletons with no memory of who they are.

In the very bottom of the trunk sit three carefully wrapped cream-colored candles, no doubt scented with night whisper. Beside those is a small box filled with white pearls, each one containing enough vengeance to fell a grown man. Last, there is a small earthenware jar of honey-colored paste nestled in the corner: St. Arduinna's snare, a poison that is used for rubbing on surfaces so it can be absorbed through the skin.

I am now as well stocked as the convent itself. Much relieved, I quickly repack the trunklet and lock it. I slip the thin gold chain around my neck and tuck the key into my bodice, out of sight.

If I hurry, I will be able to write the abbess a letter and dispatch Vanth before I must dress for the evening.

Dear Reverend Mother,

It is exactly as you and Chancellor Crunard said: there is much afoot here at court, and very little of it good. Someone has gone over the duchess's head and called a meeting of the Estates. The duchess has no choice but to face her barons under the watchful eye of the French ambassador. Anything they decide will be immediately reported back to the French regent.

Furthermore, the English king is refusing to send aid. The only bright spot is that Duval has been approached by a lord who keeps his identity hidden but claims to have a solution to offer our duchess. I will report more on this once the meeting has taken place.

One other incident of note. Duval and I were attacked upon our entry into the city. The men's blades were coated in poison, so it was no mere robbery. (And I am saddened to report that Nocturne fell victim to their treachery.)

I pause for a moment and run the feathers of the quill along my chin as I consider whether to tell the abbess of Duval's nightly visits so she will see that I am not shirking my duties. I fear if I do she will write back wanting more detail, so I say nothing.

I have met our duchess and can clearly see the hands of the saints upon her. Truly, they have chosen well, for she is wise and strong beyond her years. Honesty compels me to tell you that she appears to trust Duval completely and values his counsel above all others'.

I eagerly await your next orders and pray that Sister Vereda will See some way I may be of service to my god and my duchess.

Sincerely,
Ismae

The next letter is much easier to write. I know Annith will find a way to read the letter to the abbess, so I do not waste time repeating what I have already written there.

Dear Annith,

I wish someone had thought to tell me Duval was one of the duke's bastards! You might mention to Sister Eonette to include the bastards' names when she speaks of them. It would prevent future misunderstandings.

I saw Sybella! There was a mob of people trying to enter the city when we arrived, and she was among them. She did not speak to me, but I was much relieved to see her alive and well. Alas, I have seen no marques. Soon, hopefully!

Your sister in Mortain, Ismae

The duchess is in attendance at court tonight, so Duval takes me to be formally introduced. She is surrounded by her ladies-in-waiting, the local prelates, and her advisors. I am surprised to see that d'Albret is with the duchess. No – not *with* her, but staying close, much like a wolf stalking a rabbit. She sits, rigid and tense, looking pointedly away from him, her face pale. She looks like a young child trying to pretend a monster from a hearth tale has not just sprung to life beside her. It is Madame Dinan who chats gaily with d'Albret, ignoring her young charge's acute discomfort.

Duval's hand tightens on my arm and he quickens our pace, propelling me to the duchess and her entourage. I am heartened to see Chancellor Crunard has arrived, as we need every ally we can find. Even better, he stands behind the duchess, one hand on her shoulder, as if steadying her. My heart warms toward him.

To the duchess's credit, when Duval introduces us, she greets me as if we have never met, shows not so much as a flicker of recognition. She is well made for these games of deception. "My lord Duval tells me you are fond of hunting," the duchess says politely. "Will you indulge in the sport while you are here?" As she speaks, she glances over at d'Albret, then lets her hand drift to her neck and gracefully runs one finger along the base of her throat, as if adjusting the heavy jeweled cross that hangs there.

I nearly laugh out loud and am very careful not to look at d'Albret. "If the opportunity arises, Your Grace, I would happily partake in the hunt."

"Let us hope, then, that the opportunity presents itself," she says graciously.

As we murmur pleasantries, a man-at-arms approaches and bows before Captain Dunois, then speaks quietly in his ear. The captain nods, then moves to Duval and takes him aside. "Your prisoner is awake, my lord."

Duval turns to me with an eager gleam in his eye. "I must go and question him."

"Surely I should come with you."

"Surely you should not. How would I explain allowing either my young cousin or my mistress to be in the presence of such a criminal?" As he speaks, he searches among the gathered nobles. "No, you will stay here and play your part and keep your ears open." He releases my arm and to my utter horror calls out, "De Lornay!"

"No!" I whisper to Duval, but too late. The young lord disentangles himself from a group of admiring women and heads our way.

Duval glances down at me in surprise. "You cannot just stroll about unattended. People may turn a blind eye to a discreet liaison, but a lone woman wandering on her own is no lady and will quickly find herself with a reputation that keeps her from the duchess's presence."

His words feel like the bars of a cage clanging down around me, and I suddenly feel trapped in a prison of silk and velvet. He looks faintly amused. "Do not act as if you've been consigned to the executioner's block. Most women are quite fond of de Lornay's company."

"I am not most women, my lord," I say, and I assume his snort is one of agreement.

De Lornay bows in front of us, and I am gratified when his eyes move past me, then sharpen.

Duval gives his friend a wry grin. "She cleans up nicely, does she not? I have something I must see to and I would leave her in your tender care."

De Lornay's dismayed look mirrors my own. "What, pray tell, am I to do with her?"

Duval waves his hand in the air. "I don't know. Whatever it is you do with your lady friends."

"Not *that*, surely," de Lornay murmurs.

"Dance then." Duval casts a worried look at me. "You do know how to dance, do you not?" he asks.

"Yes, but—"

"Good." Before de Lornay or I can issue another protest, Duval abandons us and walks away.

De Lornay and I stare at each other with twin expressions of distress before we both quickly look elsewhere. Even as I plot an escape, the music starts up and the dancers move to the floor. With an ungracious sigh, de Lornay gives me a perfunctory bow. "Let us dance then."

I dip a shallow curtsy but do not take his offered hand. "I appreciate this noble sacrifice you are making, but rest assured, it is not necessary. I have as little desire to dance with you as you do with me."

He reaches out and snags my hand. "Nevertheless, Duval said dance, so dance we shall."

I try to pull my hand away, but his grip turns to iron. I set my teeth and tug harder. "Do you always do what he tells you?"

"Always," de Lornay says as he begins dragging me toward the dance floor. "I would ride into the fires of hell itself upon his command."

Forgetting our tug of war, I glance at his face to see if he is serious. "Does he demand such things of you?"

De Lornay looks at me then with a fierce expression on his face. "If he did, I would do it gladly and welcome the chance."

The music begins in earnest, and the other bodies around us fall into the steps of the dance. Even though my mind still mulls over de Lornay's fearsome loyalty, I move easily into the opening reverence. As I go through the steps of the dance, I cannot help but wonder why de Lornay dislikes me so very much. Indeed, I have never found dancing so painful. He glares at me over the other dancers' heads and I am surprised our mutual loathing does not set their hair on fire.

When the music finally ends, I nearly shout with joy. De Lornay takes my arm and escorts me from the dance floor. "You dance very prettily." *For a lowborn assassin.*

The actual words do not cross his lips, but I hear them all the same. I pay them little mind, for we have danced as Duval has commanded and surely now he will leave me to my own devices.

I curtsy with as much gratitude as I can muster. "Thank you for the courtesy you have shown me." I keep my head down so he does not see the resentment in my eyes, and I begin to move away.

Once again, his hand clamps down on mine. "Oh, we are not done, demoiselle."

I jerk my head up and snatch my hand away. "We most certainly are."

He shakes his head. "Listen. The musicians are readying their instruments for another dance – a basse dance, I think. I am quite fond of the basse dance. Are you?"

I stare at him. Does he intend to blindly follow Duval's orders until he returns? "No," I say flatly. "I am not." Then, before he can reach out and grab my hand again, I turn and leap away from him, putting as much distance between us as I can and hoping that he will not lunge after me and cause a scene.

I quickly worm deeper into the crowd and lose myself among the gathered nobles. As I move through the richly dressed and heavily perfumed bodies, I try to decide how best to make use of my hard-won freedom. I wish a marque of Mortain would appear on any one of these silly, vain nobles, but alas, it does not.

I spy François flirting with a venomous-looking lady dressed in peacock blue. His mother is in the far corner, laughing gaily and flirting with the half-dozen barons who surround her. Is that why Duval is so angry with her? Because she is not wasting any time finding a new paramour? If he was close with his father, then mayhap he considers it a betrayal of his memory that his mother is seeking a new bed to warm so soon after his death.

Madame Dinan, Count d'Albret, and Marshal Rieux have left the duchess and now stand together, buzzing among themselves like busy little bees. That could prove a most interesting conversation.

I shift directions and move toward them, determined to hear what they are plotting. I am nearly halfway there when a tall figure steps boldly in front of me and I must stop suddenly or plow right into him.

The French envoy, Gisors, looks down at me from his towering height. "Demoiselle Rienne," he says.

"Milord Gisors." I give a small curtsy.

"It occurs to me that I did not greet you as warmly as you deserved yesterday. You must forgive me, as I had weighty matters on my mind."

"But of course, my lord ambassador. I understand completely." Indeed, I am a marvel of restraint and cunning.

"You are young and innocent of the ways of court, even such a small court as this one. I would be honored if you would allow me to act as your guide in some matters."

"That is very kind of you, my lord, but that is what Lord Duval has promised to do."

Gisors's green eyes seek out Duval. "And yet he is not at your side. And you may not realize it, but a small flock of young cockerels are lining up behind you even as we speak. I would help you learn who it is wise to associate with when your Duval is otherwise occupied."

I open my mouth to demur, but he steps closer – far too close – and places his hand across my mouth. The boldness of the gesture shocks me into silence. "Do not say no, demoiselle. I only ask that you think about it. I can make it worth your while. Living at court is very expensive, and no woman should be without her own resources. Especially since you cannot be sure just how long Duval's protection will last."

I push his hand away. "What do you mean?"

"I mean, once it becomes widely known that Duval's mother is plotting to put her son on Anne's throne, you will find yourself a pariah at court. I wager you will not be too proud to accept my friendship then." And then he moves away, back to whatever rock he has crawled out from, and I am left breathing hard, shock simmering in my veins.

Duval and his family are plotting treason.

Chapter 23

I cannot sleep. My mind worries and gnaws at this newest revelation about Duval like a rat on a bone. A week ago, I would have been thrilled with the discovery, eager for the proof needed that would compel my god to act against him. But tonight – tonight it does not feel like a victory at all. I tell myself it is because the duchess trusts him so much and has so few allies left, but that is a lie. I fear my lack of pleasure has more to do with Duval himself, and it pains me that my heart has been so easily swayed.

It is also possible – likely, even – that he is not involved in his mother's schemes. Indeed, it would go a long way to explaining the rift between them. So too would acting as if they were estranged prevent suspicion from falling on him.

There is a faint click at the door and everything inside me stills. I have no idea if I will confront Duval with what I have learned. I am torn between wanting to leap out of bed and rail at him for his duplicity and wishing to hide in shame because I was so easily misled. Instead, I pull the covers up under my chin and close my eyes, hoping he will think me asleep. I will my heart to slow its beating and my breathing to become deeper. My elaborate efforts are foiled by a muffled curse exploding out of the darkness. "God's teeth! What is this you have used to barricade the path to the window?"

His good-humored discomfiture befuddles me. "What?" Disoriented, I sit up and push the hair out of my eyes. "'Tis Vanth's cage. You can just move it out of the way."

"I already have," he grumbles. "With my shin." He flops into his customary chair and glares at me. "Who, by the grace of God, is Vanth, and why must he be kept in a cage?"

The darkness in the room is not absolute. I hug my knees while trying to read his face, but it is too hidden in shadow. "He is the crow sent by the abbess so that she and I can communicate."

"Ah, did she have any news for you? Any assignments that I should know about?" Is that a note of concern I detect in his voice?

"Why, my lord? Are you afraid she has learned of your mother's plot to put her son on the throne?"

His head snaps up and I can feel the intensity of his gaze. His silence is proof enough of their guilt.

"When were you planning on telling me? Or did you truly believe I would not find out?"

"No, I knew that you would eventually, and when you did, I hoped that you would ask me about it."

"Then I am asking you."

He leans his head back against the chair, and when he next speaks, his voice sounds impossibly weary. "My mother got it into her head that what our country needs is a duke, not a duchess. She does not believe that Anne will be able to weather the current crises with both France and the barons. Instead of risking the duchy going to one of them, Madame believes it should go to one of the duke's sons, bastard or no."

There have been bastard dukes before, but not in a long while. "Why François and not you?"

"Can you not guess?"

"I can, but I want to hear it from you."

"Because I refused." His words are clipped.

"Which is why you and she are estranged."

"Exactly so." He sighs and runs his hand through his hair.

"Then why did you not tell me?"

"And seal their death warrant? Perhaps I am not as cold-blooded in my pursuit of justice as you and the convent. Until I understood your full orders and how you would act, I did not dare tell you." There is a moment of silence, then he speaks again, "So, are they marqued for death by your god?"

"No," I say. "Not that I can see."

He lets out a long slow breath. "Then how did you learn of their plans?"

"The French envoy, Gisors. He not only tried to purchase my loyalty tonight but also warned me that once your family's plans were known, I would be a pariah at court."

Duval swears. "If nothing else, this should prove to you how badly I want Anne crowned duchess. Aside from the love I bear her, it is also the only way I can be certain my mother and François will put aside their ill-conceived schemes."

"But I have only your word that that is so."

There is an impatient whisper of velvet as he leans forward. "We must call a truce, you and I. If we are constantly at each other's throats, it will serve only our enemies, not our duchess. I would ask that you set aside your abbess's suspicions and listen to your own heart, for even though you pretend you don't have one, I know that you do. I ask not for my sake, but for my sister's.

"D'Albret presses her to honor her father's promises to him; the Holy Roman emperor wants her hand but does not have the troops to secure her realm once she agrees to that betrothal. The French are breathing down our necks, and there are very few options open to her that do not either plunge her country into war or consign her to a marriage too horrible to consider. If we do not work together, we further reduce those options."

Of course he is right, but, even so, it is a dangerous bargain we strike. I cannot help but think the abbess would never approve. I do not know how dearly she holds her belief in Duval's guilt or whether she and Crunard will thank me if I prove them wrong. But I have searched high and low for any signs of treachery to give weight to their suspicions, and the only evidence I found has just been neatly explained. It also has the convincing ring of truth to it, especially as I have witnessed the open animosity between him and his mother.

It is a narrow line Duval asks me to walk, seeing to both the duchess's needs and my convent's. For although their goals are the same, I fear their methods are very different. If I am wrong, I risk losing the convent's trust, which is surely the thing I value most in this world. Even so, there is no other choice. Not with the duchess in such dire straits, for if she fails to maintain her country's independence, the convent will surely suffer. "Very well, milord."

He smiles then, and even though it is well past midnight, it is as if the sun has just come out. "Excellent," he says. "This is what I need you to do."

Early the next morning Duval and I ride out into the country. Louyse asks him to repeat himself twice when he requests a hamper to take with us. Clearly, this is out of character for him, and she slides her wise old eyes to me, a look of pleased speculation in them.

De Lornay and Beast are waiting for us outside, their horses fresh and pawing at the morning. Duval is lending me a dappled gray mare of his for the day, and I slip her a bit of apple I snuck from the table.

Our horses' hooves ring out on the cold cobbles as we ride toward the north gate. The town is even more crowded than it was the day we arrived; every Breton noble – and many French ones – are tucked up inside its walls, waiting to see what drama will play out at the Estates meeting. The tension in the city is thick enough to slice with a knife and feed to the peasants.

As we ride through the streets, de Lornay tosses his head back and laughs, as if Duval has said something clever. Duval himself grins, and Beast turns his ugly face to me and smiles. I smile back. We are, for all the world, a happy little party out to enjoy the fine autumn day.

But of course, we are not.

Duval is well aware we may be riding into a trap, but the duchess's situation is desperate enough that we will take our chances. De Lornay and Beast are the muscle of the operation. I have been brought along as a decoy, for surely the serious, stalwart Duval would not leave town at a time such as this unless he was utterly besotted with his new mistress.

Once clear of the city, we head north through the woods that surround Guérande, and our gaiety falls from us somewhat. It is a crisp, chill morning and I am grateful for the fur-lined cloak Sister Beatriz has sent. My thoughts hop and flutter, just like the nearby birds searching out the last of the season's offerings before winter arrives. I tell myself that if the abbess learns of this outing, I will simply explain I am being her eyes and ears, just as I was instructed. She has no need to know I have agreed to work with Duval. Indeed, I do not know myself if I truly meant it or just agreed in order to placate him and be included in his plans. Either way, until it requires that I do something in direct conflict with the convent's orders, it seems harmless enough.

We ride for nearly an hour before Duval sends de Lornay to double back and check if we are being followed.

"Who do you think would follow us?" I ask.

Duval shrugs. "Anyone who saw us leave. The French envoy would dearly love to know what we're about, as would my mother. D'Albret. Anyone on the Privy Council who is jealous of the trust Anne places in me."

"So very many," I murmur.

He cocks an eyebrow but says nothing as the sound of galloping hooves reach us. De Lornay rides into view, nods his head, and holds up five fingers, then one. Six pursuers. Duval mutters an oath. "How far back?"

"Not far at all," de Lornay says.

"Could you tell who they are?"

De Lornay shakes his head. "They are men-at-arms, wearing no identifying tabards or colors."

Duval nods grimly, then waves us off the road and into the surrounding forest. His eyes search the area until he spies a small glade with a log and dappled sunlight. He steers his horse toward that, and the rest of us follow.

By the time I reach the glade, he has dismounted and is waiting to assist me. He lifts me from my saddle, then grabs the bag slung across his horse's neck. He points Beast and de Lornay to a flat boulder that sits closer to the road, then takes my hand and leads me to the log.

He lowers himself onto the grass and then leans back against the log and tries to pull me down beside him. "My lord!" I squeak as I nearly tumble into his lap.

He looks at me. "Would you rather I put my head in your lap?"

"Can we not just sit side by side?"

His eyes glitter as brightly as highly polished steel. "We are besotted lovers, remember? I, who never leave the duchess's side except on *her* business, am out lolling around with my mistress. Or so we must make them believe."

I glance away, ashamed. It is the plan we concocted last night, but it is harder than I expected to play this masquerade. I clear my throat. "If I must choose, I would rather sit and have your head in my lap." I will feel less helpless that way.

He rolls his eyes but quickly switches positions. I have hardly settled my rump to the ground before he is stretching his long body out beside me, and then his head is in my lap.

It is heavy and solid and warm, and for a moment, it consumes all of my attention. Embarrassed, I glance over at de Lornay and Beast, but they are busy doing their part, sprawling and dicing, looking for all the world like bored attendants waiting on their lingering lord.

When Duval's hand closes around mine, I jump like a startled rabbit, and his eyes crinkle in amusement. "How long must we stay this way?" I whisper.

"Until they are satisfied that we are naught but the besotted lovers we claim to be."

It is my turn to roll my eyes.

"Do not scowl so." His voice is amused, tender. "Pretend I am de Lornay, if it is easier."

I snort in disgust.

"My brother, then, if you fancy him. I do not care, but God's teeth! Paste a smitten look on your face or our ruse will not work."

I soften my eyes and force my mouth into a smile. "I do not care for your brother, either," I murmur, as if it is a declaration of love.

Something in Duval's face shifts. "Good," he whispers, and I must remind myself he is but playing the game. It should not surprise me that he is so very, very skilled at it.

Then our pursuers are upon us. Beast and de Lornay spring up and draw together, as if trying to protect us from prying eyes. It is no great struggle for me to look discomfited by the intrusion, especially when the mounted soldiers do their best to peer around the two men. Lewd curiosity has replaced their suspicion, and after slowing down to gawk, they quickly ride on.

As they canter away, some of the tension leaves my body and I allow myself to sag against the log at my back. When I open my eyes, I find Duval staring up at me. "We really must work on your skills of seduction," he says.

Without thinking, I reach down and hit him on the arm. He laughs, and reluctantly, I smile. I *am* bad at this, but only with him. I was able to play the flirt with Martel and even François. It is only with Duval that my skills leave me.

Duval reaches up and brushes away a strand of hair that has fallen across my cheek. I expect to see amusement or jest in his eyes, as if he is trying to teach me how to play this game. But there is no hint of amusement there – only his gray eyes, which are deep and serious.

I hear a quail call just then, the signal Beast was to give once the soldiers had ridden out of sight. As if some master is pulling on my strings, I leap to my feet, nearly sending Duval's head thudding to the ground. He looks at me as if I have lost my wits. Perhaps I have.

I brush the grass and twigs off my skirts as Duval rises. De Lornay and Beast join us. "Did you recognize them?" Duval asks.

Beast shakes his head. "But now that they have passed, will you tell us where we are meeting this mysterious fellow of yours?"

Duval glances down the road, as if assuring himself they are well beyond hearing. "At the church in St. Lyphard."

At his words, all the blood drains from my face. Not wanting the others to see, I turn and lead my horse to a stump so I may mount. But Duval – damn his eyes – misses nothing. When I am settled on my horse, he nudges his own mount closer to me. "Are you all right?" he asks.

"I am fine, my lord."

"Then why is your face the color of chalk?"

I manage a crooked smile. "It is just that I was born in St. Lyphard and have not been there in years. It was not a happy place for me."

"You mean you did not spring wholly formed from drops of sweat off Mortain's brow?"

I smile. "Not wholly formed, no."

No longer teasing, he looks at me in concern. "Will you be recognized, do you think?"

"No, it was many years ago, and I have changed much. Besides, they would never think to look for the turnip farmer's daughter in such finery or among such exalted company. People see what they want to see." Perhaps if I repeat it enough, it will be true.

His eyes hold mine a moment longer. They are filled with understanding and I want to slap such kindness from his face. Does he not realize it erodes my defenses just as surely as salt erodes his armor? I look away abruptly. "If you do not wish to be seen, I know a shortcut to the church," I say, eager to be out from under his shrewd gaze. When at last he nods, I put my heels to my mare's flanks and fly.

Chapter 24

As we draw near the church, I catch a glint of sunlight on steel behind a wall of shrubbery. I slow my horse so that I fall back alongside Duval. Dipping my chin, I look up at him as if flirting. "There are armed men in the trees," I tell him in a low voice.

A quail calls just then, and Duval flashes a quick grin. "They are mine," he says. "I had them ride out at first light to watch the place in case any trap was laid."

I say nothing, but I admit to myself that I am impressed.

The church in St. Lyphard is an old one, made of solid Breton stone and thick wooden timbers. Small alcoves are set into the walls, each housing one of the old saints. My eyes are drawn immediately to the carving of Mortain. This statue is old, older than any I have seen, and shows Mortain at His most skeletal, clutching an arrow with which to warn us all that life is fleeting and He could strike at any moment.

While Beast and de Lornay take up positions on opposite ends of the churchyard, Duval dismounts, then comes to assist me from my horse.

"Why this place?" I ask in an attempt to distract myself from the sensation of his hands at my waist.

He sets me on my feet. "Because the priest here still makes prayers and offerings to the old saints and I can be certain he is loyal to his country. Besides, men are less likely to plot treachery in a church."

The arch over the front door is covered with more carvings, this time of cockleshells and sacred anchors of St. Mer. Some pious soul has hung a sheaf of wheat for Dea Matrona. Duval pulls open the door, puts his hand on my back, and nudges me through.

The inside of the church is dark and damp and filled with the rich, smoky scent of incense. The shimmering, golden halos cast by the burning candles do nothing to lift the chill of the place. I can feel the weight of all the souls that have passed through here, feel the pull of the thousands upon thousands of prayers that have been said inside these walls. The pulpit is carved with scenes of the early lives of the saints, the copper gone green with age and dampness. Behind that, above the altar, is an exquisite, if newer, sculpture of the Resurrection.

I make my way to the niche of St. Amourna and take the small loaf of freshly baked bread from my pocket. It is the traditional offering all young maids make when asking for true love, the disguise Duval and I have devised for our trip to the church. In order for the offering to work, it must be fashioned by the maid's own hands. This one is not, but even so, the old saints are thick in this place and I do not like putting a false offering before a saint for a blessing I do not wish. To ease my conscience, I pray instead that the duchess will find happiness in whatever match she is forced to make.

When I am done, Duval motions me to a back doorway, one only the priest uses. I am to stand here and be certain no one approaches him from behind.

We wait in silence for what seems an eternity before I hear the scrape of a boot heel upon the stone step. Harsh light slices through the darkness as the door opens.

A lone figure enters the church. His hair is blond with a reddish cast to it, and his clean-shaven jaw is strong. While he is clearly of noble blood, he is neatly dressed in a breastplate and vambraces. Not just some court dandy then, but a man with soldierly experience. The two men greet each other cautiously, then the stranger gets right to the point – yet another thing to admire about him. "Thank you for agreeing to see me."

Duval nods. "Your caution was well founded. We evaded a party of soldiers following us."

The stranger smiles. "Ah, yes. My own men intercepted them just before we split off the road for the church. They are even now leading them on a merry chase toward Redon."

Duval tilts his head, studying the man. "I know you," he says at last.

The young man smiles. "You have a good memory. I am Fedric, Duke of Nemours." He bows deeply.

Duke of Nemours! My mind scrambles back to Sister Eonette's lessons. Nemours is a small but rich holding that, like Brittany, pays only nominal homage to the French

Crown. The old Duke of Nemours had fought alongside Duke Francis in the Mad war, and died there. The young lord before us was one of the many men betrothed to the duchess.

"I come to offer to reopen negotiations for the hand of your sister," Nemours says.

"But I thought you were already married."

Nemours's face grows somber. "I was. My wife and young son died of the plague that passed through Nemours at the end of the summer."

"I am sorry to hear that," Duval says.

Nemours's grin is somewhat forced. "Which is why I come to you seeking a new bride. When word of your sister's circumstances reached me, I thought to approach you."

"What have you heard?" Duval asks warily.

Nemours barks out a humorless laugh. "That the French regent has bribed half your barons to join France's cause and that the Holy Roman emperor is too mired in his own wars to come to her aid. And the duchess's own barons are too busy fighting for her crown to fight on her behalf."

"You have heard the right of it, I'm afraid."

"So I offer a way out. I propose the same terms as the original betrothal agreement, so you will see that I am not trying to take advantage of your situation."

Duval is suddenly cautious. "Why? What is in it for you that you are so chivalrous?"

"Is chivalry not its own reward?"

"Not in my experience, no."

Nemours shrugs, then smiles. It very nearly reminds me of Beast's maniacal grin. "In addition to the great fondness I bear your lady sister, is not beating the French at their own game enough? My father died at their hand."

"How many troops can you lend to enforce the betrothal? For the French regent will move quickly once she learns of it."

"Three thousand," he says, "which I know is less than d'Albret's considerable numbers, but at least I can guarantee they will be loyal to the duchess."

"And that is worth much, I think."

"There is more," Nemours adds. "My cousin, the queen of Navarre, will send fifteen hundred pikemen to aid our cause."

Duval's brows shoot up in surprise. "Not that we would not welcome them, but why would she bestir herself on our account?"

A grim note creeps into Nemours's voice. "Do not forget that she also is married to a d'Albret. She knows only too well what marrying into that family entails."

A dark look of understanding passes between the two men. "Very well then," Duval says. "I will put your proposal before the duchess." And although he tries to hide it, the relief in his voice in plain.

It takes me a moment before I recognize the feeling burbling through me. It is not trepidation, or even apprehension, but joy. I am nearly giddy with relief that we may have found our duchess a solution to her tangle. And while it is not the task I was trained for, I savor it all the same.

I tell myself that my happiness has nothing to do with coming that much closer to removing the suspicion that clouds Duval's name.

On our return trip to Guérande, Duval does not use the shortcut I showed him but instead leads us through St. Lyphard itself. If this is a test, it is easy enough to pass. I know in my bones that no one will recognize me.

The town has not changed at all since I left nearly four years ago. We pass the blacksmith's forge and the small square where we held our meager celebrations, the weaver's home, the herbwitch's cottage and that of the tanner. In no time at all, we have reached the town's outskirts. A lone cottage sits there with smoke rising sluggishly from the chimney and a few threadbare linens hanging on the line.

In the fields beyond the house, a man works, his back bent as he struggles with the hard ground. Even though he is a turnip farmer, in the winter he sows a crop of rye. I am surprised at how old he looks, how grizzled his hair, how stooped his shoulders. It is as if only his hatred of me had kept him going. Now the monster of my childhood nightmares is nothing but a broken old man struggling to eke out a living, while I have been chosen by a god to do His bidding.

As if sensing my eyes upon him, the man looks up, surprised to see four nobles prancing through his fields. When he bows his head and tugs at his forelock, I know that my disguise is complete. Even my own father has not recognized me.

Duval brings his horse closer to mine. "Someone you know?" he murmurs.

"He is no one," I say, and for the first time I realize it is true.

Chapter 25

Before the walls of the city come into sight, we are met by an outrider looking for Duval. Captain Dunois has sent him to tell us that the footpad has not only awakened, but escaped. I glance sharply at Duval, briefly wondering if that could have been his purpose, to lure me from the city long enough for our assailant to escape. But since he is doing a fine job of looking poleaxed by the news, I dismiss that idea.

We ride to Guérande with all due haste and hurry to the dungeons beneath the palace.

"How?" Duval asks as he steps inside the small prison chamber that is now empty. It is made of four solid walls with no window and only the one door. "How did he escape?"

The captain of the palace guard shrugs uncomfortably. "He was not bound or manacled, and the key hangs on the hook outside. Anyone could have opened the door."

"But why? Is the question."

With reluctance, one of the guards steps aside so that I too may enter the chamber. The minute I am in the room, I know. Death has visited; the man did not walk out alive.

"My lord," I murmur to Duval. "I would speak with you alone."

His eyes widen in surprise. "Now?"

"Now."

Understanding dawns and he pulls me away from the others.

"He did not escape," I murmur. "He was killed first, then taken from here afterward."

His dark eyebrows shoot up. "You can tell this merely from being in the room?"

I nod.

His eyes narrow in thought. "That at least makes more sense." He turns back to the guards. "Find everyone who visited this room within the last two days, then bring a list of those names to me." He sighs heavily. "Let us go speak to the duchess. At least we have one piece of good news to trade for this latest setback."

We find the duchess in her solar, sitting with her ladies and Madame Dinan, embroidering an altar cloth for the new cathedral. A young girl lies on the couch beside her. Isabeau, her younger sister, is delicate and frail-looking and cannot be older than ten. Both of their faces light up when Duval steps into the room.

He bows and I drop a deep curtsy. "Your Grace; my lady Isabeau."

"Hello, Gavriel." Young Isabeau smiles at him. "What brings you out from behind your stuffy desk?"

"Since the sun is not shining today, I thought to catch sight of your face instead."

I have to look twice to be certain this is the same Duval I walked in with for I have never heard such pretty words fall from his lips, not even when he was with the duchess. But young Isabeau throws back her head and laughs, amused by his flattery. Before long, her laughter gives way to coughing; great, racking coughs that shake her frail body. Instantly the duchess is at her side, rubbing her back and trying to soothe her.

Madame Dinan slaps her needlework down and hurries to Isabeau. She scowls at Duval. "Your teasing is unseemly, my lord Duval. It is too much excitement for the girl."

"Nonsense, madame," Anne snaps back. "Isabeau coughs like this with or without my brother's words, and at least he brings a smile to her face." She turns to her ladies-in-waiting, who hover nervously. "Leave us, please." With rustling as faint as butterfly wings, the ladies set down their embroidery hoops and leave the room. But not Madame Dinan, who boldly stands her ground.

A look passes between Duval and the duchess, and then Anne turns to her governess. "Madame, sit with Isabeau, if you please, as I must speak with my brother."

Dinan wishes to argue, it is there in her eyes, but Duval does not give her the opportunity. "Walk with me, Your Grace." He holds his arm out and the duchess takes it. He leads her to the far window, and I stand there like a bump in the floor, unsure if I should follow or stay and distract Madame Dinan. Anne glances over her shoulder and gives a quick motion for me to follow. I lift my skirts and hurry after them, Madame Dinan's scorching gaze fair burning a hole through the back of my gown as I go.

The three of us gather in front of the oriel window. It is a large room, and Duval speaks softly enough that his voice will not carry back to Dinan. "I bring interesting news, Your Grace."

"That is good to hear, as there is a desperate shortage of that just now."

Keeping his voice low, Duval tells her of our meeting with Nemours. When he is done, she clasps her hands together, hope lighting her young face. "Are my prayers being answered in such a fashion?"

When Duval smiles at her, I realize that I have never seen him truly smile. Not like this, where it warms his entire face. "It would appear so, dear sister. But I would warn you not to speak of it to anyone. Gisors's men followed us today, but we evaded them." Duval glances over to where Madame Dinan is attending to Isabeau. "Nor do we want word to get back to d'Albret. Who knows what mischief he could make for our plan."

The duchess quickly nods her understanding. "I will say nothing to anyone, but I cannot deny it will give me something to cling to during the meeting with the barons tomorrow. I cannot tell you how much I am dreading it."

Duval's face settles back into seriousness. "I think the simplest course is to plead your grief over our father's death. It is too fresh right now for you to consider marriage to d'Albret or anyone else."

The duchess's mouth trembles ever so faintly. "It is not even a lie," she says, and I am struck by how few choices she has for all that she is a duchess.

Chapter 26

The great hall, which once seemed impossibly large, now seems impossibly small, stuffed as it is with this many bodies. Oh, they are noble enough bodies, but ripe with sweat and perfume and unbridled anticipation. I cannot tell if they are expecting disaster or farce. My sincerest hope is that my god will marque all the traitors today and my duty will be clear.

I worm my way to a spot by the far wall, and my shoulders press painfully into the carved paneling at my back. Even so, I am glad for the space and am all too happy to defend it with my elbows when others press too close.

As the main players assemble on the raised dais in the front of the room, I scan the crowd. The men have left their swords with guardsmen at the door so that none may be drawn during the meeting, but no one has been searched for knives or daggers. My hand drifts to my own hidden weapons at my wrists, and I wonder just how many other blades are nestled inside sleeves or hidden in folds of satin.

Once all of Anne's councilors have taken their place, the assembly rises and the duchess herself comes into the room. Her chin is high, her spine rigid with determination. Of their own accord, my eyes search out Duval, who sits at the far end of the dais. He is dressed in his customary black and is the very picture of somber reason. De Lornay and de Waroch stand near him at the front wall. They have kept their swords, most likely at his insistence.

D'Albret sits directly before the dais, sprawling in his chair, trimming his nails with a knife, either a subtle threat or a sign of just how uncouth he really is. I study him carefully, but no matter how much I will it, there is no visible marque upon him.

Chancellor Crunard calls the meeting to order, and the room grows quiet. Before the chancellor has finished the formal opening remarks, Count d'Albret puts away his knife and rises to his feet. There is the swish of skirts and creak of boot leather as the courtiers lean forward to hear better. The duchess eyes him shrewdly but gives him her full consideration, much as one gives a venomous serpent.

"My lords." He runs his gaze along the dais, then turns to the crowded room. "I am here to collect what was promised to me by your late Duke Francis. Namely, marriage to his daughter – my rightful payment for lending aid against the French last fall."

"A war we lost," Chancellor Crunard is quick to point out, and I cannot help but think of his two sons who died in that war.

A rumble reverberates around the room, but whether it is one of outrage or approval, I cannot tell.

The duchess's clear young voice carries over the crowd and they grow quiet once more. "My lord d'Albret. While your offer is worthy of our consideration, I am afraid I am too consumed by my family's recent loss to turn my thoughts to marriage, and I beg your understanding a little while longer in this matter."

"You do not have the luxury of time, my lady. Your very country is at stake."

"You do not need to remind *me* of that, sir," the duchess snaps.

"But perhaps I need to remind you of your duty. Dukes and duchesses do not have the luxury of long mourning periods. The needs of their kingdoms come first, even before their grief."

Of course, he is right, and the duchess knows it as well. "I have always put my country first." There is true anger in the duchess's voice now.

D'Albret's tone softens in an attempt to coax. "With this marriage I offer, you will be able to turn your attention to more womanly concerns and let me shoulder your burdens. Then you may mourn all you want." He glances briefly at the dais, but I cannot see who he is looking at. Madame Dinan? Marshal Rieux?

There is a long quiet moment during which it looks as if the duchess is considering the idea. "I see you have thought of all my needs, Lord d'Albret. Even so, I must beg more time."

The count's face grows red as he tries to keep his anger in check. He turns to address the barons directly. "This is a dangerous time for our kingdom. War beckons, and enemies circle. It is no time for young girls or old men to whisper behind closed doors and plot and plan. It is time for action. Time to face our enemies on the field of battle."

But at what cost to the duchess? I wonder, as I watch all the color drain from her young face. Duval's mention of the man's six former wives rustles through my head, as does Nemours's disturbing whispers of his cousin's marriage to a d'Albret.

There is a disturbance in the middle of the room as the French emissary Gisors steps forward. The crowd opens up around him, much as it would if a wolf were emerging from its lair. "It seems to me," he says into all that silence, "that this would be a good time to remind you of the Treaty of Verger, which clearly states that Anne may not marry without France's approval. I'm afraid her marriage to Count d'Albret is out of the question. She is a ward of the French Crown and thus everything must be negotiated through us."

And praise the saints for that small mercy, I think.

"How did *he* get in?" Duval asks no one in particular. To Beast and de Lornay, he says, "Get him out of here." With grim, satisfied smiles they begin making their way through the throng of nobles. Before they can reach Gisors, however, he turns and heads to the back door. Before him, the crowd moves aside quickly, eager to get out of his path before de Lornay or Beast catch up to him.

It is as elegant and unhurried a retreat as one can imagine, but it is a retreat nonetheless.

"And see that he is confined to his chambers!" Duval calls out after them. By the way the councilors on the dais snap their heads round to stare at Duval, I am guessing this is a great overstep of his duties or a disregard of protocol.

D'Albret moves smoothly into the breach created by Gisors's departure. Ignoring Anne, he speaks once more to the nobles. "If you wish to keep your independence, you must support my marriage with the duchess. I will keep you safe from the French." He smiles, but there is no warmth or humor it in. "Me and my five thousand troops."

He turns to face the duchess and council, his voice growing hard. "But if you do not support this marriage, I will have no choice but to hold the house of Montfort in breach of contract and will use all of my considerable resources to get by force what I could not gain by reason."

The room explodes in an uproar. I lean forward slightly, hoping that the count will now bear a marque. But there is nothing. I turn my attention to the dais, hoping that a marque will at least appear on whoever called this meeting and set this trap for the duchess, but again, nothing.

Chancellor Crunard rises to his feet, his cheeks flushed with anger. "You are but one of many who was promised the duchess's hand in marriage; there is no way we can honor all such agreements. Indeed, if we were to take them in the order they were made, yours would be the fifth in line."

D'Albret's face is expressionless, but his eyes burn with an intensity that is most disturbing. "But do all those others have an army of five thousand just outside your borders?"

The blood drains from Chancellor Crunard's face. Satisfied at the effect his words have had, d'Albret turns on his heel and quits the chamber.

The newly adjourned courtiers erupt in excited, nervous voices. Crunard motions for the guards and they throw open the large doors at the back of the chamber so the nobles may begin filing out of the room. I do not have a clear plan, but unable to help myself, I move to follow d'Albret. I am like a small boat moving against the tide of the crowd, but I ignore the bumps and stares that come my way, my attention never leaving my target.

A practical knight-at-arms opens the small door to the side of the chamber in order to allow some people out that way. D'Albret moves in that direction, and so I too begin making for that door, silently cursing the laggards and dullards who stand between me and d'Albret. I cannot accept that Mortain has not seen fit to marque d'Albret for his threat – for after all, he is half Breton and owes some allegiance to the rightful duchess.

When d'Albret steps out into the hall beyond, he is surrounded by nearly a score of his own men-at-arms. *Merde.* I cannot take on that many armed men.

"Demoiselle Rienne!" There is a tug on my skirt and I glance down to find a young page. "What is it?" I ask.

"Chancellor Crunard requests you attend him immediately."

I cast one last frustrated glance at d'Albret's retreating back, then give my full attention to the boy. "Did he say what it was about?"

"No, milady, but please come."

Hoping that the chancellor has received news from the convent, I let the boy lead me to his chamber. The page knocks once on the door, then opens it. If Chancellor Crunard is ruffled by the disastrous estates meeting, he hides it well. "Come in, demoiselle," he says as the page scampers away.

His desk is nearly as large as a bed and has a neat stack of correspondence on one side and three maps on the other; there is also a small pot of ink and a handful of quills. He does not offer me a seat. Instead, he rises and moves to the window. After a long moment of silence, he turns to face me, his expression impassive. "Where were you hurrying off to?"

I meet his gaze steadily. Only my promise to Duval of utmost secrecy prevents me from telling him of the duchess's newest suitor and the hope he offers her. "To see if I could convince Mortain to give me permission to remove Count d'Albret."

He blinks in surprise. Whatever he expected me to say, it was not this. His face relaxes and I detect a glint of humor in his eyes. "By all means, search d'Albret for one of those marques. Then we can be done with him and move on to equally pressing problems."

While I am surprised to learn that Crunard knows of the marques – he is even more in the abbess's confidence than I realized – I am pleased that we are in agreement on this. He turns back to the window. "Have you learned anything further of Duval and his true motives?" he asks.

"No, my lord. I have found nothing to warrant your or the abbess's suspicions." I am aware that I must tread carefully here. "He seems most devoted to the duchess, and she seems to trust him above all others."

"And does that not seem highly suspect to you?" he asks. "That she would trust her bastard brother above all her others? It speaks to me of undue influence."

"Or perhaps he just puts her interests before his own," I suggest, thinking of Madame Dinan and Marshal Rieux.

Crunard's head whips around and he fixes me with a piercing stare. "As do we all."

"I meant no disrespect, my lord, only that Duval appears to have her best interests at heart."

"And you trust his word on this?"

"No, my lord. I trust my own eyes and ears. Everything I have seen and heard speaks of his absolute loyalty to his sister."

"But is that not the best way to avert suspicion? To profess deep and abiding loyalty?"

I do not know what to say to this. I have no words with which to convince Chancellor Crunard of what I feel in my heart to be true.

"Nevertheless, it is not wise to place too much trust in Duval." His voice drips with contempt. "I know him to be an oathbreaker."

I bite back a gasp. That is no small thing. "What oath did he break?" I ask before I can stop myself.

The chancellor brings his steepled fingers to his lips and

studies me. "The one he made to his saint," he says. "I was there when he broke it, saw his blasphemy with my own eyes." When I say nothing more, he nods his head curtly. "You are dismissed. Inform me as soon as you hear anything from the convent."

For a moment, the briefest moment, I consider telling him of the wonderful new possibility Duval has found for his sister, but something holds me back. What if the chancellor fears that I, like the duchess, have fallen under Duval's spell and sends me back to the convent? Instead, I promise him I will keep him informed, and then take my leave.

If the duchess is still up to the task, it is time for her to meet Nemours.

Chapter 27

The duchess has withdrawn to her solar, surrounded by her ladies of the court. Her younger sister, Isabeau, is well enough to join them and reclines on a couch that has been pulled next to Anne's chair. The atmosphere in the room is tense and nervous, everyone's mind on the claims and accusations heard in this morning's meeting. Even though the duchess's face is pale and the skin around her eyes drawn tight, she greets me as if we are old friends. "Demoiselle Rienne! Come join us and let us see your pretty handiwork."

Would that I had thought to warn the duchess of my inept fingers. "Thank you, Your Grace. You do me great honor, but my handiwork is not worthy of such compliments."

She pats the chair next to her. "Come. Sit. It cannot be that bad."

From behind her sister's shoulder, Isabeau gives me an impish grin, and I wonder if her sister has confided in her. I return the smile and take my place next to the duchess.

"What are you working on, demoiselle?" she asks.

"Well." I pull the basket onto my lap and begin to rummage through it, looking for a suitable project. "Ah, here it is. An altar cloth for milord Duval, to thank him for sponsoring me here at court." I stumble painfully through my words, like a toddler learning to walk. I have less talent for small talk than I do for embroidery.

The duchess and Isabeau make a kind fuss over my embroidery pattern while the other ladies eye me with distrust. To them, I am nothing but an interloper, a cuckoo bird who has come to nudge them from the duchess's favor and take their spot.

At last everyone turns back to their needlework, and I am left to blunder on with my own. As I try to decide how best to approach it, the duchess leans close so that only I will hear her words. "It will cause the linen no pain if you stick it, demoiselle."

I bite down on a small bubble of laughter.

"Have you no practice at needlework?" she asks.

"Only with a much larger needle," I mutter.

She smiles grimly at my joke. "Ah. Perhaps we can find some larger pieces for you to practice on."

I incline my head solemnly. "Any project you desire, Your Grace."

Then she winks at me and adjusts her arms so that I may watch her hands at their work. Biting my lip, I study the angle at which she applies her needle, the twist of her wrist as she brings the thread through, the easy rhythm with which she sets the needle to the piece again.

I turn to try it on my own work. I am able to poke the needle through the cloth well enough, but when I try to pull the thread through, it snarls and knots so that I have to set the needle aside and untangle the mess. I catch Madame Dinan watching me with her cold eyes, a hundred questions lurking in their depths. Angling my shoulder to block her view of my clumsy work, I pray for the hour of the chapel visit to arrive.

In the end, I manage well enough, but I am heartily glad when the hourglass runs empty. The duchess notes the direction of my gaze and smiles. "Demoiselle, I would grant you a boon and free you from your embroidery so you may accompany me to chapel. Perhaps you can pray for more nimble fingers."

"Your Grace," Madame Dinan says sharply. "I do not think—"

"And you, Madame Dinan, may sit with Isabeau," the duchess says. Ignoring her governess's raised eyebrows, she rises to her feet.

"Thank you, Your Grace." My thanks are heartfelt enough as I set aside my embroidery, only too glad to follow her from the solar.

Once alone in the hallways, we exchange glances and some of the strain leaves her face. Even so, I am compelled to ask, "Are you sure you wish to do this today?"

"Now more than ever," she says, her voice firm. "The only path open to me is one I cannot take. It is weak of me, I know, but..." Her voice falters and she turns stricken eyes on me. "I cannot," she whispers. "D'Albret terrifies me."

"I do not blame you, Your Grace. He terrifies me as well. No one should ask such a sacrifice from you."

She is somewhat comforted by my words, and we walk in silence a short way before she speaks again. "You have seen

Lord Nemours, yes? How did you find him?" She is every bit the twelve-year-old girl eager to meet her new suitor.

"Were you not betrothed to him once before?" I ask.

She shrugs. "Yes, but I have not ever *seen* him."

"We-ell, he is quite old, with a long white beard and crooked back. And his teeth are yellow."

Her look of horror turns to one of exasperation when she realizes I am joking, and then she laughs. "You are as bad a tease as Duval," she says. But my jest has worked. When we reach the chapel, the remnant of her laughter lingers in her eyes and plays about her lips.

The chapel is small and nearly empty, and I am pleased to see the nine niches under the crucifix honoring the old saints. The only other supplicant in the chapel wears a dark green cloak with the hood drawn close around his head. At our approach, he rises to his feet and pulls the hood from his face, revealing the red-gold hair and handsome face of Fedric of Nemours. He and the duchess stare at each other for a long moment, and then he gives an elaborate, courtly bow.

"Lord Nemours?" she says, a small spark of hope lighting her face. "You may wait by the door," she murmurs to me, then lifts her skirts and joins Nemours in a pew at the front of the church.

I take up position at the door, folding my hands and trying to look as if I am praying rather than pining of curiosity.

Their voices are but soft murmurs, and Anne's manner is somewhat awkward at first, but Nemours quickly puts the duchess at ease. Once I see their heads draw together and hear soft laughter, I turn my thoughts to my own plans.

Chancellor Crunard's words still echo in my ears: *By all means, search d'Albret for one of those marques.* Why had I not realized that I must search d'Albret before I can be certain there is no marque upon him?

Because I am a coward, that is why.

But surely Crunard is correct in where my duties lie, and the abbess would want me to create every opportunity to determine if d'Albret bears a marque anywhere on his body.

A strike to the head is not the only way to kill a man.

Unwilling to face her fractious barons that evening, the duchess decides to dine in her chambers with her sister. I cannot help but wonder if it is also to hide the smile she now wears. Truly, she and Nemours are well matched, and his suit is a gift from both God and the saints. Even better, if there is no formal court tonight, it will be easier for me to go in search of some answers.

My brief meeting with Chancellor Crunard and an afternoon of prayer have convinced me that I have made a grave error in assuming Mortain would marque d'Albret in plain sight. As the abbess is so fond of reminding me, that is not how our saint works. Indeed, the man may well have been marqued for days – someplace where I cannot see it.

I glance around the dim hallway, trying to get my bearings in the east wing of the castle, the section assigned to d'Albret. A pair of doors stand wide open. Raised voices and laughter spill out into the hall along with the candle-light. The laughter has an unpleasant edge to it, a faint tinge of cruelty that makes my heart beat faster and my hands long to reach for the knives at my wrists. Instead, I force them down to my sides, where they grip the heavy velvet of my gown.

I have given much thought as to how I will extricate myself should d'Albret not bear a marque but have yet to come up with a satisfactory plan. I would like to believe I can just turn and walk away, but I fear it will not be that easy. The boys in the village had ugly names and taunts for girls who promised kisses but never delivered them. Even so, I take a deep breath and slip silently into the chamber.

The room is full of noblemen and their retainers, and half the nobles sprawl in chairs drinking wine. D'Albret himself sits in the middle, arrogance apparent in every line of his body, from the way he lounges in his chair to the disdainful gaze with which he surveys the room.

Even as anticipation surges through me, my mind whirs. I know I cannot just glide up to him and ask that he unlace his doublet so that I might peer at his chest. Once again I curse my awkward, graceless nature. Sybella and even Annith would know what to do.

And then it comes to me. I have only to pretend I am Sybella.

She would find an excuse to approach her target, then she would wrap her delicate web of seduction around him. I glance at the room, pleased when I spy a half-full flagon of wine on one of the chests. I pick it up and make my way toward d'Albret.

Feeling more sure of myself now, I slip around the knot of men so that I can approach d'Albret from behind. The fact that he and his men have eyes only for their own magnificence makes this easier than it should be. I take a deep breath and remember Sybella's throaty laugh, the way her lip curls delicately so that you cannot be certain who she is laughing at, the tilt of her head and the slant of her eyes as she peers at you, trying to decide if you are worth her efforts.

At my approach, the man on d'Albret's left looks up. Having been spotted, I can delay no longer. Even though my fingers are desperate to pull away, I force them to rest lightly on d'Albret's shoulder. He smells of wine and sweat and the braised venison he had for dinner. I curl my lip in a knowing smile and lower my voice. "My lord," I purr. "May I refill your wine cup?"

He lifts his head and somehow manages to look down his haughty nose at me even though I stand over him. He holds up his goblet, and his eyes narrow in recognition. "Ah, what do we have here?"

As I pour his wine – slowly – my eyes inspect every inch of exposed flesh, looking for the faintest hint of Mortain's dark shadow. There is none. *Merde.* That means I must take this even farther. When his goblet is full, I clutch the flagon to my chest and cast my eyes downward. "It is just as you said, my lord. I fear I am left alone far more than I would like." I glance up from under my lashes in time to see a triumphant smile spread across his thick lips. My heart skips a beat and I look down once more so he will not see how badly I wish to strike that smile from his face.

"Leave us," he tells the others abruptly. There is a moment of surprised silence, then, with knowing winks and a bold comment or two, the other men file out of the chamber. The last one to leave shuts the door behind him.

I can feel d'Albret's eyes on me, as cold and hard as winter hail. "Now it is just us, demoiselle."

I carefully set the flagon down, and my mind scrambles for the best way to get him out of his shirt and doublet as quickly as possible. However, before I can say anything, d'Albret rises to his feet and reaches for me. As his thick, coarse hand clamps down on my arm, I am nearly overcome with fear and loathing.

"Jumpy, demoiselle?" His voice is mocking.

As I start to answer, the door behind me bursts open. D'Albret's head snaps up and his eyes narrow. Before I can turn round, there is an iron grip on my other arm.

It is Duval, tight-lipped and glaring at me, and I am ashamed at how glad I am to see him, how relieved I am to be kept from completing this task I have set for myself.

The count's expression shifts when he sees who it is. "Eh, Duval? Have you lost something?" I do not know why d'Albret's good humor returns. Does he take that much pleasure in taunting Duval? "Perhaps we can make a little trade, you and I," d'Albret says, letting go of my arm. "I will return your mistress to you if you will give me your sister."

"They are not horses to be traded at the fair," Duval growls.

"No? Is that not a woman's role, to act as broodmare to a sire?"

The pulse in Duval's jaw beats fiercely. "We must agree to disagree on that point." He gives a curt, shallow nod, then drags me from the room. I feel d'Albret's chilling gaze at our backs until we are well clear of him.

Out in the hallway, Duval releases me with a little shove. "Sweet Jesu, do not poison him so openly! Has the convent not taught you any better than that? Why not just create a trail of blood leading to my door?"

I glare back. "I was not poisoning him."

All the color drains from Duval's face. "What were you planning then?"

When I do not reply, he reaches out and shakes me. "Have you heard nothing I've told you about Count d'Albret?" His voice is low and urgent and tinged with fear. Fear for me.

Suddenly it is all too much. His concern, my relief at being found. Frustration and impotence boil up inside me. I reach out and push Duval – hard – so that he stumbles back.

"This is *my* job, *my* calling. It is why I am here. My duty is to my god, not to you and your political maneuverings. I am here to do His will, not yours." I turn away from him. My frustration is so great, I am afraid hot angry tears will spill from my eyes, and I will not let Duval see that.

When he speaks, his voice is filled with certainty, and I so envy him that certainty that I want to hit him all over again.

"Whatever it is your saint demands of you, I am certain it is not what would have happened in that room."

I glance back at him. "What do you know of gods and saints?" I ask, filling my voice with scorn.

His fingers drift to the silver oak leaf of Saint Camulos on his cloak. "I know that what our saints want is not always made clear to us. Sometimes, it is their wish for us to flail and struggle and come to our own choices, not accept ones that have been made for us."

Easily enough said by one who forsook his own vows.

"Everything I know of the saints and old gods," he continues, "is that they and Brittany are one. Anything that serves our kingdom, and by extension our quest to remain independent of France, serves them."

I am sorely tempted to throw his forsaking of his saint in his face, but something stops me. Instead, I spin on my heel and begin making my way toward the main door of the castle.

Outside, the night is cool, but the moon is full, casting a bright, silvery light on the streets of Guérande. We walk in angry silence, using back ways and alleys, both of us clinging to the shadows, our dark cloaks rendering us nearly invisible. Small tendrils of mist have begun to creep in from the sea, bringing with them the moist tang of the nearby salt marshes.

When we have nearly reached his residence, Duval speaks. "The duchess is well pleased with Nemours's offer." His voice is wooden, formal. "We will put the proposal before the Privy Council in a few days to gain their approval."

And though I have vowed never to speak to him again,

I am surprised into looking up. "Is that wise? I thought secrecy was of utmost importance."

He grimaces in frustration. "We do not have much choice. She has not yet been crowned duchess, so she does not yet have the ability to act on her own behalf. We must have the Privy Council's signatures on any agreement we enter into. After that, we will move quickly to maintain the element of surprise."

When we reach his residence he takes us through the front door, merely nodding at the surprised man-at-arms. He pauses at the bottom of the stairs and motions for me to go on ahead. "I think we have shared each other's company enough for one night. Besides, I have much to prepare for tomorrow's council meeting."

I am all too happy to bid him goodnight. When I reach my room, I do not undress but instead go to the window and kneel in the puddle of moonlight spilling onto the floor.

I pray to Mortain for the insight and clarity to see my way through the thicket of loyalties and alliances that surround me. I pray for the wisdom to discern His will in this matter. And most of all, I pray that I am not falling in love with Duval.

I do not know why I am drawn to him. He is not as pretty as de Lornay or as easy to be with as Beast. His brother has more charming manners, and yet...

It is Duval who sets my heart to racing, who addles my wits, who makes me short of breath. For even when he is angry, he is kind, and not the mere surface kindness of good manners, but a true caring. Or at least, the appearance of true caring, for I am well aware it could all be an act. An act designed to earn my trust. And just like some poor, dumb rabbit, I have stumbled into his snare.

Chapter 28

It does not take but three days for the duchess and Nemours to fall in love, and who could blame them? Nemours is young and handsome and kind, but there is a depth to him as well, for he has known sorrow, just as our duchess has. It does not hurt that he has come to rescue her, nor that she is a true damsel in distress, surrounded as she is by fire-breathing barons. It is as romantic as any troubadour's tale.

But she does not let this go to her head. During these three days, she and Duval hammer out the most favorable betrothal terms possible. If they can present a strong, solid contract for marriage to the Privy Council, it will be all the harder for her councilors to refuse.

Everyone is in an uproar over d'Albret's threat of war. There are meetings upon meetings as the council and barons discuss how best to address this newest menace. Meetings the duchess begs off from now and then, pleading a headache. Her ambitious guardians are all too happy to have her out of the way while they plot and plan her duchy's future.

The Privy Council meets in the duchess's private chamber, away from the prying eyes and straining ears of the court. Two men-at-arms stand at the door to her rooms. However, no matter how well trained they are, they cannot see round corners, and there is an antechamber that abuts the solar that could easily be used to eavesdrop.

Duval has put me in this room to act as secondary guard. But there is no rule that says I cannot guard and listen at the same time.

This wall is every bit as thick as the last one I tried to listen through, so I head directly for the window and perch myself on the sill. The murmur of voices is stronger here, although I will be hard-pressed to explain why I am embroidering while hanging out the window if someone should happen upon me. Even so, I know the abbess will want a full report on the deliberations.

Chancellor Crunard's deep rumble calls the meeting to order. Someone wants to know why this unexpected meeting has been called, and by the way his voice sets my teeth on edge, I am sure it is Marshal Rieux.

"*I* have called this meeting." Anne's voice is easy to discern. "But I will let my lord Duval explain the why of it."

When Duval finishes telling of the Nemours offer, there is a small uproar from the council members.

"How has this happened?" Madame Dinan asks, as if it is a disaster and not a boon. "There has been no envoy from Nemours."

"No open one, no," Duval says. His words cause another wave of outrage from the council.

"Why did Nemours come to you?" Marshal Rieux asks, his vanity and pomposity sorely pricked by this breach in protocol. "You are not regent here; stop acting like one. Or is that what you are angling for?"

"If he wanted to seize a regency, I doubt he would be putting this before all of us," Captain Dunois points out.

"Enough," Chancellor Crunard says, and they all quiet down. "This is good news for our duchess and our country, let us not forget that. How much aid will Nemours bring?"

"Three thousand men-at-arms and fifteen hundred pike-men."

There is a long, painful silence. "Surely you jest," Marshal Rieux says at last.

"That is not nearly as many as d'Albret has offered," Madame Dinan points out.

"Madame." There is a faint tremble in Anne's voice. "As I have said more times than I can count, I will not wed him. He is more than fifty years old and a grandfather." She does not say that he is ugly and coarse and makes her skin feel as if it wants to crawl off her bones, but I know that is so.

"But he brings with him an army compared to Nemours's paltry offer!" Rieux sputters. "An army we will need to stand against the French."

"Let us put it to a vote," Crunard says. "All in favor?"

Anne's voice is first to answer "aye," but Duval's "aye" is a close second.

"Nay," says Rieux, followed by Madame Dinan's softer "Nay."

There is a pause, then Captain Dunois speaks. "I am sorry, Your Grace, but as captain of your army, I must point out that without d'Albret fighting by your side, we will need to find additional allies, and as yet we have had no luck in convincing others to our cause. But as a father, I cannot help but be glad of this newest development."

"Chancellor?" says Anne. "What say you? How will you vote in this matter?"

"I am most pleased at this new development," Crunard says. "Although it does create problems of its own. Even so, I vote aye."

I sigh in relief on the duchess's behalf. Just as Duval is reminding them to speak of the Nemours offer to no one, there is a faint whisper of sound behind me. I whip my head around in time to see the latch lifting.

Moving quickly, I pull my long dagger from my ankle sheath and cross the room to stand behind the door.

It creaks open, momentarily blocking my view and trapping me between it and the wall. *Madame Hivern again?* I wonder. *Or perhaps François?*

Or maybe Sybella, for why is she in Guérande if not to protect our duchess?

Almost as if sensing the relaxing of my guard, the intruder slams the door into me. I swear as my shoulder crashes into the unforgiving stone, then I spring forward, dagger ready.

Too late. The intruder is already fleeing down the hallway. I step into the corridor in time to see him disappear round a corner. Determined to catch up, I break into a run.

The labyrinth of palace hallways work to my advantage,

for every time he turns a corner, he must slow down just enough that I can catch sight of him. One of the circular stairways looms ahead, and the spy takes the steps two at a time. Cursing my cumbersome court garb, I lift my skirts and follow. When I am but halfway up the stairs, I hear the click of a door opening and then shutting.

When I gain the landing, I am dismayed to see a dozen chambers stretching out as far as the eye can see. Swearing in frustration, I approach the first one on my right but sense no spark of life behind it. The first room on the left is similarly empty. I pause at every door until the fifth, where I sense a pulse of life.

I stop long enough to draw my knives, then, moving as silently as possible, I lift the latch and push open the door.

There is a whisper of movement at the open window, then nothing. I race over and peer outside just in time to see a dark figure disappearing through an archway at the side of the courtyard.

At least he is limping. Hopefully, he broke his damned leg when he jumped. I sheathe my knives and return to tell Duval of this new twist.

Two days after Duval informed the Privy Council of Nemours's offer, his brother François invites me to play chess. I accept, wondering if there is some ulterior motive to the invitation.

François is waiting at a table in the grand salon, his attention on setting up the chessboard, which gives me a moment to study him unobserved. That he would betray his own sister makes him dishonorable. That he is Duval's brother makes him fascinating.

He glances up just then and I smile shyly, as if I have been caught admiring him. He rises to his feet and bows. "Good morning, demoiselle."

"Good morning," I reply as I take my seat.

"Duval let you out for the morning?"

"Duval is busy with the duchess and her councilors." I grimace with distaste, and François clucks his tongue in sympathy.

"What will you choose, my lady, white or black?"

I look down at the ornately carved pieces in front of me. "Black, I think."

His brows raise in surprise. "You give up the first move then?"

"Is not the defensive position the stronger?" I ask sweetly.

He laughs. "You have been spending too much time with my brother and his strategies. Very well, I shall go first." He reaches for his king's pawn and moves it forward two paces. I respond by moving a knight's pawn forward one pace.

François gives me a sly look. "No hesitation; I like that in a lady." It would be hard to miss the double meaning in his words.

"I hesitate when it is called for, my lord, and your game has not called for it yet."

He laughs, and I am pleased at how artfully I fall into this flirtation. "A challenge," he says, his eyes glittering at the prospect.

I let my face grow sober. "Speaking of challenges, what did you think of the Estates meeting? Were you as shocked as everyone else with Count d'Albret's threat of war?"

François's cheerful face turns grave. "I was. He is not known for idle threats."

I cannot tell if he is concerned for the duchess or his own aspirations. "Your poor sister already has her hands full with France, she does not need d'Albret's rebellion on top of everything else."

"Indeed, she does not." He smiles tightly. "But I am certain Duval will take care of it. He always does." He sneaks his bishop out from behind the pawn and takes my knight. When he looks up, our eyes meet. "Your move," he says softly.

I keep my expression light and turn the conversation to other matters. "Your brother serves St. Camulos," I say as I consider the board. "What saint do you serve, if any? St. Amourna, perhaps? Or St. Salonius?" The moment the name crosses my lips, I wish to take it back. As François is a bastard, there is a very real chance he was dedicated to Saint Salonius, patron saint of mistakes.

Overlooking my blunder, he claps his hand to his heart. "You wound me, demoiselle! Armourna?"

I shrug. "You are most charming, so it seems fitting to me."

François's brown eyes grow serious. "There is more to me than that, demoiselle."

"Is there now?" I ask, putting just a touch of doubt in my voice so that he will be compelled to prove it to me.

In spite of the seriousness that has fallen over him, he smiles. "I was dedicated to St. Mer," he says, "with the hopes that I would have a naval career." He gives a self-deprecating grimace. "Until we discovered that I become deathly seasick and am of absolutely no use to anyone on a boat."

I laugh, as he intends me to, but I am more than a little surprised to find that I grieve for him as well. It is no small thing to be dedicated to a saint you cannot serve. "And your sister the duchess?" I ask.

"Ah, Saint Brigantia," he says, then falls silent.

Of course. The patron saint of wisdom.

"You are not close to your sister, are you?"

He looks up at me again, and this time his normally open gaze is unreadable. "I was not given a chance. From the time of her birth, Duval was her champion; I could never get close."

I study him. It is not the faint bitterness in his voice that surprises me but the faint echo of abandonment. "You miss him," I say in surprise.

François picks up his rook and studies it. "Aye, I miss him. We spent our youth doing everything together. He was my older brother, the one who taught me how to hold a sword and how to draw a bow and where to fish for the fattest pike. When Anne was born, that all fell away, and he became consumed by duty." He moves his rook down eight spaces. "Check," he says quietly.

I study the board a moment, trying to force my mind back

to the game. At last I move a pawn. It is a feeble move, and François looks at me with mild amusement. "Does speaking of my brother distract you so very much?" he asks.

"No," I say, managing a dismissive laugh. "It is just that I am so very bad at chess, as I warned you."

He smiles, but it does not reach his eyes. Something behind me draws his attention. "Gavriel, you finally decided to come up for air?"

I look over my shoulder, surprised to see Duval glowering in the doorway. "No," he says shortly. "I came because I must speak with Demoiselle Rienne. If you'll excuse us?" His voice is filled with ice and I cannot fathom why.

"But of course." François stands.

As soon as I reach Duval's side, he takes my elbow in an iron grip. I wince as he begins walking me to the door. His face is unreadable and I have to quicken my pace lest I end up being dragged. Even so, something compels me to glance back at François. His eyes are fastened hungrily on Duval and filled with yearning.

Once Duval and I are in the hall, I pull away from him. "Have I done something wrong?"

He stops, twirls me round to face him, then backs me up against the wall. His eyes spark in fury as he leans in close. "Did you receive orders from the convent that you did not share with me?"

Before I can utter so much as a word, he gives me a little shake. "Did you?"

"No!"

"Do you swear to it? Swear on your service to Mortain, if that is what you hold most dear."

I frown at him. "Yes, I swear it. Tell me what's happened."

He stares at me a long moment. "Better," he finally says, "I will show you."

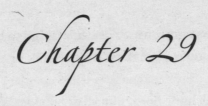

Chapter 29

Duval tucks my arm through his – none too gently – then leads me deep into the castle. His face is set in harsh lines and there is a grimness I have not seen for a number of days. "How long have you been in the grand salon?" he asks.

"An hour. Maybe more."

"Has François been with you that whole time?"

"Yes, my lord, but—"

"What of my mother? Did you see any sign of her while you were there?"

"No. What is amiss?"

He does not answer as we hasten through the hallways, past closed doors and empty chambers. "Why are we in such a hurry?" I ask, breathless.

"Because there isn't much time before news begins to spread through the castle faster than the plague."

We finally reach a closed wooden door. Duval nods at the guard posted there, who steps aside to let us enter. Duval leads me into a well-furnished room with an outside balcony. Winding steps lead from the balcony to a private courtyard. Duval points to a still, twisted body on the flagstones below. "Fedric, Duke of Nemours."

"No!" I whisper, then lift my skirts and hurry down the

staircase. I curse my sense of death, wishing to hold out hope one moment longer, but there is no mistaking that Nemours is dead.

When I reach the body, I kneel at his side. "When did this happen?"

"I was hoping you could tell me."

I glance sharply back at Duval. One eyebrow is raised in a sardonic question that does nothing to mask the fury and disappointment he feels.

"You cannot think that I did this!"

"I cannot?"

"No, milord. I have received no instructions from the convent, nor has my god revealed His will to me. Are you so very certain he did not fall?"

Duval grunts. "I am not."

Nemours's body still holds traces of warmth. He cannot have lain here long. "Who found him?"

"I did."

When I raise my eyebrows in inquiry, he shoves his hand through his hair. "Do not look at me so. We were to meet to review the final betrothal arrangements, but when I arrived his chamber was empty."

"Did you question his men?"

"Yes. They confirmed he spent the morning alone and had no visitors." He glances up at the window, two floors above us. "When I found his chamber empty, I looked out here to see if he was waiting in the courtyard and saw his crumpled form."

Our eyes meet. "But he told no one of his true identity; he introduced himself as a wool merchant from Castile. Only the Privy Council knew who he was..."

"Precisely." His lips twist in a smile that has nothing to do with humor. "After yesterday's meeting, they all knew about Nemours, and any one of them would have had time to act."

"So one of the duchess's closest advisors must have been involved with this."

Duval nods in agreement. "Although, it is not impossible that Gisors learned of Nemours's identity through one of his many spies. Or perhaps he paid off one of the council members. Nor is it beyond the bounds of reason that d'Albret arranged this in retaliation, for I can very easily believe Madame Dinan told him of Nemours."

"No matter which of those is correct, you still come back to the fact that someone from your Privy Council said something. To someone. With ill intent."

Duval's jaw clenches. "Does his soul still... linger?" He waves his hand awkwardly. "Can you speak with it?"

"I will try."

I turn my face from Duval and bow my head. Do the people of Nemours worship the same gods and saints as we do in Brittany? I have no idea, but it is worth trying.

I close my eyes and allow this world to fall away until I no longer feel the hard stone beneath my knees or see the fading light of the sun against my eyelids. The faint chill of Death caresses my cheek, like a loving mother who has greatly missed her child.

When I peel away the thin veil between life and death, Nemours is there waiting. His distress at being outmaneuvered is thick and solid, a veritable wall of grief. But it is the despair he feels at leaving the duchess without a protector that touches my heart, for his last thought proves what an honorable man he was. I, too, am filled with despair. Why must the honorable die when so many dishonorable live?

Sensing the presence of life, Nemours's soul moves toward me. I gently reach past the cloud of grief and misery that surrounds him, searching for more of his last thoughts in this world, looking for something that will help us. There: the solid feel of a hand against his back, a sharp push, the sense of falling. The force of his landing sends me reeling. I do not realize that I have almost fallen myself until I feel Duval's hand on my shoulder pulling me back into life and breaking the connection with Nemours. A gasp escapes me and I open my eyes.

Duval stands over me, his warm, solid hand grounding me in this world, his face full of concern. "Are you all right?"

"Yes, my lord. I am fine," I say.

Duval's free hand touches my cheek. It feels far warmer than Death's caress but is just as gentle. "Then why are you so pale?" he asks softly.

"I am not." I shove his hand away and cast my eyes down to avoid meeting his. "Nemours was pushed. From behind. He does not know whose hand it was, for he never saw it." We are both silent as we digest the full implications of this news.

Someone on Anne's Privy Council is a murderer.

Chapter 30

Duval stays late at the palace so he can inform the duchess of the events and see to the necessary letters and arrangements required by Nemours's death. I sleep not a whit. I am furious that this chance at happiness has been snatched from the duchess, that such an honorable man has died by such a dishonorable hand. I want to fix it, to put things right, but it is beyond even the skills of Mortain.

But perhaps I can grant the Duke of Nemours a small mercy.

At daybreak, Louyse bustles in with a full pitcher of water and a cheery "good morning", shutting the door behind her with her ample hip. "After I lay out your clothes, I will bring a tray to your room to break your fast. Also, my lord Duval left you a note."

"A note? Is he not here?"

"No, demoiselle. He and the other lords have gone off on a hunt to stock the castle larders."

She hands me the note and turns to my garderobe. I am torn between opening it at once and using the moment to slip into my fresh chemise. Shame wins over curiosity, and my scar is securely hidden by fine linen by the time she returns. Once she has helped me into a gown, she excuses herself to fetch my tray. I tear open the note, cracking the seal and spilling small bits of red wax to the floor.

Ismae,

I have decided that we will be moving into the palace to be nearer the duchess. If last night's activities are a sign of things to come, I would be close at hand when she needs me.

Also, after much discussion, the council has decided to go on with the planned hunt – indeed, all court activities – as if nothing has happened. There is no reason the death of an unannounced stranger would alter our behavior, and thus are we bound and trapped by our own deception. It is better that as few as possible know the extent of this disaster.

Be well, Gavriel

He is right. No one but the Privy Council and he knew Nemours's identity, so it would not make sense to accord Nemours any particular honors. But in denying him those, surely we are adding to our grievous insult against the man.

I move toward the bed and fetch the sacred bone dagger from under my mattress. The reverend mother has given it to me for some purpose. Perhaps easing Nemours's death is precisely what the misericorde is to be used for. I do not know if it is some whim of my own or some higher purpose of the god, but I am filled with an urgency to grant Nemours a small act of mercy.

Even as I secure the misericorde at its customary place at my waist, a plan begins to form in my mind. I go to my small trunk, unlock it, and withdraw a long, thin dagger. I place it in a supple leather sheath and then strap it to my left ankle. I slip the plainest garrote bracelet on my wrist, and last, I remove the small crossbow and attach three of the quarrels. The bow is designed to be carried by a thin chain at my waist, under my overskirt. If someone were to press close against me, they would feel it, but other than that, it is undetectable.

I do not expect to be questioned at the palace, but I have an excuse prepared just in case. I carry a small offering to leave on Saint Arduinna's altar in the chapel in the hope that she will smile on today's hunt.

The castle is nearly empty since all the nobles are off chasing stag or boar or whatever it is that has caught their fancy today. The servants and attendants are busy at their tasks, relieved, no doubt, to be spared from dancing attendance on so many nobles and courtiers.

I pause for a moment, wondering where Nemours's body might be. Remembering the strange, unerring way I found Martel's grave, I cast out my senses, searching for Death.

It is harder here, with so many sparks of life flickering about their duties, but, even so, I am drawn to Death like a moth to a flame. As I follow the trail, I quickly realize the path leads to the small chapel where Anne and Nemours first met.

The chapel is empty and I make my way to the bier, the soul's despair guiding my steps more surely than the small, sputtering candles in the nave. When I reach the body, the soul seems to recognize me and rushes toward the familiarity and life that I offer.

I open myself to it, let it warm itself against me, surprised when it curls up and settles into me like a despondent hound with nowhere else to go.

We sit together for a while, this soul and I. When I am certain no stray mourners or triumphant gloaters will appear to pray over this mystery corpse, I allow myself to turn my mind fully inward to Nemours's soul.

I have brought with me the means to unite you with your god at once, if you wish it.

When the soul stirs hopefully at my words, I rise to my feet and step closer to the bower. The poor twisted body has been straightened, but the grimace of shock is still on his face. I slip my hand through the slit of my gown, and my fingers close on the handle of my misericorde. My hope, my small plea to Mortain, is that by my setting this dagger on Nemours's flesh, his soul will be able to depart immediately.

Before I can draw the dagger from its hiding place, a scrape on the stone behind me stays my hand. "What an interesting surprise." Count d'Albret's deep, grating voice destroys the sanctity of the chapel. "I had not thought to find Duval's cousin grieving next to a lowly wool merchant from Castile."

Stiffly, I turn and face the count. I have not seen him since my attempt to examine him for a marque and I brace myself, unsure whether to expect mockery or anger. I find neither. Instead, his dark eyes glitter with unholy mischief. I cannot help but wonder if it was his hand that pushed Nemours. "Surely not a surprise." I keep my head bent low, as if reluctant to cease my prayers. "I was convent raised and have been taught to honor the dead and pray for their mercy." I blink innocently. "Have you come to pray too?" I know full well he has not. Whatever he has come for, it is not prayer.

"I am afraid I have come out of morbid curiosity, demoiselle," d'Albret admits without a hint of shame. "I confess to being fascinated by this poor merchant who met his death in our fair city. Besides," d'Albret continues, "I have little belief in accidents." He looks pointedly at me. "Or coincidence."

"Ah," I say. "Then you and my lord Duval have something in common."

There is a movement back by the door of the chapel, and the duchess and her governess enter. I drop into a deep curtsy. "Your Grace."

Out of the corner of my eye, I see d'Albret sketch a perfunctory bow. "My dear duchess," he says. "Have you come to pray for a lowly wool merchant as well? Surely he is blessed beyond his station."

The duchess meets d'Albret's insolent gaze. "I would pray for any poor soul who met his death under my roof." Her voice is sharp with disapproval. "And you, sire?"

D'Albret shrugs and throws his arms out to his sides. "I have been found out! My motives are nowhere near as fine as you ladies'."

The duchess smoothly changes the subject. "I am curious

as to why you chose not to join the others in the hunt today."

D'Albret's hooded eyes capture Anne's and I feel my pulse quicken at the affront in them. "They do not hunt for prey that interests me."

The duchess pales; her fingers gripping her prayer book turn white. My hand hidden on the dagger in the folds of my gown tightens as well, and I imagine what it would feel like to stick d'Albret like a pig.

Perhaps he senses my thoughts, for he makes another short bow. "I will leave you to your prayers."

Still pale, the duchess nods, and d'Albret departs. Anne turns to Madame Dinan. "You may leave us as well. I know you have no love for this task I have set myself. I shall pray with Demoiselle Rienne."

And while it is clear her governess does not want to be here, she wants the duchess left to my influence even less. "But Your Grace—"

"Leave us." The duchess's voice brooks no argument. After a moment's hesitation, during which a multitude of resentments cross Madame Dinan's lovely face, she curtsies and leaves. When she is gone, the duchess turns to me. "She does not like you, you know."

"She no doubt thinks you should not be in the company of Duval's dubious cousin, Your Grace."

A smile of satisfaction crosses her lips and I am suddenly aware of just how much she enjoys thwarting her overbearing governess's wishes. Then her smile disappears. "So, why *are* you here?"

"You do not believe I came to pray for the man's soul?"

"Oh, I believe you pray, but I cannot but wonder if it is something else that brings you."

The Breton court – indeed, all the kingdoms of Europe – would do well not to underestimate this duchess. "There is something else that brings me, Your Grace." I look down at Nemours's still form. "Did you know that he cared deeply for you? Not just your duchy or your power, but you. He was filled with a desire to rescue you from an unpleasant fate."

The duchess blinks, then looks down at the man who would have been her husband. "I had begun to hope so." Her pale cheeks blush. "It seemed as if he cared. I sensed within him an enormous capacity for kindness and felt I would be able to grow to love him. That is a great blessing for someone such as myself, who feared love would have no place in a marriage between two kingdoms."

I say nothing. Since the age of four, she has been dangled before half the kingdoms and duchies of Europe, like bait at the end of a stick. The best she had hoped for was a marriage of mutual respect and no cruelty. But to have the potential for love snatched away by a false hand...

She looks up at me and says again, "So, why are you here?" Her firmness of manner will not tolerate any falsehood or evasion.

"I had thought to release his soul from the misery of his death." I am careful to keep my voice pitched low so that any lurking outside the chapel will not hear it. "Souls must linger near their bodies for three days after their deaths before moving on. But Lord Nemours's soul is so tormented by what he sees as his failure to protect you that I thought to hasten him to his forgiveness."

The duchess's eyes widen. "You can do that?"

I think so. "Yes."

She nods. "Do it then. And may his soul rest in peace."

"As you command." I am pleased with this authority she has given me. Neither Duval nor the abbess can find fault with me for acting under her order.

"What are you waiting for?" the duchess whispers.

I meet her clear brown gaze. "Solitude, Your Grace. The rites of Mortain are most private."

Arguments and orders flit across her face, her desire to watch and know these mysteries at odds with her desire to honor the sanctity of death. "Very well," she says at last. "I will leave you." She reaches across the body and clasps my wrist. "Thank you," she whispers. With one last look at her betrothed, she turns and quits the chapel. "Madame Dinan?" she calls as she reaches the doorway.

Her governess appears so quickly that I am thankful we kept our voices low. The two women make their way down the hall, their voices echoing faintly behind them.

Once again I grip the bone dagger. Using my other hand, I pull aside Nemours's shirt collar and the fur trim of his doublet. It is best if this scar remains hidden.

Casting up a brief, heartfelt prayer to Mortain to guide my hand, I lift the dagger and run the edge lightly across Nemours's neck.

I feel, rather than hear, a gasp. Not of pain or shock, but of release.

"Go in peace and with our prayers," I whisper. There is a rustling sensation, as if a score of doves are flying past my cheek, their pale wings filling the air with a joyous sense of flight. *Protect her,* his soul begs me as it departs.

I will, I promise. Then there is naught but silence and I am left alone to stare at a thin cut along his dead white flesh that does not bleed. I carefully put his collar back in place.

Chapter 31

Upon leaving the chapel, I am pulled toward Nemours's chambers, almost as if tugged by an unseen hand. I have no idea why, but an insistent itching at the back of my neck bids me hurry. Mayhap my god is on the move at last.

Just outside Nemours's apartments, the itching at my back grows stronger. Without bothering to knock, I reach out and open the door.

One of Nemours's men-at-arms is behind a desk, rifling through a saddlebag. He is dressed in riding leathers and a breastplate, and his helmet is tucked under his arm. A small black marque sits in the middle of his forehead. Smiling, I close the door behind me.

He does not start guiltily, as he should, but frowns in annoyance. "Who are you?"

I slip my hand through the slit of my overskirt, and my fingers close around the hard wood of the crossbow tiller. "Vengeance," I say softly.

His eyes widen slightly at my words, then he grows alarmed as I draw the crossbow from its hiding place. Within the space of a single heartbeat, I cock the bow, fit the quarrel to the string, and level it at his head, aiming directly for the marque. For a moment I am torn, balancing the duchess's and Duval's need for information against my desire to prove myself to my god and my convent. I decide it cannot hurt to ask. "Who paid you to push your lord to his death?"

The man's face pales. "I don't know what you're talking about."

"No? I think you do. I think you are the man who betrayed the Duke of Nemours. If you tell me what I need to know, I will kill you as quickly and painlessly as possible. If you do not, it will be slow and lingering. Your choice. Either way, you *will* die." My blood is singing in my veins, so happy am I to be doing my god's work.

Keeping his eyes on mine, the man comes out from behind the desk. "Who says I killed my lord Nemours? Do I get no chance to defend myself? Be tried and judged?"

"You have been," I say. "By Saint Mortain Himself. And found guilty. Now, I will ask you one last time: on whose orders did you push?"

I see in his eyes the moment he decides to rush me. Grunting in annoyance, I release the bolt. It flies straight and true and strikes him in the forehead, precisely where Mortain has marqued him. As he falls, his eyes shift from my face to the door behind me. Swearing, I drop the crossbow and go for the knife at my ankle.

The action saves my life.

There is a breath of air at my back followed by a searing pain, then I am turning toward my assailant, thrusting upward with my knife before I have even laid eyes on him.

My aim is good, and the knife plunges into his gut. His brown eyes widen in surprise, then in pain, as I shove the blade upward, hastening his death. In spite of my threat to the other man, I do not deal in long and lingering deaths.

Before I can do more, however, the soul of the first man flees his dead body. It rushes at me, swirling with cold hostility. I force myself to concentrate on the myriad images it sends flickering through my mind, desperate to find some small tidbit of information that will tell us to who is behind this disaster. While I am distracted by this task, the second man's soul also rushes at me. I gasp as if I have been plunged into a frozen river and stagger back against the wall, shivering so hard I can barely stand. As the second soul floods me, I am filled with anger and pain and regret. An aching sense of loss. A sense of fear so thick it coats the back of my tongue with its bitter taste.

Then, as quickly as they came, they leave, and I sag against the wall. The faint, faraway blare of the hunting horns sound outside. The hunting party has returned.

I kneel on the floor next to the second body long enough to retrieve my knife and wipe it clean on his tabard. When I rise to my feet, I am surprised at the small wave of dizziness that passes through me. I turn for the door, then blink at the smear of red where I leaned up against the wall. I am injured.

Desperate to be away from here, I grab a rough woolen cloak from the bed and use a corner of it to wipe the wall clean as best I can. Then I throw it around my shoulders and hide the crossbow beneath my skirts once more. I can hear the faint clatter of horses' hooves on cobbles and the excited barking of the hounds. Satisfied that everything is as it should be, I step from the chamber out into the hall and begin the long walk down the corridor and away from the evidence of my actions.

As I wind my way through the palace corridors, I debate whether to return to Duval's residence or meet him outside. In the end, I decide he must know what has transpired sooner rather than later, and better from my own lips than a stranger's. Besides, someone must clean up the mess.

The wetness at my back spreads as the injury burns and pulls.

I glance behind to be certain I am not dripping a trail of blood behind me.

Outside in the courtyard is a confusion of prancing, blowing horses; dismounting men; barking, wagging hounds; and shouts of greeting. Two large stags hang from poles and I find myself smiling. Today was clearly a good day for hunting, inside the palace and out. I hang back, searching for Duval.

Almost as if I have called his name, his head comes up and his gaze latches onto mine. I do not care for this connection between us.

Duval dismounts and makes his way to me. "What are you doing here?"

I say nothing, but simply stare at him.

"God's teeth!" he says. I would be heartily impressed by his ability to read my thoughts if it were not so exasperating.

He leans in closer, dipping his head as if he will kiss me, and I must remind myself that it is simply so no one will overhear. "Who?"

"Nemours's guards."

One dark eyebrow shoots up. "More than one?"

"One because he was guilty of treachery; the other was in self-defense."

"Did the convent send you orders?"

"No. I went to pray for Nemours's soul. Then I was drawn to Nemours's chambers. There I saw a guard who bore a marque, and so I acted."

I cannot read the expression on Duval's face. "I *did* try to question him first, my lord, but he gave nothing away. At least, not then."

Duval pounces on that like a wolf on a fallen bone. "Did you read his soul?"

I nod, then swallow before continuing. "He was paid a bag of ducats, and those who paid him held his wife and child. His last thought was of them, a quick prayer that they would be allowed to live now that he had done what he had been asked."

"He spared no last thought for those who had ordered him?"

I shake my head, then wince, as it pulls the cut on my back. "He did not know. The man he dealt with wore a deep hood, and they always met in the shadows."

Duval sighs. "Where are the bodies? I assume you need me to clean up after you."

"They are in Nemours's chambers. If you will see to them, I will be on my way."

For the first time Duval notices the unfamiliar cloak I wear. "Whose cloak is that?"

I start to shrug, then wince again. "One of the men I—"

With a sound of impatience, Duval lifts the cloak from my shoulders, then sucks in a breath. I look round to see the gown beneath is soaked through with blood. "We must get you attended to," he says, letting the cloak fall back in place.

"Shouldn't you see to the bodies first, before someone discovers them?"

He thinks for a moment, then gently cups my elbow with his hand. "We will do both," he says, then leads me toward the palace.

"Where are we going?"

"To my rooms here. We will tend to your wound and I can oversee the clean-up. Although I will now owe Beast a favor."

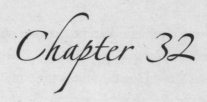

Chapter 32

Once inside the palace, Duval snags the first page he sees. "Here." He gives the boy a coin. "Go find the Baron de Waroch, the one they call Beast. Do you know who he is?"

The boy's eyes shine as he nods his head.

Duval ruffles his hair. "Tell him to come immediately to my chambers in the north tower."

The page sketches a quick bow, then takes off at a run, neatly dodging around mingling courtiers and servants, who barely notice his passing.

Duval is quiet as he escorts me through the palace to his rooms in the north tower. When we reach them, he leads me through a jumble of trunks and furnishings in the outer rooms to his bedchamber, where a valet is unpacking his clothes. Duval brusquely waves the man away, and I blush when I realize what the servant will think.

Duval sits me on the bed and angles me so that my back is to him.

"I am not a doll, my lord. If you but tell me what you wish to do, I can do it myself."

His only response is a grunt, then the mattress dips as he sits down behind me. His body is so close I can feel the heat rising off it. Chilled by the wet blood on my gown, it is all I can do to keep myself from leaning into that warmth.

He removes the borrowed cloak from my shoulders, and I hiss as the cold air sets the cut stinging.

He is silent for so long I nearly squirm, except I worry the movement will bring me more discomfort. When I feel his fingers on my neck, I pull away before I can stop myself. "What are you doing?" My voice sounds unnaturally high to my ears.

"Removing the ruined bodice so I can tend your cut."

"No, milord!" I jump up from the bed and spin round, putting my back safely out of his reach. Panic flutters in my breast. *He cannot see it. He* mustn't *see it.*

Duval looks at me as if I am mad. "Would you rather I send for a physician?"

"No!" I say, beginning to feel trapped. I have no love for the court physicians, and they will ask questions I do not wish to answer. But I cannot bear for Duval to see my ruined back. "If you will leave me, I can tend it myself."

He snorts in disbelief. "Is that yet another miracle of Mortain? That His acolytes are able to contort themselves enough to tend their own backs?" His voice turns gently chiding. "If you are worried about the gown, I am sure the reverend mother will understand."

But of course, it is not the gown that worries me. The sense of panic in my chest grows until I can hardly breathe. Every taunt thrown at me by the village boys, every slur cast my way, every insult echoes in my head. And those were all from villagers and peasants, people much accustomed to ugliness and deformity. Duval is of noble blood, was raised amid the beauty and finery of court. I cannot bear that I will be the ugliest thing he has ever seen. "No." I take a step backwards, determined to stay out of his reach. "I do not need your help."

He frowns at my unreasonableness. "If we do not tend your injury, you could well lose the use of your shoulder and arm, and how would that serve your god or your duchess?"

I hiss in frustration. Trust Duval to find the one argument that will remind me of my true purpose here. My *only* purpose here. My service to Mortain comes before all else. There is no place for modesty or shame. Perhaps the god is testing me even now to see if my vanity is stronger than my duty to Him. Feeling raw and exposed, I cannot help but grumble. "What would a man know of stitching anyway?"

Duval laughs outright at that, and a small hidden dimple winks briefly at the corner of his mouth. "If a man expects to survive in battle or help his fellow men-at-arms afterward, he will indeed learn to stitch, and to stitch well, if not prettily. Now quit putting this off."

Slowly, I return to the bed, sit down, and turn my back to him. I feel hollow inside and remind myself that what Duval thinks of me or my scar is of no importance. Indeed, perhaps his disgust and revulsion will help rebuild the barrier that once stood between us. The words he spoke when we left the convent echo through me. *Being sired by one of the old saints puts your lineage into a class all its own, a class as untouchable by the nobility as the nobility is by turnip farmers.* He may claim such lofty ideals, but it is another thing altogether to see with one's own eyes what marks such parentage leaves behind.

I hold myself rigid as he unlaces my bodice. It starts to fall forward and I catch it with my hands, hugging it to me like a shield.

There is a rustle of movement as he takes a dagger from his belt. The tearing sound as he cuts away my ruined chemise is loud in the quiet room, and the rush of air against my damp back makes me shiver. I clutch the front of my gown tightly and steel myself against what must surely happen next.

The silence grows impossibly long, and I am painfully reminded of the hideous silence when Guillo saw my back. Of his fear and anger and revulsion. I force myself to breathe.

"Ah," Duval says. "So this is what you didn't want me to see. Poor Ismae." His voice is as soft and tender as a caress. I square my shoulders and stare straight ahead. "How did you come by it?" he asks.

"'Tis where the herbwitch's poison burned me when my mother tried to cast me from her womb."

When he touches my shoulder again, I bite back a yelp of surprise, and my skin twitches beneath his fingers. Slowly, he traces my scar. It is exquisitely sensitive, and pleasure unfurls across my skin, so intense and unexpected that it feels as if I have been brushed by an angel's wing.

It is all I can do to keep from leaping from the bed and bolting.

Perhaps sensing this, Duval speaks, his voice low. "There is no shame in scars, Ismae."

I long to laugh at his gentle words, to throw them back in his face and claim I do not care what he thinks. But I do care. Far more than I have any right to, and his acceptance undermines every last defense I possess.

"We'll need to wash this," he murmurs, and even though I welcome this practical task, when he rises from the bed I am torn between relief and disappointment.

He pours water from a ewer into a shallow basin, then carries it back to the bed. After settling the basin in his lap, he dips a piece of linen into the water and uses gentle, efficient strokes to wash the blood from my wound. It is a practical, matter-of-fact touch, much like Sister Serafina would use were she tending to me. Even so, my entire back is alive with awareness. Every inch of my skin, every knob of my spine, and even my scar seem to gain pleasure from his touch. Indeed, the whole world narrows so it is all I can think of.

I close my eyes and try to break this spell he is weaving. "Do you have scars, milord?"

"Oh yes." He removes the cloth from my back and wrings it out in the basin. "One received in service to my lord father, and another received in service to my sister." He touches the re-wetted linen to my back and I shiver. I want to lean into that touch, lean into *him*, feel his warmth wrap around me. Instead, I force myself to pull away. "I'm sure it is clean by now."

His hand clamps down on my good shoulder. An unwelcome thrill flutters somewhere deep in my belly. "Aye, it is clean, but deep enough that it will need to be stitched.

It did not tear the muscle, though, so it should not take long to heal. You are not afraid of a few stitches, are you?"

"Of course not." His taunt works and I hold myself still.

I welcome the bite of the needle as it jabs my flesh. Pain, at least, is familiar to me. Each little prick and burn helps clear away the heady intoxication of Duval's more gentle touches.

"This is the last one," he says. I feel an extra tug as he knots the end. He leans in close, his breath warm upon my skin, then bites the thread with his teeth. "There. Done. Raise your arm, but slowly. I want to see if it pulls."

Still clutching the front of my dress, I lift my arm. The stitches bite and burn, but not unbearably. Just enough to remind me to use caution until it heals.

"It will do," he says gruffly. "Although I shall refrain from moving onto fancy stitchery anytime soon."

"And here I imagined you embroidering altar cloths with the duchess and her ladies in the afternoon."

Duval snorts. "Hardly. But it would be wise for you to do that for a few days while this heals."

"Methinks not. In case you hadn't noticed, the schemes and plots around here are beginning to thicken."

"It has come to my attention, yes," Duval says dryly.

"May I stand up now?"

"If you wish."

I rise to my feet, careful to keep the loose bodice clasped firmly in place, then spin round, anxious to remove my naked back from his view.

But facing him is worse, I realize, for his expression is soft, unguarded, and there is a tenderness there that I have only seen when he is with the duchess. Our eyes meet, and in that moment everything alters. It is as if he has only just now realized that we are alone in his bedchamber with me barely clothed. The tenderness in his face turns to something else, something that makes me aware of the cold air on my bare back and of my tattered bodice. He takes a step closer, then another, and suddenly we are almost touching. His eyes never leave mine, but his hand comes up and brushes a strand of hair away from my collarbone. Without even realizing what I am doing, I lean toward him.

His hand moves up to cup my face. Slowly he draws me closer, lowering his head to meet mine. His touch is careful, as if I am fragile and precious. And then his lips are on mine, firm and warm and impossibly soft.

A fierce heat rises up inside me, as sharp and bright as a blade. I move my lips against his, wanting more, but more of what, I cannot say. He steps closer, until our bodies touch, then his other hand comes up, the warm fingers grasping my waist, pulling me even closer still. I am lost in his kiss, and all my defenses give way before this hot, hungry mystery that lies between us.

And then he pulls away, slowly, as if loath to do so. That is when I hear the rap at the door. I blink, reality crashing in around me. I take three giant steps back until I reach the cold stone wall, my lips still tingling from Duval's kiss.

"Coming!" Duval calls out, his voice somewhat hoarse. Like a drawbridge being pulled up and slammed into place, he composes himself, and the sure, practical Duval is back. He takes his eyes from me and goes to answer the door. I lean against the wall and try to pretend my entire world has not just tilted in the heavens.

He stands there talking with whoever it is, blocking the view into the room with his body. After a moment he closes the door and returns to where I stand. I cannot meet his gaze.

"That was Beast," he says. "He found the bodies and removed them. As best as he can tell, they were simply two of Nemours's guards, one of whom was responsible for the treachery."

I nod but do not trust my voice just yet, so I say nothing. He is silent for a long moment. I risk glancing at him. He stares sightlessly at the bloodied chemise on his bed, his hand raking through his hair as he thinks.

I clear my throat. "My lord, what would you have me do?"

He pulls himself from his distant thoughts and returns them to our predicament.

"Can we patch my clothing together enough so that I can return to your residence? Perhaps with a cloak thrown over it?"

He glances ruefully at the ruined linen. "I do not think so. But maybe they have begun to move your trunks into the palace. I'll check. Sit, before you fall down," he orders.

I lock my knees and press my back against the wall, welcoming the bracing cold of it. "But the servants..." I protest.

"Even though I am a bastard born, I am also the son of a duke. It is not my servants' place to question me or what I ask of them."

Stung by this rebuke, I simply nod and wave him away. Once he has left the room, I do indeed sit down, although not on the bed. I perch on one of the unopened trunks.

I should do something. Search through his things, or try to escape to my own room, or... in truth, my wits have left me, for I cannot think what I ought to do. My back is burning and my heart still races. In the end, I decide to remain seated and try to compose myself. Surely recovering my wits is the highest priority.

Duval returns a short while later, a look of triumph on his face. He carries a wad of clothing in one arm – my clothing, I realize. "One of your trunks has been delivered," he says. "Let's get you dressed, then I must go follow up on Nemours's guards and inform the duchess of this latest development."

"Surely you do not intend to help me dress, my lord?"

He shrugs. "Neither Agnez nor Louyse is here just now. What do you suggest? Who would we risk giving explanations to?"

"I can do it myself." Even as I mutter the words, I know I cannot.

In the end, I have no choice but to let him assist me. The most awkward task is getting into a clean chemise without fully exposing myself to him. I finally order him to lay it on the bed and then turn and face the far corner of the room. Even though he cannot see me, I move quickly, not caring if I rip the stitches he has so carefully made. I let go of my bodice, which falls to the floor, step around it, slip my good arm into my chemise, then slither in the rest of the way, grimacing as I wriggle my bad shoulder to get my arm through the sleeve. "Very well," I say when it is securely in place.

"Here." His voice and manner are matter-of-fact as he holds out my bodice much as a squire holds out a chest plate. I thrust my arms in, then turn round so he can lace up the back. Next I untie my skirt, let it fall to the ground, and step out of it. He takes the new skirt he has brought, shakes it out, then holds it open for me to step into.

With the bulk of my clothing in place, we become less awkward, and our movements cease fighting each other. The rest of the task goes smoothly until he pulls my last sleeve up my arm and his knuckles brush against my breast. I wrench away at the unexpected touch, tearing the sleeve from his fingers. He sets his teeth, takes up the sleeve again, and ties it in place.

When he is done, he gives a short, formal bow. "I will leave you to compose yourself." While I am pained by his formality, I also welcome it. "Meet me in my study when you are ready."

I nod – for I still do not trust my voice – and he departs.

I am blessedly alone. Even though I am fully dressed, my skin feels raw and exposed. Tender, like the new skin under a blister that has ruptured. Even as a giggle threatens to climb up my throat, tears form in my eyes. What madness is this? Something has changed – something dark and alarming now sits between us.

When I am finally calm enough, I leave Duval's private chamber and go in search of his study. It is not difficult to find as he has been given only a handful of rooms here at the palace. I pause in the doorway. He sits brooding in front of his chess set. "Milord?" I say softly.

His head comes up and his face relaxes somewhat. "There you are."

I blush and try to pretend it has not taken me the better part of an hour to find my composure. Ill at ease, I pluck at the silver threads embroidered on my skirt as I move to join him at the chessboard. "Where do we stand?" I am anxious to discuss strategies and tactics, troop levels – anything but what has just happened between us.

"That's what I am trying to discern."

The white queen sits with but a handful of white pieces around her as she faces a board full of black. "Someone on the council bribed Nemours's guard or told someone else who did." Duval's fingers rest lightly atop the queen. I shiver, remembering the feel of those fingers on my cheek, the weight of his hand on my neck. They are strong, capable fingers, and yet he held my face so gently. Irritated, I shake off this pall that has fallen over me. "Madame Dinan could easily have confided in d'Albret," I point out.

"True enough, but they are our known enemies. It is the ones we do not know who concern me more. Has France bought someone on the Privy Council, and if so, who?"

"Why would anyone on the council want the French to know?"

"That is the question, is it not? That and what their next move will be."

"What is *our* next move?" I ask. "What is the duchess's second best option, now that Nemours has been removed?"

Duval answers without hesitation. "The Holy Roman emperor."

"Then perhaps a visit with his envoy is in order," I suggest.

"Clearly." Duval thinks for a moment longer. When he lifts his eyes from the board, I see how tired he is. "Beast needs help with the clean-up. I took the liberty of ordering a supper tray to be brought to your room so you wouldn't have to dine in the great hall with the others tonight."

"That is most welcome, my lord."

He gives a brisk nod. "Do you need anything before I go?"

I want you to return my wits, I long to say. Instead, I merely ask if I may use his desk and quills to write to the abbess of the most recent events.

"But of course," he says, then takes his leave.

Once he is gone from the room I can breathe again. In an effort to prove he has no hold over me, I make a cursory search of his chambers, but I find nothing of interest. No secret correspondence, no hidden weapon, nothing to indicate he is anything other than what he claims to be: Anne's devoted half brother.

When that is done, with a heavy heart, I turn to the letter I must write. There is much I need to tell the abbess, but there is much more I long to ask. Does she have any counsel to give as to who would have assassinated Nemours? Has

Duval's name been cleared of suspicion yet? May I work with him on our duchess's behalf? And what of love? Is loving someone a sin against our god? Surely not, for according to de Lornay, there was love of a sort between him and someone from the convent.

Or perhaps that was merely lust. I suspect the convent does not mind if we take lovers, for the nuns have spent much time training us in that art and no doubt wish us to practice. But to fall in love? That, I fear, is a grave offense. One heart cannot serve two masters.

Of course, I put none of that in my letter. Instead, I explain all that has happened over the last few days: d'Albret's announcement that he would force Anne to fulfill her betrothal promise and the Duke of Nemours's stepping forward with a new offer. Sadly, I must also inform her of Nemours's subsequent murder and of Mortain's guiding me to the guard who betrayed him. By the time I am done with it, the letter is weighty and full of grim tidings.

After I finish that letter, and with no pressing duties to attend to, I take the time to write to Annith. The quill flies across the parchment, the questions and concerns pouring out of me. I ask her if she knows of the misericorde and the grace it bestows upon Mortain's victims. I tell her of the small, green shoot of love that sprang up between the duchess and Nemours, and how cruelly it was struck down. Last, I ask her if she knows if any of the initiates had a special lover outside the convent.

When I am done writing, I am nearly limp with the effort.

I fold and seal both letters, then return to my room to wait for Vanth to be brought along with the rest of my things.

The remaining afternoon and evening drags by and I spend it torn between wanting and not wanting. I do not want Duval to come to my room tonight; I am drained and weary and more confused than I have ever been. And yet...and yet I fear that he will not. The truth is, I can no longer imagine my nights without him.

I need not have worried, however, for Duval is as steady and constant as the tides. He even comes early so he can see how I and my wound are faring.

"You're not asleep," he says, slipping in silently through the door.

"No." I start to sit, then wince.

"Do not get up," he says sharply, and hurries to the side of the bed.

The fire has been built up in my room to keep me warm, and I can see him clearly in the faint orange light from the flames. The stubble on his face is heavy, and I long to touch it, to see what it feels like. I quickly busy my fingers with the rich silk of my coverlet instead.

"Do you need anything? For the pain? To help you sleep?"

"No, milord."

He is quiet for a moment, and I can feel him looking down at me. "I should check your wound to be sure it isn't festering."

That shocks me enough to look up at his face. "No! I could tell if it were. I am sure it is fine."

He smiles wryly. "I suspected you would say that." He reaches toward me and I freeze. A lone finger touches my cheek, as soft as a snowflake falling. "I do not think it wise for me to linger." His voice is full of longing and regret. "Not tonight," he says, then he takes his leave.

Sleep is a long time coming.

Chapter 33

In the morning, Duval and most of the other nobles and courtiers are off on another hunt. Even though it is Advent, and fasting is required for three days each week, the castle supplies are quickly being depleted. The nobles are ill-tempered and tense, and it is hoped a hunt will release some of their pent-up humors as well as fill the larder.

I have been assigned to attend to the duchess in her solar. I am loath to spend the day under Madame Dinan's critical eye, but I am not good for much else. I had thought to skulk about the palace, spying on those I could until Duval pointed out that nearly everyone would be on the hunt.

The duchess sits in the cold winter sunshine spilling in the solar's windows. Her sister, Isabeau, lies on a couch that has been placed beside her. The rest of her ladies-in-waiting are perched about the room. The mood is somber, and the duchess is pale and drawn. Only Madame Dinan seems to be in cheerful spirits.

I look at her anew. Could she have ordered Nemours's death? Is she that committed to placing her half brother d'Albret on the Breton throne?

Young Isabeau sees me first. She waves shyly, and the duchess's head turns to follow the movement. "Come in,

Demoiselle Rienne!" the duchess calls out in her high, musical voice. I curtsy quickly, then enter the solar. The younger ladies stare at me in open curiosity, while Madame Dinan's eyes glitter with challenge. "What brings you here, demoiselle?" Madame Dinan's voice is distant and cool, meant to send me scurrying for cover.

I grip my sewing basket tightly and raise my chin. "I am here at my duchess's command," I tell her.

Madame turns her head to the duchess and raises one elegant eyebrow in question.

"I invited her to join us." The duchess's impatience makes me think all is not well between her and her governess.

"Your Grace." Madame Dinan lowers her voice, pretending she does not want me to hear. "I know that she is a special friend of your brother's, but it is inappropriate for someone in your position to include her in your pastimes. You have your rank to consider. Besides, have you not enough friends here to keep you company?" Her graceful hands gesture to include the other ladies, and I find myself wondering just how many of them are beholden to Madame Dinan in some way. Perhaps even loyal to her outright.

The duchess keeps stitching and ignores her governess, not deigning to address her protests. As the long silence draws out, one of the ladies-in-waiting clears her throat nervously. "Did they ever learn who the man was that fell to his death?" she asks the room at large. "They say he was quite handsome."

What little color remains in the duchess's face drains away, and she concentrates carefully on her stitching. Madame

Dinan clucks her tongue. "No such morbid talk today, ladies. What do you wish for them to bring back from the hunt? Venison or boar?"

As the ladies turn to discussion of the hunt, I take a seat next to young Isabeau.

She smiles, and I smile back. She is pale and wan and it seems to me as if her life spark burns but dimly. I rifle in my basket and retrieve the altar cloth I worked on last time. I pick up the needle threaded with blood-red silk and vow to try harder this time. I intend to be capable of stitching any wound of mine I can reach. I grunt and stick the needle into the linen.

The ladies talk of the upcoming Advent festivities and discuss the court poet's latest romantic verse. I ignore their voices and focus on my embroidery, pleased to see my stitches are growing neat and even.

After they have thoroughly discussed every aspect of the upcoming holiday merriment, Madame Dinan speaks with a casual, artful slyness that raises the hairs on the back of my neck. "Your Grace, my lord d'Albret did not ride out with the hunt this morning. He thought this afternoon would be a good time for the two of you to discuss some things. Alone," she says, glancing at the rest of us.

Remembering how she squawked when Duval requested similar privacy, I cannot help but poke at her hypocrisy. "Alone?" I put one hand to my lips, as if scandalized. "You would leave her alone with him, madame?"

"No, you fool," Madame Dinan all but hisses. "I would remain here as chaperone."

"It does not matter," the duchess says primly, "because I will not see him."

"But, Your Grace, you owe it to him to let him plead his ca—"

"He has done so," Anne says sharply. "Before all the barons of Brittany, if you remember. I refused him then and I refuse him now."

Madame Dinan stops sewing and leans forward. "You must marry someone. He is half Breton and has the troops you need."

"He is also old and fat and crude. He has seven children and is a grandfather!"

Madame Dinan's nostrils flare in annoyance. "Your marriage must strengthen the duchy."

The duchess keeps her eyes on her embroidery, but she is stitching blindly. "While I know that I must marry for duty, I do not think I must bear *him*."

Beside me, Isabeau begins to wheeze slightly. She has grown even paler, and her eyes are fastened on the two women arguing. I quickly stitch a small frowning face on my linen square. I nudge her with my elbow and she looks up at me, then down at my embroidery. The silly face – or perhaps it is my poor stitching – manages to coax a smile from her lips.

Madame Dinan leans farther forward, her eyes burning with intensity. "You have a duty – *a duty* – to your country and Count d'Albret to honor the agreement your father made."

The spell of my trick with Isabeau is broken, and the child begins to cough. With a cluck of frustration, Madame Dinan throws her embroidery down. "Fetch the court physicians," she says.

Isabeau shrinks back onto her couch. "No, please, no," she whispers. "I'll stop coughing."

Madame hurries over and smooth the child's brow. "It is not a punishment, child. They merely want to make you well."

"But I hate the leeches," she whimpers. "See?" she says, her face brightening. "I stopped now. I don't need to see the doctors."

Anne leans close and brushes a few strands of hair from her sister's face. "She is not feverish," she tells Madame Dinan.

The governess pinches her lips. "Very well, but if it happens again, she will need to see them."

Dinan returns to her chair, and the rest of us stitch silently, none of us wanting to be the one that sends poor Isabeau into another coughing frenzy that brings the court physicians down upon her.

It stays quiet for so long that the little girl dozes off. Anne smiles in relief, and her shoulders lose some of their tension.

Madame Dinan rises to her feet. "If you will excuse me, Your Grace, I have something I must see to." She speaks softly so as not to waken Isabeau.

Anne nods her permission for the governess to leave. As Dinan slips out of the room, I look at the duchess and raise my brows in question.

One corner of her mouth quirks up. "Did you see your saint's marque upon her?" she asks so quietly that it takes me a moment to be certain I have heard.

I blink in surprise. "No, Your Grace."

"Pity," she murmurs, then nods her head, indicating I should follow Dinan. I drop a quick curtsy, then hurry after the governess.

I am careful to stay well behind the older woman. With her headstart, it is not difficult. The lack of courtiers also works to my advantage, for with so few others about, her footsteps echo, making them easy to follow even when she slips out of sight.

At the east tower of the palace, she pauses to look behind her, and I quickly duck back around the corner. I hear her rap on a door. A man's voice greets her, and then her voice fades as she moves into a room. I poke my head round the corner just in time to see which door shuts.

Giving thanks once again for the deserted hallways, I hurry to the door and lean in close.

"What do you mean she refuses to see me?" It is the rough, coarse voice of d'Albret.

"She is but a young, foolish girl, my lord. Do not take it too much to heart."

"I thought you and Marshal Rieux were her appointed guardians. How much influence do you hold if she sees fit to ignore your counsel?"

"It is that brother of hers. I believe he encourages her stubbornness."

"Do you need me to take care of him?" The casual way in which d'Albret asks this sends a chill up my spine.

"No, no. Do not worry. At the next council meeting, I will make it plain she has no other choice."

"Well, do it before the French eat up the entire countryside, will you? I grow bored waiting for this spoiled child to agree to do what she has already promised. If she is old enough to rule a country, certainly she is old enough to marry." There is a moment of silence, then d'Albret speaks again. "And what of Rieux? Is he still in favor of the match?"

"Absolutely, my lord. He believes joining your forces with Anne's is the only way to keep the duchy safe from the French. When it is time to act, Rieux will support us. You can be certain of it."

D'Albret's voice drops lower then, and I can no longer make out the words. Shaking with anger, I back away from the door and hurry down the hallway.

It is worse than I feared. Madame Dinan does not simply wish Anne to marry d'Albret but has fully committed herself to his cause. Indeed, she has promised him that he shall marry the duchess. And what can she possibly say at the council meeting that will prove Anne has no choice? I am so deep in thought on my way back from the east tower to the solar that I almost stumble upon Sybella before I see her.

She is thinner than before, more drawn and pale. Her features are sharper, as if she has grown even more brittle and fragile since I saw her enter the city gates. She has a fresh scar upon her cheek, and I am certain I can see madness lurking in her eyes. It is hard to believe she is the same person who coaxed Annith and me into all sorts of mischief at the convent, from stealing jugs of wine to teaching us how to kiss when Sister Beatriz said too little on the subject.

"Ismae?" she whispers as if she has seen a ghost.

"Sybella!" Suddenly, I am afraid for her, although I cannot say why. Without thinking I throw my arms around her, hugging her close, whether for her comfort or my own, I cannot be certain.

For a brief moment, she relaxes into me, returns the embrace as if drawing strength from it, but then, too soon, she pulls back, her eyes unnaturally bright. A thousand questions crowd my mind, and nearly as many worries, but before I can voice a single one of them, we hear the echo of boots upon stone. Sybella looks frantically toward the sound, true fear flaring in her eyes. "Trust no one," she finally whispers. "No one."

And then she is gone, her light, hurried steps carrying her out of sight just before Chancellor Crunard rounds the corner.

"My lord chancellor!" I say with a curtsy.

He frowns for a moment, as if he can't quite place me. "Demoiselle Rienne," he says at last. He glances at the empty corridor. "What are you doing in this part of the castle?"

I debate how much to tell him. "My convent's business, my lord."

"Indeed? My correspondence with your abbess did not indicate you were to take any action against Count d'Albret."

I blink, wondering how deep in the abbess's confidence he is. And how he knows that I am spying on d'Albret. "I am not only to act, my lord, but to be the convent's eyes and ears as well."

He purses his lips. "True enough. Have your eyes and ears given you any answers in the Nemours debacle?"

"What do you mean, my lord?"

The chancellor spreads his hands, rings glittering. "I mean, Duval handled this Nemours matter most poorly. The Duke of Nemours is dead, is he not? Furthermore, I have just heard a most disturbing rumor." He leans in close, his breath stale against my cheek. "His mother is plotting even now to put his brother on the throne in Anne's stead. Could there be any connection?" He cocks his head like a bird and studies me with a piercing eye. "And how is it that you have been here nearly a fortnight and have not learned of this?"

My heart begins to beat painfully. He knows! "I have only just discovered this myself, my lord, but I've heard rumblings only. I have been trying to ascertain Duval's involvement, but he and his mother are most estranged. I do not believe she speaks to him of her plans. Indeed, they barely speak at all."

Crunard's eyes glitter coldly. "That you know of. What if the estrangement is feigned? Perhaps Duval is only waiting for Hivern to line up enough barons behind François, and then he will make his move, displacing his brother and claiming the throne for himself."

"Why would you think that, my lord?"

"Why would I not? What possible evidence do you have that he is trustworthy?"

None, except my own heart, and that is not nearly enough.

"Someone close to the duchess is working for the French. It could very well be Duval. Do not let your youth and naïveté cloud your vision, demoiselle."

"I assure you, my vision is clear, my lord."

"Good. See that it remains so. Be vigilant, demoiselle. Do not let his charm or good manners sway you to his cause. The abbess would not be pleased to hear of it." And with that final warning, he takes his leave.

That night, when I get in bed, I do not lie down but instead lean back against the bolster and wait for Duval. Once again, I cannot be certain of my own desires. I do not care for this new awkwardness that has sprung up between us, even as I know I should use it to my advantage and sever the fragile ties we are beginning to form. This seems especially prudent, given Crunard's warning earlier today. My wanting to trust Duval does not make him trustworthy.

And yet I feel in my heart that he is.

I try to be honest with myself, to remember when I first started trusting him. Was it before I began to have feelings for him? Or after?

It is clear the chancellor wants me to keep Duval under suspicion, which in and of itself makes me hesitate. I have no good reason for my reluctance and would be hard-pressed to justify this to the reverend mother. The truth is, while I take great pride in serving Mortain and the convent, I do not wish to be a political pawn of the chancellor's.

The faint snick of the door pulls my thoughts away from the chancellor, and my pulse quickens as Duval slips into the room. "Ismae," he says, then closes the door behind him. Instead of going to his customary chair, he makes his way toward me. Twin bolts of panic and anticipation shoot through me. Does he think to kiss me again? Pursue something more than a kiss? I hardly dare to breathe, waiting to see his intent.

When he reaches the bed, he looks down at me, his soft expression stealing the breath from my lungs. "How are you feeling?"

"Fine." The word comes out in a whisper. I clear my throat. "The stitches hardly pull."

"Excellent." He gives a crisp nod, and I wonder if he will ask again to see how the wound is healing, but he does not. Instead, he lowers himself onto the small, thick rug on the floor and leans back against the bed. My whole body stills, and my heart beats even faster. His head is so close that I could reach out and touch his hair. What would it feel like beneath my fingers? I clench my hands into fists. "How was the hunt?" I manage to ask.

He smiles then. "Fruitful. I sent the Holy Roman emperor's envoy a message late last night, suggesting it would be worth his while to attend the hunt. He did, and we were able to snatch a few moments together and arrange for a more formal meeting. This way, we evaded Gisors's spies and lackeys."

"Were none of them on the hunt?"

"I am sure they were, but since I had a few moments of private conversation with any number of men today, my discussion with the emperor's envoy will not appear overly significant."

"That is good then."

"The Privy Council has called another meeting tomorrow. Isabeau has requested you attend on her while Anne and Madame Dinan are in the meeting."

I study him with narrowed eyes. "Did you put her up to this as a means of having me close by?"

"No. Apparently she's become fond of you all on her own. It seems you grow on a person," he says dryly, then changes the subject. "And you? What did you learn today?"

"Nothing good, I'm afraid. Madame Dinan met with d'Albret and spent most of the meeting assuring him that Marshal Rieux would support him when the moment was ripe."

He sighs. "I fear his duties as marshal are overshadowing his duties as Anne's guardian. All he can see is d'Albret's military might."

"I also ran into the chancellor today. He was most aggrieved with me for wasting my time on d'Albret. He wanted me instead to focus on your mother and brother."

"And me," he says.

"And you," I agree.

"Did you tell him we decided to work together in this?"

"No, I did not. It did not seem . . . wise. Although I cannot say why I think so."

"Your instinct is good. Better we keep our own counsel till we sort out this mess." He begins to rub his forehead and I am filled with a desire to run my hands through his hair and soothe the pain from his brow. Instead, I tuck them safely beneath the coverlet, away from such temptations.

When he speaks again, there is a hint of amusement in his voice. "You cannot will it away, you know. Pretend it never happened."

I open my mouth to ask what he means, to indeed pretend it never happened. Instead, I surprise myself by saying, "But I do not know what else to do with it." My voice sounds small and lost, and I am grateful for the darkness of the room.

"It is not convenient for me, either." His voice is dry and he addresses his words to the fireplace.

"I imagine not," I concede.

"However, it appears we have both been pricked by St. Arduinna's arrow."

St. Arduinna, the patron saint of love. Is that what he thinks is between us? And is the fluttering in my belly panic or joy? I cannot help but think uneasily of the false offering I made to her a few short days ago at St. Lyphard.

"We are both bound by other duties, other saints," I remind him. "Our hearts are not ours to give."

He turns his head to look at me then. "Is that what they teach you at the convent? That the gods demand the hearts from our bodies?"

"I fear it is what my convent expects," I tell him. "They

may train us in the arts of love, but in their minds our hearts belong firmly to Mortain."

"I disagree with your convent," he says. "Why give us hearts at all then?"

Slowly, as if afraid I will bolt, he reaches for my hand, which has somehow escaped from the covers. When he laces his fingers through mine, my heart does its now-familiar panicked flight, bumping painfully against my ribs. My shoulder twitches as if to pull my hand back, but my heart overrules it.

His hand is warm, the skin firm. We sit together in silence. I do not know what is going through his head, but my own mind is unable to form a single thought. At least, not a coherent one. After a long while, he squeezes my hand, then leans down to kiss the back of it. His lips are warm and soft and I am filled with the memory of them on my mouth, my throat. Slowly, as if with great reluctance, he pulls away, and I shiver. "Perhaps," he says. "When this is all over."

"Perhaps, my lord."

He gives my hand another squeeze, then rises gracefully to his feet. "Until tomorrow," he says, then leaves. I am alone in the darkness.

Knowing I have done exactly what the convent would want brings me little comfort.

Chapter 34

When I arrive at the duchess's solar the next morning, one of the older ladies-in-waiting ushers me into Isabeau's smaller chamber. The young princess is in bed, sitting up against the pillows, clutching a doll in one hand. A cup of warm, honeyed milk sits nearby. Her cheeks have two bright spots of pink, and her dark eyes are glassy with fever. "Hello, demoiselle," she says shyly.

"Hello, my lady." I curtsy, then draw close to her. "My lord Duval said I should sit with you while the others are in their meeting." The assignment is a good one for me, for although my shoulder is healing, it is not yet fully recovered.

"Yes, please, demoiselle."

I sit on the stool by her bed and try to think of something to say. "Are you looking forward to Christmas?" I ask, then want to bite my tongue. It will be her first Christmas without her father.

"My sister says we are to have a feast and a mummers' parade." Her face glows with excitement.

"Truly?"

She nods. "Will you be there?"

"If the duchess wishes it, yes."

"I am sure she will. She likes you quite a lot." She is

overcome by a fit of coughing just then, and her small, thin shoulders heave with the effort. When she is done, there is a faint sheen of sweat on her brow. "Do not call the physicians," she pleads.

"No, no. I will not," I say, smoothing her hair back. There is little the court physicians can do for her. Little anyone can do for her, her life spark flickers so weakly. "In fact, I have brought you medicine of my own, from the convent where I was raised. It is very good at settling coughs, although it might make you sleepy."

"I will gladly suffer sleepiness if it means no physicians, demoiselle."

"Very well." I pull the small vial of Mortain's caress from my pocket. It is a poison, true, but Sister Serafina used it on the younger girls when they were sick. It is good for coughs and lung fever, for it allows the patient to rest and get much needed sleep, but only if it is given in small doses. I carefully measure two drops – no more – into her milk, then swirl the cup to stir it all around. "Here." I hand her the cup. "Drink it all down now."

She takes the cup from me and does as she is told, draining the last drop from it. She hands it back to me. "It does not taste bad. Just a little sweeter."

"That is because I do not believe in foul-tasting medicine," I say. She smiles, which pleases me more than it should. The muffled voices coming from the other side of the thick wall call to me. I would dearly love to hear what they are discussing, judge the inflections and timbres of their voices.

But as I look into Isabeau's shadowed eyes, I find I cannot leave her to struggle for breath on her own.

"Do you know any stories?" she asks as I settle myself on the stool once more.

I hate to disappoint her, but I have no stories. No one told them at my house when I was growing up, and the stories told at the convent are not meant for such young, innocent ears. Just as I start to shake my head, I remember one tale. One of Annith's favorites. Perhaps Isabeau will find some comfort in it. "Have you heard the story of how St. Amourna captured St. Mortain's heart?"

Isabeau's eyes widen. "The patron saint of death?" she whispers.

"It is not a frightening story, I promise you, but one of true love."

"Oh." Her face relaxes. "Very well, then. I would like to hear it, please."

"One fine moonlit night, Mortain and his wild hunt were riding through the countryside when they spied two maids more beautiful than any they had ever seen before. They were picking evening primrose, which only blooms in the moonlight.

"The two maids turned out to be Amourna and Arduinna, twin daughters of Dea Matrona. When Mortain saw the fair Amourna, he fell instantly in love, for she was not only beautiful but light of heart as well, and surely the god of death needs lightness in his world.

"But the two sisters could not be more different. Amourna

was happy and giving, but her sister, Arduinna, was fierce, jealous, and suspicious, for such is the dual nature of love. Arduinna had a ferocious and protective nature and did not care for the way Mortain was looking at her beloved sister. To warn him, she drew her bow and let fly with one of her silver arrows. She never misses, and she didn't miss then. The arrow pierced Mortain's heart, but no one, not even a goddess, can kill the god of death.

"Mortain plucked the arrow from his chest and bowed to Arduinna. 'Thank you,' he said. 'For reminding me that love never comes without cost.'

"Such gallantry surprised Arduinna, and, in the end, she let her sister ride with the god of death to his home, but only after Amourna promised she would come back and visit her twin at least once a year."

"Wasn't she scared?" Isabeau asked, her voice naught but a whisper. "To go with death?"

"No." I reach over and tuck her hair behind her ear. "For death is not scary or evil or even unmerciful; it is simply death. Besides, His realm has much beauty of its own. There is no hunger, or cold, or pain. Or nasty leeches." This last makes Isabeau smile.

"Is she happy there, do you think?"

"She is." I do not tell Isabeau the rest of the story, of how Arduinna grew so jealous that she vowed that from then on, love would always bring pain. Or of how in the sorrow of missing her daughter, Dea Matrona brought bitter winter to our land.

By the story's end, the medicine has begun to work, and the young girl's eyes drift closed. Her chest rises and falls easily, and her breath is no longer labored. Perhaps I fool myself, but she looks more at peace. If I trusted Madame Dinan at all, I would leave some of the medicine with her, but I do not. If only I had coltsfoot or hyssop. Even comfrey or balm would help, but all I have is poison, and I am loath to give it to the girl's governess.

In the quiet of the room, I hear the muffled sound of raised voices in the next chamber cease suddenly, and then the sound of a door being thrown open. I rise quietly and go to the solar, shutting the door to Isabeau's room behind me.

Anne strides into her antechamber, face white. Duval storms in behind her. "How dare she?" he explodes.

At his display of temper, I hurry forward, putting my finger to my lips. "Isabeau has finally fallen asleep," I say. "We do not want to wake her."

That checks Duval's outburst somewhat, but I can still see his pulse beating, furious and erratic, in the hollow of his throat.

"I cannot believe she has done this." The note of heart-break in Anne's voice is harder to bear than Duval's anger. "She is supposed to serve *my* interests, not her own."

A look of pain crosses Duval's face, as if he is saddened that she has had to learn this unpleasant lesson so young. "Your Grace has enough experience with the Breton court to know just how little truth there is in that notion."

"But she was my governess," Anne says. "I was her charge.

Not the treasury or the armies or the royal household."

"For the love of Mortain, will someone please tell me what has happened?" I ask.

Duval whips his head round and spears me with his intent gaze. "Have you received no orders from the convent?" he asks.

"No! Why?"

"Perhaps your crow is not working properly," he mutters.

I dismiss his jab at the convent and turn to the duchess. "What has happened?"

"My governess, Madame Dinan, has plucked from her sleeve a betrothal agreement between my father and Count d'Albret. One that, apparently, I signed."

This is well and truly disastrous. I glance quickly at Duval and he gives a nod of confirmation. So far all the betrothal agreements have been verbal, giving them all equal weight in the eyes of the law. But if there is a signed agreement with d'Albret, that may very well be more legally binding. The duchess might have no choice but to marry the brute. "Did you get a chance to speak to them of your plans with the Holy Roman emperor?"

Duval and the duchess exchange a look, one I do not care for at all. "They would not hear of it," he says. He lifts his finger and wags it at me. "'Not so fast,' they said. 'You were wrong about the English sending aid and you gave us false hope with Nemours. We shall make the decisions now and you shall merely carry them out.'"

"It is worse even than that," the duchess says, following

Duval's pacing with worried eyes. "They flayed Gavriel with their lying, twisted tongues, and blamed him for Nemours's death."

"What?"

Duval drops his head and rubs his eyes with the heels of his hands. "They said it was my fault for having kept Nemours a secret, for not having assigned a larger body of guards to him."

"Did you point out that Nemours was perfectly safe until they learned of his existence?"

"Oh, yes, and you can imagine how well that went over. Marshal Rieux nearly flew across the table to strike me, and would have if Crunard had not held him back."

We are all silent as we consider the full magnitude of this disaster. When the duchess finally speaks, her voice is laced with desperation. "Surely there is something we can do."

"Oh, there is much we can do," Duval says grimly. "But each action will have a cost. We can begin negotiating with the Holy Roman emperor now, the Privy Council be damned, but it will turn them more firmly against me. We can send a letter to the ecclesiastical council pointing out that the agreement was made without your consent and you had no idea what you were signing."

Anne halts her pacing and whirls round to face Duval, determination writ plainly on her face. "Yes!" she says. "Yes to both of those things."

"The rest of the Privy Council will not be pleased. They already think that you and I collude too much and that I am overstepping my station. They may follow through on their threat to bar me from your meetings."

The duchess lifts her chin. "Then I will consult with you in private."

Duval hides a smile. "Very well. I will arrange a preliminary meeting with the Holy Roman emperor's envoy tomorrow, and if you will show me where you keep quill and ink, we shall draft your letter to the ecclesiastical council. D'Albret shall not have you. Not while I still draw breath."

A chill scuttles across my shoulders just then, and I wish Duval had not made such a vow. It is never wise to taunt the gods.

Chapter 35

I am scheduled to attend the duchess this morning, but when I arrive at the solar, Madame Dinan will not let me in. She informs me that Isabeau took a turn for the worse during the night, and Anne is with her. Her refusal to allow me access is sharp and pointed and intended to make clear to me that I am not welcome. Ever.

The old familiar shame nearly chokes me as I return to my chamber. Duval is off meeting with the envoy, so I cannot vent my anger and frustration to him. Instead, I spend the morning tending to my weapons: oiling and sharpening the blades, replacing the poisoned pearls on my golden hairnet, generally making ready for whatever comes. My healing shoulder itches fiercely. Perhaps that is the cause of this sense of restlessness that plagues me. I feel as if we are on a vessel moving inexorably toward some unseen destination. There is no one steering or tending the sails; only the dark tides and currents carry us to their preordained destination. It is not a pleasant feeling and there is little I can do to prepare myself.

Just as I am putting away the last of my knives, there is a knock at the door. My heart lifts. Is Isabeau feeling better then? When I open the door, a page thrusts a sealed parchment in my hand, flops a short bow, then scampers away. Puzzled, I close the door and turn the message over.

The wax seal is black, and the handwriting Sybella's. I rip it open and read the loose, looping scrawl.

Meet me where we last spoke, at noon.
S

Immediately I remember her drawn, pale face, her brittle manner. Is she in trouble? As it is nearly noon now, I grab my cloak and head for the east tower.

The church bell strikes noon just as I enter the main hall in the palace, and I quicken my steps, keeping my eyes peeled for signs of Sybella as I hurry toward the east wing.

At the top of a wide staircase, I nearly bump into Madame Dinan. "Madame," I say, dipping a curtsy and cursing my ill luck. She is in a hurry herself, however, and barely pauses to acknowledge me. "Demoiselle Rienne. The duchess asked that I fetch her embroidery," she says in passing.

I frown. She has never explained herself to me before, and I cannot fathom why she would do so now. "Very well," I say, then continue down the stairs.

She stops. "Are you on some errand for Duval?" she asks.

I decide it is as good an excuse as any. "Yes, madame," I say, and start to leave, but she speaks again.

"Where is Duval? I have not seen him all day," says this woman who has ignored me most of my time at court. That is when I realize she is trying to detain me.

Without bothering to answer, I turn and race down the

stairs, a sense of dread growing within me. I am nearly there, only one more corridor. As I turn into the last hallway, I hear a man's voice – a deep, cajoling rumble that slithers across my skin. D'Albret! Every instinct I possess comes alert. I hear another voice then, a young girl's voice. Not Sybella.

Anne.

Pulling my knives from my sleeves, I rush forward, panic pounding in my breast. When I round the final corner, I see the duchess backed against the wall and d'Albret looming over her. One of his hands is braced on the wall, trapping her. The other grabs at her skirts as she furiously tries to bat him away.

At the sight of his filthy hands on her, fury explodes in my heart, and a red mist rises up before me. I must make a sound, because d'Albret jerks his head up and swears. He snatches his hands away from Anne as if he's been burned. The duchess sags in relief against the wall, her face pale as death.

D'Albret's eyes widen at the sight of my daggers, and he holds his arms out wide, far away from his sword. "Do all Duval's mistresses walk about armed to the teeth?"

My eyes never leave his face. "Surely it does not surprise you that Duval does not cavort with simpering maids."

His tone turns cajoling. "Now, demoiselle, my betrothed and I were merely having a private moment. It is not so very unusual as all that. There is no need to overreact."

"I am not your betrothed," Anne tells him coldly. Her face is pale, but her voice is strong and steady, and I have never been more proud of her. "I have no memory of signing that agreement, and I have written to both the pope and the ecclesiastical council asking that it be nullified."

D'Albret whips his head back to Anne. Something frightening glitters in his eyes. "Be careful, little duchess, for I will not give you many more chances to spurn me."

"I will never marry you." Her voice is low and furious.

I take a step closer. "You heard Her Grace. She has given you her answer. Now move away."

With one last furious glance at Anne, d'Albret turns his attention back to me. "You are making a grave mistake."

"Am I?" I draw even closer, my eyes searching desperately for the marque of Mortain. Surely assaulting the ruler of our duchy counts as treason. But there is no marque on his forehead, nor on his neck above his fur-lined collar. Perhaps that is not where his deathblow will be. Perhaps Mortain intends for him to be gutted like a fish.

Before I have fully thought it through, I reach out and slash at him. His scarlet doublet parts like a wound, exposing his fat white gut. It is pallid and covered in coarse black hair, but there is no marque. A thin red line wells up where the tip of my knife has scored his flesh.

Disbelief and rage clouds his face, and his eyes burn with something that looks like madness. He reaches for his sword, but I bring my dagger down on his hand. "I do not think so."

His eyes narrow, and the rage in them nearly flays the skin from my bones. "You will pay dearly for this." The cold flatness of his voice is somehow more terrifying than his fury.

Footsteps sound behind us and d'Albret looks up. Fearing

some trick, I do not remove my gaze from his face, but my shoulders itch in warning.

"Madame Dinan!" Anne calls out, her voice hitching in relief.

The governess ignores Anne and hurries toward d'Albret. "What have you done, you stupid girl?" she asks me.

"I have kept our duchess safe. What have *you* done, madame?" Our eyes meet and she knows that I see just how heinous a betrayal this has been. The duchess catches the accusation in my voice and takes a step back from her governess, her features stark with disbelief.

I am unable to act against either of these two traitors, and my temper flares. "Get out." I gesture with my knives. "Both of you." I make no effort to hide the contempt I feel for them.

"But the duchess..." Madame Dinan starts to say, then trails off.

In that moment, the balance of power shifts. I have caught her in an act of rank betrayal, and she knows I can use this against her. "I will tend to the duchess. You, my lady, have lost that privilege."

Dinan's nostrils flare. She raises her chin and glares down at her charge. "If you had but listened to your advisors, Your Grace, and not acted like a stubborn child, all of this could have been avoided."

"And if you had but honored the sacred trust placed in you by the duke," I point out, "this could have been avoided." I wave my knives as if I am about to lose my patience, which in truth I am. "Go."

D'Albret pulls his tunic over his belly and holds it in place with his arm. "You have just made the biggest mistake of your short life," he says. "Both of you." He turns and storms down the hallway. With one last reproachful glance at the duchess, Dinan follows the count, fluttering nervously behind him.

When they are out of sight, I turn back to Anne. Slowly, she slides down the wall until she is sitting on the floor. A single tear escapes her bright eyes, and she swipes it away angrily with a trembling hand. Gone is the proud, brave duchess, and in her place is a young, frightened girl, using anger as best she can to shield herself from what has just happened. Not stopping to think of stations and rank, I kneel beside her on the floor and put my arms around her shoulders, hugging her to me. I have no fine or fancy words to bring her comfort, so I say the only thing I can. "You are very brave, and he will think twice before trying that again. On anyone, I hope."

Anne takes a great, shuddering, sobbing breath. "Madame Dinan said she needed to fetch a page, as she had a message to send. I thought it odd, but she has been much distracted of late, and there has been great discord between us. I never thought . . . never suspected such a . . ." Her voice falters as her throat tightens up, closing off her words.

"Come," I say gently. "We should get you back to your chambers. Can you walk, do you think?" I do not know what I will do if she says no. I cannot carry her, and I dare not leave her side to fetch help.

"I can walk," she says, her face full of steely resolve. I stand first, then help her to her feet. We slowly make our way back to her solar. We pass a few courtiers and nobles, and when we do, Anne makes an effort to straighten up and raise her head proudly; her regal bearing drives away any curious glances.

When at last we reach the solar, I am relieved to find that Madame Dinan has not returned. A handful of ladies-in-waiting are in attendance.

"Leave us," Anne orders. I have never heard her speak so sharply, and neither have her ladies, for they look startled, but they do as she demands nonetheless. "Wait!" she calls out. They stop like dogs that have reached the ends of their leashes. "Have water sent up for a bath. Hot water."

The ladies-in-waiting look among themselves. One brave soul finally speaks. "Shouldn't we stay here to assist Your Grace?"

Anne glances at me, a silent question in her eyes. I nod my assent. "No, Demoiselle Rienne will attend me. Now go."

Flustered as a flock of pigeons disturbed from their roost, they scuttle from the room. As soon as they are gone and the door firmly shut, the duchess begins ripping off her fine clothes. At first, I fear she is having a fit, until I hear her words: "I can still feel his fingers on me." Her voice catches, and I hurry over to help her.

She claws at the collar and tears at the sleeves, pulling the gown off before I have the lacings undone. The fabric rips and there are tiny pinging sounds as a dozen seed pearls fall and scatter across the floor. "Your Grace, you will destroy your dress," I murmur.

"That is the point," she whispers, staring at the tattered gown at her feet. She kicks at it. "I will not wear it again. Not ever." She is shivering in her shift, looking younger and more vulnerable than even poor Isabeau.

There is a knock at the door. I remove my cloak and wrap it around the duchess's shoulders, then admit the attendants so they may set up her bath. They politely fill the copper tub with hot water, stoke the fire, lay out fresh linen towels, then hover uncertainly.

"Leave," Anne says, her voice weary.

When they are gone, I turn my back to give her a moment of privacy to step into the bath. As a person of rank, she has always had ladies to attend to her, to scrub her back, hand her a towel, brush her hair. Except when she needed them most, I think, anger rising up again. "Would you like me to wash your hair for you, Your Grace?"

A corner of her mouth tilts in a valiant attempt at a smile. "Part of your assassin's training?"

I smile back. "No, merely something my sisters-in-arms and I used to do for one another."

Her dark brown eyes meet mine. "Today I feel as if we are sisters-in-arms, and I would be honored if you would do for me what you have done for your friends."

I bow my head low, humbled by this gesture. "But of course, Your Grace."

I retrieve the ewer and fill it with warm water from the

tub, then pour it over her long brown hair. I have never seen her without her headdress, and her hair is as rich and thick as mink. We scrub and rinse in silence; the soap she uses smells of roses.

When she speaks again, her voice is steadier. "Once I am clean and dressed, I must send for Gavriel."

"He is whom you would speak with first?" This pleases me, this trust she has in him.

She turns to look at me. "Above all others," she says, her face and eyes solemn. She turns back round, and I pour another pitcher of water on her hair to rinse the soap from it.

"When I was born, my father took Gavriel aside and explained that I was to be his first duty from then on. My happiness and my safety were his to guard."

"How old was he then?"

"Twelve or thirteen, I believe."

Not much older than she is now. "So much responsibility for one so young."

"Ah, but he welcomed it. It gave his life purpose. He now had a reason to excel at his lessons, beat his tutors in chess, practice for hours in the sword yard." Her voice changes, growing softer. "And he doted on me. He told me once that from the moment he first held me, he was besotted. I demanded no cleverness or victories of him, asked only that he love and protect me. And that he has done ever since."

"Were there so many demands on him at that age?"

"Have you not met his mother, demoiselle?"

I laugh outright at that. "Yes, I have, Your Grace."

"She has been working on schemes and plots since his birth, most involving him. Until I was born, he tolerated it. Once I was put in his charge, he would have nothing to do with her plots. Even then, his honor shone brighter than most men's. I believe she quite hates me for it."

"No doubt," I murmur, captivated by this peek at the young Duval.

"And if ever I had any doubts – which I did not, although others did – they were erased when I was five years old. Did you know I was betrothed to the English crown prince?"

"Yes, Your Grace. At the convent we study the actions of your family, as your safety and well-being is our first priority."

She looks around and dimples prettily at this. "Truly?"

"Truly."

"No wonder that you and Gavriel are so well suited," she says, turning away again so I can continue rinsing her hair. I frown at this, but before I can protest, she is speaking again and I am loath to interrupt her.

"Anyway, the betrothal enraged the old French king, who had spent years fighting the English and had no wish to see Brittany come under English rule. So he hatched a plot to send his agents into Nantes and abduct me so that I might become his pawn rather than such a liability.

"We received news of this even as they entered the city. As my father's advisors stood around arguing about what action to take and how best to respond, Gavriel grew impatient, fearing the French would knock down our door any moment. Instead of listening to their arguments, he came to our nursery and roused Isabeau and me from our beds. He tucked one of us under each arm and, accompanied by his staunch companion de Lornay, spirited us away to safety. Even as he galloped out of the stables, the French plotters broke into the nursery. I will never forget the terror of that night, the feeling that my whole world had been turned upside down. Nor will I ever forget the safety of Gavriel's arms as he carried us out of harm's way."

I stare at the back of her head, my mouth open in surprise. And yet, some small part of me is not surprised. It all fits with the Duval that I see, if not the one seen by Crunard and the abbess.

The duchess shakes her head. "I still do not know how he managed two young girls on that horse of his." She turns round to look into my face. "How could I not trust such a man as that, Demoiselle Rienne?"

"Indeed, how could one not?" I whisper.

"I know some call him oathbreaker, for although the oath he swore to Saint Camulos required him to stand and fight, he turned his back on the fighting and instead carried me to safety. But, as he explained to me later, what good is fighting if what you are fighting for is lost?"

"True enough, Your Grace." Then we both fall silent, consumed by our own thoughts, while she finishes her bath. My heart feels lighter now that I know the circumstances behind Duval's oathbreaking. From what I am learning of my own god, it seems just the sort of thorny trial they love to torment us with.

When all the traces of d'Albret have been scrubbed from her skin and she is dressed and warm and calm, we send a page to find Duval.

He arrives shortly after, tugging off his riding gloves and looking slightly mussed, as if the wind is blowing mightily outside. His gaze darts from her to me, then back again. "What has happened?"

The duchess grips her hands together tightly. "There has been an incident," she says, then falters and looks to me for help.

"D'Albret assaulted her in the hallway."

Duval grows impossibly still and I am reminded of a viper before it strikes. "What do you mean, *assaulted*?" His voice is deceptively quiet.

"I mean, he backed her up against the wall and fumbled at her skirts." Anger at the memory makes the words come out harsher than I intend.

Duval's face grows pale.

"Mumbling all the while about how I would like it if I would only give it a chance," the duchess adds.

I look at her in horror. "I did not know that."

"You were too far away to hear."

Duval's entire body is as taut as a drawn bowstring. Rage fills his eyes, but he tries to tamp it down for his sister's sake, as concern wars with fury. "Are you all right?"

"I am fine. Ismae arrived in time."

He turns then and bows low to me, which shocks me to the core. "Our debt to you is immeasurable," he says. When he rises, his face is calm and still. "We will kill him," he announces, then looks at me thoughtfully. "Unless you already have?"

"Alas, no, milord. He ceased his attack when I approached, and he did not bear the marque."

"Saints take the marque! Look harder." He begins to pace.

A faint glimmer of amusement touches the duchess's features. "She fair gutted him looking for it," she says.

At her words, I feel sheepish. "I admit I did not stop to give thought to maintaining the deception we had in place."

"Good," Duval says. "Perhaps others will think twice before trying something similar."

I clear my throat. "There is more."

Duval stops pacing and stares at me. "More?" Even the duchess looks at me curiously.

"Madame Dinan set the duchess up. She made an excuse to leave her alone in the hallway when she knew d'Albret would be there."

"How do you know this?"

"I met her on the stairs. I was heading toward the duchess and she was moving away. She tried to detain me."

Duval explodes. "That traitorous sow!"

The duchess looks uneasy at this rare display of temper from Duval. I try to say something to turn the conversation to strategy rather than anger, though Mortain knows I have plenty of that as well. "We knew she favored her half brother, but I never guessed she would go this far in pursuit of his claim."

"None of us did," Duval says. "We must ban him from court. Her too."

The duchess promptly agrees, but this plan worries me. "Excuse me, Your Grace, but I think we must tread carefully here."

Duval's head snaps up. "What do you mean?"

"We cannot risk word getting out that the duchess was assaulted. In this world of ours, it matters not what actually transpired. The mere suggestion that she was exposed to such a situation could be enough to bring her virtue into question. What would that do to her chances of marriage?"

All the blood drains from the duchess's face, and Duval swears a black oath and resumes pacing.

"I will not marry the baron, no matter if he is the last man in Christendom!"

"Nor would we let you, Your Grace." Duval's pacing is making me dizzy. I keep waiting for him to step in and say something helpful, to come up with some strategy that will find us a way out. Instead, he is indulging in a fit of temper.

"I know," he says suddenly, and I breathe a sigh of relief. "We will issue an edict stating that you repudiate the betrothal agreement with d'Albret and have no intention of marrying him. If we do so publicly, he will have no choice but to accept it."

I shake my head. "Will that not simply back him into a corner and cause him to take even more drastic measures?"

Duval spears me with a feral gaze. "What do you suggest instead?"

And there he has me. I have no brilliant strategy or clever tactics. That is Duval's gift, not mine. "I have no better plan, my lord. In truth, I am sorely disappointed in my god's justice so far."

Duval stares at me a long moment, his eyes bright as if with fever. "Perhaps that is because you mistake death for justice, and they are not the same thing at all."

In the morning, Vanth arrives bright and early, pecking at the window even before Louyse comes in to stoke the fire. I throw off the covers and hurry over, my toes curling away from the cold stone floor. When I open the shutter, Vanth hops in and cocks his head as if to ask what took me so long. "I was sleeping," I tell him, then grab for the note on his leg before he can peck me.

He squawks in annoyance when I retrieve the missive, then flutters off to his cage and puts his head under his wing.

Much to my frustration, it is not instructions from the abbess but instead a note from Annith. I check the seal, then crack it open and read.

Annith writes to say she has never heard any rumor or gossip about initiates of Mortain taking permanent lovers but begs that I tell her why I wish to know. Luckily for me, she spends little time pressing me on that issue; she is much preoccupied with her own situation.

Sister Vereda has taken ill, she writes, *and has not had a vision in over a week.*

Is that why I have received no orders from the convent? Because Sister Vereda is ill? If that is the case, then surely I must be even more watchful for Mortain's marque.

The nuns have been meeting behind closed doors more than usual, so of course I had to listen to see what they were about. Ismae, I overheard the reverend mother herself tell Sister Thomine that she thinks I will be able to serve as the convent's seeress once Sister Vereda passes into the realm of Death! A seeress! After all that I have trained for, all that I have studied and practiced. I have spent my whole life preparing to step outside this convent in service to Mortain – and now she thinks to lock me up inside these thick stone walls forever. I won't do it. I can't do it. Indeed, the thought has kept me up the last four nights. Just the idea of it makes me feel as if I am suffocating. So, please, in your spare moments, pray for Sister Vereda that she may recover and that I will not be consigned to the convent's inner sanctum for the rest of my days.

Yours, in misery,
Annith

Poor Annith! Can the reverend mother be serious? Does she intend never to let Annith step outside the convent? Annith's plight is so dire, it takes my mind off my own misery, but eventually, I have no choice but to dress for the special meeting of all the barons that the duchess has called.

As the church bells strike noon, Breton nobles, courtiers, barons, and the Privy Council file into the great hall. Duval takes special care to be certain that Gisors attends. "Let him read it as a gesture of goodwill, even if it is nothing of the kind," he says.

I scan the faces of the gathered crowd. There is much gossip and speculation as to why this meeting has been called. Many glance at d'Albret, no doubt wondering if it has something to do with the betrothal he has been boasting about for the past two days.

The back door to the chamber opens and two men-at-arms stride in. The duchess comes next, followed by her Privy Council. The privy councilors are clearly disgruntled that such a meeting has been called without their approval. My gaze goes to Madame Dinan, whose face has an annoying air of smugness to it. Does she really think she has won? Can she know so little of the girl she helped to raise? Once again, Sister Beatriz's words come back to me: *People hear and see what they expect to hear and see.*

Madam Dinan smiles at d'Albret and he smiles back. I am eager to see just how long those smiles hold.

The duchess takes her seat and motions for Duval to hand her the parchment. As she unrolls it, the room falls silent. I cannot help but admire her fortitude – it is not an easy thing to renounce a man in front of his peers.

"I, Anne of Brittany, do hereby declare that the betrothal agreement made between me and Count d'Albret is null and void, as I did sign it with no knowledge of the commitment I was making. While we appreciate the count's valiant service during my father's reign and continue to value him as an ally, I will not now nor ever enter into a marriage arrangement with Lord d'Albret."

When she is finished, every head in the room turns to

Lord d'Albret. His face is a deep, mottled red, his jaw clenched so tight I fear his teeth will snap. Next to him, Madame Dinan sways a little. Marshal Rieux surges to his feet and opens his mouth, but Chancellor Crunard puts a hand on his arm and holds him back with a small shake of his head.

Aware that everyone's attention is on him, d'Albret makes a small, mocking bow to the duchess, then turns on his heel and strides away. The crowd parts before him like butter before a hot knife. Madame Dinan rises to her feet, lifts her skirts, and hurries after him, two bright spots of color burning in her normally pale cheeks. Moving as if in great pain, Anne rises to her feet and turns to leave the hall.

Chapter 37

Two days after the duchess reads the edict against d'Albret, she, Duval, and I stand at her window and watch him ride away. He has so many retainers and attendants that it feels as if half the castle goes with him. I fear Sybella is among them. How else would she have been able to warn me of the trickery planned in the corridor?

The idea that the abbess would place Sybella in d'Albret's household is so repellant that I thrust it aside and pray to Mortain that I am mistaken.

If d'Albret has taken a large part of courtiers with him, he has also taken a fair amount of the court's gloom. The serving maids in particular have a renewed bounce in their step now that they no longer have to endure his pinches. Even young Isabeau's health seems to improve, as if it were d'Albret's presence that had clouded her lungs.

One week before Christmas, the duchess calls for a full court dinner, complete with entertainment. The night before the feast, Isabeau is so excited she nearly makes herself sick. At the duchess's request, I give her another tisane so she can sleep.

The castle steward has spared no luxury for tonight's feast.

The tables are covered with rich damask cloth embroidered with silver thread. Liveried servants stand near the walls, and gold and silver vessels adorn the table. In an especially fancy touch, notes from a horn summon us to the great hall. We are all, as ordered, dressed in our gayest finery. Long fur-trimmed capes mingle with embroidery-encrusted waistcoats and colorful slashed sleeves. Shoes of brightly dyed leather or rich velvet peek out from beneath thick satin skirts.

The duchess and Isabeau take their places at the high table on the raised dais, and the privy councilors join them. And while it seems as if I have done nothing but drink Duval in with my eyes for the past two weeks, tonight he looks different. He has grown thinner, and there are deep shadows under his eyes as well. The negotiations with the Holy Roman emperor have been fierce. Both the duchess and Duval know they bargain for the very life of their country. The Holy Roman emperor's envoy knows it as well and tries to use it to his best advantage. I worry that the strain is getting to Duval. He grows edgy and has taken to checking the doors and windows, certain that someone is listening in.

Most likely someone is.

I am shown to a seat at one of the lower tables with the lesser ladies and knights, but I do not mind. In truth, I need to pinch myself, for I fear this is all a dream. I can scarce believe that one such as I has been allowed into so fine a celebration.

Once we take our seats, servants bring us basins of warm water scented with verbena so we may wash our hands before eating. While we dry them on soft linen towels, the food is carried in on platters. Meat carvers set to work slicing venison and roasted boar, peacock and pheasant. There is also braised rabbit and roast goose, pork pie, pastries, and frumenty.

I am pleased to find myself seated next to Beast and wonder if Duval had something to do with this. "I have not seen much of you of late," I say.

His face creases into a grotesque smile. "Duval has kept me busy overseeing scouting parties. We scour daily, looking for signs of d'Albret making good on his threat or of the arrival of the French."

"Which is the greater danger?"

Beast shrugs his huge shoulders. "I do not know. If d'Albret has retired to his holdings in central Brittany, all he must do is prevent loyal barons and their armies from answering the duchess's call for troops. That will play havoc enough with our defense."

I take a pinch of salt from the salt cellar and sprinkle it on my venison. "And the French? Where do you anticipate they will come from?"

"From the north and east. They still hold Saint-Malo and Fougères per the terms of the Treaty of Verger. They will use those as strongholds and strike out from there. But enough of this depressing talk, demoiselle. Surely you have spent your days more pleasantly than I?"

I grimace. "Actually, no. I am not overfond of either embroidery or the chattering of ladies-in-waiting."

"What would you rather be doing?" Beast's eyes sparkle with mischief.

"Something helpful," I mutter, then I take a sip of wine to wash the sense of helplessness from my tongue. It is not a feeling I relish.

His face grows somber. "Is it not helpful staying by our duchess's side, offering her peace of mind?"

"But of course, if my presence brings her peace of mind, it is most worthwhile. In truth, she seems most vulnerable since her governess's betrayal."

"What of young Isabeau?" Beast's eyes turn to the high table. "She looks frail to me."

"Her health is not good. Her lungs are weak, and, I suspect, her heart."

Beast sends me a strange look. "Does your assassin's training tell you this?"

His bold question makes me sputter on the wine I have just sipped. I look around to be certain no one has overheard. "No, my lord. But I worked closely with our herbalist at the convent, and it was she who tended to our illnesses."

"I had hoped she would recover by now. That she has not is unwelcome news," he says, then tosses back the contents of his goblet. The lord on his right asks him a question, and Beast begins talking with him. Remembering the social pretenses I must uphold, I turn to the knight on my left, but he is leaning so close to the lady next to him that I fear he will fall in her soup. Only too happy to ignore him, I look out among the feasting nobles, their chins greasy with meat, eyes slurry with wine. This celebration has the doomed feel of trying to raise a Maypole in a thunderstorm. I can only hope an order from the convent comes through. This entire room stinks of desperation and betrayal.

Madame Hivern sits between two of the coastal barons and I wonder just how close she is to making her move. Her hand was brilliantly played; she waited for d'Albret to quit the field, and now her opposition has been reduced by half.

My gaze then turns to François, who is always at the heart of whatever festivities are taking place. Twice he has tried to pull me into his merrymaking, but both times I have politely refused. I do not have the heart for his flirtations.

The blare of a sackbut heralds the arrival of the evening's entertainment, and a parade of masked performers troop into the great hall. The leader wears a donkey-headed mask and is followed by an ape, a lion, and a bear. The bear is real and reminds me uncannily of Captain Dunois.

An old bent-over man pushes a cart holding two fools. Another fool gambols in, a pig bladder hanging from the stick over his shoulder. It is mayhem as they cavort and frolic, looking both humorous and grotesque. The fools draw up to the tables and begin dicing with the diners.

The duchess has eyes only for Isabeau, who laughs and claps her hands, delighted. Another mummer comes in rolling a great barrel. There is a rapid beating of drums, a dark, primitive sound. A stag-headed man bursts out of the barrel and leaps into the fray; he represents the patron saint of horned creatures, Dea Matrona's consort. He is killed every year at the end of harvest so he may rise again when Dea Matrona gives birth to the new year.

The music changes yet again, and a man dressed as a young maid and holding a bouquet of flowers frolics between the tables. The music deepens, grows more terrifying. Out from the shadows steps the black-robed, skeletal figure of Death Himself. Everyone gasps.

The maid tries to run, but four masked men leap out of the shadows riding four stick horses. Their red and black masks obscure their faces, and I shudder. They are hellequin, the wild hunt who came for Dea Matrona's daughter and carried her away to Death's underworld, leaving Dea Matrona to make our world stark and barren in her sorrow.

The maiden evades them. Once. Twice. But the third time, the hellequin surround her. My heart begins to beat faster. Surely this is too frightening for young Isabeau?

I look to see how she is faring, and my breath catches in my throat when I see how close the hellequin have drawn to the high table. Some inner alarm – perhaps Mortain's own whisper – sounds in my head, and I am on my feet, pushing through the cavorting mummers, reaching for the crossbow hidden beneath my overskirt.

The entire court gasps as a hellequin leaps onto the table in front of the duchess and draws a knife. Most think it is part of the play. Duval and Dunois know better and reach for their swords, but they are too far away. With a heartfelt prayer to my god, I slap the quarrel in place and pull the trigger.

The quarrel catches the hellequin in the back of the neck, just below the protection of his mask. He freezes; the knife drops from his spasming fingers, and hc topples forward.

The duchess just manages to leap away in time to keep from being crushed by his falling body. Dark red blood splatters onto her pale face.

The pandemonium is instantaneous.

Ladies scream, courtiers shout and scramble away. Men-at-arms pour in from the corridor and surround the mummers, who look in shocked silence at the dead hellequin.

Captain Dunois's eyes widen in admiration. "Excellent shot."

I incline my head in acknowledgment of his compliment. "Catch Isabeau," I tell Duval just before she crumples. But Duval's reflexes are quick and he snatches her before she hits the floor. "Waroch! De Lornay! Question them." He nods his head toward the stunned mummers. "Your Grace, I think we should get you back to your quarters," he says to the duchess.

Pale and trembling, the duchess nods shakily and follows him as he carries their sister back to the solar. Marshal Rieux stares at me as if he fears I, too, have sprung from the mummer's drum. "What is the meaning of this?" Rieux thumps his hand on the table.

Chancellor Crunard steps in to smooth things over. "I think explanations are best made in private. Perhaps we should all adjourn to the duchess's chambers." His eyes seek out mine. "You as well, demoiselle," he says.

Now that the moment is over and the danger passed, my body begins to tremble. So close. *Too* close. Ignoring the whispers and the pointing, I follow them out of the hall. Was the assassin a parting gift from d'Albret? Or an opening shot fired by some new enemy?

Chapter 38

"Who is this woman?" Marshal Rieux demands.

I ignore his question, go to the ewer near the duchess's canopied bed, and pour water into the basin. I grab a linen cloth from the stand nearby, wet it, then carry it to her. "May I?"

She looks at me in puzzlement.

"You have blood on your face," I explain.

Her eyes widen in horror and she gives a frantic nod. Gently I begin sponging the spatters from her cheek. Now that she is safe, I am calm. The god truly guided my hand, for I could never have made that shot otherwise. Let the others say what they will, they cannot take that away from me.

"Who is she, Duval? We knew she was not your cousin. I, for one, did not begrudge you a lightskirt—"

"Careful." Duval's voice is a warning growl.

"But clearly she is much more than any of us guessed."

"Some knew." Duval shoots a glance Crunard's way. It is an excellent strategy. This whole idea was cooked up between the chancellor and the abbess, so let Crunard answer to his irate fellow council members.

"Chancellor Crunard? Did you know about this? Who is she and what just happened out there?"

Out of the corner of my eye, I see Crunard's signet rings flash as he steeples his fingers. "She has been sent to court by the abbess of St. Mortain."

I feel all the eyes in the room staring at my back.

"I thought they were the stuff of nightmares," Rieux mutters quietly.

"But no," I say innocently. "I am saint-sent to aid our duchess and our country, Marshal Rieux. Unless our duchess's triumph is your nightmare, you have nothing to fear from me."

He turns accusingly to Anne. "Did you know her identity, Your Grace?"

The duchess raises her chin. "I knew that she served St. Mortain and that He had sent her to me in my hour of need."

"Why were the rest of us not told?" the marshal asks.

Crunard shrugs. "We thought the fewer who knew, the easier to keep her identity hidden. Surely, Marshal, you do not tell me every bit of your military strategy?"

Rieux's face reddens, but he cannot deny the truth of Crunard's words.

"I do not see why you are so angry." It is the duchess herself who speaks. "If it were not for Demoiselle Rienne's quick actions, I would even now be lying in a pool of my own blood."

There is a resounding silence, then Marshal Rieux rushes in. "You misunderstand us, Your Grace. We are overjoyed that you were not injured. But are we so sure that poor man was not merely part of the entertainment?"

"We are sure," I say.

Rieux whips his head round to stare at me. "How?"

My eyes meet his. "Because St. Mortain guided my hand."

Rieux's lips flatten into a thin line and he takes a step closer to me. I do not know what he intends, but Chancellor Crunard stops him. "Marshal Rieux!"

Nostrils flaring in annoyance, Rieux checks himself. "Whoever this woman is," he says, "she should not be privy to our council meeting. You are dismissed, demoiselle."

I make a great show of ignoring him and look to the duchess. It is she whom I serve, not him. "I await your command, Your Grace." I can hear Rieux's teeth grinding in frustration.

I see plain on her face that she is loath to dismiss me because Rieux has ordered her to. "If Your Grace allows it," I explain gently, "I have duties I must see to regarding your assailant."

She nods her head graciously. "By all means, demoiselle. See to your duties."

"Where has the body been taken?" I ask Duval.

His eyes narrow as he realizes what I am planning. "I will show you myself," he says. "We are done here."

"We are not done, Duval!" Marshal Rieux says in frustration.

"I am," Duval says, then takes my elbow in an iron grip and escorts me from the room. When we are alone in the hallway, I shift my elbow. He immediately lessens his hold and grunts an apology. We go the rest of the way to the dungeon in silence, the twitching under Duval's left eye discouraging any questions. There is a lone guard standing outside a row of cells. "Where is the body?" Duval asks.

He points to a larger cell. "In there, my lord."

Duval leads me inside. If the guard thinks this odd, he is wise enough to keep it to himself.

The hellequin's body has been laid on the floor, the crossbow bolt removed from his neck. No one has thought to remove the ugly red-and black mask. I kneel on the hard stone floor and gently lift it from his face. What strikes me most about the man is his ordinariness. He is neither handsome nor plain, looks neither high born nor of peasant stock. It is as if he is a blank canvas, waiting for an artist and his paints to bring him to life.

Duval comes to stand beside me and stares down at the body. "Do you know him?"

"No, my lord. I have never seen him before."

Duval frowns as he ponders this. "Where did he come from then?"

"I will do my best to find out."

It takes him a moment to realize my intent. "Is it safe, do you think? With someone as dangerous as this?"

Even though his concern pleases me, I shrug, pretending a confidence I do not feel. "Anyone could have sent him. We are no closer to knowing who moves against the duchess than we were a sennight ago. What other path is open to us? Besides, he is dead now, what danger can he be?"

"Even so," he says, his face grim. "You will be careful, Ismae."

"Always, my lord." I give him a reassuring smile, then turn back to the dead hellequin. I close my eyes, take a steadying breath, then slowly lift the barrier between life and death. At first, there is nothing, so I step more fully into death. Still, there is nothing but a great, black abyss, and then I realize that the hellequin has no soul with which to communicate – I feel only a gaping void. Is that the price of acting without Mortain's blessing? To be emptied of our divine spark?

There is a slow, deep tug from the void. To my horror, the darkness reaches out to me, embracing me and pulling me into its nothingness. I struggle to resist, but its grip is firm, unyielding. It is like night falling, only darker, blacker, more absolute.

And so very chilling. Just as one's skin sticks to ice atop a pond, so does my soul cleave to this freezing emptiness. In no time at all, the normal chill of death disappears, and in its place I feel numbness. Emptiness.

Hands are on my face, slapping gently at my cheeks, a voice murmuring. I feel a faint trickle of warmth begin to work its way into my body. With immense effort, I open my eyes.

Duval is kneeling beside me, his eyes wild with concern. I shiver uncontrollably. "Praise God!" he says, then hauls me up into his arms and holds me close against his chest.

His heart beats strongly against my ribs, its rapid rate nearly matching my own. Warmth pours from his body into mine.

"There is color in your face again," he says. Indeed, I can feel the blood moving under my skin once more. He places a hand on my cheek and turns my face to his, searching to be certain I am all right.

I give him a reassuring smile that does nothing to ease my own dread. I have seen my own destiny now and know precisely what will happen to me if I step outside Mortain's grace.

The corridors are empty as Duval escorts me to his chambers; all the feasters and revelers having returned to their own rooms. Once we reach his apartments, he tucks me up in a chair near the fire and orders hot spiced wine to warm me. Between the fire and Duval's cloak, I finally stop shivering and am able to hold the wine when it arrives. I take a sip, savoring the rich, sweet taste on my tongue. "What is our next move?"

"We must finalize the betrothal agreement with the Holy Roman emperor and find a way to get the entire council to agree to it."

My mind goes immediately to Madame Dinan and Marshal Rieux. "What if they will not?"

"Then we must get Anne crowned so she may act in her own sovereign interest."

"Do you have a plan to evict Gisors from the palace so he will not interfere with her coronation?"

Duval snorts. "I am still puzzling that part out," he says, then takes a sip of wine.

"Why *can't* you simply evict him? Escort him out and bar

the door behind him? At least long enough to have Anne crowned?"

"The French regent has plenty of other spies who will inform her soon enough, and they will undoubtedly use that as an excuse to invade."

There is a knock on the chamber door. Duval and I exchange a glance, then he goes to answer it.

It is Captain Dunois, looking uncomfortable as he nods to Duval. "I must speak with you. Alone," he adds, shooting me a glance. Duval waves his hand in dismissal. "She will only listen at the door."

Captain Dunois's lips twitch ever so slightly. "The council continued to meet after you left," he explains. "The news is not good. They feel that, whether by accident or by design, your counsel and influence have placed the duchess's life in grave danger."

If Duval feels any pain at being stabbed in the back by the council, he does not show it on his face. I set my wine down, afraid I might spill it or hurl it into the fireplace in outrage. "On what do they base this accusation?"

Dunois looks even more uncomfortable. "On the attempt made on the duchess's life this evening."

"How is that Duval's fault?"

"I can speak for myself," Duval mutters.

Dunois ignores us both. "They believe it is the inevitable result of all the decisions and moves Duval and Anne have made so far. Consorting with the known traitors Runnion and Martel, bringing an assassin to court without informing anyone, negotiating a betrothal agreement with Nemours, without authorization, that resulted in his death. And, finally, encouraging the duchess to publicly repudiate one of our most powerful barons.

Not to mention your mother's planned treachery. They are still not convinced you are not part of it."

Duval does not react to this long list of crimes until he hears the last one. "Who brought that up?" he asks sharply.

"Marshal Rieux."

Duval buries his head in his hands, but whether in defeat or frustration, I cannot tell.

"Surely the duchess or the chancellor spoke on Duval's behalf?" I ask. "Explained the true nature of his actions?"

"The duchess did," Dunois replies. "But since the issue before the council was whether Duval was exercising undue influence over her, no one listened."

"But what of Chancellor Crunard?" I ask. "It was largely his decision to install me in Duval's household. He also knows the reason Duval was meeting with Runnion and Martel. And he voted for the Nemours alliance rather than the d'Albret one. Did he not explain any of that?"

"Not in detail, no. He argued forcefully on Duval's behalf, but the others would not be swayed."

"What do they plan to do?" Duval asks.

"They think to arrest you in the morning. At the chancellor's suggestion, they are considering putting you under house arrest rather than sending you to a prison cell. We will meet first thing in the morning and take a vote."

The rank unfairness of this has me gaping at Dunois. "How can they ignore all those who have moved so openly against the duchess but lock up Duval based on a thin web of unfounded accusations?"

Dunois glances uneasily at Duval. "Because they feel powerless and wish to take *some* action, even if it is not the right one."

When Duval speaks again, it is as if he dredges up the words from some great hollow pit inside himself. "And that is the true danger," he says. "They will think they have addressed the threat when they have not. Whoever planned that attack will be free to act again." He looks up and meets Dunois's gaze. "Thank you for the warning." Something solid and bittersweet passes between them.

When Dunois leaves, Duval rises to his feet and begins pacing in front of the fireplace. I wait for him to speak. When he doesn't, I cannot keep silent. "Why did the chancellor not explain the reasons behind your actions to the council?"

Duval shrugs. "He is a wily old fox and plays a deep game. Perhaps he did not want the others to see his own hand in this and cause them to direct their accusations and suspicions his way. Who would be left to see to Anne's safety then? Or perhaps he simply knew he was greatly outnumbered and did not wish to fight a lost cause."

"It was he who told me of your breaking your oath," I blurt out.

Duval stops pacing and snaps up his head. "He told you of that? When?"

I shrug. "When I was in his office after the meeting of the estates."

"And yet you said nothing."

I shrug again, not sure I can explain my reasoning. Not even to myself. "I did not ask you because it was clear that he wanted me to."

Duval barks out a laugh. "My little rebel."

I ignore the small flush of pleasure his words bring. "But it also seemed to me that I had no right to ask you of your saint when I have refused to tell you anything of mine."

The look he gives me is long and considering.

"And," I am compelled to add, "the duchess herself told me of the incident. But later."

"Did she?"

"Yes, when I was tending to her after d'Albret's attack."

Duval's eyes stay on mine a long moment before he pulls himself away and heads for the chessboard. I join him there and together we look down at the meager forces left protecting the white queen.

"What will happen if they remove you?" I ask.

Duval studies the board intensely, as if trying to conjure secrets from it. "Then there is no one left to speak on Anne's behalf. Beast cannot do it, nor de Lornay. They are not high enough in rank to sway the council."

"What of Dunois?"

"Captain Dunois is as solid and loyal a man you could ask for, but politics and treaties and the games of kingdoms are not his gifts. Leading men in battle, grasping tactics and strategies of war, those are his strengths."

I stare at the board, thinking of the poor duchess surrounded by an entire council that has so little interest in her personal welfare. "Then you must not be taken," I say.

"But if I leave, it ensures the same result, does it not? It is a brilliant plan they have concocted. Perhaps they even wished for Dunois to speak with me. Whether I am arrested or leave of my own accord, the result is the same: I am unable to help Anne. Unless..." Duval begins tapping at his chin with his finger.

"Unless what?" I ask impatiently.

He turns to look at me, his face alight with a touch of unholy glee. "Unless there is some way to remove myself yet not. What if they think I have left, but I haven't?"

"You mean to disguise yourself? Surely your face is too well known—"

"No. I will hide under their very noses." Duval turns to stare at the fireplace. More accurately, the wall beside the fireplace. "The castle holds a number of hidden passages. With our country so often at war, the ducal palaces have always had escape routes out of the castle."

"You would live in those tunnels and passageways?"

He shrugs. "It cannot be worse than being imprisoned. And it will give me a chance to finalize the agreement with the Holy Roman emperor's envoy, Herr Dortmund, and send him on his way with a signed contract. I fear that is Anne's last chance if she does not wish to end up in the arms of either the French or d'Albret."

"But will you not need the privy councilors' signatures?"

"I will forge them. This is only the preliminary agreement anyway. Hopefully, when the final document is ready, Anne will have been crowned and can act on her own behalf."

It is a desperate plan but the only one available to us. We spend the next several hours working out the details, trying to anticipate all the obstacles that could lay waste to our strategy.

Duval will continue to visit my chamber each night. He does not think the council will go so far as to post sentries at my bedchamber door. I am not so sure.

While he is in hiding, I will pretend to mope and will ask for my meals in my room, which will make it easy enough to set aside food for him.

"What shall I tell the others when they ask where you have gone? For Crunard, at least, will surely question me."

"Simply tell them the truth. You do not know where I am. For you will not. I could be anywhere in the castle, I could even leave it, and no one – including you – will know where I have gone."

"And the duchess? What will she think when you disappear?"

"The passageways open up into the royal bedchambers. I should be able to get to her. But it would not hurt for you to try to get a message to her as well."

"What shall I tell her?"

He looks down at the chessboard again. "Tell her we no longer know whom she can trust. We will keep her apprised as we learn more." He glances at the window, then back at me. "I have a few preparations I must make before I go."

We are close enough to kiss, and for a long, heart-stopping moment I think that he will do just that. Instead, he runs his knuckle along my cheek. "Until tomorrow night, then."

I shiver. "Until tomorrow."

He turns to leave, then stops and snatches the white queen from the board, wrapping his fingers around it as if to keep her safe.

It is not surprising that I cannot sleep that night. I lie awake and think of Duval crawling around the hidden tunnels of the castle like a rat trapped in a wall. I think of the duchess abandoned by every one of the guardians her father appointed for her. But mostly I think of the council, of Chancellor Crunard and Marshal Rieux, and wonder who is telling the truth and who is lying.

Chapter 39

When I draw aside the curtains the next morning, the icy fingers of winter come through the glass and pinch me awake. The true season of Mortain is upon us, everything cold and barren and gray.

Behind me, the door opens and Louyse bustles in. "My lady! Come away from there before you catch your death!"

Her words bring a smile to my lips. Does she think Death is some small bird with my name written on it, beating at the window in the hope that I will catch it? "Something subdued," I tell Louyse as she moves toward the garderobe. "I am feeling somber today."

"Aye, you and the whole palace," she mutters darkly.

I turn from the window and rub some warmth back into my arms.

When she has set out the gown, I send her off to fetch a breakfast tray and hurry to dress, a plan forming as I do. My first task is to write to the abbess informing her of the attempt on the duchess's life.

I pause partway through the letter as I realize that not once did the Privy Council discuss who might be behind the assassination attempt. At least, not in my hearing.

It cannot be d'Albret, for if Anne dies, there is no way he

can become duke. France, then? Do they assume Isabeau is too weak to hold the crown?

The only one who gains by Anne's death is France, at least as far as I can reckon. And no matter how I turn that over in my mind, I cannot reconcile it with Chancellor Crunard's lukewarm support of Duval. Hoping the abbess will be able to shed some light on the possibilities, I finish the letter and send Vanth on his way.

With that task done, I turn my attention to the rest of the day and try to think what to do with myself. I have already oiled all my weapons, and Madame Dinan will not admit me to the solar. Besides, the Privy Council is meeting there this morning.

And then I have my plan.

With everyone in the Privy Council meeting, it is easy enough to slip into Madame Dinan's and Marshal Rieux's chambers unobserved. All it takes is a well-chosen moment and the twist of a needle-like blade, then I am inside. Dinan's apartments are much like the woman herself, coldly beautiful but containing no warmth or heart. Marshal Rieux's rooms are grand and sumptuous, which is no surprise. He seems the sort to demand luxury, not so much for his own pleasure but because it is befitting for someone of his stature. Even so, his chamber holds no proof or evidence of any treacherous dealings.

That leaves only Crunard.

Fear scuttles across my shoulders at the thought of searching his rooms. He is the convent's liaison, after all, and appears to be a great confidant of the abbess. Somehow, I doubt very much she will thank me if I expose him as a traitor.

But she is hundreds of miles away, and the young duchess is running out of options. Her needs seem more urgent than the tender sensibilities of the abbess.

I make my way back through the halls to the chancellor's office. It is early afternoon and I fear their council may well be over. Not to mention they have no doubt discovered Duval's absence by now. Even so, I must try.

As I reach the chancellor's door, I cast my senses out and realize he is in there. And he is not alone. Since there is no one else in the hallway, I put my ear to the door. The two male voices are close. With a start, I realize they are at the door itself. Less than a second later, it opens. I try to look surprised, my hand raised as if to knock. "Chancellor Crunard," I say.

He scowls. "Demoiselle Rienne. What are you doing here?"

I try very hard not to look at the man Crunard is escorting out of his office. "I have come to see if you know where my lord Duval is." It is a bold move, but I can think of no other reason to explain my presence at his door.

"No, I do not know where he has gone," Chancellor Crunard says. "I was going to send for you to ask the same question."

Unable to help myself any longer, I glance at Crunard's visitor. It is the French envoy, Gisors. His brilliant green eyes study me intently.

Crunard follows my gaze and gives Gisors a brusque nod. "I think I have said all there is to say." The heat of his anger comes through clearly in his voice. Gisors's nostrils flare, then he gives a precise bow and strides off. When he is out of sight, Crunard turns back to me. "Have you really not seen Duval today?"

"No, my lord." Since it is no lie, I am confident he can hear the ring of truth in my words. "I have not seen him since last night after we left the duchess's solar. Did you not find him in his chamber?"

Crunard shakes his head. "He has not been there all day. His steward said he was gone this morning when he went in to wake him. If you see him, tell him I am looking for him, will you? Remind him that running away only makes him look more guilty." His eyes are cold and hard upon me and put me in mind of a bird of prey's.

I tip my head to the side and crease my brow in puzzlement. "Guilty, my lord? Running away? I am not sure I understand you."

His face relaxes and he looks somewhat less fierce. "It is nothing, demoiselle. Only leftover arguments from the council meeting. That is all."

"Very well." I sink into a curtsy and then turn and head down the hall, careful to keep my steps slow and measured, as if I have nothing to hide.

When I reach my room, I quickly shut the door, then lean against it. That was a near thing.

A scratching at the window makes me jump. When I see

that it is a crow, my pulse quickens in anticipation. Once I open the window, the crow waits patiently for me to remove the message.

Dearest Daughter,

I have received much information from Chancellor Crunard but very little from you, although perhaps your message is even now on its way to me.

The chancellor has informed me of the French whore's plot to put her youngest son on the Breton throne. There is no question that this is open treason and the French whore must die. See to it immediately.

It has been so long since I have used the name that it takes me a moment to realize the note means Madame Hivern.

The convent is ordering me to kill Duval's mother.

Chapter 40

No matter how long I stare at the note, the order simply makes no sense. The threat Hivern and François present is small compared to all the others the duchess faces. Nor have they made any open moves.

Has Sister Vereda recovered, then, and Seen this? Or is the decision based solely on Chancellor Crunard's report? My head is so full of questions it feels ready to burst.

When Louyse brings a dinner tray, I do not so much as glance at it. Instead, I sit staring into the fire, tying myself in knots over this problem that should not be a problem at all. The convent has given me an assignment, one made all the easier because I do not care for Madame Hivern in the least. I find her annoying and pretentious, and yet... to kill Duval's mother? He may be violently at odds with her plans, but he cares deeply for his family.

And why Hivern? Why has Mortain decided I am to act against her when He has let d'Albret remain unmarqued? Is it because she is fully French? But if that was the reason, why did he not marque Gisors?

And how can I tell Duval?

In the end, I cannot. I am the worst sort of coward and pretend to be asleep when he comes. As the heavy wooden door by the fireplace creaks open, I lie as still as death, forcing my breathing to be slow and even, willing the blood to move more slowly in my veins.

I feel Duval draw close to the bed, feel him looking down at me for one, two, three breaths, then he moves away. He pours a cup of wine, swallows it in one gulp, then pours himself another. He is restless and I am filled with remorse. He has been cooped up inside the stone walls of the palace all day and is no doubt eager for news, but I do not know how to speak to him without telling him of the convent's orders. I fear I have forgotten how to lie to him, which disturbs me almost as much as my new assignment.

When he finally stops pacing long enough to eat the dinner I left by the fire, I begin to relax. My cowardice has been rewarded and I will not have to tell Duval that I must kill his mother. At least not tonight.

The next morning I tell Louyse I am not feeling well and am not to be disturbed. The first thing I do is write to the abbess explaining that I was waiting for confirming evidence before sending her the reports on Hivern's plot. I assure her I will take this lesson to heart and will inform her of events in a more timely manner from now on. Next I write to Annith and ask how angry the abbess is with me. Best to know just how much trouble I am in.

I spend the rest of the day planning how I will kill Madame Hivern.

Normally, we do not worry overmuch about hiding our

kills. The main purpose of the deception of posing as Duval's mistress was to allow me easier access to the court. If the barons and nobles had learned I was from the convent, they would have been cautious and wary around me. Usually the convent feels it is wise to announce Mortain's justice as a warning and a deterrent. Even so, in this case I decide it is better to be discreet.

Poison, then. I am certain that would be Hivern's choice if she were given one.

I take the thin gold chain from around my neck and use the key to unlock the trunklet. There is a faint tinkle of glass as I open the lid. The pearls would be easiest, but they leave signs of poison behind. Martyr's embrace and scourge are far too painful. Amourna's woe, so named for the pair of star-crossed lovers who were forbidden to wed, might work. So might Arduinna's snare.

I stare down at the small clay pot of thick honey-colored paste nestled in the corner of the trunk. Arduinna's snare is subtle and easily absorbed through the skin, but it is too imprecise for my taste. One can never be sure who will touch the poisoned object or if enough will be absorbed to kill one's victim.

Nocturne's malaise is painless. Hivern would simply fall asleep and never wake up, waste away into nothingness, but Madame Hivern would hate for her carefully tended appearance to wither so.

I scowl. What do I care how she feels about her death? This is what happens to traitors.

I reach for the bottle of nocturne's malaise, but my hand grows still when I see the slender white candles beneath. Night whispers. Painless death by an intoxicating perfume, the perfect death for Madame Hivern.

If for no other reason than so I will not be filled with remorse when I tell Duval how his mother died.

Chapter 41

It is well past dark when I set out for Madame Hivern's quarters. Luck is with me, and she is not there, so I let myself in. I fortify myself with the thought that she is likely out plotting treason. I choose a hiding place behind a thick tapestry that hangs on her wall and settle in to wait.

It does not take long. She and her maid come into the room, chatting about the charming necklace an admirer has given her and guessing its worth. I wait as the maid undresses her and brushes her hair. I block out the sound of their low murmuring voices as they talk of the recent Christmas festivities and what Madame Hivern will be giving François. Instead, I focus on Hivern's spitefulness toward me since we first met and how cruel she is to Duval.

At last the maid leaves and I hear the rustle of covers as Hivern settles into her bed. *Now*, I think, just as surely as if Mortain had placed His hand on my back and pushed. I step out from behind the tapestry, take the candle laden with night whispers from the folds of my skirts, and approach the bed.

As my shadow falls across her, Madame Hivern starts, then sits up. "What are *you* doing in here?" Her voice is sharp with surprise, perhaps even fear. Ignoring her question, I hold the deadly candle against the small flame from the oil lamp on her nightstand until it catches. Slowly, I turn to face her. There is just enough light in the room that I can see the marque of Mortain upon her; a faint trickle of darkness begins just under her chin and trails down her throat. The marque spreads, like a bruise just beginning to form, across her neck and the swell of her chest that is exposed by her low-cut chemise. This comforts me greatly, for if Mortain has marqued her, then the convent's order cannot be due to some trickery of Crunard's.

"You are a spy, aren't you?" Madame's voice still holds a note of alarm. She looks younger, more vulnerable, without all her fine jewels and fancy headdresses.

"Some might call me that, but it is not what I am."

She barks out a laugh. "I should have known Duval would not be taken with a mere maid."

"My lord Duval is not taken with me at all," I say tartly. "We merely work together. Our love and duty to the duchess give us much in common." I realize I should move closer so the fumes from the candle can work more quickly, but my feet are leaden and reluctant to move.

"Whoever you may be, you are quite wrong if you think Duval is not taken with you. If there is one thing I know, it is men. And I certainly know my own son. He is smitten."

"That is not so!" It is demeaning, this arguing with a victim while waiting for Death to claim her, and my voice is sharper than I intend.

She cocks her head to the side and studies me, as if we are

simply having a tête-à-tête over spiced wine. "Ah," she says, her voice full of wisdom nearly as old as Mortain's. "You love him back."

I grit my teeth but say nothing.

"I do not blame you for being distraught, Ismae. It is no comfortable thing, having your heart in thrall to a man, especially one such as Duval."

I am unable to help myself. "How do you mean, one such as Duval?"

"One who will put duty and honor before everything, no matter the cost to him. Or you."

Her words please me, for if even she says such things about him, it confirms what I myself have come to believe: that he is loyal and true to the duchess. "Too bad you do not hold your own honor so highly, madame."

A delicate frown creases her brow. "What do you mean?"

"I mean that you are a traitor to the crown of Brittany, and for that you must die. St. Mortain has willed it."

She puts her hand to her forehead. "Is that why it grows warm in here?"

I am impressed that she does not faint or scream or cry out for help. "Yes, my lady. That is the poison beginning to work."

"Poison?" Her face relaxes somewhat. "Thank you for that. I am not overfond of sharp things. Or pain."

Her composure surprises me, as I have always thought her high-strung and overwrought. "Who besides François is involved in your plots and conspiracies?"

At her son's name, she grows rigid with fear. "No! Not François! Do not lift your hand against him!" She rises up from the bed, crosses the distance between us, and grabs my shoulders. I wince as her slender fingers bite into my still tender wound. "It was me, all me. François wanted nothing to do with it. You must not kill him. Promise me!"

"I cannot make such a promise. If my saint bids me act, I must, but if François is innocent, Mortain will not raise a hand against him."

She pushes away from me, her cheeks flushed. "Do not sit in judgment of us, stupid girl. You do not know what it is like, having your life run by men. Men who care not one whit for you beyond the pleasure you can bring them in bed or the pretty way you decorate their arms." She clenches her fists. "You have no idea what it is like to have no choices, not one thing to call your own, not even your children."

"But I do, madame," I say softly. "I assure you, no woman has the choices you speak of. She cannot choose whom she marries or which family she is born into or even what her role in this world will be. I do not differ from you in that regard, only in what I did with what I was given."

"What could I do when I was but fourteen and the aging French king decided he must have me in his bed at any cost? What choice did I have when he died? So I chose the duke. He was young and handsome and kind and, most of all, smitten with me. That power – the power to attract men – was the only weapon I had."

To my horror, I find myself sympathetic to her.

"And once I'd borne children – do you know how hard it can be for a bastard? How dispensable they are? I tried to do all in my power to assure them some measure of respect and safety in their lives."

Her words make me think of my mother for the first time in years. Would that she had tried to protect me as well as Madame Hivern protected her children.

Madame Hivern shoves her golden hair out of her eyes and gives me a scornful look. "This love you feel for Duval is nothing to the love you would bear your child. Believe me in that, if nothing else."

A child. Something I have never even allowed myself to think about. Knowledge wells up from deep inside me. If I did have a child, I would protect it and serve it with every breath I drew.

It hits me with the unwelcome force of a crossbow bolt: we are alike, Hivern and I. Both women, both powerless over our own fates. Who is to say I would not have done exactly as she if I had been born into her circumstances? The life I would have led with Guillo spreads out before me, his offspring hanging from my skirts. Would I have grown to love them? Protect them? Could I have done any differently than Hivern had?

She sways on her feet, then stumbles over to the bed, all the will and fight seeping out of her at once. "How much longer will this take?" she asks, and I find I am nearly drowning in my reluctance to kill her. Not fully understanding my own intentions, and with a quick movement I am not sure is my own, my fingers reach up and snuff out the flame. I go to the window and throw it open, letting the cold, cleansing air rush in and chase away the cloying, sweet scent.

Hivern's teeth begin to chatter. "W-what are you d-doing? It's c-cold."

I want to shout at her that I do not know what I am doing, that mayhap I have gone mad. Instead, I cross to the bed. "Stand up." I grab her by the arm and haul her to her feet. "Walk."

She looks at me as if I am addle-brained, and perhaps I am. "I don't want to walk. I want to sleep. Isn't that what you want?"

"Walk!" I command. "I have an idea, a plan to protect you and François." *That* gets her feet moving.

Her gaze fuzzily tries to focus on mine, urgent. "What is it?"

"You say you lack choices in your life, and I would give you a choice. But we must walk while I do it in order to chase the poison from your body, or else you will have no choices left to you at all."

She looks at me, her lovely blue eyes confused and hopeful. I give her a shake. "Move. I need your head clear when you make your choice." But that is only partially true. I also need time to marshal my thoughts.

I cannot believe I am refusing to carry out an order from the convent. I glance at the marque upon Hivern's face. It is one thing to agree to work with Duval on behalf of the duchess, one thing not to tell Crunard of Duval's whereabouts, but this . . . this is to move in direct opposition of the convent's orders – and Mortain's.

But my mind has affixed itself on my first kill, Runnion, who also bore a marque. Duval maintained that Runnion was working for the duchess in order to cleanse his soul. That knowledge has haunted me ever since, the idea that I robbed him of forgiveness.

What if I can give Madame Hivern the choice I took from Runnion?

What if I can convince Hivern to renounce her sins and thus gain forgiveness? Surely that is not going against the convent, or the saint, but simply finding another way to do His will?

If He does not remove the marque from her, it will be easy enough to set up a second kill. And then I will also know that my actions against Runnion did not cost him forgiveness.

After three turns about the room Hivern is still shivering, but it is only from the cold now, not the effects of night whispers. Only then do I lay my offer of salvation before her. "My lady, if you and François will appear in front of the full court and swear an oath of fealty to the duchess, then perhaps I can spare your lives. But only if the oath comes from your hearts and you mean to keep such a vow, for while I might not know if you are lying, Mortain surely will, and He guides my hand in all things."

"If you will spare my son, I will promise you anything," she swears.

"If François is innocent, then he should have no hesitation swearing fealty to his sister."

She grabs my arm and falls to her knees in supplication. "He will have no problem with such a thing," she says. "Indeed, he will be glad to do it. As will I."

I watch her closely, but the marque does not fade. Hoping I am not making the biggest mistake of my life, I take her arm and pull her to her feet. "Very well then. Here's what we will do."

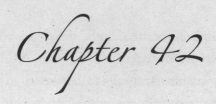

Chapter 42

That night, the duchess once again takes dinner in her chambers, so the rest of the court does the same. I am not hungry, which is just as well since Duval will need all the food Louyse has brought me.

I dismiss the older woman early under the guise of having a headache and take the precaution of locking my door. Then I take a seat by the fire and wait. I go over my actions of the afternoon for the hundredth time hoping – praying – I have made the right choice.

When Duval arrives, his doublet is unlaced and his shirt sleeves rolled up. His hair stands on end, as if he has spent the day running his hands through it. When he sees me fully dressed and sitting by the fire, his hand goes for his sword hilt and his eyes dart around the room.

"Much has happened since we last spoke," I say quickly to reassure him. "I did not want to risk falling asleep or missing you."

Satisfied there is no trap waiting, he comes fully into the room and takes a seat in the chair next to mine. He shoots me a cunning glance, then pulls the white queen from the leather pouch at his belt and sets it on the arm of the chair. "It is done," he says.

"What is done?"

A smile plays at the corners of his mouth as he fills a cup with wine. "The betrothal terms between the Holy Roman emperor and the duchess have been agreed upon." He lifts the goblet to his lips in a jaunty manner and drains it.

"But that is good news!"

A wry smile flickers briefly across his face. "You were expecting bad?"

"In truth, I was. Things seem to turn against the duchess at every opportunity."

His head snaps round. "Has some new disaster befallen her?"

"No, milord. Indeed, I have good news as well."

He lifts the flagon of wine and refills his cup. "Then tell it so I may hear."

"Your mother and brother have agreed to swear their fealty to Anne before the Privy Council and all the barons at court."

He sets the flagon down with a thump. "They have?"

"They have."

Watching me closely, he asks, "And how, pray tell, did this miracle come about?"

I look away from his piercing gaze and stare at the flames dancing in the fireplace. While I have every intention of telling him the truth, I fear he will see far more than I want him to. "I received orders from the convent."

There is no sound but the faint crackle and hiss of the fire. "I see," he says at last. "Or rather, I do not, for if you received orders from the convent, surely they would both be dead?"

"The order came only for your mother, and when I went to . . . visit her, another option presented itself."

"Go on."

"You do not sound especially surprised, my lord."

"I am not surprised, no. I knew this was a possibility from the moment I brought you here. Remember, I have known of her plans all along."

Perhaps that is why he fought so hard against my coming. "It occurred to me that if she was consigned to death for her plots against the duchess, then perhaps by renouncing those plots, she could earn herself a reprieve and the saint would unmarque her."

"And did he?"

I clear my throat. "Not yet. But I do not think He will reverse His judgment until the oath passes from her lips." I risk a quick glance at him. His face is flushed, but whether from my words, the heat of the fire, or the wine he has downed so quickly, I do not know. "Just as Runnion's marque had not left him before he performed his act of contrition – it is the act of atonement that removes the marque, not simply the wanting to atone. Or so I believe."

"Does the convent know you have taken matters into your own hands in such a way?"

"No." I smile wryly. "Not yet."

"And Crunard?"

I shake my head. "What actions the convent does or does not take are no concern of his. Or shouldn't be. But I suspect he will figure it out soon enough, since it was he who reported your mother's plot to the convent."

Duval eyes me curiously. "Not you?"

Embarrassed suddenly, I rise to fetch his dinner tray. "I had not had a chance to write to the abbess yet, no." Still feeling his eyes upon me, I fiddle with the tray, rearranging the food and dishes. Only when he looks away do I feel comfortable enough to turn round. Even so, I am careful not to meet his eyes as I set the tray before him.

When I do manage to glance up, he is holding the white queen and studying her, his dark brows drawn together.

"I must find a way to tell the duchess of Madame Hivern's and François's need to swear fealty to her. I was hoping you might have some insight on how I may do that without letting her know the full extent of their betrayal."

He tilts his head, reminding me for a moment of Vanth. "You wish to keep that from her?"

"I wish to protect her young heart from any more bruises. Truly, how many more people can betray her?"

"How many more barons are there?" is his unsettling reply.

And so it is that on Christmas Day, Madame Hivern and François kneel before the duchess and swear everlasting fealty to her. And mean it.

Madame Hivern has come within an angel's breath of her own death and is aware of the mercy that has been granted to her and her son.

As I watch her swear the oath, the purple, bruised marque slowly fades from her throat. My breath leaves me in a rush, and my knees grow weak with relief. Mortain has indeed granted her mercy. Which means I did not fail Him or subvert His will. Joy fills my heart as I realize I have not stepped outside His grace.

When the ceremony is over, I slip away and return to my room, eager to give the news to Duval. The servants are enjoying their own feast, and my chamber is dark except for the reddish glow from the fireplace. It is nearly full dark outside, and little light comes in through the windows. Just as I turn to light some tapers, there is a scritch of sound at the window and a faint caw. Vanth.

I hurry to the shutter. When I open it, the crow tumbles in, a scramble of black feathers and rushing wings. At least he no longer tries to snap my fingers off.

Vanth lands near his cage and cocks his head. He caws and ruffles his feathers before going in. I take my time teasing the note from him, not sure I want to read the scolding I am certain the reverend mother has sent me. At last I snag the message from Vanth's leg, break the seal, and unfold the parchment.

Daughter,
Once again I have received no word from you on the most recent developments at court and must rely on Chancellor Crunard to guide me. What he has told me is so shocking that I can scarce credit it. Not only does the French whore still live, but you have neglected to inform me of Duval's true allegiance. The chancellor has laid out the case against Duval and there can be no doubt that he is

guilty. He has driven away all of the duchess's allies, one by one, and when that failed, he arranged an assassination attempt on the duchess. Have you known all along that he was spying for the French regent? Or have you been blinded to his real purpose? Indeed, the only reason I do not judge you an accomplice in this matter is that the chancellor informed me that it was you who saved her life.

Duval must pay for his crimes, and you must pay for your negligence. Dispatch him immediately, then pack your things and return to the convent at once so I may decide what is to be done with you.

My heart stops beating for one – two – long beats and the note falls from my numb fingers and flutters to the floor. I press the heels of my hands to my eyes, hoping to expunge the words from my mind. But it does no good. I have been ordered to kill Duval.

The desires of my convent have collided with the path of my heart.

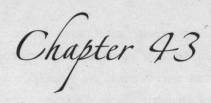

Chapter 43

Slowly, as if every bone in my body has turned to melted wax, I sink to the floor. How can this be? Did the abbess not get my most recent letter? And what of Crunard? Does he believe his own argument, or is there some darker purpose here? For everything he accuses Duval of could also be laid at his own feet.

My mind begins turning over every conversation I have had with the chancellor, looking for rips or tears in the cloak of loyalty he wears with such sincerity. Was it he who first suggested Duval might be guilty? Or the abbess? He was most insistent I turn my attentions away from d'Albret and back to Duval. And it was Crunard who informed the convent of both Runnion and Martel. Could he have purposefully brought about those kills in order to work against the duchess? But why?

And most important, is Sister Vcreda well enough to have Seen this? Surely not, for Mortain would not send a false vision, and I know that these accusations are false. Even hearing it from the abbess does not persuade me otherwise.

When my brain has exhausted itself with questions for which I have no answers, I turn to prayer. I open my heart to

Mortain and pray as I have never prayed before. But as I listen for His voice, all I can hear are those of Chancellor Crunard and the abbess.

After a while – a long while – I stand up and straighten my skirts. I am so hollow inside that it feels as if I have left some vital piece of myself on the floor. I know – *know* – that the convent is mistaken. They have been fed false information or have drawn the wrong conclusions. Or both. My own arrogance shocks me, and yet I know they are wrong. That the convent can make such a mistake unnerves me. The nuns are not supposed to make mistakes.

There is a scraping sound by the fireplace as the heavy door begins to swing open. Duval! without thinking, I crumple the note into a ball and toss it into the fire. I watch the convent's orders turn to ash as Duval strides into the chamber. Much to my surprise, he heads straight for me and wraps his arms about my waist, then whirls me round the chamber as if we are dancing. "The tide is turning!" he says, his eyes bright. "D'Albret is gone, the agreement with the Holy Roman emperor is finalized, the English king grows closer to meeting our terms, and my family's plotting has ended!"

I am breathless with his whirling and try to smile back, to act as if nothing has changed, but my face feels frozen. I push at his hands, but they do not budge from my waist.

"Truly," he says, slowing down, "your saint can work miracles." As he looks into my eyes, his smile fades and his eyes grow dark with emotion. Slowly, he leans toward me.

His lips are soft and warm as they touch mine. His mouth moves urgently, as if he is trying to experience every nuance and curve of my lips. The utter rightness of this fills me, for it feels I have waited all my life for just this moment.

His mouth opens slightly, and he shifts the angle of his kiss, nudging my mouth to do the same, and I am lost in a whole new world of sensation. His mouth is soft compared to the strong, callused hands that grip my waist. He tastes faintly of wine and victory and something bitter and astringent.

Even as the realization dawns, my lips begin to tingle, then grow numb. "My lord!" I gasp and pull away.

He looks at me, his eyes full of desire, his pupils grown so large they have swallowed up nearly all the gray in his eyes. It cannot be! I lean in close again, press my lips to his, then run my tongue lightly over his lips and inside his mouth. Even as he responds by pulling me closer, the acrid tang fills my senses.

I pull away and take his hands from my waist. "My lord," I repeat, hoping he will hear the urgency in my voice. "Stop. Think. What have you had to eat today?"

He stares at me intently, trying to make sense of my words, as if I have spoken in some strange language from a far-off land. "Nothing but what you gave me last night. Why?"

I lean in and press one last soft kiss against his lips – to be certain, I tell myself. "You are poisoned. I can taste it."

His pulse beats frantically in the hollow of his throat. "Poisoned?" he repeats, as if the word is new to him.

I hold my fingers to my lips, tasting them again. "Yes," I whisper.

His eyes fill with unspeakable sadness. "You—?"

"No!" I grasp his face with my hands, his whiskery stubble rough beneath my palms. "It is not I who have poisoned you. I swear it!" I hope he does not push me further and ask if the convent is behind it, for I do not know the answer. Did the reverend mother not trust me to do as she ordered? Or has someone else taken matters into his own hands?

He smiles then, a quick fey thing that displays the small dimple I have seen only twice before. Nearly stupid with relief that he believes me, I smile back. His hands reach out and cup my face. "I should not have doubted you," he whispers, then he lowers his mouth to mine.

The taste of poison is strong on my lips and yanks me back to the matter at hand. "Are you sure you haven't eaten any food or wine other than what I gave? Did you notice any strange taste?"

He snorts. "No and no. If so, I would not have eaten it."

But of course, there are hundreds of poisons, many of them too subtle to be detected by the tongue. Others are administered by different means. "Then perhaps it passed through your skin."

He holds his arms out to his sides. "As you can see, all I have left to me are the clothes on my back."

"I know, and that is what I would like to inspect."

"What?"

"Poison can be placed in your gloves, on the inside of your

doublet, your shirt, your hat, anything that touches your skin."

He blinks, at last understanding what I am saying. With a sudden movement, he reaches down and tears the gloves from his belt and throws them on the floor. Frantic now, as if his clothes are coated in stinging nettles, he pulls off his belt, then yanks his doublet over his head and tosses it onto the chair.

I hurry over to inspect each piece, all of them still warm from Duval's body, but there is no trace of poison. No waxy residue, no trace of scent.

"There is nothing on any of these," I tell him. "May I see your boots?"

He recoils in horror. "You are not going to smell my boots," he tells me flatly. He tramps to the chair, drops into it, and pulls off his boots. "What would it smell like?" he asks.

I shrug, hating this helpless feeling. "It depends on which poison was used. It can smell sweet as honey or like bitter oranges. Some have a metallic tang." My heart falters at all the possibilities, for how can I cure him if I do not know what is being used?

He sticks his nose into his boot. "They smell nothing like that," he says.

I am not sure if I should take his word, but he looks ready to come to blows over it, so I let it be for the moment. "Here, let me hold that one while you check the other." I brace myself for another argument, but he grunts at me and shoves the boot into my hand. While he is busy with his other foot,

I let my fingers brush against the inside of his boot. There is no tingle, no numbness, nothing.

"This one is fine too," he says, shoving his foot back into it. He holds out his hand for the other one and I return it to him.

"Now your shirt, my lord."

He gapes at me. "You want to examine my shirt?"

I let my impatience fill my words. "Did you not just hear me say it could be on anything that touches your skin? There are no end of ways to poison a man. You must trust me to know this better than you."

However, there is another reason I wish him to remove his shirt. I need to see if he bears a marque.

His eyes on mine, Duval rises to his feet, undoes the lacings of his shirt, then pulls the fine cambric over his head.

I swallow back a gasp, my eyes fixed on the map of silvery white scars that crisscross the left side of his ribcage. A deep, puckered scar sits just inches from his heart. Unthinking, I step closer, my fingers reaching out to touch the pale tracks some keen blade left. He flinches as if in pain. "Do they still hurt?" My voice comes out as a whisper.

"No." His voice sounds strained.

I trace the longest of the scars that spans his chest. "How close you came. How very, very close." I shiver, unbearably warm and chilled at the same time. Surely Mortain did not spare him then only to have me kill him now.

His skin under my fingers twitches and suddenly I no longer see the scars, but the shift of taut muscle and the broadness of his shoulders. Heat rushes into my cheeks and, unable to stop myself, I look up to meet his gaze. He lifts my hand and kisses it. "Dear, sweet Ismae."

The longing and wanting that rise up inside me is as sharp as any blade and cuts as deep. It is also more terrifying. I snatch my hand out of his grip and turn to fumble for the shirt he has so carelessly dropped on the floor.

I busy myself with picking it up and turning it inside out. I can feel his eyes on me, the room full of unspoken dreams and desire. I concentrate on the shirt, checking the seams carefully, the cuffs, any place a smear of poison might hide. However he is being poisoned, it is not from his garments.

"It is clean," I say, then slowly turn round to hand the shirt to him.

Duval is all business and takes the shirt and slips it over his head. I use that moment to inspect him for a marque. Other than his scars, there is nothing on his chest or his throat, which confirms he has not eaten nor drunk this poison. But the room is lit only by the fire and a brace of candles, so I cannot tell if the grayish pallor to his skin is due to the poor light, the effects of the poison, or the marque of Mortain. But of course, it does not matter. I cannot kill him, marque or no.

"If it is not you poisoning me, who is it?" he asks as he tugs his sleeves into place.

"There are so many who wish you ill, my lord, it is difficult to say."

He gives a wry grimace, then shoves his arms into his doublet. "What is the antidote?" he asks.

"I won't know until we determine which poison has been used." Even then I might not know. I was not taught how to remove the effects of poison, only how to best administer it. It will also depend on how much he has taken in and how much damage it has done to his body.

"How long do I have?" he asks.

I wrap my arms tightly around myself and keep my voice calm. "That you are not dead yet bodes well. Many poisons that will kill you in large amounts only sicken you if taken in small doses." I do not tell him that some of those small doses can have lasting results.

The grim lines about his mouth lead me to believe he knows I am honey-coating my words. "The best we can do for now is keep your strength up. Eat and sleep, my lord, for the stronger you are, the better you will be able to fight the effects."

When he sits down to the tray, he attacks his dinner as if it is an invading army he must vanquish. When he is finished, he lies down in front of the fire and falls immediately to sleep. But I do not. I spend the long, dark hours of the night fighting despair and looking back over the past few days, trying to pick out symptoms I may have missed.

What I told him is true; there are hundreds of possibilities. Many noble houses in France and Italy have their own poisoners on staff, each with his own secret recipe or concoction. There are dozens upon dozens of poisons that can be taken in through the skin alone. How will I ever determine which one is being used against him?

And if I cannot figure it out, he will die.

Chapter 44

When morning comes, Duval is gone. I tell myself that his being well enough to leave is surely a good sign.

The night has brought some clarity but no solutions. I do not think the convent is behind Duval's poisoning, for who would they use to do it? I have not seen or heard from Sybella since d'Albret left. Besides, the note from the abbess made it quite clear that this task was my last chance to prove to the convent I was serious about my duties and my vow.

Which means someone else is behind the poisoning.

I think of Duval's chessboard and how the white queen stood surrounded by fewer and fewer allies. The answer, of course, has to be one of those left standing: Marshal Rieux, Captain Dunois, and Chancellor Crunard.

Of those, only Crunard has free access to the convent and only Crunard has accused Duval of spying for the French regent. Even angry as Marshal Rieux was, he suspected Duval only of acting in his own self-interest rather than Brittany's. And, of course, what better way to deflect suspicion from one's own actions than to lay the blame at someone else's feet.

Like the tumblers in a lock, my mind shifts and moves. With hindsight, everywhere I look I can find traces of Crunard hidden in the background or under layers of deceit.

He was one of the few who knew I was traveling with Duval to Guérande and would know extra assailants would be needed. The lone captive from that attack was killed immediately after Crunard returned to the city. I even saw him meet with the French ambassador. And while the chancellor spoke with Gisors sharply, he himself has pointed out how easy it is to fake that.

If all of that is true, then he must also be behind Duval's poisoning. I assume such poison can be found in a town of Guérande's size. Or perhaps he obtained some directly from the convent. Or...

I hurry to my trunklet, take the key from my neck, and fit it to the lock. I remove the tray of weapons and look to the poisons beneath. Frantically, I examine the bottles and jars. They are all full except one: the jar of Arduinna's snare. That is half empty.

All the symptoms fit: rapid pulse, dilated pupils, dry fever, disorientation, paranoia, numbness in the extremities, and, in the end, death.

Crunard has used my own poisons to destroy Duval.

He had access to this very trunk when he traveled with my things when they were sent from the convent. A lock is easy enough to pick.

With shaking hands I return the vials to the trunk and lock it. I push to my feet and try to think. If it is Crunard, then to what end? Did he not think that the convent would issue the order? Or is it more than that? It is possible he has been feeding the convent false information all along, but again, to what end? And while I do not fully understand how the marques work, I know they are more complex than I – and perhaps even the convent – first thought. It would be easy enough for him to feed us information that supports his claims and withhold information that does not. When my own reports contradict his, how easy it is to dismiss them as the work of an unskilled novice.

But how do I tell the reverend mother that?

She will not like the suggestion that he has used her for his own ends. Nor am I certain she will believe me. Even so, I fetch a parchment and quill and do the unthinkable. I write a letter to the abbess to tell her why she is mistaken and that her liaison has given her false intelligence.

When I have poured out all my suspicions regarding Crunard, I seal the missive, then begin a second one. This message is for Annith and begs her to write to me with the antidote for Arduinna's snare. Sister Serafina must have something, some antidote she can send. If she does, Annith will surely find it. I also inquire after Sister Vereda's health, wanting to know if she is still having visions.

When I finish, I approach Vanth's cage. He is sleeping with his head tucked under his wing and is sorely put out at being wakened. I mumble an apology and secure the notes, then carry him to the window. "Fly fast, if you please. Much depends on this." Then I toss him out the window. He spreads his wings and rises into the gray sky, and I watch until I can no longer see him.

That done, I dress quickly. There is one possible antidote

I know of: a bezoar stone. I am not certain if it will work on poison passed through the skin, but it is worth a try. And there is only one person I can think of who might possess one.

It is nearly half a day's ride to the herbwitch's cottage, and even though I have never come this particular way, I have no trouble finding it. I have feared the old woman for most of my life. When I was younger and Mama had first sent me to her for tansy to treat my sister's fever, I had hidden nearby, crying for hours. I was certain the woman would take one look at me, know that her poison had failed, and finish the job then and there.

Of course, she had not. She had merely beckoned me from the shadows, coaxing me with a bit of honeycomb dripping with golden honey – a rare treat I could not resist. When at last I believed she would not harm me, I had managed to stutter out what I had come for, which she gave to me and then sent me on my way. I had believed that she did not recognize me, and so my fear had left me.

But clearly I had been wrong, for it was she who came for me years later and whisked me away to my new life.

When I reach the small, squat cottage surrounded by a riotous garden, I dismount, tie the horse to the fence post, then open the gate. A merry little bell sounds, making me jump. I weave my way through the hawthorn hedge and the waist-high bushes of lavender until I reach the front door. It opens before I can knock and the herbwitch herself peers up at me through her rheumy eyes. "Still hovering, after all these years?" she asks. "Come in before you let all the warm air out."

The cottage hasn't changed much, nor has she. Her hair is still white, flyaway strands of thistledown; her eyes perhaps a bit more faded, her skin more wrinkled. Herbs hang from the ceiling, their sharp, peppery, sweet scents assailing my senses. Three small cauldrons bubble on the hearth, and all manner of clay beakers, pots, and copper dishes cover her tables. It is surprisingly similar to Sister Serafina's workshop.

"What brings Death's handmaiden to my humble door?" she asks, not looking the least bit humble. Mayhap she even gloats somewhat.

I open my mouth, then hesitate. It was she who sent me to the convent three years ago. Will she know that by seeking an antidote, I am going against their wishes? Will she care?

Ignoring my gaping silence, she begins to speak. "I always expected to see you again someday, wanting to know about your mother, no doubt."

My mother. It is not until she says the word that I realize I *am* hungry for such knowledge. What had caused my mother to lie down with Death in the first place? Had she been forced? Or had He taken her by the hand and led her away from her harsh life for a few stolen moments of... What? Pleasure? Love? Respite? What could Death offer someone such as my mother? And if it had been love, why had my mother sought to expel me from her womb?

The old woman takes a seat near the fireplace and waves her gnarled hand for me to follow. "The first time I saw your mother was when your father – no, not your real father, but that lout she married – brought her to me. He marched her up to my doorstep, holding her arm so tight she had bruises for two weeks after. Gave her arnica root for that, by the bye."

"And?"

She settles back into her chair, savoring her hungry audience. I do not imagine she gets one all that often. "And he demanded I do something to expel the babe in her womb."

My mother hadn't wanted to get rid of me, then. It had not been her choice. Some great, dark weight lifts from me.

The herbwitch shrugs. "I thought about faking something, but he stood there and watched me mix the brew himself, asking after each thing I put in. I soon realized that if I gave him a false potion, he'd be back again, like as not. Best for everyone to get it over with as soon as possible.

"But in spite of my best efforts, it didn't work. That's when I knew you were god sired. Two weeks later, he was back pounding at my door, demanding another dose. But Matrona's curse is harsh and had already sickened your mother almost to the point of death. I told him I would not have the killing of her laid at my feet and that considering who her lover had been, he should think twice about inviting Him back." She turns her watery eyes from me to the fire, and I can see the flames reflected in them. "Your mother did all she could to protect you from that man's wrath. Reminded him often of who your true sire was. But even with that, you did not have a smooth time of it."

We are both quiet and stare into the flames, but we see very different things, no doubt. I struggle to adjust to the world reformed. The knowledge that my mother had not hated me shifts everything. It is as if all my life I have been looking at the world through a pane of thick, distorted glass, and now that glass has shattered, and I can see clearly. "How did you come to find me the day" – I cannot bring myself to say *the day of my wedding*—"the day my father sold me to Guillo?"

"I had promised your mother I would try to keep an eye on you. Although it was unfair of her to ask, me being the only herbwitch for miles around and too busy besides. But I did what I could."

"It was you who had me sent to the convent."

"Aye."

"What is the convent to you?"

She turns her head sharply to me. "You think those nuns are the only ones who know Death? What do you think I do all day besides dance with Him, bartering for a life here, a few extra months there? Chasing Him from this old man's lungs or that young boy's fevered brain? No, the convent is not the only one to partner with Death."

That the dance goes two ways is not something I have ever considered. "So, you are Death's handmaiden too," I murmur.

She looks surprised, then cackles in delight. "Aye," she says, sitting up somewhat straighter. "I guess I am at that."

"But you do not serve the convent?" I ask, just to be certain.

"No, but it was the only place I thought you'd be safe."

I weigh the risk carefully, but I do not have any choice.

Wanting to avoid her sharp gaze, I study the back of my hands. "Do you have a bezoar stone?"

The herbwitch gives me a sly look. "Surely the convent has antidotes for their poisons."

"We spent our energies creating poisons, not antidotes, and while we did have bezoar stones in case any of the girls ingested some, I do not have one with me now."

Out of the corner of my eye, I see her frown. "So now you step outside the circle of the convent and begin your own dance with Death," she says, and I curse her old eyes that see too much. She rocks back in her chair. "Alas, I have no such stone. Never seen one of them, truth be told."

I ask her if she knows an antidote for Arduinna's snare, but she has never heard of it. Furthermore, she has no antidotes at all for poisons absorbed through the skin, as purgatives do not work in those cases. My shoulders sag as my last hope crumbles to ash. Seeing my distress, the old woman pats me on the arm as she bids me goodbye. "It is a dark god you serve, daughter, but remember, He is not without mercy."

As I travel back to Guérande, the herbwitch's words roll around in my head like loose pebbles, clattering and bumping, shaping and smoothing. I walked into that cottage as one person but left as another. There is now a thin blanket between me and the harsh, cold abandonment I have felt ever since I was old enough to understand what my mother did to me in her belly.

My mind flows over old memories. With this new bit of

knowledge, many of my mother's small gestures and comforts are suddenly clear. They were expressions of the very love I thought she had denied me. They were not simply duties borne but small rebellions of her own as she thwarted her husband in the only way she could.

Even though one burden has been lifted, I return to the palace exhausted and defeated and out of ideas. I pray that I will not meet anyone on the way to my chambers, and I do not.

Once I am in my room, I see a crow sitting outside the window. My heart clutches in my chest. My message of that morning cannot have reached the convent yet. Is it new orders from the abbess? A reprieve?

When I open the shutter, the crow flies in. He is a large fellow with a crooked left wing. Sybella's crow. He is tame only for her, so it takes me a moment to wrest the message from his leg. When I do, I see that it is indeed Sybella's writing, and I am filled with foreboding.

I tear the message open and read the words scrawled within.

Rieux and d'Albret have taken Nantes. They entered the city with men-at-arms, seized the duchess's palace, and manned the ramparts. We are besieged from within.

My heart ceases its racing and gives one slow, painful thud in my chest. The very men who are supposed to support and guide our duchess have risen up in open rebellion.

The implications of this are huge. Nantes was the duchess's fallback position, the biggest, most fortified city in Brittany.

Her home. Indeed, she has only been waiting for the plague to leave the area so she could return.

But now it is taken from her. And without a sword raised or shot fired. The only piece of good news I can wrestle from the wreckage is that with Rieux removed to Nantes, there is no longer any doubt that Crunard must be the traitor.

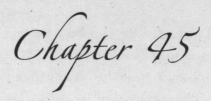

Chapter 45

Crunard is alone when the guard ushers me into his chambers. I drop a respectful curtsy. "My lord, I have received urgent news that I must give the duchess and request you accompany me, as she will need your guidance once she has learned what I have to tell her." I had considered waiting to discuss the news with Duval before taking it to the duchess or her council, but I do not know how quickly we must act. Plus, it is hard to say what condition Duval will be in by this evening.

"Have you news of Duval?" Crunard asks sharply.

I meet his eyes steadily. "No, milord, I am afraid not."

A spasm of irritation crosses his face. "Well, you have piqued my interest. Of course I will accompany you to the solar."

"We should send for Captain Dunois to meet us there, my lord."

Crunard raises one gray shaggy eyebrow but sends a page to fetch the captain of the armies.

Captain Dunois reaches the solar just as we do. The duchess takes one look at our grim faces and dismisses her ladies from the room. "What is it?" she asks, clasping her hands together, as if praying it will not be as bad as she fears.

Chancellor Crunard smiles wryly and shrugs. "It is not I who called this meeting but Demoiselle Rienne."

Everyone's eyes turn to me, and it is all I can do not to twitch and squirm out of my skin. I have been trained in subterfuge and concealment, not this standing out in the open like the town crier. To calm myself, I address my words to the duchess. "I have received grave news, Your Grace. I have learned that Marshal Rieux and Count d'Albret have taken Nantes."

There is a moment of stunned silence, then Captain Dunois asks, "Are you certain?"

"How have you learned this?" Crunard asks, and I cannot help but wonder if he is behind this newest disaster.

"The ways of Mortain are both glorious and mysterious. I may not divulge how I know, but it has most definitely happened. If you do not believe me, send a scout to verify my claim."

Crunard looks to Dunois, who gives a sharp nod. "Consider it done."

"If it is so," Crunard says, "this is well and truly a disaster."

He looks visibly shaken, so either he is a superb liar or this is not part of whatever game he is playing.

"Marshal Rieux?" the duchess says to me, her brown eyes filled with distress. "Are you certain?" she whispers.

Meeting her gaze, I nod solemnly. The man who was appointed by her father to guard her has just betrayed her instead. She draws in a long, shaky breath, then asks, "What does this do to our position?"

Crunard and Dunois exchange a bleak look. "It is not good," Captain Dunois says. "As marshal, he commands the troops. It will be hard to raise the barons to fight against him. If Marshal Rieux and d'Albret combine their troops, well, our only hope will be to hunker down and prepare for the coming siege."

The duchess glances in alarm from Dunois to Crunard. "Not our *only* hope, surely?"

"I am afraid so, Your Grace," the chancellor tells her, and even though he but agrees with Dunois, I find I cannot trust his counsel. "It is as Captain Dunois says; the marshal commands our troops. It will be hard to raise them against him. Indeed, it will be hard to raise them at all without his help."

"What about Baron de Waroch?" It is only when everyone turns to stare at me that I realize I have spoken out loud. Flustered, I continue. "Did he not go through the countryside raising the peasants and farmers to revolt against the French in the Mad war? Why could he not do that again?"

Chancellor Crunard sends me a dismissive look. "It will take more than peasants and farmers to repel the French, demoiselle."

"Ultimately, yes," Captain Dunois says, his voice thoughtful. "But perhaps they can hold off the French forces long enough for help to arrive."

"What help?" Crunard asks sharply.

That is when I realize that Duval – dear, ever-suspicious Duval – has told no one of the preparations he has been laboring over.

"Even as we speak," the duchess says, "fifteen hundred

troops are en route from Spain and another fifteen hundred from Navarre."

Crunard is nonplussed, but hides it with a snort of derision. "That is too few."

"But if combined with the peasantry," Captain Dunois points out, "they may stand a chance."

Hope shines in the duchess's face. "Might this work?"

"A long shot, Your Grace, but within the realm of possibility," Dunois tells her.

Crunard shakes his head. "I think it is but a dream, Your Grace."

With my new suspicions filling my head, it is all I can do to keep from shouting that whatever Crunard counsels, we must do the opposite. I am saved from such drastic measures when the duchess puts her hands to her head as if it aches. "Enough. I will think on this and we will meet again tomorrow morning."

As we all file out of the solar, the duchess catches my eye. I nod, letting her know I will discuss this with Duval before then.

I spend the evening pacing, turning every possible idea over in my mind, looking for any small opening or crack in the walls that hem our duchess in as surely as any dungeon. But there are none. None that I can find. And it was clear in today's meeting that none of the duchess's other councilors can think outside the well-plowed furrows of their own thoughts.

There is a scrape at the wall behind me and I turn round to see Duval lurch out of the passageway. His hair is mussed, his face is covered in dark stubble, his eyes arc wild. "My lord!" I hurry toward him, afraid he will fall to the floor. "What has happened?"

"Nothing, dear Ismae." He waves his hand in a wild, expansive gesture, then stumbles. My heart sinks as I help him into a chair. Alarm inches along my skin. His symptoms are worse, which means he must have come in further contact with the poison. If it is not removed from his body, he will surely die.

Once in the chair, he leans forward and puts his face in his hands. "My head feels as if it is spinning on a wheel."

"'Tis one of the effects of the poison, my lord."

He glances up at me with a heartbreakingly confused look. "Poison?"

Not his memory. Sweet Mortain, not that. I kneel at his feet and put my face close to his. "Remember? We talked of this last night? You are being poisoned."

He grabs my hands in his as if they are a lifeline that will lead him back to sanity. In a moment his face clears as the memory comes to him, and I breathe a sigh of relief. "Do you remember what else we talked of?"

His grip tightens. "Yes. Of course."

I pull the tray of food close to him. "Are you hungry? You should eat."

He pushes it away. "I have no appetite."

I shove the tray back. "You must eat. Your body and your

mind need food, my lord. You must stay strong in order to fight the effects of the poison." Indeed, he has grown thin from his days in the tunnels. To appease me, he takes the cup of tepid broth I hand him and fiddles with a wedge of cheese. I do not tell him of the latest news until he is done eating, not wanting to risk destroying his already diminished appetite.

Once he has finished, however, I can put it off no longer. "I have much news, and none of it good." Duval leans back slightly in his chair, as if bracing himself for a physical blow. "Nantes has been taken by Marshal Rieux and Lord d'Albret."

"Taken?"

I nod, then tell him of the message I received. Fury and frustration spur him out of his chair, but he stumbles. He looks down and scowls at his feet. "What did the Privy Council recommend?" he asks.

"Dunois and Crunard think we should close the city gates and ready ourselves for a siege."

"They are mistaken," he says. "Guérande will not withstand a siege for long."

"Dunois hopes the troops from Spain and Navarre will arrive in time."

He is silent a long moment. "Ismae, I'm sorry..."

"No, my lord. You were right to keep your own counsel. I do not fault you for it. Besides, there is more bad news you must hear. I believe it is Crunard who has been working secretly against the duchess all this time. I do not think he can be trusted."

Duval looks at me as if I am the one who flirts with madness.

"The chancellor? But why, and to what purpose? The man is a hero who has fought in three wars and lost all four of his sons to the cause. He and the late duke were the closest of friends. Why would he do something that would render all of their sacrifice for naught?"

"I do not yet understand the why of it, but look at the evidence. He was one of the very few who knew to send enough footpads to attack us when we first came to Guérande. It was also just after he arrived that the sole remaining assailant disappeared." I fold my arms in front of me to keep from wringing my hands. "Furthermore, it is my own poison being used on you, and Crunard is the only one who has had access to it."

Duval blinks, as if my arguments are finally reaching him. Then he shakes his head, trying to clear it, and rubs his hands over his face. "But look how he has supported Anne all this time! Backed her refusal of d'Albret, voted for the alliance with Nemours. I cannot see what purpose lies behind his actions."

Frustration bubbles through me and I cannot tell if my own logic is flawed or if Duval's mind is too far gone. "My lord, he told the convent that you were involved in your mother's plot of treason – that you were a traitor."

His head snaps up and a bewildered look crosses his face. "He did?"

"Aye."

"Then why did they not order my execution?"

I say nothing, but his addled wits are not *that* far gone. "Oh." He looks down. "Is that why my feet are numb?"

"No, my lord. I swear it. I have ignored their order. Here, you need rest." I jump up to catch him as he stands and sways. He sags against me and I propel him to my bed. Louyse has already turned back the covers, so I lay him down in my place. Propping his legs on the bed, I yank off his boots and, after checking them one more time for traces of poison, let them drop to the floor. Then I swing his legs under the rich, thick quilts. He tries to push up on his elbows to argue with me, but I place my hand gently on his chest and push him back down. It takes frighteningly little effort. His eyes flutter shut, and my heart leaps into my mouth. I lean in close to check his breathing.

"Are you trying to steal my breath?" Duval asks.

"No, milord. Only trying to—"

"Kiss me?" The yearning in his voice shakes me to the core.

"Yes, my lord. That is it." And I lean in and kiss him, a long, slow kiss, as if I would drink the poison from his body. His eyes close again, and his breathing grows steadier. The lines of tension ease somewhat, but not altogether. The shadows under his eyes are darker; his cheeks are more gaunt. He is in need of a shave, and the color is high in his cheeks. My heart is so full – full of love and full of sorrow – that I fear it will burst.

His hand twitches and spasms, so I reach out and cover it with my own. He grows still then, and turns his hand up so that our palms are touching, our fingers linked. "Don't leave."

"I won't," I tell him. *Nor you, either,* I long to say, to make him promise not to die. But I cannot insist he make a promise he cannot keep. Instead, I lower myself to the floor and keep watch over him through the night.

I awake to a faint kiss on the back of my hand. I open my eyes to find Duval's head propped on his hand as he watches me. "Good morning."

"Good morning," I mumble, embarrassed. I try to disengage our tangled fingers, but he holds on long enough to give one last squeeze, then lets go.

I rise to my feet and try to ignore the various aches and pains from sleeping in such a cramped position. As I smooth my skirts and try to regain my composure, Duval gets up from the bed and crosses to the ewer and basin, where he splashes cold water on his face. His legs are steadier than they were yesterday, and I can only hope this is a sign that a decent night's rest has done him some good. When he turns round, beads of water still dripping from his face, I see that his eyes have cleared somewhat.

I hand him a linen towel. As he dries himself, I move to the tray of food. "You really should try to eat some more before you go."

"I will." He puts the towel down and comes to grab a wedge of cheese from the tray. He looks to the window to check how close to dawn it is.

Very close.

As he stuffs his pockets with the rest of the food, I frown

in puzzlement. He appears much better this morning. Surely that is a hopeful sign.

When his pockets are full, he comes and puts his hands on my shoulders, his eyes alight with urgency. "They must get Anne to Rennes. Guérande is not strong enough to withstand a long siege, but the citizens of Rennes will rally around her, and the town has the means to defend itself. It is the best place for her until help arrives. Convince them, Ismae."

"I will try, my lord."

"And beware of denouncing Crunard in front of the others. They have known him far longer than you and will be more likely to side with him should it come to that. You will need solid proof to convince them of your accusations."

There is a sound outside my door. Louyse. He brushes a quick kiss on the top of my head, then disappears into the passage in the wall.

A moment later, Louyse bustles into the room, full of her usual morning cheer. She pauses briefly and looks confused when she sees I am wearing my cloak over my night shift. I rub my arms and give a little shiver. "It is cold this morning."

"That it is, demoiselle!" As she sets out my clothes, a plan forms in my mind. The remaining members of the Privy Council will be meeting first thing this morning. It will be the perfect time for me to search Crunard's chamber. Surely I can find something that will convince the others of his guilt.

Chapter 46

When I arrive at Crunard's chambers, the door is closed and there is no guard posted. I knock and call out, "Chancellor Crunard?" There is no answer. I glance down the hall in both directions. It is clear. Indeed, the palace is very quiet today, and I wonder how many courtiers have heard what has happened in Nantes. Assured that there is no one to see, I try the door. It is locked, but that does not stop me.

I slip one of the needle-thin daggers from my wrist and slip the tip inside the lock, as Sister Eonette showed us. I gently press against the metal insides, nudging the iron to do what I want. When I hear a satisfying click, I straighten, check for witnesses, then slip silently into Chancellor Crunard's office.

I do not know how much time I have, nor do I know what I am looking for. Something – anything – that will confirm my suspicions.

The papers on his desk are what I expect: correspondence with the barons, maps of Brittany and France, everything that a chancellor needs to perform his duties. I open the cupboard that sits behind his desk and quickly rifle through the pages of the books stored there, but none of them hold hidden letters or carved-out compartments. Nor is there any damning correspondence rolled in along with the rest of the maps. It would help if I knew what I was looking for.

Frustrated, I turn back to his desk, my eyes landing on his writing box. When I try to open it, I find it locked. Why would he lock away his writing supplies?

My pulse quickens as I take out my dagger once more and work the lock. This one is smaller – and trickier – than the door's, but in the end it gives way. I lift the wooden lid and peer inside. Quills, ink pots, a small paring knife, red sealing wax, a heavy gold signet ring...

I pick up the ring and examine it carefully. Crunard wears so very many rings, why would he lock this one away? Something about it niggles at the back of my mind. It takes a moment for me to recognize it.

It is the very ring I glimpsed when Martel's soul passed through me. Which means... What?

That the French spy Martel had seen Crunard's ring, whether it was on the chancellor's finger when they met face to face or it was sent to him with some lesser courier. If it was sent as a sign, then Martel knew to trust Crunard.

It is not Duval who has been working with the French regent but Crunard.

I close my hand around the heavy gold ring, savoring the solid feel of actual evidence in my hand. But the only one who would give weight to this proof is the abbess, and even that is doubtful. None of the remaining Privy Council will understand how I know this; they will not favor my word over Crunard's.

Even so, I slip the ring in my pocket. Surely flimsy evidence is better than no evidence at all.

Because I am late for the Privy Council meeting, I must suffer a scowl of disapproval from Crunard, but I smile coolly at him. Now that I know he is a traitor, I do not care what he thinks of me.

Neither Dunois nor Crunard has changed his mind during the night. As they run through their reasoning for the duchess, I study Crunard carefully, looking for any sign of a marque, but his bedamned fur collar comes up to his ears and hides any marque he might bear.

"What counsel do you have for us this morning, demoiselle?"

I blink and find the duchess looking at me politely. Crunard, too, is watching me with his cold blue eyes and I realize I must play this very carefully. "Would it not be better to use this moment of time before all our enemies descend on us to get you to a more secure location? Rennes, perhaps? The people there are loyal. They have a defensible position and the troops to defend it, as well as a bishop who can see you safely crowned duchess."

Crunard regards me, his face carefully blank. "What makes you think that Rennes is so very loyal, demoiselle?" There is a challenging tone in his voice, and I fear I have said too much or said it too baldly and have made Duval's hand in the strategy clear to him.

I meet his gaze. "The convent has always thought highly of them, my lord chancellor." There. Let him make of that what he will.

"That is not a bad idea," Captain Dunois says thoughtfully.

Chancellor Crunard opens his mouth to argue, which makes me favor the idea all the more. But before he can begin his arguments, there is a knock on the door. "Yes?" he calls out, making no attempt to hide his annoyance.

De Lornay opens the door, bows low, then comes into the room. All signs of the seductive courtier are gone; he is sweat stained and travel weary. He falls to one knee before the duchess and lowers his head. "Your Grace. I beg forgiveness for interrupting your meeting, but I bring grave news that cannot wait."

The duchess's face pales. "Go on."

"The French have taken Guingamp in the north. The city has fallen."

Behind me, Captain Dunois swears under his breath, but de Lornay continues. "That is not the worst of it. The French army has crossed our northern and eastern borders as well. They have taken three of our cities, Ancenis, Vitré, and Fougères."

Even though we have all been awaiting this news, it is different to actually hear it. There is a long, stunned silence as we realize our country has once again been invaded. The duchess is white as snow, but she gracefully inclines her head. "Thank you for bringing us word of these events,

Baron de Lornay. Pray go refresh yourself."

He rises to his feet and leaves the room.

Crunard speaks first. "It seems we are suddenly out of time."

The duchess looks up at Captain Dunois, her eyes wide with fear she is trying so desperately to hide. "How long can we withstand a siege if it comes to that?"

"Three weeks, four at the most."

"Is that long enough for any of the help on the way to reach us?"

"No. It is not," he says, his voice heavy with defeat.

She gives a sharp nod. "So staying here buys us nothing, not even enough time."

Captain Dunois starts to speak, but she silences him. "How long would it take us to reach Rennes from here?"

"Four or five days, Your Grace."

"At best," Chancellor Crunard points out. "We will be greatly hampered by the baggage carts and household that cannot travel by horse. Our party will be stretched out for half a mile, a ripe target for all our enemies."

Captain Dunois nods, conceding the point. "Besides, Rennes is close to Fougères. The French could easily cut us off and might even now be marching on the city. However, these bad tidings also bring a small gift."

The duchess frowns. "How is that, Captain?"

He spreads his hands. "Ancenis is Marshal Rieux's own holding. If the French have seized his lands, what better rallying cry to call him back to our side? Surely he will wish to put aside this petty alliance with d'Albret in order to protect his own lands."

A small ray of hope appears on the duchess's face, but Crunard stares at him stonily. "Do you mean reconcile with Marshal Rieux?"

Dunois nods.

"Do you think that is possible?" the duchess asks.

Dunois shrugs. "He is a good man at heart, Your Grace, and no doubt thinks he is doing what's best for his country."

"By holding my own city against me?" the duchess asks tartly.

"By allying with the strongest of your suitors. However, now that the French are on the march, he will no doubt see the need to face them with a united front and will abandon this path he has taken."

Her face creased in thought, the duchess begins to pace. "How would we do this?"

"We would take a small party and ride for Nantes to parley with him."

Crunard takes a step toward the duchess. "I do not think it is safe for you to leave the city, Your Grace."

She glances at Captain Dunois, her arched brows raised in question.

"I think it is worth considering," he says. "Whatever Rieux may hope to get from this rebellion of his, he will not want it at the cost of his own holding."

The chancellor sighs heavily, as if deeply worried. "I think you are making a terrible mistake."

But his is only one vote among three and he is overruled by both Captain Dunois and the duchess herself. And so it is decided. The duchess and her small party will ride for Nantes tomorrow.

Chapter 47

Duval is late. Either that or he is not coming. I pace in front of the fire and try not to fret, but the most likely explanation is that he has become too ill to move. That he is huddled in some corner on the verge of death.

This idea so distresses me that I grab my cloak and head for the door. If the hidden tunnels and corridors run the full breadth and depth of the castle, I will need help searching them. Besides, I will not be able to carry him back by myself.

The sergeant-at-arms will not let me into the garrison, but he sends a lackey to fetch Beast for me. A short while later, he and de Lornay arrive. I have caught them dicing. De Lornay still holds a pair in his hand and is rubbing them together cheerfully. When they see it is me, the casual smiles and laughter drop from their faces and they hurry forward. "What is it?" Beast asks.

I glance at the nearby sergeant-at-arms, and Beast takes my elbow and moves us outside. When we are standing in the middle of the training yard, far from any corners or doorways that might conceal an eavesdropper, de Lornay asks, "Has something happened to Duval?"

"He was supposed to come to my room tonight and he has not. He has told you where he is staying, yes?"

Beast nods slowly.

"Well, I fear he is lying somewhere in there. Have you seen him in the last few days? He is very ill. He—" My throat grows so tight that it is hard to get the words out. In the end, I cannot tell them I am afraid Duval is dying but say instead, "I fear he is too weak to move."

De Lornay's whole manner changes and his gaze sharpens. "It is not my doing," I tell him, but I do not think he believes me.

"We will help," Beast says before de Lornay and I can come to blows. "Show us."

The hour is late and the court subdued, so there are few people about to see us. When we reach Duval's apartments, I hesitate. It would not do for loyal Louyse to see me leading two men into my bedchamber. She would never forgive such a betrayal of her master.

But there is no one in the main chamber, so I motion to Beast and de Lornay and they move through the room, silent as shadows. When we reach my chamber, Duval is still not there. "The door he uses is here," I say, showing them the wall by the fireplace. "But I do not know the mechanism that opens it."

Neither, apparently, do they, for they poke and grunt and prod at the wall for long frustrating minutes, until finally there is a solid thunk, and then the wall gives way. Beast puts his shoulder to it and shoves. Cool, dank air wafts into the room. "We'll need light," de Lornay says.

I hurry to the table and use the lone candle burning there

to light three more tapers. I hand one to de Lornay, another to Beast. They glance at the candle I clutch in my own hand but do not try to keep me from coming.

The blackness inside the corridors is absolute, and the faint glow from my room is swallowed up in a matter of seconds. There are no windows, no doors, no openings of any kind. Just thick gray stone pressing down on us from all sides. It reminds me of the crypt at the convent, and I do not know how Duval has stood it all this time.

The main corridor branches off in many directions. Carefully and methodically we explore each one. It is slow going in the dark, with few landmarks to guide us. We do not dare call out his name for fear of being heard in the bedrooms and chambers on the other side of the walls.

The corridor twists and turns like a writhing serpent, and just when I fear we will never be able to find our way back, there is an "*Oof*" from Beast, followed by a voice in the darkness: "I think I would rather die of the poison than be trampled by a great oaf like you."

"Duval!" My breath hitches in my throat and I dart around de Lornay and Beast. Duval leans against the stone wall, his face alarmingly pale. "You are alive," I say, and do not add, *but barely*. It is as witless as anything I have ever uttered, but relief sings so sharply in my veins it has chased away my wits.

"Alive," he says, then grimaces. "But unable to move my legs."

I turn my gaze to his lifeless legs so he cannot see my face. The poison has seeped further into his body and has begun paralyzing his limbs. Surely, his lungs and heart will soon follow.

Beast shoulders past me, shaking his head and *tsk*ing like a nursemaid. "Never could hold your drink." De Lornay goes to the other side of Duval and I see they mean to haul him to his feet and carry him. I know he would not want me to watch, so I take the men's candles from them and turn back toward the corridor, ready to light the way once they have a solid hold on him.

I use the moment to compose myself. *Why have I not heard from Annith? Could it be that the abbess has intercepted my note? Or is my request so contrary to the teachings of the convent that Annith will not honor it?* A note of hysterical laughter comes close to escaping. I, a mistress of poison, am willing to trade my soul for an antidote, if only I could find one.

Now that we have located Duval, I find the passageway does not seem so impossibly long or hopelessly dark. In a matter of minutes we are back in my chamber. I set the candles down and busy myself with stoking the fire, giving Beast and de Lornay a chance to settle Duval on the bed.

The men murmur softly among themselves as I take a pot of broth from the hearth. I am close to throwing myself on Duval's ruined body and weeping. Instead, I square my shoulders, put the warm broth on a tray, and carry it to the bed. "There is much news," I tell him.

He tries to push the tray away, but I glare at him. "And I will not tell you a word of it unless you eat something."

He exchanges a glance with Beast, and in that glance I see

he thinks it a pointless exercise. He accepts that he is dying. Not only accepts it, but prefers it. He does not want to be carried like a scarecrow for the rest of his days. But *I* do not accept it, so I hand him the spoon.

"Tell me," he says, lifting it to his mouth.

"The French have crossed the border into Brittany and taken Ancenis, Fougères, and Vitré."

The spoon stops in midair. "Marshal Rieux's own holding?"

"Aye," I say.

Off to my side, Beast whistles.

"Keep eating." When he puts another spoonful of broth into his mouth, I continue. "Captain Dunois thinks we have a chance of using this to reconcile with Marshal Rieux."

"She must not reconcile with Rieux," Duval says, his voice fierce. "She must demand that he come to her to beg forgiveness; she must not go to him."

I cannot help but wonder if this is the poison talking, for surely the duchess is in no position to demand anything. "As much as I detest Marshal Rieux and what he has done, if there is a chance to reclaim an ally, mustn't she at least consider it?"

"How do they propose to effect this reconciliation?" he asks.

"They will ride to Nantes and attempt to persuade him to return to Anne's side so he can lead her armies against the French."

"What does Crunard say?" Duval asks around a bite of bread.

"He wants to keep her safe in Guérande, but Dunois and the duchess overruled him."

"When do they leave?"

"At daybreak tomorrow," I tell him. "They want to get underway before word of their plan leaks to Nantes or the French regent."

Duval swears a black oath. "Do they not realize they are most likely riding directly into a trap?"

"Not to mention that the French are inside our border, and there is no way of knowing how many scouts or sorties they have sent out," Beast adds. "How large a company will they be taking?"

"A small one. Not more than twenty."

"Easily overpowered by a large scouting party then," Beast says.

Duval drops his head back against the wall in frustration. The loud thud makes me wince but he barely even registers the blow. "By the five wounds of Christ, this is a wretched time to be poisoned."

"Poison!" De Lornay's fist clenches around the dice he has been fidgeting with and he takes a step toward me. But it is Beast's reaction that cuts me to the quick. He lifts his great head and looks at me with wounded eyes, as if I have betrayed him as well as Duval.

"It is not by my hand," I snap. When they say nothing, I grow agitated. "Think! Would I have fetched the two of you if I wanted him to die?"

That seems to convince them somewhat, although de

Lornay keeps casting dark, sullen glances toward me as I carry the empty tray back to the table by the fire. Behind me, Duval starts to put together a plan. "Beast, de Lornay, when you leave here tonight, go to Dunois. Tell him you want to be in that party that leaves for Nantes. Do not let him refuse you. Ismae!" he calls out.

I stop what I am doing and turn to face the bed.

"I want you to go as well. Attach yourself to the duchess as if you were her shield, for in truth, you may be. Do not leave her side."

My hands grip my skirt and I hurry back to him. "My lord, that is not what my convent has ordered." I do not let myself think on what my convent actually wants me to do. The herbwitch's words rise up in mind and I cannot tell if they are meant to taunt or comfort: *It is a dark god you serve, daughter, but remember, He is not without mercy.* Is this His mercy, then? That I will not have to slay Duval with my own hand because he is already dying from poison? A dark god indeed.

"Perhaps not," he says, "but surely it is what they would want you to do if they knew of her plans." When I do not speak, he turns to Beast. "Make her go with you. No matter how sick I am or what Crunard or Dunois say, make sure she rides out with you. Carry her if you have to. Swear it."

"I swear it." Beast's deep voice rumbles through the room.

Duval turns to me, his voice more gentle now. "This is what I have worked for my entire life, Ismae, the duchess's safety. I cannot finish this task, so I ask that you do it for me."

And, of course, I cannot say no. Not to his dying wish. "Very well," I whisper.

A faint tremor shudders through Duval's body, as if it is only his determination to make these last arrangements for his sister that has kept him going. Our eyes meet. "Thank you."

When Beast and de Lornay take their leave, Duval leans back against the pillows, his face taking on a grayish pallor. I have spent the day longing to share my news of Crunard's signet ring with him, but he is so ill, I do not have the heart to add to his cares. "You really must sleep, my lord. You can give us more instructions when you wake up."

He says something I cannot make out. "What?" I ask, coming closer to the bed.

"If," he says. "*If* I wake up."

I reach down to caress his cheek, his week-old whiskers rough and scratchy against my palm. He is burning as if with fever.

"Do not cry," he says.

I scrub at my face with my free hand. "I am not crying, my lord."

"Lie with me," he says, and I do not know if he means to lie next to him on the bed or rather to lie with him as a woman lies with a man. "They say it is the most glorious way to die, lying with Death's handmaiden."

There is a hint of the old Duval in his smile and it fair breaks my heart all over again. I want to tell him he is not dying, but my throat is so tight with grief I cannot force the words out. Even if I could, he would surely know it as a lie. I kneel beside the bed. "My lord," I whisper, "you are too ill."

He falls silent then, and regret pierces me so sharply it is all I can do not to cry out.

Too late, too late. Everything is too late. I want to raise my voice and shout and rant at all the gods and saints in the heavens. Instead, I step out of my gown and let it puddle on the floor. I remove the sheaths at my wrists, then the one at my ankle. When I am left in nothing but my shift, I lift the bedcovers and climb into bed beside him.

His arms are waiting, and as I slip into them, the rest of the world falls away. The skin and muscle in his arms twitch and spasm, damaged as they are by the poison, but he pulls me close until my head is on his shoulder and our chests are touching through the thin linen of my shift.

His heart beats impossibly fast, as if he has just run some great race. Wishing I could slow his heart by my touch, I place my hand on his chest, the ridges and bumps of his scars rough beneath my fingers. He smiles and captures my hand. He tries to bring it to his lips, but his grip is too weak and he drops it. I snuggle up against him, my arms draped around his neck and shoulders, determined to stay as close to him as humanly possible.

It is all that we have left to us. And while it is more than I ever dared dream, it is nowhere near enough.

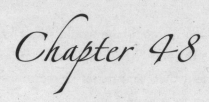

Chapter 48

I do not sleep at all that night, afraid to lose one single moment I have left with Duval. Just before dawn I peel myself away from him, one small inch at a time, so that he does not wake. I hold my breath as I put my full weight onto the mattress, afraid the shifting movement will disturb him, but it does not. Indeed, he is sleeping deeply, his breathing shallow. His pulse beats in his throat, thin and thready. Truly, this is a small mercy that my god has granted me. I do not have to even raise my hand and Duval will be dead by nightfall.

Perhaps Mortain knew I could not kill him even if he bore the marque. I cannot kill the only man I have found it in my heart to love.

And no matter how much I long to stay by his side, I have promised all my choices away; to the convent, to the duchess, to Duval himself. I am caught in a web of my own making, my crisscrossing promises ensnaring me as neatly as any trap. Only duty, which once held such joy for me, is left. It is as sharp and bitter in my mouth as bile.

I am dressed and ready before Beast comes to collect me. I have no wish to be dragged from the bedside and have no doubt that Beast will do exactly as he promised. Leaving

Duval is as painful as cutting out my own heart and giving it to the crows to feed on. I do not look at Beast when he arrives. I do not dare meet his eye, for if I see one drop of sympathy there, I fear I will splinter into a thousand pieces like shattering crystal.

While Duval has not been seen around the palace for the last few days, it is only the duchess and the Privy Council who know he has gone into hiding. With the rest of us en route to Nantes, he should be safe enough in my chamber. My eyes are dry as bone, my face as still as the cold marble floor beneath my feet as I move through the palace in a daze. Beast sends me a number of worried glances, small flickers of concern that prick against my skin. I barely register their existence.

How much has Duval told Beast? I wonder. *Will he believe me if I confide my suspicions of Crunard to him?* In the end, I decide it is worth the risk. If something happens to me, no one will know where the true danger lies. "We cannot trust Crunard," I say without looking at him.

His head does not move, but I feel his eyes swivel in my direction. "In what way, demoiselle?"

"I believe it is he who is poisoning Duval, and that he is behind much of the misfortune that has befallen the duchess. I fear he is in league with the French regent."

He is quiet a long moment, then asks the same question Duval did. "To what purpose?"

"I do not understand the why of it, I know only that his actions point to his guilt, and I want someone other than myself to have this information. Mayhap you can help keep a close eye on him on the trip to Nantes."

Beast turns and looks at me fully then. "He is not going with us."

I stop walking. "What?" Apprehension makes my voice sharp.

"Isabeau is too ill to travel, and the duchess was reluctant to leave her side. Crunard offered to stay with her."

"Duval!" I turn to head back to him, but Beast grabs my arm.

"There is little more Crunard can do to Duval," he says gently, and I remember his promise to carry me if need be.

After a long moment of weighing my options, I nod, and he releases my arm. We continue walking. "Do you think Isabeau will be safe?" I ask.

Beast scowls. "I cannot believe he would harm a poor, sick child."

I can only hope he is right. Trying to see to Isabeau's safety is yet one more thing that is at odds with my promise to Duval.

In the courtyard, a score of men-at-arms are mounted. Four horses wait beside them. Crunard is there but dressed in his robes of office rather than for travel. "The duchess was not comfortable leaving Isabeau on her own, and my age will only slow down your progress," he explains, which is in itself suspicious, for he owes me no explanations. I cannot help but wonder what he gains by staying. No matter how I poke and prod the question, I can find no answer.

"We will miss your wisdom and counsel on the road, Chancellor Crunard," I say sweetly. "I'm sure Isabeau will be glad of your company."

"It will be poor comfort while her sister is gone. But it is some small way I can assist."

Beast helps me mount my horse, then climbs into his own saddle. The duchess will ride perched in front of Captain Dunois, his thick, sturdy arms keeping her safe as he guides the horse.

As we ride out of the courtyard, I keep my face forward, afraid to look back at Crunard lest something in my expression gives me away. When I hear the gates of the city clang closed behind us, I finally dare to look over my shoulder. Crunard has climbed up on the ramparts to watch us depart. Across the distance, our eyes meet.

"Demoiselle? Are you all right?" I turn to find that Captain Dunois and the duchess have pulled up alongside my horse. The duchess's eyes are upon me, such a deep liquid brown and so very young. I wonder how I can tell her that she and I have just left the two people we care most about with yet another traitor. Coward that I am, I cannot. I have no proof with which to convince them. And even if Dunois believed me, what action could he take? Since I do not know Crunard's purpose, I cannot be sure he wouldn't slaughter us while we stood arguing the issue. Besides, I am hemmed in by my promise to Duval: to get the duchess to safety. If I tell her of my suspicions, she will surely not leave Isabeau. "I am fine, Your Grace. Merely pondering what awaits us at the end of this journey."

She wrinkles her brow. "Nothing pleasant, that is certain."

"As you say, Your Grace."

She looks inclined to linger and I feel something stir in my chest, some small bird of panic that threatens to take flight. I cannot keep up this masquerade all morning if she chooses to ride beside me.

Captain Dunois sends me a sympathetic glance and makes some excuse to ride ahead. As they draw away, Beast moves to my side and hovers there, as if he is afraid I might even now turn and gallop back to the palace. "Leave," I tell him sharply. "I will not forget my promise."

This seems to satisfy him. He turns and gallops to his place at the back of the party, and I am left alone.

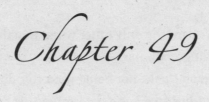

Chapter 49

We are two days on the road, a somber, cheerless troop, each of us lost in misery – except perhaps for Beast, who wears a faint maniacal grin the entire time. When I ask him why, he says he is imagining what he will do when he gets his hands on those who have betrayed the duchess. For the first time, I glimpse the brutal, savage part of him that earned him the name Beast, and it is fearsome.

Every time I consider telling Captain Dunois of my suspicions regarding Crunard's treachery, he is busy giving orders, seeing to the duchess's safety, or consulting with his scouts. There is no moment in which he is not rushed and pressed for time, no moment for him to quietly hear my arguments and give me a chance to convince him, so I keep silent.

Late in the afternoon of the second day, we reach the village of Paquelaie. These winter days are short, and we make it to the village just as darkness overtakes us. Dunois leads us to a stone hunting lodge that had belonged to the late duke, stopping only long enough to dispatch a spare soldier to fetch a village woman to cook for us.

Even though we are a small party, it takes a fair while to get all the soldiers quartered and the duchess comfortable in her rooms. As I am the only other woman in the party, I find myself attending upon her.

She is tired and pale, not being used to riding for so hard or so long, but her face has a determined set to it. There are no servants, so Dunois assigns the solders to bring hot water up to her room.

We do not speak much as I assist her in her evening toilette, for I am afraid if I open my mouth all the secrets I am holding will spill out. After she has washed away the two days' travel, a simple meal is sent up. I keep her company while she picks at her food, then I help her into her bed, and she dismisses me for the night. But my time with her has brought all my secrets swarming to the surface. I must now do my best to convince Captain Dunois of my suspicions.

I find him in the great hall with Beast and de Lornay finishing off the remnants of a meal. The men look up from the demolished duck and capon. "We assumed you would dine with the duchess," Captain Dunois says sheepishly.

I nod. Let him think I ate upstairs with her. It matters not, for I have no appetite and am not sure I could choke down a single bite. "I must talk with you."

Dunois glances at Beast and de Lornay. "Alone?"

"No, they know some of it already." I slip my hand into my pocket and close it around the heavy gold signet ring. "I believe Chancellor Crunard has betrayed us all."

"Crunard?" His eyes widen with astonishment and disbelief, but I am relieved he does not dismiss me out of hand.

"Yes, my lord. It is a long and complicated story, one that Duval did not think you would accept without proof."

"You have this proof?"

"Of a sort." I have had two days on the road to arrange my thoughts into some semblance of order, so I am sorely frustrated to find myself groping for words. "I first grew uneasy about him when you told us of the chancellor not better defending Duval on the night the council discussed his arrest, for the chancellor was behind much of Duval's actions. I grew even more suspicious when I received word from my convent that Crunard had told them Duval was involved in his mother's plots, as that was blatantly false."

Dunois's thick brows draw down in a scowl. "The chancellor told them that?"

"Yes, but there is more." I spend the next hour laying out all my evidence against Chancellor Crunard: the footpad attack on us, the signet ring, the death of Nemours, and the outright lies he told the convent.

When I am done, Dunois sits silent and brooding for a long time. At last he shakes his head. "While I can see how your reasoning has led you to believe this, I cannot help but feel there is some other explanation we are missing."

"But what of the signet ring? Surely that is proof."

Dunois rises to his feet. "It is strange, I'll grant you that, but proof of treason? And on such a grand scale?" He shakes his head again. "I cannot bring myself to believe that of the chancellor. What does Duval think?"

"Duval's mind was too consumed by the poison Crunard has given him to use reason."

His head snaps up at this. "Poison? Duval is being poisoned?"

"Yes, my lord. Yet another betrayal to lay at the chancellor's feet."

His face turns to chalk. "I thought he had merely gone into hiding."

"It is quite advanced," I tell him gently. "He cannot move his legs. The paralysis will move to his lungs next, then his heart. Perhaps it already has."

The silence is filled with the crackle and hiss of the fire.

"Sweet Jesu!" Dunois says, scrubbing his face with his hands.

"If what you are saying is true, we cannot return to Guérande should this gambit fail. And Isabeau . . ." He looks up at me, his face haunted.

"You make certain this gambit does not fail," I tell him. "I will think of something to free Isabeau once we have finished here."

Chapter 50

The next day is Sunday, and the duchess spends the morning in prayer, but I am far too restless for such pursuits. I cross to the window and stare out at the rich woodland that surrounds the hunting lodge, wondering if my letter has reached the convent and, if it has, if the abbess believes me. I wish bitterly that Annith had written to me before I left. Even if she has learned the answers I seek, Vanth will never find me here.

Like a tongue poking at a painful tooth, my mind goes back to Duval. At our parting – should I have done something different? And what of Crunard? He has always been suspicious of Duval's disappearance. Will he come looking for him once I am gone?

Or perhaps Duval will die of the poison before Crunard finds him.

That thought is like pouring salt into a fresh wound and prods me to grab my cloak and go outside. Le Palais is on a ridge that overlooks the Loire River and the valley below. The chill wind whips at my hair and tugs at my cloak as I stare down at the city ramparts. *What are those traitors plotting?* I do not trust them, and I do not like Anne being this close to whatever they have planned.

I hear a step behind me, and I turn to find the duchess

bundled up in her ermine-lined cloak, picking her way along the path. "Shouldn't you be resting, Your Grace?"

"I cannot. My mind will not hold still." She comes to stand next to me and together we stare down into the valley, to the imposing high walls of Nantes and the blue and yellow banners flying from the ramparts.

"I was born there, you know," the duchess says. "The night I came into this world, my father carried me to those very ramparts and held me aloft so I could behold my kingdom and so his subjects could behold their next ruler." She sounds bemused, as if she cannot quite understand how she came to be here while her enemies are there.

"That gate," she says. "See? That far one? That is the very gate through which Duval carried Isabeau and me to safety nearly eight years ago." Her voice catches in her throat. "I wish he were here," she whispers fiercely. "If ever I had need of his counsel, it is now." She sends me a stricken look. "I had thought he would ride out and meet us on the road. Dunois will not honor the call for his arrest; surely he knows this. Why did he not come, Ismae?"

As I stare into her unflinching brown eyes, I find I am unable to keep secrets from her any longer. It is exactly what her other advisors do, and I do not wish to repeat their mistakes. "He is ill, Your Grace. Gravely ill."

Her hand flies to her mouth. "The plague?"

I shake my head. "He is being poisoned."

Her eyes grow round with horror and she takes a step back. "Poison?" she says faintly.

"Yes, but not at my hand," I rush to assure her.

"Why did no one tell me of this sooner?" she demands.

"Because he did not wish for you to know, and I was hoping to find an antidote or cure before having to give you such dire news."

"But I take it you have found no cure."

"I have not."

She is silent as she stares down at the city below us, gathering her courage to ask the next question. "Is he dead?"

"Very likely he is by now, as he was at death's door when we left Guérande." Remembering how I left him fills me with a nearly overwhelming urge to grab the nearest horse and ride back to Guérande to protect his unconscious body from Crunard's further machinations.

She turns on me then, her voice harsh with anger. "Who would do such a thing?"

I take a deep breath. "Chancellor Crunard, Your Grace." And then I tell her all the ways her most trusted guardian has betrayed her.

The next day, Anne sends an officer to Nantes to request that she be allowed to enter her own city so that she may talk with Marshal Rieux. She chooses de Lornay to carry her message into the city. He is well liked for his beauty and smooth manner, and she hopes he will turn the people of Nantes to her cause.

We ride out with de Lornay as far as a small ridge that overlooks Nantes. From this vantage point we watch him ride down to the city gates. "You don't think they will slay him unheard, do you?" I ask Beast.

His brows fly up in mock surprise. "Do not tell me you've developed a soft spot for our Lord Dandy."

"Not at all," I say coolly. "I merely want to be certain the duchess's message has a chance of being heard."

"Ah," Beast says, but he is not fooled. "Since Rieux and d'Albret hope to use Nantes as leverage to force the duchess to accept their terms, I think they will be more than willing to speak with de Lornay."

Just as Beast predicted, one of the city gates opens and a small party rides out to meet de Lornay and the two archers that have accompanied him. It is a distressingly short meeting.

When de Lornay returns there is thunder in his eyes, and my heart sinks. "Marshal Rieux will not discuss terms with me. He insists on meeting the duchess face to face and will speak only with her. He suggests noon tomorrow. We are to meet him on the field below. We may escort her as far as the field, but only the duchess and ten archers will be allowed into the city. Neither Captain Dunois nor the Baron de Waroch nor myself are to accompany her. Neither is the assassin."

It takes a moment to realize he means me.

"I do not like it," Captain Dunois says at once. "It stinks too much of a trap."

"Then we will just have to make sure he does not catch us unawares," the duchess says. "Tell Marshal Rieux I will meet with him then."

The next morning dawns crisp and clear. Captain Dunois was afraid that the mists would move in and obscure our view of the city, thus hiding any treachery Rieux or d'Albret have planned, for he is sure that they are planning something. But the gods have smiled on us in their choice of weather for today.

The duchess has her heart set on speaking to Marshal Rieux. She has even decided to apologize to him for appearing to dismiss his counsel. It is a big step for her, but she wants him to see that she is willing to bend on some things.

Our entire party rides with her into the valley. We stop a short way from the city walls and wait. At noon exactly, the city gates open, and Marshal Rieux rides out with an escort of four men-at-arms. We all draw around the duchess, waiting to be certain it is not a trap. When no more riders appear at the gate, we give way so that Anne and the marshal may talk.

Marshal Rieux reins his horse in a few feet from the duchess.

"Your Grace."

"Marshal Rieux."

"If you will leave all but ten unarmed archers behind, I will be happy to escort you into the city."

Dunois has made her promise she will not enter the city without her full guard in attendance. "But it is *my* city, Marshal, my men, my home. I will be received in the manner befitting a duchess, not snuck in like some thief in the night."

"Then we are at an impasse, Your Grace." He starts to turn away, but her clear young voice stops him.

"Did you know the French have crossed our borders?"

He cocks his head to the side. "Hopefully, that will spur you to come to your senses and reconcile with Count d'Albret."

Captain Dunois gives a snort of disgust, but the duchess holds out a hand to silence him. "Did you know they have taken Ancenis?"

Marshal Rieux slowly wheels his horse round. "Ancenis?"

The duchess nods. "At this very minute, they occupy your own holding."

Her announcement has the desired effect. Shock registers on Marshal Rieux's face, then disbelief. "You lie."

"Marshal Rieux! Remember who you are speaking to," Captain Dunois reminds him.

"Why should I believe this claim?" the marshal asks.

"Why would we lie?" the duchess says. "It is easy enough for you to confirm. Send a rider, if you like."

Rieux hesitates a moment, then nods at two of his men. They peel away from the party and turn their horses toward the road for Ancenis. "It will still gain you nothing," he says, but his voice rings less certain.

Captain Dunois spurs his horse forward. "Jean!" he says. "Surely you do not mean to let the French benefit from this rift between you and the duchess."

The marshal says something I cannot hear, for the two men have drawn closer now and speak in low, urgent voices.

I cannot say what compels me to look away from these fierce negotiations, but something does, some small flicker of premonition, or perhaps it is Saint Mortain Himself whispering in my ear, saying, *There. Look there.* However it happens, my gaze is drawn to the ramparts of the keep and I see a slender shadow detach itself from the stone wall. The slim figure walks to the very edge of the ramparts, so close that I fear she will throw herself off the crenelation to her death.

But no. She stays just inside the edge of the stone and looks out across the river and the fields and the fighting men. At me.

Even from so far, I feel when our gazes meet, and in that moment I know that it is Sybella. The furtiveness of her movements tells me she has put herself in serious danger by being there. When she is sure she has my attention, she draws her arm across her body, then flings it out, as if she were throwing something. Scattering seed to the wind, perhaps? Or casting crumbs on the water of the moat? I glance down at the moat to see if there is some clue there. That is when I see the postern gate open and two columns of troops pour out. Troops clad in blue and yellow tabards. D'Albret's colors.

I look back up at Sybella and she makes the gesture again. She is not throwing something. She is telling us to flee.

Chapter 51

A dozen men, two dozen men. I stop counting as I near fifty. "Captain Dunois!" I cry out.

At my warning, Marshal Rieux looks up. His eyes register the reinforcements, and then he and the rest of his party wheel round and gallop back for the city. Their job is done; they have distracted us long enough for d'Albret to spring his trap. Dunois's normally ruddy complexion pales when he sees the troops pouring from the gate. "Your Grace, we must get you to safety." He begins barking orders. "Waroch! De Lornay! You take the men to meet the approaching line. You three" – he points to the two largest of his guardsmen and myself—"come with me. We will guard the duchess's retreat."

As we turn our horses round, the south postern gate opens and a second column of mounted soldiers streams out. They mean to box us in.

And then Beast's horse is next to mine. A wild gleam lurks in his eyes and I wonder if he is already drunk on the prospect of battle.

"A kiss for luck, demoiselle?"

I look into his dear, ugly face. He is not coming back. Neither is de Lornay. They will buy the duchess some time, and that is all they can do against the two hundred soldiers riding toward us. If he wants a kiss from me before he goes, I will give it willingly. I nod, and he slips his great tree trunk of an arm around me, pulls me close, and plants his lips on mine. The force of the kiss bends me back over the saddle, his thick arm nearly pulling me from my horse.

It is a magnificent, lusty kiss and I feel nothing but deep regret that it may be his last.

Just before he pulls away, he whispers in my ear. "Duval said to give you that should I get the chance. It is from him."

He puts his spurs to his horse and rides to the small group of men he must lead to their deaths. De Lornay draws near then. He says nothing but unties one of the two crossbows that hang from his saddle and hands it to me. "This will strike from greater distance than the peashooter you carry." He winks, then turns and gallops to Beast's side.

Captain Dunois is already riding away, leaning low in the saddle and protecting the duchess's body with his own. The two rear guards have taken up position behind him. Even as I fall in with them, I cast one last look over my shoulder.

Battle fever burns bright within Beast now. He shouts an order that divides his men into two parties so they can delay both vanguards of the oncoming forces. "On my signal!" he says. But before he can give it, a long blast from a trumpet stops him. My head turns toward the sound.

Soldiers on horseback are riding hell-bent toward us. De Lornay is the first to recognize their colors. "The garrison from Rennes!"

He and Beast exchange an elated grin, then Beast gives

the order to charge. Beast looks back and sees me hesitating. "Go!" he roars.

And, of course, I must. I cannot waste this chance he has given us. I spur my horse and gallop after the others.

When I gain the copse of trees, I allow myself one backwards glance, just in time to see Beast rise up in his stirrups, battle-axe in one hand, sword in the other. Then d'Albret's forces are upon him. The sound when they meet is deafening, the clash of weapons, the scream of metal, the terrified whinny of the horses.

I urge my mount forward and continue on, the sounds of their terrible fighting echoing in my ears.

Not half a league later we reach the main bulk of the forces from Rennes. Dunois barely has time to rein in his horse to avoid plowing into them. Reinforcements flow around us like a river of safety, encircling the fleeing duchess and her meager guard. Even if d'Albret's soldiers were to reach her, they could never fight through the superior number of troops from Rennes. I rub my eyes for a moment, surprised to find that my cheeks are wet. As I quickly dry them on my sleeve, I am shocked to see a familiar figure riding toward us.

"François!" The duchess's voice is full of joy at the sight of her brother. My own heart lifts too. François has done far more than simply swear fealty to her; he has provided for her in what is surely one of her greatest hours of need.

"It was you who brought these men to our rescue?" she says.

He bows from the saddle. "Only in part. It was Gavriel's idea to send for them. I was simply the one he dispatched."

I am not sure I have heard him correctly. "Duval?" I repeat stupidly as the duchess looks at me hopefully.

He bows again. "Duval, my lady."

"But he was so ill when I . . . When we left. He could not even move from the bed!"

François shrugs. "He was indeed ill-looking, but I can vouch that he was able to move. The night that your party left, he came to my room and gave me urgent instructions to ride for Rennes as if my sister's life depended on it, for surely it did."

I can still scarcely credit what he is saying, but the commander from Rennes is already regrouping so that they may ride back to the city and get her behind its walls. Everyone agrees that the first priority is to get the duchess to safety.

Before they ride away, the duchess directs Dunois to steer their horses to me. "Go," she tells me in a fierce, urgent whisper. "Find de Lornay and Waroch. If they are wounded, have them brought back as soon as can be arranged."

I know full well they are all dead by now, bleeding from a hundred different cuts, but I say, "I will do as you command, Your Grace, with all my heart."

I lean in low over the saddle and urge my horse to go faster. Every moment that those I love must suffer, languishing above their wounded, broken bodies, is a sacrilege to me. For I have realized that I love not only Duval, but also Beast and de Lornay, each of them in a different way. I do not think on how I will reach them or how I will dodge any enemy that still lingers on the field. I know only that I will do so with my last breath if necessary.

When I break free of the trees beyond the ridge, I am surprised by the silence. There is no sound of battle, no clashing swords, no screaming horses. It is completely, eerily quiet. I pull back on the reins so the horse will not take the ridge in one bone-jarring leap, and he stumbles to a halt.

D'Albret's fighting force has already withdrawn back behind the city gates. Once they saw their trap was ruined, they retreated. Only bodies remain on the field. I climb off my horse and tie him to a tree. My hand moves to the misericorde at my waist as I go the rest of the way on foot, gripping Mortain's own dagger firmly.

I wade among a sea of shattered limbs and bleeding wounds. I try not to let my gaze linger too long, for it hurts. Even though half of them have betrayed their country, in death they are naught but dying men, their lives leaching out of them to water the grass. I am surprised to learn that I have not left all of my heart back in Guérande, and I am not strong enough to steel the small remaining piece of it to their plight.

Or their cries. Soft, pitiable cries float over the sea of the fallen. I wrap my cloak around myself, wishing for wax to stop up my ears so I won't have to hear the quiet, broken noises they make. I scan their faces, bruised and bloodied, grimacing with the rictus of death. As I draw closer to the walls of Nantes, there are a few men that I recognize as our own, and none of those still live. Until there, finally, a familiar face.

I lift my skirts and run to de Lornay. He lies on the ground, his body scored with cuts. Two arrows stick out from his ribs. I fear he is already dead, until I draw close enough to hear his labored breathing.

I fall to my knees in the blood-soaked mud. "De Lornay?"

At the sound of my voice, his eyes flutter open. A look of awe fills them when he sees it is me. "Ismae?" he croaks.

I grab his hand. "I am here."

"Did she get away?"

"Yes, my lord. She is safe with Captain Dunois and two hundred men from Rennes."

He closes his eyes and I can feel the shudder of relief that goes through him.

"Have you seen Beast?" I ask.

He starts to shake his head, but stops as a fit of coughing overtakes him. Blood oozes up between his lips. "He was taken. Set a dozen men on him." He stops to catch his breath. When he speaks again, it is fainter. "Cut him down and dragged him back to the city."

Bile rises in my throat to think of the Beast of Waroch dragged through the dirt to be strung up on the city walls like a common traitor.

"I am sorry," he whispers. "I am sorry I treated you so ill. I thought only to protect Duval."

"It was not I who was poisoning him," I say.

"No, but you had stolen his heart and I was afraid you would rip it from his chest when you left."

Every ill feeling I have ever felt for this man flees, and I am filled with sorrow. Sorrow that I am only now learning his true nature. Sorrow that we did not bridge this gap earlier. Sorrow that we did not let ourselves become friends.

"I would ask your forgiveness, Ismae, so I will have one less sin to linger over."

"You have it, my lord." And he does. I hope his heart is lighter for it.

"Good." His mouth twitches in an attempt to smile. "Then I would also ask a favor of you."

"Ask and it is yours."

"Kill me."

The stark request drives the air from my lungs. "Please," he begs. "I would rather not linger here for a day while the crows pick at my guts."

I look down and see that his other hand – the one I am not holding – is clutching his stomach together.

"It does not need to be a coup de grâce. Any killing blow will do."

"No, my lord," I say.

Hope leaves his face. "It was too much to ask."

I lift my finger to his lips and hold them still. "That is not what I meant. A hero such as yourself deserves the misericorde, and all our thanks besides. I know the duchess would wish it as well."

He smiles weakly and squeezes my hand, but it is a feeble grip.

Unwilling to watch him suffer any longer, I take the misericorde from my waist. I bend over and press my lips to his bruised and bloodied cheek, a kiss as gentle as a mother gives her child, then put the tip of the misericorde to his neck.

His soul bursts from his body, a joyous exultation as it rushes past me and I feel as if I am awash in holy light. The body on the ground is nothing more than a shell, a husk, and I am filled with a sense of peace. Yes, I think. *Yes.* This is what I want to be. An instrument of mercy, not vengeance.

I stand and survey all the fallen around me. I know what I must do.

I move to the closest fallen soldier next to de Lornay's now empty body. I bend over and put the tip of the misericorde to his shoulder. In a rush of grace and gratitude, his spirit leaves his body. Once again I feel the touch of that holy light. "Peace," I whisper as his soul departs.

I go on to the next, and then the next. As I move through the fallen, I notice something: they each bear a marque. And Death has found them even without my aid.

It is not until I have released the last soul from the battlefield that I see a tall, dark figure standing under the nearby trees. I try to get a better look, but the light is failing now and I cannot be sure if I truly see something or if it is just one of the lengthening shadows. But no. Something – some*one* – is there, and he has been watching me move from one body to the next.

He is tall and cloaked all in black. And still. He holds so very, very still. My hand does not move to my knife, for I now recognize His presence, a light, lingering chill and the faint scent of freshly turned earth. With my heart thudding painfully in my chest, I rise to my feet, my gaze never wavering as I walk toward Death.

"Daughter." His voice is like the rustle of autumn leaves as they fall from dying trees.

"Father?" I whisper, then fall on my knees and bow my head, every particle of my being trembling. I am afraid to look upon His face, fearing His wrath, His retribution for all the wrongs I have committed, from loving Duval to disobeying the convent to releasing these fallen men's souls.

And yet, in this copse of trees, with the shadow of Death so close, I feel neither wrath nor retribution. I feel grace. Warm and flowing like a river, it pours over me. I am awash in grace and cannot help but raise my face to it as I would to the sun. I want to laugh as it rains down on me, ripples through my limbs, cleanses them of fatigue and self-loathing. I am reborn in this grace, and suddenly, I can do anything.

I feel Him kiss my brow, a chill weight on my forehead. In this kiss is absolution, yes, but understanding as well. Understanding that it is He that I serve, not the convent. His divine spark lives within me, a presence that will never leave. And I am but one of many tools He has at His disposal. If I cannot act – if I refuse to act – that is a choice I am allowed to make. He has given me life, and all I must do to serve Him is *live*. Fully and with my whole heart. With this knowledge comes a true understanding of all the gifts He has given me.

And then I know. I know why Duval was able to rise from his deathbed long enough to send François to Rennes, and I know how to save him from the poison.

If it is not too late.

Chapter 52

I gallop like the wind. It is as if Mortain has blessed my horse and lent wings to his feet. I have no idea what I will find, what further mischief Chancellor Crunard will have wrought, but even if I am mistaken about Duval, I will have the opportunity to face Crunard, and that is worth much.

My mount may ride as if he is a winged messenger of Death, but in actuality, he is not, and I must stop for the night so that both of us may rest. I choose a clearing next to a stream within sight of a small stone cottage. I walk the horse to cool him, then let him drink from the brook.

I try to rest as he does, but I cannot. I can hardly accept this gift I've been given, although I dare not question it for fear my doubts will cause it to evaporate. Instead, I focus on the sense of unending possibilities I had when in the presence of Death and hold on to that.

In the morning, I am up with the birds and we are off again. I am a light load for my horse, accustomed as he is to long marches with heavily armed knights, so we reach Guérande in excellent time.

I rein in just outside the city. The gates are open, and people are coming in and out. No one seems to be subjected to any extra scrutiny. Even so, I cannot bring a war horse through the gates; that would raise unwelcome questions. In the end, I leave him with one of the cottagers who live outside the city, giving him a handful of coins to keep the horse safe for me.

And promising him retribution if he does not.

As we make our transaction, his wife stands in the corner of the yard where she had been taking her laundry from the line. I throw in an extra two coins and my own fine gown in exchange for the homespun dress she has hanging there.

I slip out of my own clothes, eager to be free of the convent's finery. As I step into the rough brown garb, something inside me shifts. I am no longer a creature of the convent but my own true self, naught but a daughter of Mortain.

Leaving the trappings of the convent behind, I depart from the cottage on foot dressed as the peasant I am. I keep only the weapons.

The guards at the gate hardly glance at me as I pass into the city. These are not guards I have seen before, but as I have passed through the gates only a handful of times, that means nothing. They do seem to be paying closer attention to those who are leaving rather than to those who enter.

My heart races as I move through the city. I long to break into a run and hurry to Duval's side, but that would draw far too much notice. Instead, I force myself to walk sedately and keep my head down, as a modest serving woman would. But it is hard. So hard.

I approach the palace from the back, where the kitchen

deliveries are made. I pause long enough to grab a basket of cabbages from a wagon and then carry it inside. No one pays me any heed – truly all my actions seem god-touched – and I slip into the palace unobserved.

It is a long, tense walk from the west wing to the north tower, where my old chamber is, but that is the only entrance to the hidden tunnels that I know.

I keep my head down as I move through the hallway, but even so I can see much has changed. The pages stand at rigid attention, no longer cheerful and good-natured. The servants hurry on their business, all of them with glum countenances.

I am filled with relief when I finally reach Duval's apartments, especially when I see they are deserted. There are no servants, no Duval, nothing.

I let myself into the main chamber, then quickly cross to my own room. Once inside, I shut the heavy door and bolt it.

My bed is empty but messed, as if it has not been made since the day I left for Nantes. There are candles but no fire in the hearth from which to light them. I waste precious minutes setting flint to tinder so I can have some light in the dark corridors beyond. My hands are trembling so badly that it takes five tries before the tinder catches. When at last a small fire burns in the grate, I light a candle, then head for the wall near the fireplace.

I stare at it, wishing I had thought to ask Beast how he got it to work. I poke at the bricks one at a time until one gives way, just a little bit, but enough to release the spring that holds the stone door so tightly shut. I put my shoulder to the revealed door and push. It gives perhaps an inch. Grunting, I push again, bracing my feet on the floor and throwing my whole body into it until it finally moves enough for me to slip through.

I am not sure where to begin my search, for if Duval was up and walking, he could be anywhere. He could even, I realize, be gone from here. Although if Crunard had caught him, surely I would have seen his head on a pike at the city wall.

The thought has my heart plummeting like a stone, and I push away from the door and cast out my senses, searching for Death, afraid I will find it. When I do not, I allow myself to draw my first deep breath since reaching my chamber. Thus encouraged, I begin winding my way to the spot where de Lornay and Beast found Duval the first time we came here. A sharp lance of pain bites through me as I think of those two, but I push it aside. Saving Duval is my goal now.

I get lost twice, then finally the feeble light from my candle shows a corner of a blanket. Afraid to hope, but unable to stop myself, I drop to my knees beside him. He still breathes, but it is a shallow, labored breathing. I feel the beat of his pulse. It is thin and going faster than a hummingbird's wings. "My lord," I whisper.

His head turns toward my voice and his eyelids flutter weakly.

Not too late, not too late beats in my breast and pounds through my veins. I do not know if it is a prayer or a plea or a demand.

I put my hands on the sides of his face, savoring the rough scratch of his whiskers. I lean down and place my lips on his and kiss him.

His lips are dry and cracked, but I do not care. I can taste the poison. I cover his mouth with my own, deepening the kiss, kissing him as Beast kissed me – thoroughly, wantonly, as if I am gulping the finest wine from a silver goblet. My heart soars when I feel him stir beneath me.

Then he opens his mouth and our tongues meet, a shocking sensation as I allow him in. My hands upon his cheeks grow numb, as do my lips. I kiss him and kiss him, wanting to draw every drop of poison from his body into mine. When his eyes finally open and he murmurs my name against my lips, I laugh, and the exhilaration I feel spills from my mouth into his. Needing to look at him, to see his face, I pull back – but not too far.

His eyes are clouded with desire and joy. His skin already seems less pale to me. He reaches up and tucks a stray hair behind my ear. "I did not expect to find you here," he says.

It takes me a full minute to realize that *here* does not mean Guérande but that he thinks he has traveled into the realm of Death. "You are alive, my lord." I cannot help it. I laugh with triumph as I say the words.

He frowns, then tries to sit up as he remembers. "The duchess is safe," I tell him. "She is safe and well guarded by half the garrison from Rennes. You did it, my lord. François reached us in time. You saved her."

He closes his eyes and draws a deep breath. "Then I may die in peace."

"You are not dying. You were, but no longer." At his puzzled look, I lean down once again. "I will save you," I whisper against his lips.

As I slip out of the rough, dark gown, I realize I have only the vaguest idea of how a woman lies with a man. Even so, I cast my shift aside and gently push Duval back down – it takes no effort at all. Slowly, I lower my body onto his so that every part of us is touching. My head rests on his chest and my feet lie atop his shins. He is warm, too warm, and everywhere his skin flinches and trembles. My hand goes to the scars on his chest, the one just over his heart. I place my hand there, savoring the stronger, steadier beat.

I know he is growing stronger when he is able to pull me closer.

His hands roam over my back, tracing my scar. I start to pull away, then realize I do not care. As his arms gain strength, his fingers travel in delicious trails along my back. Everywhere my skin touches his, it flutters and tingles, but whether it is from the poison moving from his body to mine or simply my own response to Duval, I do not know.

Sometime later, I am the first to stir. I lay there, savoring the slow, steady beat of his heart as it thumps against my chest. When I open my eyes, I see his skin no longer has the gray pallor that heralds death. I feel damp, as if I have walked through a heavy mist. Small beads of the now harmless poison coat my skin like sweat. Just like a bezoar stone, I have neutralized its deadly effects.

As the fog of our lying passes, it clears the way for thoughts other than Duval. I sit up. "Isabeau!" Panic jolts through me, but Duval's hand clamps on my waist and pulls me back.

"She is safe," he murmurs.

I stare down at him. "How can you know? I believe Crunard—"

He lifts his fingers to my lips, quieting me. "She is gone from here."

My heart lurches. "You mean she is dead?"

He laughs and gives a rueful shake of his head. "No, dear assassin. She was spirited out of the palace while Crunard slept."

I push out of his arms and sit up. "How? How did you manage this?"

He folds his hands behind his head and looks up at me. "The morning you left, I woke feeling better. I knew Crunard must be planning a trap and that I had little time before he sprung it. I went to François and ordered him to fetch the garrison from Rennes and bring them to Anne at Nantes."

"He did it, my lord. He reached us at the very hour of our need."

Duval smiles. "Good," he says. "It is good to have him as an ally again. The next greatest need was to get Isabeau to safety." His face grows serious. "She is not well, not well at all."

"You do not need to tell me." Our eyes meet.

"Does Anne know?"

"Not the full severity of it, I do not think."

He sighs and scrubs his face with his hand. "To get her to safety, I employed the talents of the loyal Louyse, who would lay down her life for one of the duke's children, and my lady mother, who owed her life to your mercy and her newly sworn oath. It took a while to convince my mother that swearing fealty to Anne also meant endangering her life for Isabeau, but once she saw how frail the girl was and learned how Crunard had set her up, she was only too willing to ruin his latest plans."

"So you snuck them out through the tunnels?"

"Exactly." His smile is smug, and rightfully so.

"And then what?" I ask, lightly punching his shoulder. "Did you secure the entire duchy while I thought you lay dying?"

"No," he says, growing serious. "Crunard is still out there."

"What is his aim, can you guess?"

"I do not know. But I plan to find out." Our eyes meet again, and this time our own warm feelings give way before our desire to make Crunard pay. "But first, tell me of your news. What miracle have you wrought that you have saved me from this poison?"

"It is one of my gifts from Mortain." I grimace. "One the convent either does not know about or chose not to tell me of."

"And what of Beast and de Lornay?" he asks. The careful note in his voice indicates he expects the worst. I tell him of our battle before Rennes, of the falling of de Lornay and the taking of Beast. During the telling, his grief mounts and grows until it threatens to swallow us both. And then his mouth sets in a hard line. "I must get up."

When he rises to his feet, I am pleased to see that he does not sway, but he is not as steady as he once was. His body will need time to fully heal. "You cannot mean to storm into Crunard's chambers and challenge him to combat," I say.

"I cannot?"

"You are only just able to keep on your feet."

"Even so, I will face him, for I am sick of hiding in the dark while he destroys all that we have fought for."

We are silent as we make our way back through the tunnels to my chamber, both of us consumed by our own thoughts, for Crunard has cost each of us much. Even though he is still weak, Duval leads the way, for he is more familiar with these tunnels than I. Once again, I marvel at how he has stood it all this time, for the close stone walls press down on me, stealing my breath and making the hairs on the back of my neck stand on end.

At last I see a sliver of light ahead and I quicken my pace, nearly treading on Duval's heels. He grunts, then stumbles forward. When he reaches the doorway, he freezes, then puts out his arm and shoves me back into the tunnel. "Crunard," he says loudly, and every nerve in my body comes alert.

Chapter 53

"Ah, you *are* still alive. I thought as much. It was the only explanation that made sense."

Careful to stay well out of sight, I press my back against the stone wall, heart hammering in my chest as the chancellor's cold, hard voice fills my ears.

"Come in, come in, don't hover at the door." At first I think he is talking to me, then I see Duval move away from the tunnel and step into the room. "Besides, you and I have a game of chess we must finish," he says coyly, and that's when I know.

I know precisely where Duval picked up Arduinna's snare. I want to bang my head against the wall in frustration.

"Is that what we have been doing, Crunard? Playing a game of chess? If so, I will confess that I did not realize it was you I was playing against, not until Ismae voiced her suspicions." Duval sounds strong and steady, and I do not know if this is because he has fully recovered or because he is simply determined not to show weakness in front of Crunard.

"The girl figured it out before you, did she? That must sting, but the convent is not known for raising fools."

"She also did not have a lifetime of memories and family loyalties to cloud her vision. I defended you against her accusations." Duval's voice shakes now, but with the pain of Crunard's duplicity rather than weakness. "I told her that one of our country's greatest heroes and my father's closest ally would never betray my sister in such a way."

Crunard says nothing for a long moment. When he speaks, his voice is so quiet I must inch closer in order to catch every word.

"Four sons, Gavriel. I have lost four sons to this never-ending war with the French. And for what? So they can turn round and invade our borders once again? In the end, do you really think it matters to the people who rules over them? Do you really think maintaining Brittany's independence is more important to their lives and prosperity than ending the constant war?"

"How can you ignore everything we've fought for for the last twenty years? How can you dishonor your own sons' memories this way?"

"*You* may not speak to me of my sons," Crunard says, his voice tight with fury. "Not when you have lived and they have died." He grows quiet, and when he speaks again, he is calmer. "I do not expect you to understand how hard it is to watch your own sons die, struck down in battle for a cause that pales when it is set next to what you have lost. Even more, I do not expect you to understand what it is like to learn that one of those sons still lives—"

"Anton?" There is joy in Duval's voice, and I remember that the chancellor's youngest son and Duval were of an age. They were likely friends.

"Anton," Crunard says. "I saw him struck down on the battlefield of Saint-Aubin-du-Cormier. So you cannot begin to imagine my joy when I received word that he still lived. All I had to do was deliver Anne into the hands of the French regent – something that was clearly inevitable – and my son would be returned to me."

Suddenly everything is clear. Every move Crunard has made, every person he has betrayed – all of it was done in the hope of ransoming his son.

"So you thought to trade my sister's life for your son's?"

"It seemed a fair exchange, since if it weren't for the blood of my sons spilled on the battlefield, none of this would be hers. Besides, I wasn't trading her life, merely her duchy. They are quite different things.

"At first it was easy. I worked quietly behind the scenes, gently bending the tides of war to France's favor without harming a soul, and then you stepped in. You and your damned strategies and tactics and pig-headed stubbornness. If you had been content to let things happen, none of this would have come to pass. But you were not. You were determined to single-handedly deliver an independent duchy to your sister along with the means to keep it. You can be certain I did not value *your* life above my son's, so you gave me no choice but to remove you. Now, sit down so we may finish this game."

"Do you always play chess with a loaded crossbow in your lap?" Duval asks, and at last I understand why he shoved me back into the tunnel.

"Only with particularly challenging opponents," Crunard replies.

But that is easily enough fixed. I take my own crossbow from the chain at my waist. It may be smaller than Crunard's, but it is just as deadly. I fit a bolt to it, and move silently toward the door.

"You shall move first, I think," Crunard tells Duval.

"No!" I shout, stepping into the room and aiming the crossbow at Crunard's forehead. "That is how he was poisoning you, by coating the chess pieces with Arduinna's snare."

"Demoiselle Rienne, I hardly recognized you in your new gown. Whatever can the convent have been thinking, sending you out in such garb? Or have you thrown away your future with them for Duval here?" even though his voice is dry and mocking, his face pales and his eyes grow wary.

As I stare at him, my anger at all this man has stolen from me rises up, nearly choking me. His treachery has tainted the purity of the convent and dragged us into his worldly struggles. He has used me – and the abbess as well – as pawns in these games he plays. He has nearly killed Duval and has come close to preventing Anne from claiming her throne. And while I have sympathy for his son, that sympathy does not come at the cost of everything I hold dear.

But even as I stare at him with death in my heart, I falter. Now that I have come face to face with His mercy, I see it in everything. For while Crunard has wronged many, the seeds of his treachery lie in his love for his son.

Killing him now would bring one sort of justice, but it would also spring from the anger in my heart. And when I moved through the battlefield, I swore to myself that I would have nothing more to do with vengeance.

Filled with equal parts wonder and disgust, I realize I cannot kill this wily old fox, no matter how much he might deserve it.

I huff out a sigh of frustration, drop the arm holding the crossbow, then swing out and clout him alongside the head with it. His eyes have just enough time to register surprise before they roll up in his head and he slumps in his chair.

Duval turns to look at me, his eyes unreadable. "Did your god guide your hand in that?"

"No," I say, looking down at Crunard's inert body. "That was my own idea. Did you have a better one?"

"Other than wrapping my hands around his neck and squeezing the life out of him, no."

There is a long moment during which I feel him watching me, so I am careful not to meet his eyes. "That option crossed my mind as well, but we need him alive so that we may clear your name with the rest of the council," I say, but I do not think he is fooled by my excuses.

I would curse at him for seeing too much, except I am too pleased he is alive to see at all.

It is two days' ride to Rennes, but due to Duval's weakened state, it takes us three.

I do not begrudge the slower pace. In truth, it is the first time we have been alone with only ourselves and our own pleasure to consider. Once we are away from Guérande, the mists lift, and the days are cold yet bright. Mortain's summer, we call it, and I feel certain it is a gift from the god Himself.

The cold fresh air chases the last vestiges of the poison from Duval's lungs, and his health improves quickly. We talk and laugh as we ride. Indeed, I have never laughed as much as this. Duval points out his father's holdings to me, and I stop and give thanks at every standing stone we pass.

The nights are our own. We sit in front of the fire Duval has built, our bodies touching from hip to shoulder, and share wine from a skin and roasted meat from a spit. We talk of small things, private things. It is a sweet, glorious time and I know it will be over far too soon.

On our last night on the road, Duval is more quiet than usual. He has pulled a ribbon from my hair and sits playing with it in his hand. "What is wrong?" I finally ask.

He looks at me, his dark eyes reflecting the flames of the fire. "We have decisions to make when we arrive in Rennes."

I look away, unhappy that the real world will intrude on this last night. "I know." I pick up a nearby stick and poke at the fire.

"Ismae, I would offer you marriage if you would have it."

My whole body stills, shocked at the honor he would do me, an honor I never dared to imagine.

He smiles. "I think that St. Camulos and St. Mortain could easily come to terms. They work hand in hand often enough in the mortal world."

I cannot help but smile, for it is such a practical Duval-like thing to say. "Perhaps, my lord. War and Death are known to be closely aligned. But I must speak with my abbess first." There are still so many unanswered questions about the convent and my service to it.

"Do you plan to remain with the convent, then?"

"I do not know yet. All I know is that if I do, it will be different, especially now that I know can no longer trust the integrity of their orders."

Chapter 54

We catch up to the duchess and the others just outside the walls of Rennes at the old abbey of St. Brigantia. Isabeau is already there, spirited out by Madame Hivern and the faithful Louyse. When Anne and Isabeau see their brother, they give cries of joy and launch themselves at him. For one brief moment, they are not princess and duchess and bastard but a family reunited.

I am surprised to find myself enfolded in Louyse's sturdy arms as she hugs me to her bosom, relieved to see me unharmed. Not knowing quite what to do with such affection, I pat her awkwardly on the back.

The sisters of Brigantia give us a few moments to enjoy our reunion, then escort us to the rooms that they have prepared for us. They assume, rightly, that we need to rest and refresh ourselves after our journey. In truth, I am travel weary and already mourning the loss of the private time Duval and I shared on the road. A novice opens the door for me, then quietly withdraws.

Alone at last, I close my eyes and sag against the thick wooden door.

A faint rustle of fabric startles my eyes open. The abbess of St. Mortain sits in a chair by the fireplace, dressed in her black ceremonial habit. Her pale face gives away nothing of her thoughts.

Fear and regret and remorse shoot through me, ugly, shameful feelings that have me falling to my knees. "Reverend Mother!" I say, my wits leaving me as my forehead touches the cold, hard floor.

"Daughter." Her voice is icy, and my mind grows blank with panic. I had thought there would be time to think upon all I must say to her. And that I would do it in a letter, which she would read while tucked behind the convent's sturdy walls, not sitting before me like retribution incarnate.

There is a rustle of parchment. I peer up beneath my lashes to see her spreading a message out on her lap. My message to her. "It seems we have much to talk about."

"Yes, Holy Mother. We do." I am pleased that my voice does not shake overmuch.

And then I remember my resolve and rise to my feet even though she has not invited me to. I take a moment to straighten my skirt and compose my features, then meet her gaze steadily. "Chancellor Crunard has betrayed us all."

Her face is still as marble. "Explain."

And so I do. I tell her of his stealth and cunning and how he hovered in the background maneuvering people as if they were pawns and destroying lives. When I am done, I cannot tell if she believes me or not.

At last she speaks. "If this is indeed true, Chancellor Crunard will have much to answer for."

I nod, accepting that what I have told her must come as a

great shock. "He is secure in the dungeons at Guérande, awaiting whatever justice the duchess and her council choose to mete out." I grip my hands tightly in front of me. "There is something else, Reverend Mother. Something I must warn you of." She raises her brows, but does not interrupt, so I continue. "I have come to believe that the marques Mortain uses to guide our hands are much more complex than we thought. I fear they are not always meant to direct our actions but are rather a reflection of what will happen—"

"Silence!" The abbess stands abruptly, cutting off my words with a swipe of her hand. "Do you think to educate your betters? You tell me nothing new. When you have served Mortain and studied His ways for a score of years or more, then you may presume to lecture me on His precepts. But not until then." Her cold blue eyes full of anger, she crosses to the window and stares out into the convent's barren garden. "And what of Duval? Do you love him?" The mocking tone of her voice suggests I wish to roll naked in the mud with pigs.

I close my eyes and reach inside for the spark of the presence I now carry, hoping to borrow its strength. "I do."

When she turns back to me, her face is pinched with fury. "You would throw away all that we have given you for a man's love?"

"Not a man's love," I say softly. "But Duval's. And I would find a way to serve both my god and my heart. Surely He does not give us hearts so we may spend our lives ignoring them."

Her head rears back, as if she has been struck. "So now you are an expert on the will of Mortain?"

I do not flinch. "I came face to face with Him on the battlefield before Nantes. He was not as I thought He would be."

Her lip curls in disdain. "You saw Mortain? He came to you in a vision?"

"No, Reverend Mother. In the flesh, or such flesh as the saints will wear. He spoke to me and called me daughter, and I found peace with Him. I wish to serve in honor of His mercy rather than His wrath."

I can tell she wishes to punish me. At first, I think it because I have defied her, and then I realize it is because I have seen Mortain and she has not. "You cannot expect to take your final vows now."

"I do not want to take my final vows, Reverend Mother." In truth, I am surprised at how much I do *not* want to. I think of Annith facing the rest of her life sealed away in the convent, never leaving its walls. I think of Sybella stuck in some hellish assignment that is surely driving her mad. Is that truly what Mortain wishes for them?

Besides, now that I finally have some choices in my life, I have no desire to hand them all back to the convent. "The convent focuses on only one aspect of Mortain's glory, Reverend Mother. I want to better understand these other parts of Him before committing to such a path."

"Clearly I was wrong about your devotion to your duties and obligations." The abbess looks at me as if I am some lowly worm, and it is all I can do to hold fast to my newfound strength.

"You misunderstand me. I am committed to serving Mortain. It is the convent I am uncertain of."

Her nostrils flare and her lips grow white. She breathes hard for a moment, then, clenching her jaw, she lifts her skirts and storms from the room.

Exactly one fortnight after her thirteenth birthday, Anne of Brittany is carefully dressed in finery befitting a duchess. When she is done, Isabeau kisses her on both cheeks, then Anne turns and leaves the abbey of St. Brigantia. A small procession of attendants accompanies her: myself, Duval, Dunois, and François.

The abbess of St. Brigantia also comes with us, as does the abbess of St. Mortain. Night has fallen, and torches light our path as we wind our way to the main entrance of the city, where the drawbridge is closed to us. When she reaches the moat, Anne steps away from our small group and stands alone before the city gates. She raises her young, clear voice and speaks the ancient words that all the rulers of Brittany have spoken and promises to guard the privileges and liberty of both the nobility and the common people of her country.

In answer, the crowd erupts in joyous cheers. They are eager to receive their new duchess, and heavy chains rattle and clank as the drawbridge is lowered. A great clang rings out when it reaches the ground, as triumphant as any bell.

The city now open to her, Anne alone steps onto the drawbridge and enters.

Trumpets blare and children shout and throw small handfuls of seeds and dried flower petals as the crowd escorts her to the great cathedral. As demanded by custom, Anne will spend the night in prayer before her coronation in the morning. The six of us will stand over her and watch her, but from a distance. This is a vigil she must keep alone. Her burden is made lighter, however, by the coronation gift Duval has given her: six thousand English troops to fight at her command.

It is a long night, but that is just as well, for every one of us in that church has much to think upon. Many times throughout the dark hours, I feel the gaze of my abbess settle on me, puzzled and brooding. I am surprised when I realize this bothers me not at all. Whatever hold she once had over me is gone.

Duval is another matter, however, and every time he glances at me I feel it just as surely as if he has reached out and run his finger along my soul. It is all I can do not to smile at the sheer wonder of it.

Although the brightly colored glass windows hide the sky outside, I can feel the moment night gives way to morning. As dawn breaks, Duval edges closer to me. When I look up at him, our eyes meet, and even in that solemn place and this most solemn of occasions, I cannot help but smile. His hand moves, and when I look down at it, I see that he is playing with the red ribbon he took from my own hair. He has tied nine knots in it, invoking the blessings of the nine saints. As he reaches for my hand, my heart begins to pound. Does he think to pledge ourselves now, before the duchess and God and all our saints? While I am certain of my love for him, I do not yet know if this is what I want.

He holds my hand gently in his and before I can snatch it back, he wraps the ribbon around not both our wrists, but mine alone. He leans in close, his whisper so quiet I can barely hear it. "Whenever you are ready, or if you never are, my heart is yours, until Death do us part. Whatever that may mean when consorting with one of Death's handmaidens."

A small bubble of joyous laughter rises up from my heart, and I lean over and seal his vow with a kiss, not caring that God and the saints and even the abbess of St. Mortain might be watching. For, while I am Death's daughter and walk in His dark shadow, surely the darkness can give way to light sometimes.

ACKNOWLEDGEMENTS

A thousand thank yous to Barbara Samuel, who helped me see that this was the story I simply had to write and helped me find the voice to tell it. Heartfelt thank yous to all the amazing fairy godmothers (and godfather!) at Houghton Mifflin Harcourt who got behind this project and showered it with their support: Betsy Groban, Maire Gorman, Mary Wilcox, Margaret Raymo, Linda Magram, Lisa DiSarro, Karen Walsh, Rachel Wasdyke, Scott Magoon, and Sheila Smallwood.

And special thanks to Erin Murphy and Kate O'Sullivan, for being true midwives to this project, gently encouraging, coaxing, and cheerleading as needed. An author could not ask for a better team!

DARK TRIUMPH

ROBIN LaFEVERS

Betrayal, treachery and danger . . .

When Sybella arrived at the doorstep of St Mortain half
mad with grief and despair, the convent was only too
happy to offer her refuge – but at a price. The sisters
of this convent serve Death, and Sybella could become
one of their most dangerous weapons. Then the convent
returns her to the life that nearly drove her mad.

But when Sybella discovers
an unexpected ally, she finds
something other than vengeance
to live for.

'An intricate, masterful
page-turner'
Kirkus, starred review

978 1 78344 824 1

MORTAL HEART

ROBIN LaFEVERS

Passion, destiny and death . . .

Annith has watched her gifted sisters at the convent come
and go, carrying out their dark dealings in the name of
St Mortain, patiently awaiting her own turn to serve
Death. But her worst fears are realised when she discovers
she is destined to be a Seeress, and for ever be sequestered
in the convent.

Annith has spent her whole life
training to be an assassin – is now
the time to strike out on her own?

'Both a powerful tale of political
intrigue and a heady supernatural
romance, this memorable
adventure will entirely satisfy
devotees of this series'
Publishers Weekly

978 1 78344 825 8

COURTING DARKNESS

ROBIN LaFEVERS

Plots, intrigue and sisterhood . . .

Sybella is searching the French court for fellow assassins
from the convent of St Mortain, placed there years ago on
undercover missions. But deadly royal politics are at play,
and she must navigate them one step ahead of her enemies.

Genevieve has been under cover for so long that she has
begun to lose faith in what she's supposed to be fighting
for. When she discovers a
hidden prisoner who may be of
importance, she decides it's time to
take matters into her own hands.

As these two worlds collide, the
fates of the duchess, Brittany,
and everything Sybella and
Genevieve have come to love
hangs in the balance.

978 1 78344 826 5